Sweet Tea
and
Anzac Biscuits

BY

JAN MARRY

Cactus Mystery Press, an imprint of Blue Fortune Enterprises

For information contact:
Blue Fortune Enterprises, LLC
Cactus Press
P.O. Box 554
Yorktown, VA 23690
http://blue-fortune.com

Cover design by BFE LLC

ISBN: 978-1-961548-23-7
First Edition: April 2025

Contents

Acknowledgements

On my multi-year journey toward finishing this book, I have been helped by more people (and animals) than I can possibly name. Thank you everyone for your valuable support, and the odd skeptical eyebrow that kept me on track.

I want to particularly thank my friend Janet Curtis, whose eagle eye has never let a typo pass unscathed. I want to thank my Johns Hopkins writing group, Mal Cole, Sarah Donahue, Kellie Schmitt, and Hanna Webster. Without the whole group's pointed but kind feedback, Jessamine would still be wandering aimlessly in her driveway. And I am grateful to my Chesapeake Bay writing group who gave great last-minute advice about one tricky chapter.

I owe a debt to Narielle Living, my publisher, for taking a chance on my book and her editorial assistance and to my friend Morag Willey for helping us meet and her valuable feedback.

My family gives meaning to my life. Thanks and love to my sister Elsa Kelly for listening to me read every word out loud and ferreting out every obscure error. Practically for this book, my husband's anguished cry of "Please make it stop" was exactly what that chapter needed at the time (and we recommended speaking to each other soon afterward.)

Prologue

Flames flickered above the trees and sparks spiraled into the midnight sky. Sirens and shouts disturbed the night. The pickup truck stopped on the bank above the river. A woman got out and turned toward the sullen orange horizon.

"Hurry up!" the truck driver called.

The woman directed the backing vehicle, then they both climbed into the bed of the truck. The woman coughed on the rancid smoke clogging the air, "The fire's getting bad. I don't think they'll be able to save the library."

"Don't worry about that! We've got to get rid of this!"

They maneuvered a bulky bundle out of the bed of the truck until it thumped on the ground. They each grabbed an end and stumbled, barely able to drag it, toward the crumbling riverbank. They tried to swing the bundle out, but it fell and lodged halfway down. The man crouched down and pushed it with his foot.

The man teetered and the woman grabbed his arm. "Careful, Frank!"

They stood on the top of the bank and watched as the bundle slid into the water with a slight splash. Caught by the current, the white shape floated a short way, and then disappeared into the dark, shiny water. They turned and the woman wiped her hands on her pants.

Search lights blazed. "Stop! Show your hands!"

The woman froze. Through the glare the Sheriff appeared.

"Jessamine Sibley, you're under arrest for the murder of Kathryn Slattery. Anything you say…"

"Oh, botherations!" the woman said to Frank and lifted her hands into the air.

Chapter 1

Jessamine smiled at the guard. "I'm starting my job at the library today. Could you please tell me—"

"No entry to the Administration Building with bags, cell phones, weapons. Please leave them in your car." The guard shifted uneasily on the sidewalk as if his feet hurt. Buttons strained on his wrinkled black uniform. He regarded Jessamine without interest and leaned against the glass doors.

"Is this Bent River County Public Library?" Jessamine asked. She had driven for three days to reach Virginia. She had studied endless online and print maps, so she didn't understand how she could be in the wrong place. "In the video interviews, they said to come—"

"Yes, ma'am." The guard gestured through the glass doors behind him. "The library's down thataway."

Jessamine peered past the guard to a looming walk-through metal detector; she couldn't see anything resembling a public library. As she opened her mouth to ask, the guard put out an arm to stop a woman in a too-big pink blouse. He raised his voice to the line of people forming behind Jessamine, now spilling off the sidewalk. "We got us a delay this morning."

A shrill, "Excuse me!" echoed across the parking lot. A tall woman in sequined spike heels clumped toward the doors. "Let me through! I work in the library. I need to get in."

Jessamine recognized her new colleague from the video interviews and stepped forward. "Drusilla! I'm starting today…"

Drusilla gave Jessamine a quick, cold look and kept clumping. People stepped aside to avoid her charge. Drusilla grabbed the metal loop of the door handle and pulled. The guard shoved the door shut with his shoulder. They wrestled briefly until Drusilla slid her spike heel down the guard's ankle. Drusilla won the door and wrenched it open. She flicked her sweeping orange and green scarves and breached the building. The guard stationed himself outside the doors, glaring at the crowd, as if to defend the entrance, and his dignity, with his life.

The gathering crowd eyed the guard, and the guard eyed them back.

Jessamine was pushed back. She didn't know what to do; she couldn't be late on her first day in a new job. "Excuse me. Do you know what's happening?" she asked the young woman in pink whose cuffs hung over her hands.

The woman looked at Jessamine. "Oh! Cute accent! Are you from England?" She moved from foot to foot. "I don't know what all they're doin'. All I know is if they don't get goin' soon, I'm going to be late for my hearing to figure out my kids' money!" She eyed Jessamine's large purse. "They won't let you take that bag in there. No cell phones or nothing."

A man behind them in a suit shook his head. "It's Bent River County all over!" He turned to the guard and called, "We all need to get in, Walter!"

"I've been told that you have to wait." The guard put his hands on his hips.

"Court starts in half an hour! And people need to get into the county building and do their licenses and business. I'm calling someone!" The man in the suit went to his car, and returned talking on a phone and glaring at the guard. "Yes, he won't let us in. There must be twenty people waiting out here!"

Within a few minutes, a woman wearing knee-high boots, dangling jewelry, and a short black dress that Jessamine thought was far too tight appeared from inside the building. She muttered in the guard's ear. He shrugged, opened the doors, and gestured for the crowd to enter.

"At last! Thank you, Kathryn," the man in the suit called. He slipped his cell phone into his pocket and walked around the metal detector.

The crowd trickled into the building, but the guard pierced Jessamine with his eye and repeated, "No entry with bags, cell phones, weapons. Please leave them in your car." The woman named Kathryn turned to look at her and gave her a quick smile and shrug before walking away.

Jessamine opened her mouth to argue, then decided it was no use. She returned to her car across the grass-studded, crookedly painted parking lot. She sat in the driver's seat for a moment and peered into the mirror behind the visor. Despite her excitement at starting a new job and a new life, purple bags under her bright brown eyes declared her exhaustion. She smoothed her short, brown hair with her fingers, wondering if she should have dressed more fashionably to start her new job. But she always wore her flowery jacket and long skirt to her library jobs, and she never wore makeup. She hoped no one would guess that she had slept in her car and squeezed her talisman, an ornate looped key on a gold chain around her neck. She shook her head at herself and snapped the visor back up.

Picking her way back, she eyed the low brick building squatting in the middle of muddy fields. She had abandoned her old life to be here, and right now the journey didn't look worth it. Rain started slashing down, and she was soaked before the guard ushered her through the metal detector.

Most of the crowd had stayed to see what was happening in the foyer. Despite her protestations of urgency, Drusilla was still there. Jessamine walked toward her with her hand out. "Hi, I'm Jessamine. I'm starting at the library…"

"Not now!" Drusilla barely glanced at Jessamine. She glared at a wrinkled, older man maneuvering a dolly under an object that towered over his head. "Frank, what in the name of all that's holy are you doing?

You'll scratch the floor."

"I was told to put this bear in here."

"This what?"

"This bear."

The man turned the dolly, and Jessamine saw that he was transporting a taxidermied bear mounted on a wooden box. It stood up straight on its hind legs, its front legs raised at an unbearlike angle, as if to start boxing with an invisible opponent. Sharp claws poked through its lustrous black fur, and its small dark glass eyes glinted with a malice that Jessamine knew wasn't possible for a long-deceased animal.

Drusilla faced Frank and the bear. "Is that a real bear?"

"Yep." The man set the dolly down and stretched his back. "I was told it's an American black bear."

"It's a mature *Ursus americanus*," the man with the cell phone added.

Drusilla gave him an impatient look. "Whatever." She turned back to Frank. "But why on earth are you bringing that thing in here?"

"Joshua Oxford wants the bear on display."

A murmur went through the crowd.

The woman in the too-big clothes shook her head at Jessamine. "Joshua Oxford lives in one of the plantations along the river. He says he's the great-great-great-grandson of Jefferson Davis." She sighed. "He makes sure everyone remembers that his family's special."

"I heard the family say they're kin to Robert E. Lee," said a man with a bushy orange beard.

"That's not right. They're descended from General Samuel Cooper," said the man with the cell phone.

"Who's that?" said the baggy-bloused woman.

"Hush!" Drusilla glared at them, standing with her hands on her hips and her chin in the air. "That's nonsense, Frank Pearson. I thought they had to kill that bear because it was in the woods by the school. Why would he want the bear displayed?"

"Joshua Oxford paid to have the bear stuffed."

"He paid for the taxidermy?" Drusilla deflated. "Well, why are you standing around not working, Frank Pearson?"

Frank took the handles of the dolly but didn't tilt it back onto its wheels. "I don't know where to put it."

The crowd looked with Frank around the tiled foyer crammed with a reception desk, racks of pamphlets about Medicare plans and the food bank, cracked vinyl seats for waiting, and a few scraggy plants in pots.

"Move that plant aside," a voice from the crowd suggested.

"Nah, it won't fit there," another voice replied.

"How about there, by that doorway?" The man with the phone pointed to a door with a glinting brass plaque that read, "Kathryn Slattery" and in smaller writing underneath, "County Controller."

The crowd paused. Jessamine thought that they took a collective breath.

Frank heaved, tilting the dolly back. Walter the guard came over to help and they pushed the bear to the door.

"Kathryn was Frank's wife's first cousin," whispered Jessamine's new friend in pink. "Five years ago, they had a big contract to reroof the school. Something went wrong, and no roof and no money! They fired Kathryn, then they brought her back. No one knows why."

"Surely that can't be true?" Jessamine lifted her eyebrows.

"Yes, and…" The woman paused and pursed her lips. "She gets paid *real* well. Our schools aren't good, so she sends her daughters to private schools in the city."

Frank and Walter eased the bear off the dolly. Frank stood back, dusted his hands against each other, and smiled. Anyone entering the county building to get a dog license or inquire about their taxes would immediately see the bear. The bear's upraised front leg obscured the polished brass name plaque on Kathryn Slattery's door.

The woman in the boots and tight dress came out of her office, pulling off headphones and ducking under the front leg of the bear. She frowned at the bear. She frowned at the assembled people. She frowned at Frank. "You can't put that there."

"Hi, Kathryn," Frank greeted the County Controller. "How's your mother? Last time I dropped in, Aunty Florence wasn't doing so well."

"Oh, she's fine. Just the same. But that thing can't go there. It's watching me!"

"I'm following orders. Joshua said, 'Put the bear in the county foyer.'"

"Really? Joshua Oxford?" Kathryn opened her mouth as if to say more. "Hmph," she said and stomped back to her office.

The crowd drifted away. The pink-bloused woman waved to Jessamine and followed the throng.

Frank came past Jessamine with the empty dolly and winked. "I don't like that thing looking at me either," he said. "It gives me the creeps." He whistled and disappeared down the hallway.

Chapter 2

Jessamine looked around, wondering where she was supposed to go.

A woman with long, dark hair poked her head out of a doorway and beckoned. Jessamine hurried toward her down a long hallway with floor-to-ceiling windows along one side. The woman held open a battered glass door plastered in yellowed fliers with last year's dates announcing, "Library Bingo!" and "Story Time Thursday Mornings!"

The dark-haired woman put out her hand. "Hi, I'm Marilyn, the library director. You probably know *that* from the interviews. You must be Jessamine. It's nice to meet you in person, not on a screen. What was that fuss in the foyer? I'm glad I was already inside. I've got so much to do! Would you like tea?"

Jessamine shook her hand. "I'm pleased to…" but Marilyn was already moving, calling over her shoulder. "It's about time to open, so we'll leave the door unlocked for Drusilla. We have a minute to grab tea. I need my tea! How about you?"

"Thanks! That sounds…"

"Great! I keep a pitcher of sweet tea in the fridge. Anyone can help themselves anytime." Marilyn led Jessamine through a room crowded with shelves, turning on lights as she went.

"Is this room the entire library?" Jessamine asked.

"Yes. In all its grandeur. We're in the process of organizing state funding and a crazy mishmash of money to build a new one. What a kerfuffle that is." Marilyn shook her head. She moved a rocking chair and unlocked a door with a key on a lanyard around her neck. "Wait there a minute. Two people won't fit in this kitchen." She pushed aside a stack of blue plastic boxes to reach the door of a small fridge and pulled out a pitcher filled with brown liquid.

Jessamine gazed at stacks of paper, books, and boxes piled on a counter, sliding off the top of a microwave, and crammed into shelves. "I hate to ask. I'm parched for a cuppa. Could I make hot tea?"

"Hot tea?" Marilyn paused and looked at Jessamine. "That's right, you're not from 'round here, are you? What part of England are you from? We've been dying to ask, but we couldn't in an official job interview."

"I'm from New Zealand, not England."

"Really? I…" Marilyn opened a cupboard above the sink and jumped as a cascade of unmatched napkins and paper plates slithered into the sink. "I know there are spare mugs here somewhere—" Marilyn's watch beeped. "Yikes! Is that the time? I've got a meeting with the Library Committee. Can you heat water in the microwave?" She pulled at her dark blue suit jacket and pencil skirt. "Is it straight? Wish me luck!" Marilyn came out of the kitchen and looked around. "Sorry. Drusilla's supposed to train you today, but I don't see her. She'll be here soon. Get to know things." She waved vaguely at the shelves. "Look at the books."

If there was an instruction Jessamine didn't need, it was to look at books. Her childhood had been full of adults telling her to stop reading under her desk, or to put down the book and go to sleep. Jessamine was distinctly damp from the rain, and she had missed her early morning tea because she had been driving, so she needed her cuppa. She negotiated the boxes and found a chipped coffee mug declaring "World's Greatest Plumber." Her favorite teabags were nestled out of reach in her lunchbox, across the rainy parking lot. She exhumed a box of elderly teabags lurking at the back of the cupboard. She wished the library had a kettle to get the water piping hot to make the best tea, but after years in America, she accepted that Americans thought microwaving water for tea was acceptable. Lukewarm tea in hand, she walked around her new workplace.

Chipped fiber board and veneer shelves bowed under the weight of tightly jammed books, with others shoved sideways across the top. As a book enthusiast, Jessamine had been guilty of cramming her own shelves full, but she'd never seen anything like this in a public library. Professional opinion varied; a faction of librarians thought it was okay to have the books fill three-quarters of each shelf, except for the middle shelf where they displayed a book or two face out. Purists went for a third full on every shelf with lots of books face out. Jessamine remembered her old colleague Rebecca, who repeated, "Studies show more books check out if there's less on the shelves!"

She ran her hand along the books and paused in the nonfiction at 567: dinosaurs. It was her favorite Dewey Decimal number and the one she found easiest to remember. The adult and children's nonfiction were mixed together in this tiny library. Jessamine couldn't tell the intended audience for a large, faded, pastel book. She pulled on it, but the books were wedged so tightly that the spine tore down both sides. She attempted to flick through the pages. They wouldn't turn. The bottom of the book was a blotchy, pulpy mass; it had been soaked, then dried. She sneezed, then forced the pages open to the beginning. "Publication Date: 1973." Her mouth fell open until she sneezed again. She managed to turn to a watercolor of a Brontosaurus. These dinosaurs had been reclassified decades ago.

Jessamine sneezed again as Marilyn hurried back, frowning and looking pale.

"We've got a video meeting in the county offices with the government people about the new library in three minutes. Why don't you come? It'll be a great introduction to what we're planning."

"This is moldy." Jessamine held up the book with two fingers from each hand. "Spores are falling off it."

Marilyn glanced at it. "Drusilla does the collection development. She doesn't want anyone else to help. I'll change the system soon. Quick, the meeting's starting."

"You mean she buys new books and gets rid of the out-of-date ones? This is over fifty years old." Jessamine turned to follow Marilyn.

"There's not much money for buying new books." Marilyn laughed. "Most of them are donations. As I said, we'll be changing the way it works soon."

"What should I do with this?" Jessamine didn't want to wave the book around too much and spread more mold spores.

"Just reshelve it. Drusilla says to send her an email if we're concerned about anything. She's pretty slow at answering emails, so you could try bringing it up at the monthly staff meeting."

Jessamine opened her mouth and shut it. She was on her first day at her new job. She tried to ease the decrepit dinosaur book back; it stuck. She pushed harder, then winced as the spine disintegrated in her hand. She regarded the torn cardboard for a second, then poked it into the shelf. She sneezed and followed Marilyn.

Marilyn paused at the circulation desk. "Where's Drusilla? She's scheduled to work today." She looked around; no other lights were on in the library. "She's supposed to be covering the desk and training you."

"I think I saw her in the foyer. She's tall and was talking about someone named John Oxbridge?"

"Joshua Oxford, do you mean? Why? He's got his nose into everything in this county. Where's Drusilla now?"

"I don't know where she went after…"

"I have to get to this meeting." Marilyn ran her hands through her hair. "It won't work if no one's covering the desk. Here, I'll sign you in on my account and you can check out books for people." Marilyn clicked on the desktop computer. "You're an experienced librarian. You'll work it out, I'm sure." Marilyn gave Jessamine a strained smile and disappeared out the library door.

Chapter 3

Jessamine poked around on the computer. She had worked in several libraries with different catalogs, but this one was strange; the interface looked clunky and decades out of date.

A few people trickled into the library. An elderly man brought up three ragged paperback Westerns. "You're new," he said, as if accusing Jessamine of trying to get something over on him.

She smiled. "Yes, this is my first day."

"Oh, you're from England." He gazed at her with more interest.

"No, from New Zealand. Do you have your library card?"

"I don't know. They don't usually ask for that," he grumbled and fumbled in his pocket for a worn wallet and used arthritic fingers to pull out a grubby card.

Jessamine was relieved that when she clicked the "Patron" box and ran the card under the barcode reading wand, and when it beeped happily, the customer's information popped up. "You have a fine, Mr. Kaufman."

The man pulled the paperback books toward him. "I can't pay it today."

"That's okay. I'm not sure how to take your money anyway."

"That's a good way to be!" He smiled. After he checked out his books, he sat in a torn vinyl armchair near the glass doors and read a well-used magazine from a nearby rack.

Few other people came in. Jessamine gazed out the glass doors and through the hallway's floor-to-ceiling windows to the parking lot. Outside, dark clouds swirled. In Kansas in January, this would signal snow to come, but it was too warm here to snow. She saw a tall woman with bright scarves laughing up at a taller man before they both got into a huge, shiny black SUV and drove away. It looked like Drusilla. Jessamine frowned. Marilyn had said that Drusilla was working today.

Kathryn Slattery came tripping into the library on her high-heeled boots. "Hi, Jennifer. I heard someone new was starting in the library. I'm the County Controller."

"Yes, I saw you in the foyer. My name's actually—"

"That's an *interesting* jacket. I prefer cheerful clothes myself. Do you like my boots?" she lifted her knee. "I bought them in Italy. Some people think it's an extravagance, but I have delicate feet, and most importantly I have a position in the county I need to keep up."

"Yes, they're—"

"I have to look right to get invited to Joshy's fishing parties. Not everyone gets to go on his boat." Kathryn paused and rubbed her fingers over the ribbing on the cuff of her tight sweater. "Honestly not everyone wants to go on his boat…" She trailed off then stood up straight and looked around. "I thought Drusilla would be here."

"I don't know where she is."

"This is very important." Kathryn looked straight at Jessamine for the first time and handed her a large, sealed envelope, with *Drusilla* written in block letters. "Don't you open it."

"I wouldn't open someone else's mail." Jessamine was taken aback.

"You'll soon learn how things are done in this county, Josephine." Kathryn waved and trip-trapped out the door.

After Kathryn left, the slow morning passed. Marilyn rushed back and waved. "Thank you for covering! I have a video meeting about the construction now. Essential!" She disappeared into a tiny office, the murmur of emphatic conversation drifting out.

Jessamine continued exploring anything she could access on the old computer. She worked out how to check out books but not much else. She jumped and knocked over her tea when a crash followed by slithery sounds echoed around the library. She wiped the tea off the desk with a crumpled napkin from the kitchen cabinet before investigating. Books and a jagged broken plank sprawled across the floor from a sagging, over-packed shelf which had given up the fight. She gathered the dull, yellow-edged mysteries.

Marilyn appeared with tousled hair. "What was that racket?"

"This shelf collapsed."

Marilyn sighed. "Drusilla will *have* to prioritize weeding them." She looked around. "Where is she? Did she get you started on your training?"

"No." Jessamine hesitated. "I might have seen her in the parking lot leaving."

Marilyn frowned. "She knew this was your first day." She helped pick up spilled books. "Let's pile them behind the desk. I have *another* meeting about the new building this afternoon that I can't miss. I was hoping you could come." She dumped a pile of books on the desk and puffed out her cheeks. "I'll text Drusilla. If she can't come, can you manage on your own this afternoon?"

"I don't think…" Jessamine started. Then she looked at her new boss with her disheveled hair and tired eyes. "Of course."

For the rest of the afternoon, Jessamine checked out books and nodded greetings to the few customers. She checked in a pile of books from behind the desk and explored the shelves to find where they went.

A few minutes later, she returned to the desk defeated. As a qualified librarian, she wasn't used to shelving books, but these call numbers were bizarre. Several James Patterson thrillers, a weighty tome about forty-year-old politics in Indonesia, and a book full of diagrams about advanced sailing techniques were classified as ABC Early Readers for small children. Even when the call number matched the book, the shelves were jammed so full that she had trouble poking the books in. She hesitated to push harder because she didn't want another shelf to collapse.

After her failed attempt at shelving, Jessamine leaned her elbows on the desk while she watched the rain slash across the parking lot in sheets. She'd thrust the book about sailing out of sight under other books. The happy people on the boat frightened her. She knew it was absurd, but boats reminded her of her husband's glowering presence filling their Kansas house with impenetrable, dark smoke. When he bought an expensive boat a few days before Christmas without consulting her, their shouting and screaming sent spiky electric pulses around the house along prickly barbed wire. Then worse, her husband sat motionless staring at the coffee table as solid plains of cracked silent ice spread around their house to their bed, where Jessamine slept alone. When she spoke, her husband turned his back on her and refused to answer. She asked about who was going to drive their youngest daughter to her dorm and he ignored her. But when their daughter wandered past and asked the same question, he answered cheerfully, as if he hadn't just ignored his wife. His absence in bed shouted louder than any of the biting, narrow-eyed comments. Jessamine couldn't sleep, her nerves oriented to the place in the bed where he wasn't. Now he didn't know where she was, half a continent away from their shared house. She shivered. She hoped to keep it that way. In this Virginia county, she owned an unseen house that she inherited from a woman in her Kansas book group. That morning she arrived only in time to start her new library job. She hoped her mysterious new home was waterproof.

At four o'clock, Marilyn rushed out of her office. "I'll be here a bit longer to finish this construction spreadsheet. You can go." She paused and smiled.

"I'm glad you came. This is going to work out well."

Jessamine smiled back, liking Marilyn, but unable to share her optimism. In the parking lot, Jessamine quickly texted her grown children that her first workday had gone well. Then she pulled up her new address on her phone. Before she left Kansas, she had scrutinized online maps and street views like she was studying for an exam, but they revealed dense forest with tantalizing driveways disappearing out of sight.

On the tree-lined roads, the GPS sent her in circles before her phone connection failed. She lost her sense of direction and wound past the same broken-down, two-pump gas station four times. A man stood by the pumps and stared at her without emotion.

When she pulled over and scrambled for the crumpled envelope covered in garbled instructions from the Kansas book group, the wavering yellow overhead car light emphasized the darkening afternoon. *Around big tree.* The instructions didn't make sense, but Jessamine had never had a chance to ask for an explanation from Eileen, the woman in her book group. Eileen had never lived in the house. She'd inherited it from a woman named Rosemary. And Jessamine knew nothing about Rosemary. *Over bridge. Wooden fence— flower. Trains!*

Jessamine's frustration grew until she returned to a dip between concrete guard rails and realized that she was on a narrow bridge. Her headlights illuminated a faded sunflower painted on a mailbox leaning on a weed-covered post-and-rail fence. The instructions clicked in her mind; here was a bridge and a wooden fence, there was a flower on the mailbox.

Jessamine eased past the mailbox and along faint tire tracks between looming trunks, the treetops lost in the gloom. Bushes shrieked against her paint and the rain thudded on her roof. As she blinked her tired eyes, her car hit a metal "No Trespassing" sign hanging from a chain across her path.

She forced herself out of the warmth of the car and shivered among soaking weeds, using the questing light from her phone to follow the chain to a thick post with a fist-sized padlock. She had no key and no means to break it.

She gulped down tears.

A barking animal cry sounded in the inky night, and she jumped, dropping her phone. She fumbled for it on the wet ground as the shadowy forest pushed at her. She suppressed mental pictures of being alone in her house in Kansas when her husband was traveling—the warm kitchen after supper while she wiped the counters and the dishwasher hummed in the background, before she relaxed on the couch under a fuzzy blanket to watch a documentary. She had *chosen* to come this far. Alone in a soaking driveway couldn't be worse than the shouts and tears and silences that she had left. There was no return.

The need for sleep hit her like a wall, so she climbed into the driver's seat and pushed the door lock button three times; the repeated clunk of the mechanism a small consolation. Then she crawled into the rear and rolled herself in winter coats and blankets. She was alone, frightened, and no one knew where she was. The forest pressed on her, but the car seat was solid against her as exhaustion dragged her into sleep.

<h1 style="text-align:center">Chapter 4</h1>

Jessamine stood in her childhood one-room Pinehollow Public Library. Her husband stormed along the shelves, punching books to the floor. As he continued, the shelves became crowded with jars of pasta sauce, bags of rice, and boxes of ice cream. He swept them to the floor and stomped on them. She rose through the fading dream into the reality of breath-steamed car windows.

She climbed out and stretched her stiff back, breathing deeply in the misty air. The tree trunks rising from the wet, rich-scented earth were decorated with fuzzy moss and tiny Post-its of gray-green lichen. Tiny buds formed on some leafless trees. Since it was January, Kansas was covered in slushy snow, and spring was a long way off. Here, the pressing silence of the night had been replaced with birds tweeting, cawing, squeaking, and scolding. "I'm with you guys," she said aloud. "Very glad to see the dawn!"

She picked up the chain across the path and the post wobbled. She put her foot against the post and pushed. With a disapproving crack, it fell over and she laughed out loud. It was too late to follow the path now; she needed to get to work.

The mist was burning off as Jessamine drove along the winding country roads toward the YMCA near the city. Before leaving Kansas, she had located the YMCA as indispensable and made certain her membership was up-to-date. Raindrops sparkled on tall branches against the blue sky, and the small gas station she had driven past so many times looked ordinary. Several pickup trucks were parked at the side, and half a dozen men sat on benches in front with their hands around steaming cups and their work boots firm on the ground. The cups gave Jessamine a surge of desire for a hot cup of tea. She'd have to wait until work.

Inside the YMCA, she swam straight lengths, combing the chaotic thoughts in her head into manageable rows, then showered and put on her black nylon skirt and black and white patterned blouse, chosen for their wrinkle-free qualities. As she left, the woman in the mirror looked like the short, round librarian that she was, not the homeless woman she had woken up as that morning.

When she arrived at the library, Marilyn stood at the circulation desk. A short, slim woman in her thirties burst through the door. "What the gol-dash is going on? Did you see that bear? Kathryn Slattery is not pleased, I'm telling you!"

"I saw them moving it yesterday," Jessamine replied. "They said that John Ox-something wanted it."

"Oh! Joshua Oxford. That explains why Kathryn hasn't already put it in the dumpster. What Joshua wants is as good as done around here." As she talked, the woman bustled about, turning on computers and stacking up books.

"This is Stephanie." Marilyn gestured. "Stephanie, this is Jessamine, our newest librarian." She frowned around the library. "Since Drusilla's not here, she'll get you started on the circulation functions. Stephanie's our star employee. Especially because we're so short staffed."

"Great to meet you." Stephanie beamed and shook Jessamine's hand. "We're short staffed alright." She put her palm on her head. "I'm five-one, Marilyn here claims she's five-two, and it looks like you're about five feet even."

Jessamine paused, taken aback by a comment about her height by a woman she had just met, but Stephanie grinned so warmly that she laughed. "No, I claim to be five-two. Maybe the rain made me shrink."

The three women laughed. Marilyn waved her travel mug. "I'll grab tea and leave you in Stephanie's capable hands. I'd better get back to those budgets."

All morning, Stephanie chatted as she showed Jessamine how the library worked. "And when a patron asks for a nonfiction book from the three hundreds to the nine hundreds, I look in the catalog of the city library and see their call number for it. It's hard if they don't own it."

Jessamine frowned in confusion. "Why don't you use our catalog?"

"This library did a big catalog update three or four years ago, long before Marilyn came, and a big chunk of data about the books didn't transfer over. We lost the electronic records for most of our nonfiction books. We're getting better at memorizing the Dewey Decimal System, but I struggle finding them on the shelf."

Jessamine had worked in several libraries of different sizes and sorts, but this library was dumbfounding her. "Why don't you use WorldCat? You should be able to find a library somewhere that owns a copy of the book you're looking for."

"What's WorldCat? Excuse me." Stephanie turned to a teenager who gave her a quick smile then looked down. "Hello, Englebert. Have you found good books this week?" Stephanie checked out four worn science fiction paperbacks. After the boy moved into the shelves, she leaned toward Jessamine. "He's meant to be at school, but he has a rough home life. If he sits here and reads quietly, it's much better than the other trouble he could get into." She looked at the screen. "What were you saying about cats?"

"WorldCat is a list of books owned by libraries all over the world. You're likely to find most books there." Jessamine paused and frowned, not wanting to be condescending. "Why doesn't this library update the electronic records of the books? Re-catalog them so you can find them?"

"We're slowly typing the records in when we have time." Stephanie shrugged. "It's supposed to be a big part of Drusilla's job. She doesn't get much done." Stephanie screwed up her eyes as if she was about to roll them, but cleared her throat and said, "Did I show you the way the babies' board books are arranged?"

In the early afternoon, Stephanie asked, "Have you found a place to rent locally? It's hard to find a place round here."

"I'm… um… staying in a friend's house." Jessamine was mortified to admit she was sleeping in a car, despite already liking Stephanie. She pictured herself as solidly respectable; her single brush with the law consisted of a speeding ticket two decades ago, and she'd apologized so much to the young cop that he'd blushed. "Er. Could you show me how to take a fine off a patron's account again? I missed that."

After they'd gone into the library's computer system to practice, Stephanie asked, "Why'd you choose Bent River County? We're losing population. People don't usually want to move here."

"It was…" Jessamine stopped. She didn't know how to explain how her family, home, and job in Kansas had grown shambolic, a word that Jessamine's grandmother had used and she found perfect for the way her life had tilted out of control. She pushed thoughts of her husband firmly away. She fought off the odd feeling that if she thought of him, he would be able to detect it and know where she was. She shuddered to think that he would be able to locate her. "I wanted a change," she said aloud to Stephanie.

"This sure must be a big change!" Stephanie laughed. "You said you worked in a university library? This might be the tiniest library in the universe. Why did you come to a small library?"

"I liked the look of the place when I saw it online, but it was unexpected that I found a new…" Again, Jessamine was overwhelmed by trying to explain how she had been stunned to learn that a woman in her book group had left her a house and land. She flabbergasted herself when she threw over a lifetime of predictability, grabbed a few clothes and her most precious books, and drove halfway across the continent to Virginia. Her mind slid past the last scenes with her husband and she shivered. She had to escape.

Stephanie must have sensed Jessamine's hesitation. "Don't worry about me. My husband's always telling me I'm too nosy. I'm glad you came to Bent River County. Our library needs new faces and ideas."

Jessamine smiled at Stephanie. "I'm glad to be here and meet you all."

They jumped as Drusilla banged through the door. She looked Jessamine up and down. "Oh, you're here." She flicked a glittering turquoise scarf across her neck.

Marilyn came out of her office. Drusilla stepped forward and towered over Marilyn. Marilyn stepped back, then turned to Jessamine and gestured. "This is Drusilla." Her voice sounded shaky. "And this is Jessamine from out west. She's finally arrived!"

"I saw." Drusilla eyed Jessamine coldly.

"Nice to meet you." Jessamine put out her hand, but Drusilla turned away.

Marilyn's hands fluttered. She gave a barking laugh and cleared her throat. "Jessamine's training can start today, Drusilla."

"I won't have time. Look, Stephanie's standing right there."

"Yes, but it's part of your—"

"I don't have time." Drusilla turned and stalked through a door marked Chief Liaison of Office and Organizational Management, closing it behind her.

Stephanie bustled about the circulation desk. "Do you want to go over the opening procedures again, Jessamine?" She turned to Marilyn. "Is that a good plan, Marilyn?"

Marilyn jumped as if she'd been thinking of other things. "Yes, that'll work. Thank you." She cleared her throat and smoothed her hair. "I've got tons to do on the budgets."

Stephanie chatted about the bear while showing Jessamine more about how to run the library. Jessamine wanted to ask about Drusilla's rudeness and Marilyn's lack of response. On her second day of a new job, she didn't know how to start.

An hour later, while Jessamine was checking in books, Drusilla came out of her office, trailing scarves and strong perfume. She stood too close, and Jessamine took a step back. "You need to do the craft program next week on the twentieth," Drusilla barked.

"Yes, we talked about crafts in the interviews." Jessamine's heart lifted. "I love doing craft programs. What are we making?"

"I don't know what we're making." Drusilla gave Jessamine a slow look. "That's what we hired you for."

"But you said next week on the twentieth. That's awfully short notice to do a craft program. Shouldn't we make a plan for several months and then schedule the programs?"

"I've already put a craft on the calendar since you were starting." Drusilla huffed. "If you don't think you can do the job we hired you for, then I guess we'll need to do it another way. I thought you said you were experienced at running library programs?"

"I *am* experienced at running library programs." Jessamine felt in the wrong, but she couldn't tell why. "Of course I'll do it!"

"Good. It's your job." Drusilla turned away.

"Where are the supplies?" Jessamine called after her. "I'll look them over to get something ready."

"We don't have supplies." Drusilla smirked.

"What budget do I have to get supplies?"

Drusilla's lip curled. "No budget."

"How am I meant to…" Jessamine wasn't sure what to say.

This time Drusilla walked away. "Work it out. It's next week. It's your job."

Jessamine stood holding the book that she had been checking in, staring after Drusilla.

Stephanie rolled her eyes. "Don't worry. She talks to everyone like that."

"Everyone?" Jessamine looked at her hands to see if they were shaking.

"Everyone she's not sucking up to. You should hear her talk to Joshua Oxford. It's so slimy it turns my stomach. We do have supplies. I can't help with the craft, though. I'm all thumbs. I run the bingo with my cousin Cyril. People love that. For now, I'll show you our poor, sad supply closet."

"Thank you." Jessamine felt better for having one ally.

"I nearly forgot—Drusilla made a sign-up sheet. It's under the desk in here." Stephanie pulled out a binder and showed Jessamine a printed sheet.

Sing up for Craft Tesday

They looked at it and burst out laughing. "She may think she's in charge, but she can't spell," Stephanie said.

"Didn't she have spell checker?" Jessamine raised her eyebrows. "Anyway, I can make another sign-up sheet. It won't take long."

Across the library, Stephanie shoved aside the cart of worn board books to reveal a door. The supply closet was piled with faded construction paper mixed with broken crayons, and bottles of dried-up school glue.

"And of course, there's the junk in the kitchen. Marilyn asked Drusilla to go through that, but she hasn't." Stephanie leaned into the closet. "There're other odds and ends at the back." She pulled out a garbage bag full of paint-spattered rags. Stephanie wiped her hands on her blouse. "A patron is waiting to check out. I'll leave you to it."

Jessamine stared at the jumble, wondering what she'd let herself in for. *I can do this. I came all this way. I left my old life behind*, she told herself sternly and began to sort the supplies into piles. This was still better than where she'd come from.

Chapter 5

Jessamine dumped an ill-assorted pile of cardstock and construction paper on the circulation desk. "Look what I found for the craft."

Stephanie poked the paper with her finger. "It's… manky."

"We can make greeting cards and bookmarks. We'll tell the patrons that the mottled effect is…" Jessamine paused. "Artistic! I thought of buying supplies out of my own money, but I can't afford it."

"You shouldn't buy supplies with your own money."

"I know, but…" Jessamine turned over more paper and shrieked as a mouse leapt out. She jumped back as the tiny creature bounced off the desk and scuttled under a nearby bookshelf. She put her hand on her chest. "Yikes! I wasn't expecting that."

Stephanie stood frozen. She dropped the book she was holding and puffed out a breath. "I wasn't either. You won't be able to use this."

"No, there's chewed paper and mouse poo everywhere."

"I'll get the dustpan." Stephanie hurried away.

Jessamine turned over pieces of cardstock with the tips of her fingers in the hope that the back was better. When Stephanie returned, she said, "I suppose we can use the paper on the outside. It's not stained. We'll tell people to wash their hands."

"I guess?" Stephanie frowned. "It's not very hygienic." She sighed. "As I always say, it's good enough for government work."

"I could cancel." Jessamine remembered Drusilla's sneer and her mind and mouth settled into a firm line. "No, I *can* work it out for next week."

"Good for you!" Stephanie piled the last of the returned books on a library cart. "Are you okay to watch the desk? I'm never far away in this library."

"That's fine. I'll keep sorting this paper." Jessamine hesitated. "I tried shelving and a bunch of James Patterson thrillers had the call number of children's ABC readers. I didn't know what to do."

"That means Drusilla entered them in the system." Stephanie laughed. "She didn't know how to use a drop-down list on the computer, so all the books were catalogued ABC since that's the first thing alphabetically on the list. We know the right place to put them on the shelves."

Jessamine stood with her mouth open and blinked.

"Yes. It's hard to believe." Stephanie laughed again. "Marilyn showed Drusilla how to use a drop-down list, and she's supposed to be fixing all the old ones. But…" Stephanie cleared her throat. "I'd better get to this shelving."

Stephanie returned with the cart half full. "I hate shelving when there's no room for the books."

"I can imagine." Jessamine hesitated again; she was worried about criticizing on her second day in a new job. "I thought the shelves were overcrowded. And I found a moldy fifty-year-old book about dinosaurs. I already mentioned it to Marilyn and she said it was Drusilla's job."

Stephanie sighed again. "Everything not done is Drusilla's job." She shrugged. "We're waiting for our new bigger and better library where everything will fit, but they've been talking about our new library for over a decade. This is the only library I've worked in. In fact, it's the only library I've ever belonged to. What do they do in other libraries? Do they add shelves to fit all the books?"

"Not in a public library. A university library keeps things longer. It's more like an archive. A public library is meant to have books that people check out—they called it a 'popular circulating collection' at library school."

"That sounds fancy. And better than what we have." Stephanie checked in a picture book with tape holding the torn cover together. "How do you get rid of books?"

"It's called weeding. And like in a garden, you need to keep at it all the time or," Jessamine looked around, "you'll get overwhelmed with books that claim the USSR still exists or have gone moldy."

Kathryn and Marilyn hustled in the door, Kathryn talking earnestly. "So, you'll work on that spreadsheet for the state and get it back to me by tomorrow?"

"Yes." Marilyn hesitated then screwed up her eyebrows. "But I think the figures for the tile need—"

"Don't worry!" Kathryn squeezed Marilyn's shoulder and grinned. "It's all working out fine." She looked around at the assembled women. "Our library is great. Thank you for your help, ladies. I'll just leave this on Drusilla's desk."

Stephanie eyed Kathryn's retreating back thoughtfully. "Kathryn Slattery thinks she deserves everything she has. She worked hard for decades, but so did lots of other people. Most people round here weren't born with silver spoons in their mouths." She laughed. "I hardly had a spoon at all. No one believes me now, but we didn't have a floor when I was a little kid. It was a step up when we moved into a used trailer after I started school. And those schools were bad. It was hard to stay away from all the drugs. Kathryn's the same as me, for all that she puts on airs and fusses about her meetings and spreadsheets."

Marilyn lifted her arms as if in surrender. "All I know is that their meetings are insane. Their budget ideas are from another *galaxy* compared with every other library I worked in."

"Where did you work before?" Jessamine asked.

"I've worked all over, in lots of libraries. I helped open a new branch of the city library." Marilyn shook her head. "They hired me from outside the county to bring my experience of libraries, so you'd think they'd accept that I know how to run this one and how to open a new one." She looked at Jessamine and Stephanie's surprised faces and laughed. "I *really* don't understand their budgeting logic."

"I was telling Jessamine that the people in Bent River County have been waiting for our new library for a long time." Stephanie gestured around the crowded room.

Marilyn leaned her elbows on the desk and sagged. "There seem to be differences of opinion about the new library. We *will* get there steadily."

"We were also talking about the crowded shelves. I can't find any room for shelving these." Stephanie patted the half-full cart. "Jessamine told me about weeding."

Marilyn drooped more. "Yes, we'll get to the weeding. We should set up a meeting with Drusilla."

"What about displays?" Jessamine asked. "We could get the better books out where people will see them. If more are checked out, there'll be fewer on the shelves. We could use the cabinet by the door with the old pamphlets."

"That's a great idea if you have time." Marilyn stood up straight. "I knew we hired you for a reason."

"And there's that folding wire display shelf behind the door in the kitchen." Stephanie looked interested too.

"I'll make a poster to go with it." Jessamine felt optimistic. "I love doing displays. What should we do for our first theme?"

"A cheerful topic to look forward to after those meetings." Marilyn stretched.

"We did a display on spring in my last library," Jessamine said. "Spring happens a lot earlier here, and we can be ready to welcome it with books about outdoorsy things like gardening and birds."

"That's a great idea." Stephanie's face lit up. She dug through the kitchen for the wire display and pulled out a box of long-forgotten glass sign holders. She held one up. "Do you think we can use these?"

"They have a definite 1970s vibe." Jessamine examined the black, glass-fronted sign holders. "You slide words into these slots. I think they're too plain for displays. They're to put on the shelves to help people find the books. I noticed you don't have anything up with Dewey Decimal numbers or call numbers and locations. How do people know where to look?"

"Oh, everyone knows where things are," Stephanie said.

"What if a new customer comes into the library? Or an old customer wants a new type of book?"

"I never thought of that." Stephanie frowned. "I guess they ask us?"

"I know they'll get a helpful answer if they ask you, Stephanie." Jessamine laughed. "I'll put up the locations and then people can find things for themselves."

Jessamine noted the books at the beginning and end of each shelf then printed the call numbers to slip into the slots. She hung the signs with sticky foam dots she found in the desk.

They cleared long-expired pamphlets off the cabinet by the front door and collected books for children and adults about gardens, spring, and flowers. They added DVDs and magazines and thought of objects to brighten their display. "I've got paper flowers. I'll bring those," Stephanie said. "And my girls have toy trowels and rakes and wheelbarrows."

"And plant pots or seed packets?" Jessamine asked.

"Yes, that'll be fun." Stephanie looked over and grinned. "I'll check what else we have at home."

Chapter 6

It was still daylight when Jessamine arrived at her sunflower mailbox. She pulled aside the *No Trespassing* sign and continued along the two-track driveway. She didn't know what the house looked like, only that it related to trains. A boxcar? An engine? It didn't sound appealing, but better than a car, and she couldn't afford anything else.

She came to a leafless tree with a trunk as wide as her car. More of the instructions: *Around big tree.* She drove to the right, but she came back to where she'd started. "Dang," she said, "I went widdershins—of course it went wrong." Knowing it was ridiculous, but in need of luck, she looped around the tree in the other direction.

She found an overgrown path where head-high weeds and thorny vines tangled around half-rotted stumps. It had obviously been cleared more recently than the surrounding mature forest. She changed out of her work clothes and tried to push past the stumps. Thorns clutched her skin and clothes and wouldn't let go. Using her sleeve as a glove, she tugged a vine but thorns pierced her hand. She pulled herself backwards and sideways until she was brought to a stop by vines stretching across her neck and face, stabbing her scalp.

Panic built in Jessamine's chest, hot and demanding. She hated to be held down, but she was alone in the woods, so she had to think her way out. She took three deep breaths. Delicately, with thumb and forefinger pinching the smooth part of the stalk between the thorns, she untangled the vines one by one, starting with those menacing her face and her neck. New vines snaked in to take their place, but she made slow progress until she tore free.

She picked thorns out of her skin, but two were lodged firmly under her fingernails. Her body was covered with red lines. They were only plants; but they felt malevolent.

Jessamine slowed her breathing and stretched her complaining back. Her eyes fell on a glinting horizontal line. *It must be the roof of the house visible in the setting sun.* Her shoulders sagged with relief. If she drove toward the house, would the car get past the stumps or bogged down in the soggy ground? And what would the thorns do to her paint? She ventured into the tall, mature forest, thinking of going around the vines. She instantly lost her sense of direction among the tree trunks. Going through the vines was her only choice.

Looking toward the house, she thought she saw tall figures, like Drusilla and the man she had seen her leaning on the day before. She took a step toward them, her mouth open to call out, but she lost sight of them. Was that a tall stump shaped like people? She couldn't be sure. She shivered alone in the forest and knew she needed to hurry.

Back at the car, she dug through her luggage until she found items to help her win this battle. When she cut at the vines with nail scissors, the stems bent and snaked around to catch on her sleeves. She dug with a rusty trowel she found near a stump, but tenacious roots and rhizomes unfurled in all directions.

She returned to her car again and munched on the cheese and crackers she'd been subsisting on for days. Should she sleep in the car another night? She groaned at the thought. Thoroughly sick of crackers, she poked in the glove box for a granola bar and found her multi-tool folding pliers her youngest son gave her last Christmas. The holiday had been a cold, awkward event, but her youngest had tried. He had given everyone thoughtful presents, probably too expensive for his first job. He had always been a sensitive child and keenly felt the tension in the house. Jessamine had thanked him warmly and wondered what to do with the tool. "You put it in your glove box. You never know when you'll need it," he said.

She gripped a vine with the pliers and swept up with her arm. A length of rhizome and vine pulled out of the ground. Victory! She wanted to tell her son about his multi-tool saving the day, but she'd have to wait until tomorrow at the library when her phone had bars.

The malevolent plants didn't surrender easily. Clearly, Velcro was based on nature, as the vines clung to their friends. It was completely dark, except for the light of the moon coming and going behind scudding clouds, when sweaty, filthy, and scratched, Jessamine stood in front of a compact building nestled in the forest. She was able to make out a sign hanging from the verandah's wooden scrollwork proclaiming *Walnut Crossing Station*. She pictured a railway waiting room with wooden benches and a ticket office.

The ornate looped key on a chain around her neck had been her talisman for five years. She had no idea if the old-fashioned key would open any doors, but it was all the lawyer sent. She climbed wooden steps to a peeling door adorned with a tarnished brass letter slot and a high window of pebbly glass. The ornate key grated reluctantly around in the lock and the door opened.

She turned on her cell phone light and entered gently, as if into a museum. An antique dial telephone and a phone book sat on a spindly, carved table in a short hallway. She'd worried that five years of abandonment would leave her owning an unlivable ruin, but under the musty smell and thick dust, the house looked undamaged.

The first doorway off the hallway revealed a bedroom containing a rumpled single bed, as if a sleeper had recently emerged from under the patchwork quilt. Cardboard boxes stood open in front of a rounded dressing table, with open drawers spilling a tangle of hairbrushes, sweaters, and makeup. The second bedroom, the living room, and the kitchen were clogged with furniture and boxes were scattered, as if the packer would return at any moment.

The kitchen transported Jessamine to the 1950s with its pastel, round-cornered appliances and swirly patterned table nestled into an alcove. More out of habit than expectation, Jessamine flicked a round metal light switch; nothing happened. It felt like an empty library that longed to be filled with people to be complete. She shook her head. She'd survived last night alone in the forest. Now wasn't the time to scare herself. She considered making her way back through the vines to her car, but the wind was picking up and through the open door she saw the glint of cold rain as muted moonlight made its way through the clouds. She closed the door.

She eyed the living room's woodstove, similar to the one her family used to heat their house and water when she was a child. Logs and matches waited in a lopsided basket, and the ash pan was brushed clean. A pyramid of sticks perched over crumpled newspaper. Jessamine had sensible thoughts of getting the chimney checked. "Being here isn't the least bit sensible," she said out loud. The living room was the only room that welcomed her with its fire waiting to be lit.

Jessamine crouched on a three-legged stool with a castle cross-stitched on top and put a match to the lowest part of the paper. She was comforted by the tang of wood smoke, overlying the deeper, earthy tones of the forest and the musty house. She placed a log across the burning sticks and watched the flames curl around it. She remembered camping with her family over a decade ago, her children elementary-school aged—able to look after themselves, but not old enough for the worst excesses of teens. "Why did you put that wood there?" her middle boy had asked. "How do you know how to build the fire?"

"You have to look at the fire how it actually *is*, not how you think it should be. Once you know how it is, you can see what it needs and give it what it needs, whether that's another piece of wood, to be stirred up, or left alone."

Her son had looked at her with her husband's eyes in a younger face. "You said something profound."

"Maybe I did accidentally say something profound!" Jessamine laughed.

She added another stick to the railway station woodstove and sighed. She couldn't remember the rest of that conversation, but she wondered if she could have been better at working out what the people in her family needed, and if she had been able to give it to them, would everything have turned out better? She poked the fire. Would her husband find her here? Would he care that she was gone?

As the fire caught and the smoke disappeared up the chimney, she relaxed on the foot stool, smiling at her worries about the chimney's soundness. She yawned and thought of Rosemary's bedroom, but it was haunted with a stranger's life. She couldn't sleep in a bed that looked like it had been recently vacated. She found a clean, folded patchwork quilt and curled up on the firm knobby fabric of the green couch while the woodstove's warmth and flickering flames lulled her to sleep.

Chapter 7

The next morning, the first thing Jessamine noticed was that the cabinet by the library door was empty. No display. She frowned. The only evidence of her glass location signs were telltale sticky spots on the ends of the shelves.

Jessamine put her purse on the desk next to a pile of books about spring.

Kathryn banged through the library door with wide eyes. "Jolene, have you seen Drusilla?"

"No, I—"

"I have to find her." Kathryn tapped the toe of her boot, then rushed to the door marked Chief Liaison of Office and Organizational Management and tore it open. "Malcolm is dead!" she shrieked.

"It's not surprising with the way he lived." Drusilla's voice was dry despite Kathryn's emotion. "We know he's been hiding and living the high life for months with all that money he owes me."

"He wasn't living at all." Kathryn sounded near tears. "The police just found his body in the Chesapeake Bay. It took them a while to identify it since it had been there for months. He must have died as soon as he disappeared."

"Died or was killed?" Drusilla sounded concerned now. "I told him not to get on the wrong side of certain people. I thought Josh's boat party was the sign of a new start."

"An end, not a start. And he was a champion swimmer. I always wondered about him drowning and —"

"Stop!" Drusilla's voice was sharp. "Some people are listening."

They both turned and glared at Jessamine, who stared at them with her mouth open until they slammed the door shut.

Stephanie appeared from among the shelves. Jessamine opened her mouth to ask about Malcolm when Stephanie bumped the library cart against the desk.

"Oops, sorry!" Stephanie stopped and put her hands on her hips. "I'm seething!"

"What happened to our display? And our signs?"

"Drusilla took them down." Stephanie shook her head.

"What? Why?"

"I don't know. Because it wasn't hers? I don't know why she was here this early."

Drusilla emerged from her office with Kathryn. "We need to take this seriously." Kathryn still sounded panicky. She glared at Jessamine and Stephanie, then trip-trapped out the door.

Drusilla came up to the desk. "I told you to put those books away, Stephanie."

"These are our display books. Jessamine's here now, so we'll rebuild our display."

"If you put them there, people can't find them. And it's a mess."

"It wasn't a mess. It's to promote the books so people can find good things to check out. And to make the library cheery and welcoming." Stephanie kept her hands on her hips. "And people can't find things in this library anyway with the ABC books all cataloged wrong."

Jessamine wanted to ease the tense situation. "Do we have a 'Display' designation in the catalog? We could check the books out to 'Display' and then we'd know where they are."

"I don't know about any designations." Drusilla sounded impatient. "I told you to put the books away, instead of making a mess with them."

Stephanie narrowed her eyes. "You're not my boss."

"I'm the Chief Liaison of Office and Organizational Management. And I say you need to put those books away."

A silence stretched out.

Marilyn came through the door. "Good morning every…" She stopped and looked at the faces around the desk. "Is everything okay?"

Jessamine and Stephanie eyed each other and didn't say anything.

Drusilla flicked her turquoise scarf with gold circles. "They are being disobedient."

"Disobedient?" Stephanie spluttered. "Plt, blt, ba!"

Marilyn lifted her hands, palms forward. "Let's sit down here and talk until the library opens."

They sat around a table among the shelves.

"What's the problem?" Marilyn asked.

The four women stared at each other silently for a moment.

Stephanie spoke first. "You know the display we talked about yesterday? Drusilla took it down."

"Why?" Marilyn looked at Drusilla, puzzled.

Drusilla sniffed. "You said yourself that this space is too small and we have too much junk. I'm trying to clean up this library. We don't need more things lying around."

"Drusilla, I asked them to make the display. As you said, there isn't much room here, and no money for pretty display shelves. We do the best we can." Marilyn paused and ran her hands through her hair. "I'm not sure I understand your objection. Displays are standard in libraries. I thought they made it look good!"

Drusilla stood up. Her face was impassive, but Jessamine saw a pulse throbbing at the edge of her scarf. For a moment, the tall woman towered over the three shorter women, then she flicked her scarf again and clumped away. "I've got work to do in my office."

As the day passed, Jessamine kept eyeing Drusilla's office door, wondering if the tall woman would stomp out, but she stayed hidden. When Drusilla disappeared out the doors at two o'clock without speaking to anyone, Jessamine's shoulders relaxed. She let out a breath and her mind wandered to returning to her new home, lighting a fire, and exploring it more. The pair of thick, paint-spattered corduroy pants and a torn sweatshirt from the bag in the library supply closet were far too big for her, but she grabbed them to wear anyway. The vines frightened her, and these felt like armor.

The next morning, Jessamine was greeted at the county building by another crowd commenting and gesturing, as Frank slid the dolly under the bear.

"You should put it *in* Kathryn Slattery's office," one voice said.

"How about back in the woods?" another voice called.

"No, on the roof so people can see it on the satellite view. That's the visibility they want." Everyone laughed.

Frank smiled and waved for the crowd to part. "I've been told to put it in the school. Then it won't be staring us in the face over here."

Walter came over to help, and Jessamine held the door open.

Frank grinned and nodded his thanks to Jessamine as he went past. "Here we go into my truck. The adventures of the Oxford bear."

The men pushed the bear over to a battered pickup truck and loaded it into the back. Jessamine wondered why they weren't using a county vehicle. She was distracted by Marilyn arriving. They walked together down the hall to the library.

"Jessamine, you don't need to share the computer on the circulation desk with Stephanie." Marilyn waved her travel mug. "There's another desk in Drusilla's office you can use."

"Okay." Jessamine grimaced inwardly. She had only worked with Drusilla for a few days, but she had no desire to share anything with her.

"You could tidy the office desk this morning, and then when Stephanie arrives, you could sit back there to work." Marilyn shrugged as she headed into her office. "Back to my infinity of reports and spreadsheets."

Jessamine switched on the light in Drusilla's tiny office. One desk was an oasis; a decorative table lamp perched on a corner of a clear desktop. A stapler, computer keyboard, and pen cup were lined up, waiting to serve their owner when she returned. The other desk was invisible under piles of books, papers, leaking pens, binders, and unidentifiable objects.

It wasn't difficult to guess which desk was hers, so Jessamine pulled out the chair. When she sat, the chair shot downwards, and she threw her arms in the air as she almost went over backwards. She stood, and the chair seat shot back up. She looked underneath and saw that the mechanism was broken, so the chair couldn't support any weight. She eased herself back onto it slowly until her chin was level with the desk. Jessamine pushed the chair aside and pulled over Drusilla's chair. She picked through the chaos.

A jumble of library books with ripped pages and broken spines were mixed with multiple copies of years-old popular titles. Jessamine sorted them into a pile to be mended and a pile to potentially add to the collection. She couldn't tell the purpose of the papers. Lists of book titles with prices fought for attention with old fliers about library programs with corrections written in pen. Jessamine needed to ask Drusilla about them. Jessamine examined a paper headed *Returns and Refunds*. She frowned. The amounts were huge for a tiny library.

"What are you doing?" Drusilla's clashing colors filled the doorway.

Jessamine jumped at the sharp voice and resisted the urge to shrink back. "I'm clearing off this desk so I can use it, like Marilyn said."

"You can't use that desk." Drusilla leaned forward. There wasn't room for her to come into the office without turning sideways and edging past Jessamine. Her voice rose. "Are you sitting in my chair? That's a special chair."

"Which desk am I meant to use? There's only one computer at the circulation desk."

"I don't know. Marilyn does the computers." Drusilla stepped backwards and held out her arm in an invitation for Jessamine to leave.

Jessamine hesitated. She felt stupid being scolded and sent out like a child, but she didn't know what else to do. "I'll talk to Marilyn about it." She gathered her dignity around her and went to the circulation desk. When she realized she was still clutching the paper, she thrust it into the pocket of her cardigan.

"I thought you were getting office space?" Stephanie asked.

"Not if Drusilla's got anything to do with it. I'd better talk to Marilyn."

"Marilyn's gone to a meeting with the Library Committee." Stephanie looked worried. "And then she has another one with the county. She said she hopes she'll be back before the library closes."

"What computer can I use?" Jessamine sagged. "I've got to work on my planning and get a bunch of fliers made."

"You can use this one when I'm not checking books in and out." Stephanie patted her on the arm.

"You need this computer to do your work."

"We can share," Stephanie said cheerfully. "We've done it before. There are always the public computers, now that Marilyn's gotten some of them working, or I've worked on my laptop before."

"Your own laptop?" Jessamine had trouble believing what she was hearing. "Most libraries have plenty of computers. It's essential! They usually have several sets that staff and patrons can use."

"Not us. When we've run programs that needed computers, we scrambled and borrowed them from everyone. We can't afford a set of laptops."

"My laptop's in my car," Jessamine said. "I'll use that for today and talk to Marilyn later."

"Tell Walter to let you through with it, since you work here," Stephanie said.

Jessamine fetched her laptop and settled down at a library table to work. She felt knocked for a six. The cricket metaphor she remembered from her childhood was the only appropriate response to the amateur bumbling of her new library. But she needed the job to keep her newly declared independence in Bent River County. She'd heard from her old boss at the university library that her husband had shown up angry and looking for her. The campus police needed to intervene. Another reason she couldn't go back.

After Drusilla left for lunch, Jessamine poked her head into the office. The piles of junk on the second desk looked higher. She shook her head. *I must be imagining it.* She stuck a removable sticky arrow on the bookshelf at the debris high tide mark. Just before closing time, the arrow was buried under fresh floes of flotsam.

"The junk is breeding on the desk that's meant to be mine," she told Stephanie. "It's weird. It can't be happening."

"It's breeding alright." Stephanie shook her head. "I saw Drusilla piling clutter from the kitchen on it." She laughed. "I thought she was finally cleaning up the kitchen. It appears not—she's trying to bury you."

Chapter 8

Jessamine used the YMCA for her showers. She worked on setting up her electricity and water as she had done dozens of times as her military family moved around, but she discovered it was more difficult in a rural area. She made multiple phone calls at work when her phone got a signal, and the power company promised to restore her electricity the following week.

The woman at the water company told her that her address was never connected to their system. When she asked the woman if there were other water companies in the area, the woman said, "Honey, if you're out in the country, you probably got a well. They should have told you that. You've got to get it inspected."

Jessamine thanked her and researched wells and septic systems. She'd need to save more money. She bought bottled water and a giant flashlight and charged her phone every day at work. Camping in her new house was much cheaper than a hotel.

She stripped Rosemary's bed and grimaced at the stained, urine scented mattress. She'd buy a new one when she'd saved money. Jessamine loved the snugness of curling up on her knobby couch in one of Rosemary's colorful patchwork quilts, but her stiff back and hips demanded that she soon sleep in a bed.

Every evening after work, Jessamine vowed to clear the back bedroom and determine if there was a usable bed in there. In the first week, she didn't get far. The door was blocked with an impassable mishmash. In the wavering beam of her flashlight, she stared at an old gramophone and a chipped statue of a flute-playing faun wearing a faded cloche hat on a broken sewing machine table before turning away.

"You can't spend so long on your phone." Drusilla stood in front of the desk with her hands on her hips.

"I just moved here. I've got to turn on the power and get organized." Jessamine turned off her phone.

"Can't you do that at home? Where are you living, anyway?"

"I can't do it at home because I've got to get the power turned on first." Jessamine didn't want to talk about where she was living. "When will I get a computer that I can use?"

Drusilla's office phone rang, and she headed into her office. "Come and see me later," she said over her shoulder. "I'll see if I can afford anything, although I don't know why you think you need one."

Jessamine didn't understand Drusilla's schedule. Marilyn told Jessamine that her job was to run programs, but Jessamine often ran the circulation desk when Stephanie wasn't there. In this library, a staff member needed to check out books for the patrons, as it didn't have a self-checkout. After Stephanie arrived, Jessamine headed to Drusilla's office. Drusilla was on the phone and she pulled faces and flicked her hand at Jessamine to enter. Jessamine squeezed into the cramped space and perched on the broken office chair, slipping down to near the floor.

"I wouldn't want to order items that you don't…" Drusilla said into the phone. "No, no. That won't be necessary. The funding will be fine. Yes, the usual arrangement. No, trust me, they have no idea. I'll work out the money. Um. There's someone here. *Being nosy!* I'd better go." She hung up the phone and turned to Jessamine. "I told you to go away while I was making a private telephone call."

"What?"

"I waved you away. You could see that."

"I thought you were waving me in. You were talking about the library."

"You should stay out of my office." Drusilla gestured for Jessamine to leave again.

Jessamine hated to feel dismissed, so she sat stubbornly on her miniature chair. Despite being blessed with short legs, her knees stuck up near her chin. "I thought this was meant to be a shared office."

"No! I need peace for my important work. I'll talk to Josh… um, Marilyn about it."

"Good idea. I'll talk to Marilyn."

Jessamine pushed herself up off the silly chair and stood with her hands on her hips, then paused. "What happened to that man who drowned? Malcolm? Kathryn was so upset."

Drusilla twitched as if stung by a bee. "None of your business." She picked up a piece of paper and her hand shook. She put it down quickly.

"I was only asking because Kathryn said he was your friend. I'm sorry he drowned."

"He didn't drown. You don't know anything about it." Drusilla blinked, then narrowed her eyes. "Don't go poking your nose in. You're a *busybody*."

Between her meetings, Marilyn didn't want to hear about their conflict.

"Can you work it out among yourselves?" Marilyn ran her hands through her hair. "I know this space isn't adequate, and the library's poor. We've got to work together and do the best with what we have."

"What about a computer? How can I work without one?"

"Yes, we'll prioritize that. Drusilla does the ordering and keeps track of the day-to-day library budget, so she'll need to order it. Talk to her."

"Drusilla's gone home for the day. Shall I choose a laptop now, or wait 'til she gets back?"

"You can select one together." Marilyn's eyes kept sliding to her computer screen. "Send her an email and you two can work it out." She ruffled her hair again. "Let's talk about it next week?" She gestured at her screen. "I've got a lot…"

Marilyn worked hard, and Jessamine hated to make her new boss's life more complicated. She typed an email to Drusilla and cc'd Marilyn. She outlined how she'd need basic equipment, such as a computer, so she could do her work. She added an exclamation point to the "thank you" in her sign-off, and a smiley face after her name like she usually did. In the past, Jessamine worried about the emoji inflation spiral. She would write satisfactory, professional, and polite emails to friends or colleagues, then on reading it over before sending it, she thought something was missing. Without a range of exclamation points, smiley faces, and clapping hands, it looked cold, perhaps angry, and she felt obliged to head back to the emoji button to rectify the situation with three cats with hearts for eyes. Writing to Drusilla, Jessamine frowned. She deleted the smiley face and exclamation points and clicked send.

The first weekend in Jessamine's new home, it rained hard again. Out her kitchen windows, she saw outbuildings poking through a soggy snarl of jungle. She would explore that part of her new domain when the weather improved. She reveled in being alone and secure. Even with the fire going, she wore two sweaters to keep warm, but there was no chance her husband's angry, demanding presence would intrude.

Her first priority was a proper place to sleep. She examined Rosemary's bedroom in the daylight, admiring faded yellow flowers meandering across dusty wallpaper. She stepped forward to touch a rounded corner. She tried to imagine why the builder added an Art Deco touch to this architecturally odd building.

"I will clear it out," she told herself firmly and unearthed hairbrushes with strands of silver hair, small bags of odd buttons jumbled with fabric scraps, and pilled hand-knitted sweaters.

As she placed items in boxes, she said, "Thank you, Rosemary," in deference to the lingering spirit of their owner. Jessamine had never met Rosemary, so she hesitated to intrude on this woman revealed to her through her possessions. But there was too much flotsam and too much of Rosemary. Jessamine hardened her oversensitive heart and pulled out the drawers, upending them into the waiting boxes. She tucked in the cardboard flaps and marched each box to be stacked in front of the faun near the back bedroom.

Jessamine tugged on a stuck drawer until it gave with a ripping sound, and she fell onto her bottom. She felt around behind the drawer and pulled out a handful of brittle paper and a small, yellowed notebook labeled *My Diary* in a childish hand. Jessamine leaned against the bed. She justified opening the diary with the thought that it might have historical importance, although she knew she was simply curious. It had been hidden, but Rosemary was dead.

Jessamine smiled at the first entries revealing the life of a well-loved child. *I got a puppy for Christmas!!! I can't, can't, can't believe it!!!! They said I couldn't have one. Now they said they were waiting to surprise me. He's the best dog in the Whole Universe!!!!* After a long time gap, the entries focused on teenage problems. *My mother won't let me go to Joshy's party!! And they have a POOL!!!! She said we should avoid those Oxfords. What century is she living in??!!??? She's so old fashioned!!! I want Joshy to see me in my new swimsuit. I love him.* Each letter o and dot for an i was drawn as a small heart.

Jessamine was about to add it to a box when she saw that later pages were crumpled. She thumbed to the back, where words slashed across the page in large red letters, *I HATE HIM. I HATE HIM. I HATE HIM.* Jessamine touched long-dried splotches in the ink and imagined the writer's tears falling on the page as she wrote. What happened to Rosemary?

She flicked through the diary but there was nothing more.

Jessamine shook her head, coming back to the present, and wrote a note to herself to email the lawyer about who the boxes belonged to. She hoped that a relative could pick them up and she wouldn't have the expense of mailing them. The job took much longer than she expected, and the cobwebs of Rosemary's anger and fear from the diary clung to the bedroom. Jessamine slept on the couch.

The next day, she drifted about the house, wondering what to do. She decided to tackle the less-personal laundry. Dim light from a cobweb-encrusted window showed a narrow tongue and groove-paneled room crowded with the sturdy barrel of a wringer washing machine, a pitted steel shower stall, and a jumble of hanging jackets and bags.

As Jessamine entered, her elbow grazed the door of a cabinet. It boomed, and she saw that the entire thing was metal. It made sense to guard against the mice she'd discovered overrunning the kitchen.

She grabbed her giant flashlight and explored the cabinet. Toiletry gift packs covered in crumbling yellowed plastic spilled out of the middle shelf. A faded washcloth tied with a pink ribbon held three rose-shaped soaps smelling faintly flowery. Jessamine's hand hovered over the trash bag when she remembered soap was on her shopping list. Why not use it? She made a pile for ribbons and dropped the washcloth into the washing machine, which she hoped would work soon. Her water could be reconnected after the electricity was connected. She'd arranged a payment plan with a septic and well system service company and put the power connection fee on the credit card she was hiding from her husband. She'd known that she'd have to connect the utilities, but she hadn't anticipated the extra expenses of the well and septic system.

She piled a gift basket with bath salts and soaps shaped into cats and hearts and set it on the side of her bath. The pale green, yellow, and pink soaps brightened the stark room and smelled of faded flowers and lemon. She transformed a piece of Rosemary's leftovers into her own.

The next shelf was crammed with still-packaged sheets and towels. She knew she'd use those, so she threw them into the washing machine for later. The entire bottom of the cupboard was covered in jars. Preserving jars with the manufacturer's name molded into the glass and rusted metal rings around the top, jostled against leftover jars from jams or pasta sauce, still with faded and scratched labels.

Jessamine sighed and sat on the floor. She wondered if there was a place in the county to recycle glass. She pulled the jars out and needed to move the pile of ribbons, cloth flowers, and paper hearts. She stopped moving and stared at them. She laughed out loud, a feeling of relief pouring over her. She hadn't realized how stressed she had been about the library craft. They could make cloth-covered, decorated jars, since there were plenty of jars and lots of ribbons. She could use the bags of fabric scraps she found in Rosemary's room. The half bottles of dried-up white glue from the library closet could be rehydrated. It would work!

Chapter 9

*O*n *Monday morning, Jessamine* pulled into the county building's cracked parking lot and unloaded boxes of jars and bags of fabric. In the past week Walter, the guard, became slightly friendlier since Jessamine had convinced him that she was a county employee. He watched her all the way to the library door, but he let her bring in her lunch of fruit, cheese sticks, and crackers, all she could manage without a working fridge.

As she clinked through the foyer with her second box of jars, Frank the custodian paused, paintbrush in hand. "You're going back and forth a lot, Ms. Jessamine."

"Hi, Frank," she said, glad to be learning people's names. "No need for *Ms.*" She adjusted a slipping box in her arms. "Just 'Jessamine' is fine. I'm bringing in these jars for a library craft that we're doing today."

Frank waved his paintbrush at the chipped doorway he was repainting. "This is my craft for today. I'm being Picasso here!" He shrugged and frowned. "They've asked me to move that bear again. Maybe we could use *it* for a craft." He grinned. "What are you making?"

Jessamine put down her box and dug out a jar with cloth tied on loosely with a ribbon. "We're making cloth-covered jars."

"Looks interesting! What do you do with a cloth-covered jar?"

"Anything you like. You can use it as a vase or to store pens or as a decoration. In one of my libraries, a lot of people used the crafts as gifts."

"Gifts? It's my cousin's birthday tomorrow. I haven't had a chance to go out and get her anything. How much does it cost?"

"It doesn't cost anything. You're welcome to attend."

"I couldn't come." Frank held up his hands. "I'd be using up your supplies."

"We're using recycled jars and cloth. We're keeping it out of the dump. Why don't you come and make one?"

"Well, I'm at work..."

Jessamine smiled. She wanted her first program to be a success. "What about coming during your lunch?"

"I don't want to use up a spot..."

"The more the merrier! I'll tell you a library secret. Libraries keep statistics on how many people attend, and we always want more. It helps our funding. Come today at one."

"Okay, I'll come along for you, Ms. Jessamine. We'll see what it's like." Frank carefully laid his paintbrush across the lip of the paint can. "You got more boxes? Let me help you bring them in."

Jessamine worried about Frank lifting at his age, but he picked up the boxes and bags deftly and helped Jessamine pile them near the circulation desk. Jessamine needed to ask Marilyn where in the limited space she could prepare. She didn't have the energy to argue with Drusilla about their ostensibly shared office.

Jessamine rewrote the sign-up sheet to remove the spelling mistakes. Only two names of their most regular patrons were on it, but experience told her she could never be sure how many people would turn up to a free program. She hoped Frank would come.

Although it was near opening time at ten, Stephanie had not arrived to open the library. Marilyn was always the first to arrive and the last to leave. Jessamine hadn't worked out Drusilla's hours; they appeared random and quite short. Jessamine poked her head around Marilyn's office doorway. Marilyn waved and kept talking on the phone. "Yes, it will have carpet tiles in the seating areas and tile by the shelves." Pause. "It's only for the library." Marilyn puffed out a breath. "Yes, I know. I can't imagine how you'd need that much tile! And the paint, it's strange…"

Jessamine quietly shut the door and went back to the circulation desk. She had gone over the opening procedures with Stephanie several times last week, and Stephanie left written instructions in a binder under the desk. She pulled out the instructions and switched on lights, signed into public computers, and collected books from the return slot.

She heard the hum of a phone conversation through Marilyn's door, and not wanting to interrupt, she unlocked the front door. She grabbed the dried-up glue and old newspapers from the supply closet and rehydrated the glue, then selected fabric and ribbons to make a sample jar.

She smiled at the few elderly people who came in and returned their books in the slot under the desk and browsed in the handmade, wooden fiction shelves. For each person who came in, she made a check mark on a slip of paper. Big libraries had automatic gate counting machines, but this tiny library kept its statistics with a pen and paper.

The first customer, an elderly woman, came up to the desk with three books. "Hi. You're new. What's all that? That doesn't look like books."

Jessamine laughed and looked down at her jumble of jars, fabric, popsicle sticks, ribbons, and glue. "I'm Jessamine. Pleased to meet you. We're having a craft this afternoon. Would you like to come?"

"Oh, you're from England!"

"No, I'm from New Zealand."

"Really? What are you making?"

"We're making cloth-covered jars. Here's the example. It's not quite dry."

"Can I come along and watch?"

"You can join in—it's free. I've got plenty of jars and fabric."

The woman wrote her name on the sign-up sheet in wobbly cursive. "Can

I bring my neighbor? She loves this sort of thing."

"Yes." Jessamine grinned. "I'm very happy for people to come to the library. I want to do programs that you'll enjoy."

The woman handed Jessamine her books and library card. "I'm Eunice by the way." She stuck out her hand.

Jessamine shook her hand and ran the library card under the bar code reader wand. Nothing happened. No beep. The red light was glowing out of the wand, so Jessamine pulled on the cords to see if it had worked loose from being bumped by craft supplies. The cords were fine, so Jessamine poked buttons on the desktop computer.

The computer made a disapproving blurping sound. "Sorry! I forgot to sign into the right thing on the computer. I'll start it up now and check out the books."

"No hurry, sweetie. I know how those computers do their own thing."

Jessamine checked out Eunice's books, then went back over the opening list. Had she forgotten more? She hated to feel unprepared, especially when customers were waiting.

Three more people checked out books, and things went smoothly. Two older people signed up for the craft. Teen Englebert shook his head and blushed when Jessamine invited him. Marilyn came past, sweating at her hairline, heading out to the county offices. She waved her travel mug decorated with cat cartoons. "I've got another meeting in ten minutes! Time for a pit stop. I need my tea! Tell Drusilla I can meet her at one."

Jessamine opened her mouth to ask where Stephanie and Drusilla were, but Marilyn was gone. Jessamine was distracted by banging noises at the door, so she hurried over. A young woman in jeans and a t-shirt was maneuvering a gigantic double stroller through the narrow doors.

"They told me not to bring the stroller in here. What am I supposed to do? That Walter isn't friendly. I knew him when he was trying to date my sister. Fat chance he had!"

Jessamine held the door open and looked into the stroller. Two babies slept, a newborn and a chubby crawler. Two toddlers perched in front of the sleeping babies, their legs poking through. A preschooler trailed through the door, dragging a big tote bag of books.

"You need the stroller. Do you have twins?"

"No twins. They're not all mine. I'm watching my sister's kids. We'll go crazy if we're stuck inside staring at each other every day."

They walked over to the children's area to a toy stove and a low table covered in tracks for wooden trains. The woman lifted the kicking, excited toddlers out of the stroller. Jessamine watched the children settle at the toys. "The library's a great place to come with the kids. I had my kids close together and know what it's like. Mine are grown now."

"Hey, we met in the line about the bear. Last week? I'm Josey."

Josey was the woman in pink who had told her about Joshua Oxford and Kathryn Slattery during the fuss on her first day. "Hi Josey. I'm Jessamine. I didn't recognize you. You're wearing different clothes." Jessamine was going to say that now the woman's clothes fit her but stopped herself in time. She'd gotten in trouble for such frankness before.

"Yes, I had to dress up for the hearing. And my sister is the only one with decent clothes."

"Did you bring the kids to the library's story times when they ran them?"

"I came once and that Drusilla was doing it. She read the book like it was a horse race and she had to gallop to the end. And she was angry. She hissed at Larsen when he didn't sit still." She patted a toddler's head. "He's an active boy, but no one needs to *hiss* at him. It was so bad, Drusilla left after only one book and Marilyn took over. That Marilyn's okay, but she's always rushing around."

As if the mention of her name had summoned her, Drusilla came through the front door in a whirl of tottering heels, dark scarves, and competing perfumes. "Jessamine! What in the name of all that's holy is going on over here?"

Jessamine smiled at the young woman. "Come to the story times when we start them up again. I'll be doing them. We'll have fun." She looked over at Drusilla sweeping an arm across her jars. "I'd better go." Jessamine hurried toward the desk. "Wait!" she called to Drusilla. "I need that."

Drusilla continued to sweep supplies into the garbage can. "Why does the desk look like a trash heap? You've got to clean this up. I would have thought you'd know better than that."

"That's the craft for this afternoon!"

"What do you mean? This is trash."

"It's not trash. I'm preparing for this afternoon's craft. We're making cloth-covered jars."

"What for?"

"What do you mean, what for? You told me I had to do a craft program."

"I thought you were going to wait and plan it out."

"You said I couldn't wait. That I had to do it this week." Jessamine could hear her own tone rising. She wanted to be accommodating with her new colleagues, but this didn't make sense.

"You can't do it this afternoon. Cancel it. You need to cover the circulation desk."

"I can't cancel it." Jessamine found herself caring less and less if her tone was rising. "There are people signed up."

"How can there be anyone signed up in such a short time?"

"Several people saw me preparing the jars and wanted to come."

"And that's the point. You can't have this big mess here where the public can see it."

"Where else could I do it? Stephanie didn't come this morning. Marilyn's been on the phone and in meetings all morning, and I didn't know where you were."

"Stephanie only works part time. I thought you knew that. I need you to cover the desk. You can't make a mess. You need to plan better and get ready."

"How am I supposed to get ready when you only gave me a few days?"

"I don't know. Work it out. You're the one we hired to do the programs. You're supposed to be so great at it." Drusilla swung one of her trailing scarves around her shoulder and stalked into her office, her spike heels flashing.

Feeling jittery, Jessamine picked up the garbage can and began pulling ribbons and pieces of fabric from around the crumpled paper and pencil shavings. She comforted herself with the thought that at least the trash didn't contain food or anything particularly nasty, then she paused. Drusilla had no right to throw away her supplies. Jessamine had a lot of time for busy Marilyn and friendly Stephanie. She was already beginning to enjoy the people who came into the tiny library, and the battered collection had so much potential, but how could she work with Drusilla? Dark thoughts of sharp words began to form, but she shook them off. She was not that sort of person, however satisfying it might be. She comforted herself with the thought of the craft happening soon and her fireplace waiting for her like a faithful hound in her home.

No one came to relieve Jessamine at noon. She could hear Marilyn talking either on the phone or a video conference, and Jessamine refused to beg Drusilla to cover the desk when she'd probably just sneer. Jessamine put her lunchbox under the desk and took furtive bites of her crackers and apple between customers.

After her quick lunch, she moved carts of DVDs and board books to make a space. A woman sat at a table reading a magazine. Jessamine looked around, but there weren't many tables.

"Excuse me? I was wondering if I could use that table? We're going to need it for the craft."

The woman looked annoyed. "I was reading. What did you say you need it for?"

"We're doing a craft. You're welcome to join in."

"I can't afford it."

"It's free. And you get to take one of these home."

The woman grunted, but she got up and let Jessamine push the tables together. Then she put aside her magazine and poked through the fabric and ribbons. "I'm Agnes, Kathryn Slattery's assistant," she said.

"I'm glad you're staying," Jessamine said. As she set out the glue, the first of the signed-up women arrived. "Hi! Eunice, isn't it? How are you? Choose a seat anywhere."

"I'm good, Jessamine, how are you? Jonquil, my neighbor, had to go to the doctor, but she wants a jar. Can I make one for her?"

"Yes, we have plenty."

"Is there yellow fabric? She likes yellow."

"We have masses. Look, here are daffodils—almost the same as jonquil flowers."

"Jessamine! Jessamine!" Drusilla gestured urgently from the circulation desk. *Josey is right*, Jessamine thought. *She does hiss.*

Jessamine went reluctantly over to Drusilla.

The tall woman pursed her lips. "What are you doing? You're covering the desk."

"I'm running our scheduled craft. Someone else will have to be on the desk."

"You need to cover the desk when Stephanie's not working. We can't afford to pay two people."

"You wanted me to do this. And Marilyn said I should do the craft and she's the boss. People are here now. Can't you cover the desk?"

"No. I'll talk to Marilyn."

Another woman arrived and looked around for help. Jessamine turned away from Drusilla and to the library patrons. "Hi, Bronwyn, isn't it? Everyone take a seat and we'll get started."

People settled and Jessamine didn't notice when Drusilla left. When she glanced over at the circulation desk, she saw Marilyn behind it on the phone, gesturing widely with her travel mug to the people on the other end of the phone.

As Jessamine demonstrated spreading the glue on the cloth and jar, Frank appeared in the doorway. "Is there room for me?"

"Sure…" Jessamine began.

"Frank! How are you? You can join us!" Bronwyn screwed up her eyes and twinkled at Frank. "It's like we're back at school! What was that? Sixty years ago?"

"It can't be sixty years!" Frank grinned. "You and me, Bronwyn, we're not a day over twenty-nine."

Eunice pulled up a chair. "Come and sit down, Frank honey. We'll show you what to do. There's plenty of room by me."

Jessamine hadn't appreciated how many people in Bent River County knew each other, and she certainly hadn't anticipated how much of a hit Frank would be.

They concentrated on the jars, choosing fabric, laughing and chatting about people they had known for decades.

"My lunch time's over." Frank stood up. "I'd better get back to work."

Bronwyn twinkled again. "You should come to all the crafts, Frank honey. Jessamine's doing a great job. And she said she'll do it every month."

Eunice held up a jar. "Have another jar to keep, Frank. This is a cheerful one."

Frank grinned. "I'll be back, ladies. You couldn't keep me away. Y'all take care, now."

Chapter 10

$\mathcal{M}$arilyn *was finally finished* with her meetings. She leaned against the circulation desk and asked, "How did the craft go?"

"It was quite nice. We had eight people. They seemed to enjoy it and said they'd come back next month."

"Wonderful! It'll be fantastic if you can inject life into the programs. Stephanie doesn't have time, and Drusilla can't… As Drusilla points out, it's not what she was hired for. She was hired before my time. The craft went well on such short notice. I was surprised you wanted to do it so quickly."

"Drusilla told me to…" Jessamine paused. "I thought I had to."

"Drusilla should be training you. She's not in charge of you. She doesn't have a library degree, bless her heart." Marilyn shook her head. "I'll talk to her."

Jessamine wondered what to say. "Do you normally get eight people at crafts?"

"That's the most I've seen for any program since I started. I don't suppose you've entered the stats for the program?" Marilyn gestured at the computer.

"We have a special form we send to the state library."

"No, I wasn't sure how."

"I'll show you. Drusilla's supposed to enter the stats, but she says doesn't understand the system." Marilyn put her hand up as if to shield her mouth. "I don't think she's exaggerating about not understanding." Marilyn giggled, but she stopped, rearranged her face into a neutral expression, and cleared her throat. "Go to the shared drive on the computer and I'll show you. The state library tells us the format they need. Gotta keep them happy to make sure we get our funding."

Jessamine took notes as Marilyn explained the steps.

"You'll be doing this over and over." Marilyn tapped a pencil on the desk. "I want to get the library programs up and running again. I'm glad you've got lots of experience at story times. And the book group is coming up."

"I love book groups! A book group is the reason I came to…" Marilyn's ever-present travel mug of sweet tea fell over and Jessamine grabbed it. In the fuss of moving books and patting with paper towels, Jessamine didn't finish her sentence. Marilyn gave a startled squawk when she saw the time and headed to her office.

A book group *was* the reason Jessamine came to Bent River County. She remembered the first time she ever heard of Bent River County five years ago when she lived in Kansas.

"Eileen is very sick," book group member Louise said. She lowered her voice and leaned toward Jessamine. "It's the end. The cancer came back."

Olivia, the kind and organized leader, came over, balancing her coffee cup and a small plate of grapes. Jessamine had found this book group from a notice board at the public library. She was touched by the members inviting a stranger into their homes, particularly when she felt adrift because her husband had deployed immediately after they moved to a new state. "Eileen is asking for you, Jessamine," Olivia said. "She wants you to visit her in the hospital."

"Me? I don't know her well." Jessamine remembered Eileen as a tiny, laughing woman who jangled with chunky necklaces and had several rescued dogs. When the group discussed a book with a character of an abusive husband, Eileen revealed that decades earlier her first husband had threatened, hit, and stalked her. Jessamine had been astonished and horrified, but the book group ladies took the story in stride; they learned Eileen's story years ago.

Olivia was tall and regal. Her intensity made her kindness an irresistible force. "Her daughter called me. She said that Eileen was adamant. I can drive you to the hospital so you won't get lost."

"Okay." Jessamine found it odd, but she didn't want to go against the wishes of a dying woman. Jessamine hadn't forged many connections in Kansas. With her husband away and her children at school, she was bored most days. "Will they let me into her hospital room if she's that sick?"

"Her family said they'd work it out." Olivia smiled down at Jessamine. "Eileen is determined to see you."

Olivia was efficient and turned up at Jessamine's house exactly at the agreed time and drove smoothly and quickly to the hospital. Jessamine was glad she didn't have to negotiate the city traffic by herself.

Jessamine was surprised by the hospital's luxurious foyer, with a fountain surrounded by shops. She was used to New Zealand's medical clinics; in old houses, often a bit wonky, with warped plywood wheelchair ramps. Olivia scanned the foyer and headed toward a slim woman wearing business clothes.

The slim woman put out her hand. "Hi, I'm Billie, Eileen's daughter. Thank you for coming. She's getting quite agitated asking for you."

"I'm sorry about your mother. Do you know why she's asking for me?" Jessamine looked at Olivia. "She knows the other women in the book group better than she knows me."

Billie shrugged and rubbed her hands through her hair. "I don't know, but she's been insisting. They're only letting family in at the moment, so I said you were a cousin. Is that okay?"

"Yes. If you're sure you want me to come in?" Jessamine hesitated.

"Yes! Please come now. I'm going to a work meeting this afternoon, and then I'll come to the hospital. I've missed so much work." She yawned. "Sorry,

I'm not getting much sleep."

Olivia pulled a library book out of her large purse. "I'll wait here."

"You're not coming?" Jessamine turned to her.

Billie hurried toward the wall of elevators. "No, she's not allowed."

Jessamine gave Olivia a last look and followed Billie. She wasn't sure what else to do.

Eileen was a small woman, but now she was a waxen, closed-eye doll against the sharp white outlines of the hospital bed. The busy noises of the hospital faded in the quiet room, leaving only the regular whoosh and click of a machine. Billie waved from the doorway and disappeared down the hall to the nurse's station. Jessamine sat on the edge of a vinyl-covered chair and picked up Eileen's hand. The bones felt as brittle and delicate as dried grass. Eileen opened her eyes. She took a shuddering breath, and Jessamine could see the remains of her immense mental strength.

"Jessamine," she whispered. Her mouth worked. "Jessamine, you need a refuge. I see that in you. You will have the train place." Eileen's eyes closed and the twist of her mouth showed she was drawing strength to go on. "I told them you need the forest. You'll be able to find it."

Jessamine leaned forward. She wasn't sure what to say. Tears pricked painfully behind her eyes. She squeezed Eileen's hand gently. "It's okay, Eileen. You can rest. I'm glad to see you." She didn't understand what Eileen said. It didn't matter. If she gave comfort to the dying woman, then Jessamine was glad to be here. Eileen didn't talk any more, and Billie came and escorted her to the foyer.

Olivia called Jessamine a few days later and passed on the news that Eileen had died. Jessamine asked Olivia what Eileen might have meant about a train, but Olivia didn't know. "She was dreaming. Rambling at the end. Thank you for going to see her. It meant a lot to her daughter."

Six months later, Jessamine eyed an official-looking envelope from a law firm in Virginia. She almost didn't open it, because it looked like a scam. If she hadn't seen Eileen's name, she would have put it in the recycling bin. *You can take possession of the real property located at Plat Number L-371* in a place Jessamine had never heard of. She didn't tell her husband about it; she wasn't quite sure why. Her husband was home between deployments, and it was a time of sharp, glass-edged silences in her house. His absences were simultaneously a burden and a vast relief, so not telling him became easy.

She took the letter to the next book group meeting and tried to show it quietly to Olivia in the corner of the hostess's dining room. "Oh, yes, it's real!" Olivia said heartily. "Eileen's daughter Billie told me about it."

"You're saying that Eileen left me land? What about Billie? Isn't she upset? Doesn't she want it?"

Several of the other book group members gathered round, selecting their snacks from the dining room table. Jessamine's secret inheritance obviously wasn't a secret. The book group ladies came closer and a couple patted Jessamine on the arm and shoulder. "Yes," jolly, round-faced Faith said. "Eileen liked you, Jessamine. She told me she had her eye on you. You reminded her of herself when she was young."

"What is this about land?" Jessamine asked. "I don't understand."

"Eileen inherited the land from a friend called Rosemary. She always described it as a refuge. That was the word she used."

"Yes, and there was a place to live, but not a normal house. Eileen was poetic about it. You know how she could get poetic." They laughed.

"Here's to Eileen!" one of the women said, and they lifted their teacups in a salute.

"Eileen was clearing the place out after her friend Rosemary died. It was difficult for her to travel so far. She said it was a place that should always be passed on to a woman who needed it. Eileen had plans, but then she got sick. And her cancer moved so quickly."

Olivia passed the lawyer's letter around the group. Jessamine began to feel that the letter represented a real place. The book group—a sensible group of women—thought it was real.

"Doesn't Eileen's family want the land? Isn't it valuable?" Jessamine clutched the solid letter, now in her hands, but couldn't imagine how the land could be real.

"Billie told me she's happy for you to have it. She knows it's legal. She doesn't need the money, and she wants to honor her mother's wishes. Billie gave me this envelope to give to you. It looks like there are instructions scribbled on the back. It doesn't make much sense." Olivia patted Jessamine's arm. "Be happy, Jessamine! Check it out with your lawyer. Be sure to tell us what you're doing. We're happy for you!"

As they discussed the book, Jessamine felt *seen* by the book group women and she clung to the gift of their friendship like driftwood.

Over the next few weeks, Jessamine went online and explored the county around Eileen's land. She looked at street views and satellite views. It was leafy and rural, so she was frustrated that most street views showed forested roads with driveways disappearing from view, and satellites showed the outlines of buildings in small clearings. She couldn't work out which was her mysterious train building.

She pictured taking her children on a holiday to the distant state. It was a long drive, but they'd be able to camp in the building. There was a lake nearby, and the sea not too far away. It filled her with hope as she dragged herself through the morning routines, when getting the children off to school felt like being at war with them. Mostly they wanted to go, but the explosion of missing lunches, lost shoes, and undone homework exhausted Jessamine. She tried various methods of organization; packing lunches at night, a labeled shoe rack by the door, homework rosters, but mornings left her frustrated and on the edge.

She wondered what it would be like to start her day by choosing her own activities and not having to deal with anyone else's chaos.

The children went on many field trips and to various camps and were individually away for days or a few weeks at a time, but Jessamine realized with a jolt that she had not had a night away from all of them for over a decade. Even if she and her husband had wanted to go away for a weekend together, they had no family within reasonable distance. Jessamine would only ask a friend to watch five children in the direst emergency; thankfully a situation that had not arisen. It had taken her a while to meet new friends in this city. To Jessamine, when the military sent her family to isolated places, the "suckiest assignments" her husband called them, then the military spouses were friendlier. They were all a long way from home with few employment options. In other new places, Jessamine had met people and made friends by having a job. Here, with her husband gone and no back-up for the children, Jessamine didn't look for a job. Her days were boring, and her evenings were full of homework and driving across the city to the children's multitudinous activities.

The military spouse groups stopped in the summer because people would go and visit family. Jessamine, the foreign military spouse, 10,000 miles away from her family and with five bored teenagers, felt hollow when the craft group ladies talked about going to their family's cabin on the lake. Hollow, but also deficient, as if she should have arranged her life properly to have family that she could drive to visit and fill the loneliness clinging to her like unwanted fat. The book group met every month, and Jessamine was the only person who attended every month for two years.

The first night her husband returned from his latest deployment, Jessamine had the letter in hand to tell him the news. The news had been too big to share electronically in a text, email, or video call. When she opened her mouth, one of the children rushed in needing help with lost homework, and the conversation went on to chores, always a bad sign, which led to angry words. Jessamine went to bed and felt completely alone on her side of the bed.

Jessamine discovered that she could get an initial legal consultation for free on the base, so she made an appointment. She gathered multiple letters from Eileen's lawyer. Her old library work clothes didn't fit; she'd put on weight while her husband was deployed, but she found a decent top to wear. The lawyer told her that the paperwork looked in order. Jessamine had inherited twenty-five acres of forest and a house in as-is condition. The knowledge kept Jessamine warm and kept her mind busy. She was surprised that her normal life went on much as before. The land and the mysterious structure filled so much of her mind; she felt everyone must be able to see and feel it.

Jessamine came to think of her inheritance as *The Train Place*. For several months, she hugged the secret to herself. The property taxes were paid up for three years, so she could keep it a secret. She went online and continued to explore Bent River County in detail; she learned about the new park around a lake, she learned about the controversies surrounding the state accreditation of the school system, and she read about the opening of a new historical research archive in a plantation along the river.

Then she got pneumonia.

Jessamine caught a bug that her son brought back from a field trip. He got better, but Jessamine coughed for weeks. One night she could hear every one of her breaths crackling and popping as her chest heaved in enough air. Her husband was away and the house full of sleeping teenagers, so she propped herself up to sleep, wondering if she'd wake up. In the morning, she called the doctor's office on the base. The nurse said to go to the emergency room on the base right away.

It was Saturday, a day she normally spent driving teenagers all around the city with musical instruments or sports gear. She felt so bad that she had sent her newly licensed daughter to drive herself to her piano lesson. Jessamine waited for her daughter to return with their only working vehicle, before she could drive herself to the emergency room.

The emergency room visit was a blur. After listening, poking, prodding, and a chest x-ray, they sent her home clutching a bag of medicines and advice to rest. They gave no practical ideas about how she was going to rest with an absent husband and five dependent children. When Jessamine asked if the military offered help, she was told, "Ask your church for help." She didn't go to church, so she went home to her children.

The children had exams, college applications, and their own problems. Jessamine wobbled down the stairs, leaning her shoulder on the wall as a coughing fit overtook her, to find the kitchen counters piled high in dirty dishes. The medicine the doctor had given her meant she could barely swallow, but she was thirsty. The cup cupboard was empty. She leaned against the counter and coughed, opening cupboards and drawers until she found a plastic measuring cup and took short, delightful sips of water.

She decided that if she had to go to hospital, she would ask the book group for help, even though she didn't know them well in daily life. The one neighbor she saw stared at her as she leaned on the car and coughed, and then he complained about the dog coming into his yard like he usually did. Jessamine was too sick to walk her, so their energetic husky cross dog misbehaved.

The pneumonia didn't get worse, and Jessamine slowly got better. The coughing eased, and she was able to do the dishes. Such a simple task exhausted her; she was used to doing it with barely a thought, while supervising homework and sibling spats and cooking dinner at the same time. She propped herself up on the counter as she took one item out at a time with one hand, turning away as a spasm of coughing wrenched her so she wouldn't spit green mucus on the clean dishes.

As Jessamine's strength improved, the total aloneness of her situation stayed in her head. The abyss had opened, and Jessamine had looked in. Her view had shifted. *The Train Place* filled her thoughts, but day-to-day life went on. The months became years. The children began to finish school and started jobs and university. Jessamine found a job in a university library. She had earned her Master of Library Science when she didn't have a work permit while her family had traveled around the world. Then after she got a work permit, she worked at a series of short-term jobs while her family continued to move every year or two. She was well-qualified for the university library job and glad to put her degree to use. As she said to herself, it was a place to go to put on decent shoes and get out of the house. She got to go through the door labeled *Staff Only*, even if it didn't touch her soul, like her public library jobs. She opened her own bank account and continued to pay the Bent River County property taxes. They weren't much.

On one of her online visits to the world around her train place, she saw the advertisement for the job in the Bent River County Public Library. She looked at the requirements and updated her resume as an exercise. She lived far too far away. She didn't tell anyone, and she didn't apply for the job.

Even though ostensibly grown and settling into jobs and futures, the children moved in and out, and Jessamine and her husband were rarely alone. On Jessamine's birthday, everyone gathered, and she cooked a big meal.

"Are you sure you want to be a nurse?" she said to her eldest daughter. "I didn't know you wanted to look after sick people. What about when I had pneumonia?"

"Oh, mom, you were just putting that on!"

"Yes, we remember you going around the house, cough, cough, cough." One of her sons laughed.

Jessamine felt a lurch. "I wasn't putting it on! I was very sick!" Jessamine snapped and tears ran down her face.

Jessamine's family stared at her, blank-faced. The babies she had gotten up for in the dark, lonely hours and fed out of her body. The glamorous foreign man she had fallen for and followed around the world. They looked at her as if she was suddenly speaking in an unknown language. Jessamine was sinking, as if she was looking up at them through a thick pane of scratched and mossy ice. She put out a hand and grabbed the back of the couch, surprised to find it was at the same level as her. She opened her mouth to protest. Nothing came out. She turned and went up the stairs, leaning on the wall, trying to get away from the crushing weight of their stares.

Chapter 11

Jessamine looked up from the books she was sponging down with a damp, soapy cloth. Library books always acquire a layer of grime. The plastic covers are designed to be cleanable, but when Jessamine asked about wipes, Drusilla said that she "couldn't prioritize buying them." Jessamine internally rolled her eyes; she thought the library would easily be able to afford wipes if Drusilla wanted them. Jessamine decided to pick her battles and didn't take up the issue with Marilyn. A few weeks passed and the awkward conflict with Drusilla dragged on at a stalemate.

"I've got your eggs," Stephanie said to one of their regulars and disappeared into the kitchen, returning with an egg carton.

"You're giving people eggs?" Jessamine asked.

"Yes, that's Casey Chilton from the Library Committee. Stay on their good side. Besides which, my girls have been *extremely* productive. Would you like eggs?"

"If you're sure, I'd love eggs." Jessamine smiled. "I've always wanted chickens. They don't fit with a nomadic lifestyle on a bunch of military bases and suburbs. How many chickens do you have?"

"We've got around forty chickens."

"You don't know how many?" Jessamine laughed.

"We have over a hundred fowl all together. We've got chickens, turkeys, ducks, and geese. And we used to have guinea fowl. My husband processes them for meat, so the numbers go up and down. And the foxes and racoons want to process them for meat. We try to avoid that if we can."

"That's a lot of birds. What do you keep them in?"

"We have old sheds that we lock them in overnight to protect them from predators. During the day they're free roaming and can go wherever they like. They are feathery homebodies and hang around with their friends and go off to bed in their coops at night. It's much easier to get a chicken to bed than a toddler."

"I believe that about toddlers." Jessamine smiled. "I couldn't cope with a hundred fowl. How could I get a few chickens that could lay eggs for me?"

"You can get chicks at the feed and seed store. You need to raise them under a heat lamp if they don't have a mama hen to keep them warm."

"A heat lamp?" Jessamine pulled a face. "Is it hard?"

"It's not hard. I'll tell you what: I can give you a few hens to get you started. And a rooster to protect them. We always end up with too many roosters. You only need one rooster for ten to twenty hens, so everyone who raises them ends up with too many roosters."

"I can't take your chickens. I can pay you for them."

"They're old hens so you can have them. They're almost five years old and don't lay many eggs anymore. My husband wants to put them in the slow cooker when they get to this stage, but I've gotten used to the old biddies by now. They have personalities and friendships. Since you've got plenty of room and only one person eating eggs, a few old hens should be plenty. You can supplement their feed with scraps and let them free range for bugs and plants when you're around to watch them. It won't cost much to feed them."

"Thank you." Jessamine smiled. "That's generous."

"I could drop them off this weekend, if you're free?"

"Okay, I'll give you my address."

Stephanie laughed. "Oh, I know where you live."

"You do?"

"Yes, in old Rosemary's place. Everyone knew when you arrived and moved in there. Frank saw you going in and out of your driveway."

"They did? I didn't know that! That's um… disconcerting."

"Yes, Bent River County is very small. Not much goes on that doesn't get noticed. That's how I knew that you'd be able to keep chickens. Rosemary has at least one chicken coop."

"You knew her?"

"Slightly. I remember her as always old. We loved Rosemary. She was Frank's mother's friend, although she was a lot younger. She was quiet and kept to herself, but she grew up here and was one of the good ones."

"What do you mean, one of the good ones?"

"People I trust knew her and liked her."

On Saturday at the appointed time, Stephanie's car wended down Jessamine's long driveway. It was strange to see another person on her land; she had become used to seeing her home as a separate place that barely existed in the real world.

Stephanie had two large plastic dog crates full of indignant feathers, sharp beaks, and watchful black, shiny eyes.

"Help me carry them to the back. Did you get the coop ready?"

Jessamine grabbed the handle of one of the dog crates, feeling excited but nervous at taking over the care of a living animal. "Yes. I couldn't find any bales of straw, and I didn't feel like driving all the way to the city, but there were lots of dry grass stalks, so I cut them."

"Do you have a tractor?"

"No, I cut it with scissors and bundled it up in the wheelbarrow and brought it in."

"You cut down straw with a pair of scissors?" Stephanie laughed. "That's what I call dedication."

They followed the path to the wooden coop.

Stephanie looked around with approval. "Doesn't that grass smell like a farm? These old girls will have a good life here. Let's release them in the run."

They walked to the wire-fenced chicken run and opened the dog crate doors. At first nothing happened, then a small, sleek, red-brown head emerged, and two beady eyes looked around suspiciously.

"Watch this." Stephanie pulled out a baggie of yellow crumbs. "Chook! Chook! Chook!" she called as she poured it into the bowl Jessamine had cleaned. A pale-yellow chicken zoomed straight to the bowl and began pecking as if she'd never seen food before. Stephanie laughed. "Greedy thing. That's a Buff Orpington. She'll get fat if she gets to eat all she wants." A red-brown chicken emerged from the dog crate and pecked the yellow chicken once on the back and pushed her aside. "The Rhode Island Red is meaner. She's the boss lady. They have their pecking order. See that bare patch on her back? As she got older, the other chickens pecked her and put her in her place. They'll settle down here since you have lots of space."

Six chickens emerged, and Stephanie and Jessamine put the dog crates in Stephanie's car. When they returned to check on the chickens, Jessamine laughed to see the round, fluffy creatures scratching the ground with their scaly dinosaur legs. "It looks like a dance pattern. They go scratch, scratch, scratch. And then step back and peer down to examine what they scratched."

"They always do that. It keeps them bus—"

"Look at that!"

In her industrious scratchings, the Buff Orpington dug up a worm. She ran clucking around the pen with it hanging from her beak, the other hens in hot pursuit. The drama finished when the first hen put her head back and gulped down the worm.

"You won't need a TV with this going on," Stephanie said. They both laughed.

"Come in for a cup of tea."

Jessamine set out Rosemary's delicate, flowery mismatched teacups on the wheeled tea cart in front of the scratchy green couch.

"This is civilized." Stephanie held her teacup with her little finger stuck out and laughed.

"Have an Anzac biscuit." Jessamine held out a plate. "They're from my grandmother's cookbook."

"Did you say *insect* biscuit?" Stephanie stared at Jessamine, the food halfway to her mouth. "Your grandmother cooked them?"

"Insect biscuits? Like creepy crawly six-legged things? No!" Jessamine laughed. "It stands for Australian and New Zealand Army Corps. ANZAC. They're from World War I. The story I was told as a child is that oats and the other ingredients were all they had left when the New Zealanders and Australians were fighting the Turks at Gallipoli in Turkey in World War I. I'm not sure the story is entirely accurate, but they're traditional down under."

"As long as they're not insects." Stephanie tried a nibble. "Oh, these are good! I like coconut." Stephanie dribbled crumbs. "I like how crunchy they are. Why are you calling them biscuits?"

"I suppose they're cookies to you," Jessamine said. "I should be used to that now. What you call biscuits, I'd call scones."

"That's confusing. Tasty cookies, anyway." Stephanie looked around. "And this is cozy. It's great Rosemary's house is getting used again."

"I'm glad to use it. Her bits and pieces seem so old. How old was Rosemary? She must have been a hundred and twenty."

"She was youngish when she lived here, so probably about your age, maybe a little older. She collected antiques. I heard stories about epic thrift-shopping expeditions."

Stephanie soon left to get on with her busy weekend with her small children, and Jessamine spent most of the afternoon leaning against the wire of the chicken run, watching the small animals explore their new home. She surprised herself by enjoying the chickens' company. When she went out to feed them in the morning, they crowded eagerly to the wire. Stephanie warned her to keep the chickens enclosed while she was at work, or she might lose them all to foxes and racoons. On the weekends, Jessamine let them out and watched them while they plowed through the weeds that grew higher than their heads; small, prehistoric monsters.

They laid brown, beige, and greenish eggs in the straw, and Jessamine cradled the delicate ovals in her two hands, warm from the chicken, hardly believing that objects so mundane felt like a miracle. "Thank you, ladies," she said to them as she collected the eggs.

Chapter 12

Jessamine crouched on a toddler-sized stool and faced a semi-circle of rapt little faces. She sang to the tune of *The Wheels on the Bus*:

The people in the library sit right down! Sit right down! Sit right down!

The people in the library sit right down! All day long!

The people in the library read a book! Read a book! Read a book!

The people in the library read a book! All day long!

Jessamine grabbed her planned book from the floor, knowing how hard it was to keep the children's short attention spans. She held the book facing forwards so the children could see the cover and read out the title, "*The Very Hungry Caterpillar*, by Eric Carle. Who's read this before?"

"I have! I have!" A girl at the front raised her arm so forcefully that it propelled her bottom off the floor.

"That's wonderful, Hailey." Jessamine smiled at the story time regular. "What about you, Larsen? Have you read it?" Jessamine asked Josey's son sitting at the back. Larsen nodded but didn't say anything.

Jessamine read stories and sang songs featuring bees and ants; the children marched as ants and brought home their baby bumble bees. Just before they became too restless to continue, Jessamine stood up and asked, "Who wants to hatch out of a cocoon?"

After conferring with her mother, Jessamine wrapped Hailey in a loose "cocoon" of toilet paper. Jessamine whispered to the prancing child, who threw her arms up and hatched out of her cocoon. The child capered and waved her flying arms. "I'm a beautiful butterfly! I'm a beautiful butterfly!" she called.

The other children lined up to get their cocoons so they could hatch.

"Come to the tables and we'll make a beautiful butterfly to take home." Jessamine gestured to the tables she had set up earlier. She held up her pre-made clothespin butterfly with coffee filter wings. "Like the one who hatched out of the cocoon. Grab your coffee filter and choose markers to color with."

As the children colored, Jessamine smiled at Josey. "I'm glad you brought everyone today, Josey."

"My sister's grateful when I can bring her kids." Josey smiled back. "She says it calms them down. And they love looking at the books they get."

"Are these your children?" Jessamine asked an older woman. She thought they were more likely to be the woman's grandchildren but hesitated to insult the woman by implying that she was old.

"No, I'm babysitting. There aren't many jobs in Bent River County. We do what we can."

"That's for sure!" A couple of people nodded in agreement.

"I like this craft," Josey said. "I haven't seen it before."

Jessamine helped a toddler pull a lid off a marker. "I did it when my kids were little. I like it because it works for kids of all ages." She looked around. "We've got babies to six-year-olds today."

"Does that matter?" another mother asked.

"Yes. Bigger libraries that I've worked in give different story times for different ages. Bent River County's small, so we put everyone together. I choose books, songs, and crafts that everyone can do."

A man added, "It works. Everyone loves wetting the coffee filters. It might make a mess!"

"Might make a mess?" Josey pulled the paper bowl of water away from the reaching hands of her niece. "The mess might be the point." She lifted the small child to the floor to toddle off to the toys.

Jessamine laughed. "I hope the point is that the children have fun." She cleared the bowls of water off the table. "We also want them to learn about getting on with each other. And colors and days of the week and numbers."

"I know it helps with that. I've noticed it." Josey picked up her baby, who was beginning to fuss. "And I'm glad you've found craft supplies. Stephanie told me the library doesn't have any budget for programs."

"I found most of it at the back of Rosemary's cupboards. Like the recycled jar craft. The coffee filters were crumpled in the library kitchen. I wouldn't want to use them for coffee. Yuk!"

Most of the children finished their craft and ran around holding up their flying butterflies.

"My caterpillar ate oranges! And cake!" said Hailey.

"Mine ate ice cream!" said another, getting her caterpillar to make eating noises on her arm.

"Come on beautiful butterflies, time to go," Josey called. The parents and children gathered their things.

"Say 'thank you' to Ms. Jessamine." Josey brushed Larsen's hair from his eyes. "Are you ready to get books?"

The shyest children didn't speak but ran over and grabbed Jessamine's leg in a hug. She heard a muffled "Fank wu" from her long skirt. Jessamine smiled, remembering her children, decades earlier, and in other countries.

Jessamine waved the book she was holding. "Remember, you can check out books about insects!" She always gathered up books on her story time theme and hoped that patrons would check them out and improve the library's circulation statistics.

She looked at her pile of books and sighed. *This was published not long after I was born*, she thought. It wasn't that the life cycle of a butterfly had changed, but the photographs were yellowed and the fonts old-fashioned. The author photo showed a woman with spreading blue eye makeup and high eighties hair. The book looked its age, but Drusilla claimed there was no funding to buy new ones. Not willing to accept that answer, in her few spare moments at work, Jessamine was busy searching for suitable grants for the underfunded library.

Jessamine also had a smaller pile of donated books, which she and Josey quietly encouraged Josey's sister's children toward. Their family had lost a pile of library books, and without paying an unaffordable fine, they couldn't check any more out. Jessamine thought it was ridiculous to charge people full cover price for decades-old books, but Drusilla insisted that the library bylaws meant the family couldn't check out more books until they paid the fine.

A crashing noise sounded at the doors and everyone swung around to see Frank and Walter heaving the bear into the library on a dolly.

Jessamine's mouth hung open. Before she could think, she burst out, "What are you doing? You can't bring that in here!"

"That's what everyone says." Frank grinned at her. "How are you today, Ms. Jessamine?" He looked around. "Hello, kiddies. Good morning, everyone! How's it—"

He was interrupted by a high-pitched scream of terror, and Larsen launched himself at his mother's legs as if he wanted to bury himself in them. She picked him up, but his screaming continued as he pressed his face into her neck, his small fist pointed toward the bear. He beat his feet on her stomach, while Josey talked to him and rubbed his back, trying to soothe him. Nothing worked. Jessamine and the other parents helped Josey negotiate out the doors with her huge stroller without checking out the stack of books her family had already chosen.

The other children stared at the bear in silence. Even exuberant Hailey stuck her fingers in her mouth and retreated behind her mother's legs, eyeing the bear darkly from her vantage point.

One of the older boys asked, "Is it alive?"

"Oh, no," said Frank. "It's as dead as a squashed possum." He poked the bear hard in the chest. "See, it doesn't do nothing."

The boy hesitated then he walked over and poked the bear in the leg. He retreated behind his little sister's stroller and let out a breath as if he'd fought a great battle.

The story time families soon left, all of them abandoning the books Jessamine had hoped they'd check out.

Frank rubbed his hands down his overalls and sighed. "We have an effect wherever we go, but that was extreme. Poor little guy." He shook his head. "How are you today, Ms. Jessamine?"

"I'm fine, Frank. At least, I was until that bear appeared. Why are you bringing it in here? I don't think it's going to work. Can't you put it somewhere else?"

"We've taken this poor bear everywhere. It's been in the county offices. It's been in the school. It's been in the fire station. This bear has traveled more than I have. No one wants the darned thing, so Joshua Oxford said that the library is the lucky winner."

"The library doesn't want it either."

"Well, Mr. Oxford has spoken. This is where we are obliged to put it." Frank sighed again.

Jessamine looked around the library. Too much had already been crammed into the windowless back room of the county buildings. "Stephanie keeps telling me that this was supposed to be a temporary location for the library, but they've been here twelve years. I can't see any possible place for it."

Frank rested the dolly. "It has to go somewhere."

"Could you tuck it in the back?" Jessamine sighed. "Beside the local history?"

"Joshua Oxford told us that Kathryn said since you keep going on and on about needing more science resources for the kids, we should put it in the children's area."

"Science resources? We need more science books, not a stuffed bear! And what about microscopes or magnets? Things that will actually help teach kids about science?"

"I don't know about microscopes, but we've got to get this moved today. Where should I leave it?"

"The only space is here. Next to the board books doesn't make sense, but at least it's not far when you take it out again. I'll talk to Marilyn about it."

"You know I'll fight to have the bear removed," Marilyn said when Jessamine asked.

"They said it was for the science education that we sent them those letters about," Jessamine said. "Do they think it will help with STEM education, or are they tormenting us on purpose?"

Marilyn shook her head. "I thought our research might convince them how important STEM is. Especially for education and jobs in poor rural Bent River County. This is not the result I hoped for." She shrugged. "They *did* agree with me that STEM was important." Her face cleared and she lifted her eyebrows. "You said you were nearly ready with your planned STEM programs? Why don't you start them and use the bear to talk about mammals? I'll see if I can help."

Marilyn didn't have any time to help with programs. She met more and more often with the Library Committee and the county administration. She returned from the meetings with her hair in disarray, as if she'd been running her hands through it, and she sucked down her sweet tea as if it was an elixir of strength. Despite longer meetings, Marilyn was able to be by the front desk more, chatting to Jessamine and Stephanie, but she didn't tell them much of what went on in these meetings.

Drusilla stayed quiet throughout this, but a couple of times Jessamine saw Drusilla eyeing an agitated Marilyn thoughtfully. And more than once when she'd gone down the hallway to the restroom, Jessamine saw Drusilla leaving Kathryn's office. Drusilla was grinning, but when she saw Jessamine looking at her, she jumped. "What are you staring at? And what are you doing out here? You should be in the library!"

Chapter 13

Jessamine steadily cleared away vines and overgrown bushes from around her house with her multi-tool and rusty shovels, saws, and secateurs from the shed. She found an old can of lubricant and got them in working, if not like-new, condition. She comforted herself with the thought that the garden had been neglected for at least five years. Once she got it into a semblance of order, she would be able to keep up.

As her place began to look less embarrassingly derelict, Jessamine thought about inviting more people around. So many had shown her kindness. An opportunity came after a cold morning a few weeks later when Marilyn approached the desk and waved her travel mug.

"Brrr. I need to take a leaf out of your book, Jessamine, and have hot tea. I'm not feeling like anything with ice today."

"Yes, I was surprised to see the snow falling last night. Is snow common around here?"

"We don't get it every winter, especially as late as March." Stephanie laughed. "My grandmother used to say that the snow here is well-mannered and leaves before it wears out its welcome."

"I'm glad it doesn't stay. I had enough of that when I lived out west." Jessamine didn't talk much about where she used to live, and Stephanie and Marilyn eyed her curiously. Not wanting to talk about her old life, she went on quickly. "The chickens are quite offended by the cold. They don't want to walk on the ground. Will they be okay, Stephanie?"

"They'll be fine. They'll keep warm by fluffing out their feathers. Feed them corn for extra energy. And they've got shelter and plenty of your hand-cut hay to stand on."

"None of the animals like the cold, but most of them do fine. Even the spoiled ones." Marilyn laughed. "My husky is complaining, and she's got thick fur." She took a sip from her travel mug, despite the drink being cold. "That reminds me. Do you know anyone who needs a cat?"

Stephanie patted Marilyn on the shoulder. "You always have lots of kittens." She turned to Jessamine. "Marilyn rescues the feral cats in her neighborhood. She gets them spayed and neutered, but there are always more kittens looking for homes."

"This is a new cat." Marilyn shook her head. "She turned up at my door on Friday a week ago, as I was leaving for work. It was that very cold morning, and she was matted and skinny and had a big sore sticking out of her ear, so I couldn't leave her. I enticed her in and shut her in the bathroom with food, water, and a litter box. She was so bad, I thought she might be dead when I got home. I think she would have been dead if I'd left her outside. I took her to the vet on Saturday. He asked what happened to her. They could tell it was an abuse and neglect situation, but they know me. She's put on six pounds in a week."

"Six pounds!" Jessamine raised her eyebrows. "That must be almost her entire body weight. How much did she weigh when you first took her in?"

"Only four pounds."

"Good gracious!" Stephanie opened her mouth in surprise. "How was she alive?"

"I don't know, but she's doing better now."

"Lucky her for finding you." Jessamine felt a prickling behind her eyes.

"Or she came looking for Marilyn." Stephanie patted Marilyn's shoulder again. "It wasn't luck at all. She knew."

Jessamine was used to being surrounded by moving, boisterous, living things; she had raised her five children and nurtured many pets across the years. She enjoyed the chickens, but they lived outside and regarded people as bringers of food or peril, not friends that she could tell. "I could take a kitten now," she said to Marilyn.

"What about the old girl?" Marilyn asked. "I'm keeping her separate. My bossy old Burmese cat will begrudgingly accept new kittens, but he's not happy about her. I'm scared he'll beat her up."

"I'd love to have the old cat." Jessamine smiled. "We'll enjoy living quietly together."

They arranged the details, and on Saturday Jessamine made more Anzac biscuits and tidied up. She thought that it was funny that her first guests made their way down her driveway with boxes of animals.

"I've called her Gabriella," Jessamine told Stephanie and Marilyn the next week. "She needed a dignified name, since she's a dignified old girl. I managed to unlock the cat door and she goes out to do her business, no problem. She prefers to be inside, especially if I've got the fire going. She's settled right in."

Jessamine didn't know if the old cat had put the word out, or the scent of her occupation of her house had gone out into the forest, but a wet afternoon a few days later, she came home from work and heard a small whine as she unlocked her front door. A medium black and white dog crouched out of the wind behind a broken patio chair, his matted plumed tail waving when he saw her looking at him. He was probably a mixed Border Collie.

"Hello, mate." His tail went faster at the sound of her voice. She crouched down and held out her hand. "Come here. Where did you come from?"

He crawled over to her and crouched, shivering under her hand. His fur was rough and muddy, and Jessamine could feel his ribs. "Come on, mate. Would you like dog tucker?" Jessamine didn't know where these words came from. She had heard them in the depths of her childhood, and never consciously said them, but they came out when she wasn't thinking.

She enticed the dog toward the house, and he slunk in, his eyes staying on her face. He jumped when Gabriella hissed and swore at him and looked away when the old cat jumped onto the back of the couch to make more rude comments.

She put a can of Gabriella's food in an old bowl. "This isn't going to make you like him any better," she said to the deeply offended cat.

As she put the food on the floor in the kitchen, the dog looked up at her as if for permission. He ate surprisingly delicately for a dog, especially one that appeared to be starving.

Jessamine asked Stephanie and Marilyn about where to report a lost dog and called the vet offices and the shelter. He wasn't microchipped and no one claimed him. Stephanie said, "It's common around here. People drop them off from their cars on the highway if they don't want them anymore. People are cruel. I don't know why they don't drop them at the animal shelter. Then the poor animals would at least get fed."

She called him Hermes because he ran as if he had wings on his feet—expressing his joy in the world through his stretched body, pumping legs, and flying ears and tail. He settled in but stayed tightly strung. When he needed to go out, he waited at the door, his small body tense with quivering eagerness, his head quirking from side to side to see if Jessamine's hand would reach for the door handle. When she bent down to pat his head, he shied away. He wasn't scared of her hand hurting him, but he was too busy for nonsense like petting, when he had to concentrate on the serious business of running.

They explored the forest together, enjoying the smells, Jessamine sucking in the deep scent of the rotting leaves and Hermes processing a million smells of fox and racoon and mouse and fungi that Jessamine couldn't hope to imagine.

Every morning Jessamine took Hermes on what she thought of as her rounds. They found a path in a gully that led near her mailbox. The gully led to a stream spanned by the small bridge with concrete barriers that she'd discovered on her first day. After a heavy rain, the path was running with water. "My path's flooded," she told Stephanie.

"It's probably an ephemeral stream. It only flows when it rains," Stephanie said.

"I love that name!" Jessamine was delighted. "My boring old path is far more enchanting now."

Jessamine found an old Adirondack chair in the jumble in the shed behind the chicken coop. She dragged it into the forest beside the ephemeral stream. On the weekends, she took her morning tea out to it and watched the wild birds flitting and twittering and going about their complex lives. One morning, Hermes yipped down at her from at least roof height in a leaning moss-covered tree. "You silly dog. What are you doing up there?"

Jessamine explored and saw that one tree had fallen, but was held up by another tree, so it leaned at a gentle climbable angle. She climbed up into a tangle of branches and found a snug fort. Broken plates, a mush of water-logged paper, and a broken doll made Jessamine think it had been a place where children had played. She looked out through the entwined branches and saw a woodpecker hopping around a neighboring tree at her height. *This place is a great wildlife hide.* She climbed into the tree house with Rosemary's binoculars and bird identification books and learned more about her forest. Jessamine felt a visceral longing for her children; she had a passion for sharing nature with them. She taught them to say *photosynthesis* when they were toddlers. "The trees eat the sunlight!" she told them.

She stroked soft moss on the tree and tears prickled behind her eyes. She realized with a lurch that she had been gone from Kansas for a couple of months. She hadn't heard from her husband, a great relief. They hadn't split in a formal way, a problem that gnawed on her mind when she let it, like a toothache she could just manage to ignore.

Before she left, three of her grown children had been living at home, returning after moving out, and another one had asked to move back to save money. Her marriage had been shaky, and at that time, she was looking forward to reconnecting with her husband after years of his military job forcing him all over the world more than he was at home.

She told her husband that she felt that every conversation was interrupted by a grown child, all now bigger than her, inserting themselves between their parents. She said that all the children should move out. The house was crowded and messy, and they argued constantly over cleaning up after themselves. Her children wanted to fall into their childhood pattern of their mother cooking and cleaning for them. Jessamine tried saying no, but it only made a marginal difference. She set up cleaning and cooking rosters, but they collapsed under the weight of various inconsistent work schedules and indifference. She nagged constantly about dishes and putting away their food mess.

"No!" became her way of standing up for herself. She convinced them to do their own laundry by simply not doing it. But they would leave their wet clothes in the washing machine for three days, even after Jessamine reminded them several times. Her husband said, "Just move it to the dryer," but Jessamine pointed out that moving it would be *doing* the laundry for them, defeating the purpose of saying she wouldn't do it. She ground her teeth as she couldn't use the machines to do her own laundry. She refused to move it and eventually her children would finish their laundry, often having to rewash musty clothes, wasting more water, soap, and electricity.

The children and her husband accused her of nagging, and she had to admit that it felt like most of their interactions were negative and about dishes and taking out the trash. "If they moved out, they would have to clean up their own mess. I don't want to argue with a bunch of twenty-somethings about the gosh-darn dishes! About every single teaspoon! We could have an interesting conversation about something else!"

One day Jessamine lost her temper and yelled at her middle son when she saw him leave a cereal bowl, a nearly full gallon of milk, spilled cereal, and two banana skins on the kitchen table and turn to walk out of the room. Jessamine left, but her husband came into the room and from the hallway she heard him tell their son that he didn't have to listen to his mother when she was in a tizzy like that.

As she sat in the peaceful forest and watched the wild birds hopping from tree to tree, Jessamine wondered why she hadn't gone and confronted her husband for undermining her and for expecting her to do all the domestic tasks. At the time, she had told herself that she was being "nice". Jessamine breathed deeply and heard the soughing of the wind, smelled the deep tang of the wet leaves, and considered if she had been "nice" back in Kansas. Or had she been a wimp? Her husband was clean cut and physically strong; he looked like a military man. He never hit any of them, but he was subject to bouts of rage when he swore and threw and broke things. His withering sarcasm had become worse and more frequent. He spent more and more money. Jessamine saw him trying to fill a void inside himself with new things. She knew it wouldn't work; she tried to fill her own void with food. He used all their savings and bought a boat without consulting her. Jessamine asked him to help get their sons to clean up after themselves, but he sneered, "Have some fortitude and do your own dirty work. You do it, if you think it's so important."

All of this became clearer to Jessamine in the snug bird-watching hide in the forest with Hermes curled at her feet. She put her hand on the dog's back, and he quickly licked her hand. From the distance of time and location, she could see it would never have worked out. She'd asked her husband to go to marriage counseling, but his icy reply had been, "You go if you need counseling. *You* need some help of some sort. *I* don't have any problems I can't handle myself."

That's when Jessamine told herself to stop dithering and applied for the job at Bent River County Library.

In the forest, Jessamine's irritation faded over the chores and lack of boundaries from her children, and she missed them with a visceral twisting. She loved the summer days when they had been at elementary school and it was a big job marshalling them around to activities and entertainments. She enjoyed the way her large family stood out and reveled in the children's enthusiasm for everything. She remembered taking them to the science museum in the city and they ran into the steam train inside the building. They gabbed and explored and touched. They tipped the water in the display of the water cycle. Jessamine played at being a molecule with them in the giant leaf, bigger than the train, painted on the wall. They followed the molecules' paths through photosynthesis, and Jessamine cherished passing on her love of nature.

When she first arrived in Bent River County, Jessamine had written a letter to each of her children. She kept in touch with emails and texts, but so far, their replies had been monosyllabic. Now she ached to talk to them. She knew that they had reason to feel betrayed, but she also knew that they needed to go out on their own. She sent them pictures of Hermes and Gabriella and explained how she had been given the cat and the dog had found her. She sent too many pictures of chickens and added funny captions, mostly involving dinosaurs. The thawing began. Royce, her youngest son, started sending her links to funny cat videos. He sent her baffling videos of round cartoon birds dancing to squeaky music. Jessamine sent him a video of a Border Collie winning an agility contest, since the dog looked like Hermes. Royce replied with a video of a husky, who looked like their family husky who had died of old age just before she left, doing the same contest but getting bored and wandering from the arena halfway through. They shared rows of laughing emojis.

Chapter 14

The next week, Josey approached Jessamine, close to tears. "Larsen won't come to the library. He's terrified of the bear," she said. "Can't you move it? I need to get these kids into the library, or we'll go stir crazy. There isn't anywhere else to go in Bent River County, especially when the weather's bad."

Jessamine patted Josey on the shoulder. "We missed you at the story time." She shook her head. "We don't want that bear here either. I'm trying to get rid of it. Marilyn is trying. We'll see what else we can do."

Other children liked the bear too much. They patted him and crooned over his soft fur. His knees became threadbare from the petting and plucking of tiny hands. Jessamine watched this development with glee and reported it to Marilyn. "They'll *have* to move it somewhere else."

"They don't care if it scares the kids." Marilyn rolled her eyes. "They *say* they care about the well-being of the people of the county…" She paused and then brightened. "But the administration is complaining that the bear's getting ruined."

"How would they know? They never come into the library."

"Someone must have told them."

Jessamine narrowed her eyes thoughtfully. "As I said, if they think the bear's getting ruined, they'll move it."

"They don't want it moved, but they told me to stop the children from touching it."

"How? It's next to the board books." Jessamine lifted her arms and rolled her eyes melodramatically. "Of course the children are touching it!"

"I'm only reporting the instructions I was given." Marilyn laughed. "I was told to put a *Do Not Touch* sign on it."

"A sign? Next to the board books? They do realize the people the board books are designed for are two feet tall and can't read, don't they? They need to touch things to learn…"

"I know! I know!" Marilyn shrugged. "I'll talk to them again. At the very least, I'll ask the county to send over Frank and his crew to move it away from the board books."

Before Frank arrived to move the bear, a tall, lithe gray-haired man in tight trousers and a polo shirt came and stood in front of the bear. He put his hands on his hips and sighed. Jessamine watched him with interest since the bear also made her sigh.

The man went outside the library doors and ran his hands over the engraved glass panels with the names of the major donors for the new library. Jessamine thought he must be there from the engraving company to do the repairs because the professionally engraved panels had been installed in front of pale wood, and no one could read the names. She went out. "Can I help you? Are you here to repair them?"

The man didn't look up. "They said they sent a new sample. Where is it?"

Jessamine remembered the sample panel that the engraving company had sent with names written in sticky vinyl letters. "I'll get it."

Jessamine rushed back into the library. "Where's that panel with the sticky letters?" she asked Stephanie.

"Under the desk, here. Why do you need it?"

"There's a workman looking at the panels."

Stephanie squinted out the door. "That's not a workman. That's Joshua Oxford." She rolled her eyes. "The one who says he's the great-great-grandson of Jefferson Davis."

"Really? That's him? I keep hearing about him." Jessamine gazed out the door with interest. Jessamine, having been born and grown up on the other side of the world, didn't recognize many of the powerful people of Bent River County, but since hearing about Joshua Oxford, she noticed his name everywhere. Oxfordville was now a crossroads boasting two gas stations and a pizza restaurant. She drove along Joshua Oxford Memorial Highway to get to the city, and local high school graduates could attend Joshua Oxford Community College. Although, the community college might be getting another name, since someone had decided they didn't want a community college named after a slave owner. She noticed this man's name on signposts and highway markers all around the county and beyond. When Jessamine had been a child, her Member of Parliament had lived in the house up the back and she'd gone to school with his children. Her egalitarian down-under soul found the county's deference to this man strange.

Joshua Oxford pursed his lips and looked around. He caught Jessamine's eye inside the library and gestured imperiously for her to come.

Grabbing the panel with the sticky vinyl letters, Jessamine hurried to the foyer and held it up. Joshua looked at the panel, not at Jessamine. "Those don't look as good as the engraved panels, but at least you can read them."

"Do you want to talk with the library dir—" Jessamine wasn't sure what she was supposed to do.

"Hold it over there." Joshua ignored her words and gestured. "Where do those words fit?"

"These black letters are bigger." Jessamine scrutinized the panel she was holding and surveyed the engraved glass, trying to work out where the panel would fit. "Here's the right place: *Library Building approved in twenty…*"

"What do you think about the panels?"

"I'm not sure. If you want to talk to the dir—"

"I'm asking you what *you* think. These plaques cost ten thousand dollars."

He looked at Jessamine over his glasses.

Jessamine was taken aback. They didn't look like they cost that much. "At least you can read these black plastic ones?"

"But do they look as nice?"

"No, I like the look of the engraved ones better."

He pointed. "That's me there." Jessamine peered, but she couldn't read it. She nodded and smiled.

Jessamine remembered the library staff's experiments with the panels on a slow day. "Have you tried putting something dark behind it?"

Joshua scrolled through his phone. "What do you mean?"

"I'll show you." Jessamine rushed back into the library. She pulled an apologetic face at Stephanie minding the desk. "Won't be long. Joshua Oxford is spending a long time looking at the panels."

"He would." Stephanie shook her head. "They might get them fixed so we can read them, but I don't want to look at their names. It's always their names in this county."

Jessamine grabbed faded blue and black paper, saved from the mice, and returned to the hallway. "If you slide this dark paper behind the panel, you can read the words. It works well in the sunlight."

"Hold it still." Joshua took a photo with his cell phone. "Now put it over there."

Jessamine moved the pieces of paper, watching to see if he approved. "Try the other one." He moved his glasses up and down. "Try over here. Put it behind the names here." He took more photos. "Okay. I've got enough to get it worked out." He turned and walked down the hallway, leaving Jessamine holding blue and black paper, staring after him.

At the desk, Marilyn held her travel mug while talking to Stephanie.

"He didn't say thank you." Jessamine blinked several times. "He didn't come in the library except to sigh at the bear. Would it hurt him to come in and check out a book?"

Stephanie rolled her eyes. "Checking out books is for us peons. He doesn't even have a library card. Those people are involved with the library *because* they'll get their names on the plaques. They're not interested in the library. They never come *in* the library. When do we ever see Joshua Oxford anywhere near here? For plaques."

"I've got to get back to updating those public computers," Marilyn said. "They're about to die. You can only update them so much. They're six years old and they were refurbished in the first place." Marilyn leaned her elbows on the desk. "Joshua is one of the ones who said, 'What do we need libraries for? I can get all the books I need on my Kindle.' And when I pointed out that not everyone has a Kindle, he said that people can look things up on the internet."

"But only half of Bent River County's residents have the internet. That's why we need the library!" Jessamine's voice rose.

"I know." Marilyn sipped from her travel mug. "Try telling them that. You'd think if they got their names on the plaque, they'd want to help the library." She paused and looked around. "It might change when they get their spectacular new building."

"Them and their building." Stephanie pulled a face. "What about books for the children? Children spend enough time looking at screens. And books for people without computers? And what about programs? We have book groups and story time. And crafts and the knitting program Jessamine's going to start. And bingo. People in Bent River County love my cousin Cyril's bingo."

"I know people love bingo. It's another sticking point." Marilyn sighed. "'What is a library doing having bingo?' they've asked me. I argue for it. I know it's a social program. I told them that library people call them anti-loneliness programs. The bigwigs don't care." Marilyn sighed again. "Those computers aren't going to update themselves. Although they do update themselves in the *rich* libraries because they can afford the software..."

Stephanie watched Marilyn leave. "I'm worried about her. She's normally so upbeat. All these meetings and spreadsheets are getting her down. But she's right. The work won't do itself." Stephanie picked up a stack of books to check in, and Jessamine picked up a rag to wipe the tables with soap and water.

Chapter 15

Bubbles *of excitement rose* in Jessamine's chest as she planned her first STEM program for the Bent River County Public Library. She briefly considered using the bear as Marilyn suggested, but after her encounter with the arrogant Joshua Oxford, Jessamine felt something stubborn gel inside her. She pictured herself as a two-year-old Jessamine, hair starting to streak with gray, stamping her foot and saying, "No! NO!" She knew she couldn't achieve everything she wanted in the library, but she didn't have to fall in with their suggestions about the bear.

"Not a single penny to spare." Marilyn shook her head sadly when Jessamine asked about a budget, but in past libraries and volunteer work, Jessamine's children's STEM programs included natural phenomena like herbs, the water cycle, soil, and seeds. She dug around on her computer for her old program outlines. For materials she poked and fossicked in closets and cupboards in the library and her house. Like the story time, the program was for multiple ages—eager fourth graders to early teens, for whom looking cool was apt to be far more important than learning anything or enjoying themselves.

After she found a jar of cicada shells in one of Rosemary's cupboards, Jessamine settled on insects for the first program. As a child on the other side of the world, she had collected jars of cicada shells. The New Zealand cicada species were much smaller, but she instantly recognized the shiny tan skins that the larvae shed. As she cleaned her new home, she kept every dead invertebrate she found, and there were plenty in the dusty house.

The turnout was good, and Jessamine eyed the children as they perched, balanced, and jiggled on the chairs around the library tables. When Jessamine previously ran STEM programs, the library gave her a separate room, usually with a scrubbable vinyl floor, or occasionally a science lab. In Bent River County, she had to hold the program in the middle of the library on a day it was open to the public.

The children were off school today, so it was a great time to try their new program. Jessamine and Stephanie had worked together for hours on perfecting Bent River County Public Library's *Science Alive: School-Age STEM Program.* Stephanie wanted to come in to help, but Drusilla wouldn't let Stephanie work extra hours, and Marilyn was too distracted to interfere.

Kathryn's assistant, Agnes, who liked to read the elderly donated magazines on her lunch hour, huffed at Jessamine when Jessamine asked if she could use the tables. Agnes now joined in the crafts and other programs after huffing, but today she was far too old to participate. Agnes sat on one of the slippery vinyl-covered armchairs and regarded them over her magazine. A few parents joined her, then wandered off.

One teen boy turned around on his chair and sat astride, as on a horse. Over the hubbub, Jessamine couldn't hear what he was saying, but it made the girls he was talking to lower their eyelids and bring their hands up to their mouths to hide giggles. Several girls were bent over the phone of one, pointing and making Os of their mouths in mock dismay.

Jessamine raised her voice, knowing it wasn't the best technique. "Who knows how many legs an insect has?"

A boy in the front threw his arm up. "I know! I know!"

"Okay." Jessamine was glad of the folded paper name plates she'd asked them to make. "Mark, can you tell me how many?"

"Six," he said, triumphant, beaming around the room to see how the other children reacted, but they weren't listening, involved in their own affairs.

"That's right." Jessamine smiled at him. The other children ignored both of them. "I have something else that's not an insect. I wonder if anyone can tell me what it is?"

Jessamine dug in her box and pulled out a dried exoskeleton of a palm-sized spider from Rosemary's kitchen. She held it on a plastic sour-cream lid and walked closer to the children. The children stared at the spider, and the volume went down.

"Is it alive?"

They reached out hesitating hands.

"Can I touch it?"

"It's a spider of course!"

The children now focused on Jessamine.

"Ma'am, you shouldn't be scaring me with that thing!" A girl shrank back. "I'm not touching it!"

"You don't have to touch it, Celeste," Jessamine said. "I'll keep it away from you. It's dead, so anyone who wants to can touch it. Be gentle, touch it with a finger. It's dried out and might break."

Jessamine pulled out her cicada shells and dried out centipedes and beetles and dragonflies. She tasked Mark to hand out paper and pencils and told them about doing an anatomical drawing. As the children worked on their invertebrate drawings, Jessamine walked around and commented and encouraged them. Celeste's aversion to "crawlies" was strong, so Jessamine let her draw a leaf.

The volume rose again, and the children drifted from their seats. Jessamine told several children to be quiet and sit down, but her quiet voice was getting lost. It became less effective when the name plates were knocked off the desks and she couldn't remember their names.

She went up to the front and clapped her hands, which they ignored, when Bobby, the Sheriff, stepped through the library doors. "Celeste Stokes, park yourself on that chair! Edward Bartlett! Are you meant to be holding that above Celeste's head? I thought not. Put it down. I know Celeste doesn't want it down her neck. And return to your seat."

"Yes, Uncle Bobby." The boy put down a cicada shell and sat down.

A hush fell over the library and the children sat in their chairs.

"Uh, thank you," Jessamine said.

Bobby smiled. "It's the magic police voice. And this uniform helps. I've known most of them since before they were born. That's a strong-willed bunch of children." He turned to leave, then turned back. "Thank you for doing this, Jessamine. Those kids need positive attention. I'm glad you've created something for them to do in Bent River County."

They all watched him leave and Jessamine turned to the children. "Finish off your drawings."

Jessamine saw that Celeste's leaf was a startlingly accurate rendition for a child of twelve. As she finished drawing, Celeste relaxed and leaned back in her chair and her eyes roved. She jumped up with a scream and pointed upwards. "Arrgh! They're on the ceiling!"

Jessamine sighed. Her two minutes of peace were over. "Sit down, Celeste. There's nothing on the ceiling."

"But, ma'am," said Mark, the eager child at the front, "there *is* something crawling across the ceiling."

Jessamine stared up, along with all the children. At first, she couldn't see anything on the stained, yellowed ceiling tiles, but if she kept her eyes in one spot, she could see movement. It looked like a caterpillar, lifting its front forward, then arching its segmented back to inch across the ceiling. Jessamine squinted. They looked familiar.

"Oh, bother." Jessamine swung around to her boxes of program materials. She grabbed a trash bag she had sealed with a wire twisty tie. Apparently not tightly enough. She pulled out a small branch from one of her sapling trees. An area as long and wide as Jessamine's forearm was smothered by thick, densely woven webs, as thick as fine cloth. These web structures had suddenly appeared in trees all over the county. Jessamine asked Stephanie about them, and Stephanie said, "They're tent caterpillars or fall web worms. I'm not sure which is which." She shrugged. "They happen every year. Some years more than others. Since it's so early—it's hardly fall in May—they might be bad this year. The trees deal with losing a bunch of leaves and just carry on."

"They're so creepy," Jessamine said. "Do they really have worms in them?"

"I guess they're caterpillars. Look inside a tent, if you find one close to the ground."

Jessamine had studied several of the webby masses on low-hanging branches and saplings. She poked their web home with a stick and stepped back as hundreds of caterpillars vibrated in disturbing synchronization. Creepy or not, they were perfect for her new STEM program, so she'd cut part of a denuded sapling and brought the caterpillars in to show the children. But caterpillars are small and apparently don't like being kept in plastic bags. She looked up.

"Cool!" said Mark. "What are they, ma'am?"

"They're caterpillars," Jessamine said. "Can anyone tell me what type of animal a caterpillar will turn into?"

"A butterfly of course," said Celeste and rolled her eyes. She glanced up and shuddered. "Are they going to fall on me?"

"And moths," Jessamine said. "No, they won't fall." Jessamine crossed her fingers in her sleeve and hoped it was true. "Does anyone know how they can stay upside down on the ceiling without falling?"

Edward stopped flirting long enough to look up at the caterpillars. "They have tiny, sticky feet, so they can stay there." He looked at Celeste. "Don't worry, I'll protect you from them."

Jessamine was relieved that Edward's attention distracted Celeste from the caterpillars; the child was genuinely scared of them. Jessamine let the children tape their finished drawings on the ends of bookshelves. Mark distributed printed sheets of butterfly life cycles. When the activity kit was new, it boasted real silk-worm cocoons and pipe cleaners for caterpillars. They were long gone and this library couldn't afford replacements, so Jessamine made-do with cotton balls and yarn from a tangle in the supply closet. The children seemed happy with it.

As they finished the project, Jessamine sighed in relief that her first STEM program was nearly over, despite unexpected visitors on the ceiling.

Jessamine had cleaned up after this sort of program before, so she had gathered old spray bottles and rags from Rosemary's cupboards. She put a trash can at both ends of each table. "After you throw everything away, wipe your tables." She pulled a spray bottle from the reaching hands of Edward and Celeste. "Anyone who squirts anything that is not a table or chair will lose their bottle," she said and looked each child in the eye. Now they looked back, and they didn't saturate each other, she saw with relief.

The children drifted toward the shelves to look at books, and Jessamine was returning the trash cans to their spots when Drusilla appeared and flicked her scarf. She looked at the overflowing trash cans, disarrayed chairs, and tables puddled with smears of mud.

"Trust you to make a mess," Drusilla said. She put her hands on her hips. "I hope you don't think I'm going to help clean it up."

Jessamine kept her face still and fought to keep herself from looking up.

Drusilla puffed out through rounded cheeks and shook her head in contempt.

A caterpillar fell and landed on Drusilla's shoulder. Jessamine thought she heard a tiny plop, but Drusilla showed no sign of noticing anything. Jessamine squinted and breathed in. There were purple marks on Drusilla's arm: four oval bruises in a row on one side and a bigger oval on the other. It had to be where a large hand squeezed so hard it left marks.

"I'm going to my office if you're just going to stare at my scarf like an idiot." Drusilla rolled her eyes and swirled toward her office.

Two more caterpillars fell on Drusilla's retreating magenta scarf. Jessamine opened her mouth to call after her colleague, then shut it and went looking for Frank. She'd have to tell him about the caterpillars so he could tell her how to clean them up.

To Jessamine's vast relief, when he got there, Frank looked up and laughed. "This county building's infested with worse than that!"

"It makes extra work for you. I'm sorry."

"Sticky traps and spray ought to do it. I've got to get up in the ceiling anyway. It's due for its big cleaning." He looked at the caterpillars thoughtfully. "I might be able to suck them up with the vacuum."

"I'm very sorry," Jessamine repeated. "Is there anything I can do to help?" She had been told in the past that she apologized too much, but this made extra work for Frank.

He waved her concerns away, so she brought him Anzac biscuits and a mint plant in a pot that she'd been growing for the next STEM program.

Chapter 16

"*C'mon. Let's whip 'round* and tidy before closing," said Marilyn as she did every afternoon. "It's not Frank's job to arrange our magazines."

The three of them piled books on carts, picked up scattered and tattered newspapers and magazines, and pushed tissues and unidentifiable detritus into a sideways trash can with their feet. Drusilla never helped. "That's what we have cleaners—sorry, facilities staff for," she sniffed when asked to help.

As Jessamine grabbed the strewn toys, she eyed the bear. She usually avoided looking at it because she was furious that it remained by the board books. She and Stephanie couldn't physically move the bear—they'd tried. The creature stared at Jessamine with its malevolent glass eyes. She knew it was long dead, but she felt like Joshua Oxford was looking at her through the bear.

"Jessamine, hurry up!" Stephanie called.

"Jessamine, did you get the trash?" Marilyn asked at the same time.

Jessamine stood transfixed in front of the bear. She jumped. "Yes. No. What?"

The library's donated toys included several mismatched tea sets of varying colors, sizes, and materials. An industrious child had selected matching, if tired-looking, plastic cups and saucers of mustard yellow with blood-red flowers of indeterminate species. Tea was set for three; cup and saucer sets were arranged neatly around the edge of the bear's wooden stand. In the middle, up against the bear's hairy left leg, the party food consisted of a knitted pumpkin, a miniature plastic box of cereal, and a molded plastic bowl of rice, whose permanent plastic grains gave Jessamine the urge to scrape them off with her fingernail. The bear had also been invited to the party; a tiny yellow cup perched on top of one of its raised paws, and a pink-sequined purse hung off a claw.

"Hey, look at this!" Jessamine called.

Marilyn and Stephanie hurried over and regarded the abandoned tea party. "That wasn't a child that put that way up there," Marilyn grumbled as she grabbed the cup and purse from the bear's paw and dropped them into the toybox. She shook her head in mock dismay. "What will Joshua Oxford say about his precious bear?"

"Wait," Jessamine said. "I'm getting an idea."

"Can't you get the idea tomorrow so we can go home?" Stephanie raised her eyebrows and headed toward the circulation desk.

Jessamine stood still. "You know how we don't have enough display space?"

"Yes." Marilyn gave the bear an unfriendly look. "And that giant, blasted bear doesn't help."

"We might…" Jessamine spluttered, trying to get her idea out. "We can use the bear for displays."

"What?"

"You know how we've got the herb program coming up? We can put an apron on the bear, because he's cooking." Jessamine laughed. "And he can be holding a jar of, I don't know, parsley."

"What?" Stephanie repeated. She stopped walking toward the desk and turned. A grin spread over her face. "I get it! He can hold a wooden spoon."

"And a chef's hat!" Marilyn put her hands on her hips and looked at the bear with narrowed eyes.

"And after that, when our book group is reading *The Maid*, he can have a feather duster." Jessamine raised her eyebrows.

Marilyn laughed and shook her head in mock desperation. "What will you come up with next, Jessamine?" She paused. "Their bear is *in* the library, and I'm in charge of the library. And we don't have enough space, and they won't buy us any shelves to use for displays. So why not?" She looked around. "Right now, we'd better get this place tidied up and closed."

That night, Jessamine looked at Rosemary's clutter in her house with new eyes. What could she use to display on the bear? She grabbed the dusty pink felt cloche hat off the chipped faun because she thought it would add a jaunty touch to the bear. She found several handmade bibbed aprons in Rosemary's kitchen drawers. She was particularly taken by a set of oven gloves and a bright red apron with a repeating pattern of whisks, bowls, and eggs.

She eyed the flowery jacket she had worn on her first day at her new job. She had bought the jacket on a thrift-shopping trip with one of her Kansas neighbors when her husband was deployed. Clusters of green embroidered stems twined upwards, sprouting orange, pink, and yellow flowers covered in fluttering butterflies, forever about to land.

The dark blue jacket caught Jessamine's eye because its bright hopefulness proclaimed a belief in the spring Jessamine longed for, but her neighbor's eyes widened. "You're going to buy that?"

"Yes, I like it."

"What for?"

"I'll wear it when I get a job. It'll cheer me up."

"You're brave. It's um… bright, as you said."

Jessamine got a job in the university library after her husband returned from deployment. She wore the oversized, flowery jacket to work, warm against the frigid prairie winters. She felt enclosed and safe when it she was wrapped in it, and she enjoyed the texture when she rubbed her fingertips over the embroidered butterflies. She thought of it as her tree-of-life jacket.

In her hurry to leave, Jessamine hadn't brought many clothes with her, so she had worn the jacket often when she started at Bent River County

Public Library. The story time children liked to point to the butterflies on her sleeves and trace the tangled stems of the plants.

One day, returning from work, she had caught it on one of the vines and the jacket tore in a V-shaped hole that she could put her fist into. Jessamine considered sewing it up, but didn't know how she could hide a tear right down the front. She knew she didn't have the skills to embroider a matching plant over the tear. Now, she put the ruined jacket in her bag for the library to see how it would fit the bear.

The next day, Jessamine and Stephanie hurried through their morning routine of checking in books from the book drop and pulling holds that had come in overnight, so they could set up their display using the bear.

Jessamine stood in front of the bear with her hands on her hips. "We should give this bear a name."

"Name the bear? Yes!" Stephanie grinned. "What should we call it? Growly?"

"Growltiger? But that was a cat," Jessamine said.

"Roger the Reading Bear? Since it's a library."

"I know!" Jessamine waved her hands. "Why don't we have a competition to name it? We did it in one of my old libraries to name the reference librarian's puppies. We could take votes at the story times or in programs."

"We could use one of your jars at the front desk to put votes in."

When they told Marilyn, she thought it was a great idea. "Why don't we take suggestions for a week or two and then vote on the best ones? Otherwise, we might get dozens. And how would we choose?"

Jessamine tapped her fingers on the desk and thought. "Okay. We've got tons of out-of-date book award posters that are blank on the back. I'll put up one behind the desk and ask for names for our bear."

The competition was far more popular than any of them expected. People who had never been library customers came in to suggest names.

"Fudge Round, since it's dark brown and fat," said Walter the guard. Jessamine found his name in the library system from when he was in elementary school, and she checked out two thrillers to him. He promised to bring in his daughters to get library cards on the weekend.

The teenager, Englebert, came in to check out his usual science fiction and fantasy. "Beorn, of course," he said and blushed.

"That's a great suggestion." Jessamine smiled at him. "It's the shape-shifting bear from *The Lord of the Rings*."

Englebert looked up. "No, it's from *The Hobbit*, actually. It's old English. 'Bjorn' with a j is a Scandinavian name. It means 'bear' in Finnish and Icelandic and other languages."

"It's perfect for a bear." Jessamine eyed the creature across the library and crossed her arms in front of her chest. "I hope that bear doesn't shed its skin and walk around at night like Beorn did."

"Beorn was hunting goblins." Englebert laughed. "That might be a good thing in Bent River County."

Jessamine was wondering how to reply to this when another customer came up to the desk and Englebert left.

The story time kids and their parents were prolific; they suggested Winnie the Pooh and Paddington and Baloo and Corduroy and Cupcake and Sprinkles.

As usual, the STEM kids argued about it.

"I think it should be Fluffy Pants," said Celeste.

"That's dumb. It should be Goldilocks. There are a lot of bears in that story."

"Goldilocks is human. That's the point. The bears could eat her."

"I like Totoro," Mark suggested.

"But Totoro isn't a bear," Celeste said.

"Yes, he is."

"He's a flying school bus with a grin."

"Nah, he's just a great big fluffy thing," Celeste said with finality. Her final word was usually accepted by the STEM group. When Mark came up to the desk to check out a biography of Feynman, he suggested Totoro and Jessamine wrote it on the poster.

Jessamine and Stephanie needed to pin up more posters to fit all the suggested names.

Marilyn suggested Booky Bear. Drusilla refused to contribute. "It's stupid. The bear doesn't need a name."

Merriam, the county lawyer who had taken his cell phone into the building on Jessamine's first day, eyed the posters behind the desk.

"What about Ursilla?" he asked.

Jessamine smiled. "After Ursula Le Guin?"

"No, because it's an American black bear, *Ursus americanus*. And I'm thinking of the other way it's spelled, 'Ursilla.'"

The next week they counted the votes squeezed into several of Jessamine's decorated jars. Ursilla was the clear winner: "By a country mile," Stephanie said. "I don't get it."

"I don't get it either." Jessamine screwed up her eyebrows. "I can't see the small children voting for the name Ursilla. It's too obscure. And from what I heard, they liked the pretty names. I thought Cupcake would win." Jessamine looked around as if someone might overhear. "Actually, I voted for Cupcake. I thought I could have one vote since I live here."

Drusilla came sweeping through the door in a puff of perfume and a flick of scarves. "I see you're making a mess again. What's all that?"

"It's the bear naming competition," Jessamine said.

Drusilla rolled her eyes. "I'm not sure Josh… I mean Mr. Oxford will like that competition. It impinges on the dignity of his bear."

"If he came into the library, he could have voted," Stephanie said. "Too late now. I guess he must accept that the bear is named Drus… I mean Ursilla." Stephanie held her hand in front of her mouth, but the puff of a suppressed giggle emerged.

"What?" Drusilla stood, as if unsure of what to do for once. A red stain rose from her neck and up her face. "You can't name it that! It's ridiculous." She flicked her scarf again. "I'm going to talk to the Library Committee about it. After all, it's their library." She sniffed and stalked off to her office, leaning forward on her four-inch heels.

Chapter 17

"*O*uch." *Jessamine stretched.* "*My* back hurts."

"Did you wrench it clearing your yard?" Stephanie pulled her mouth into a sympathetic O.

"It might be," Jessamine hesitated, "because I'm sleeping on the couch."

"Holy moley, Jessamine!" Stephanie put her hands on her hips. "You've been here for *months!*"

"Why are months significant?" Jessamine was cautious.

"I saw two perfectly good bedrooms in your house." Stephanie tapped her foot. "Why aren't you sleeping in a bed?

"It doesn't feel right, or hygienic, to sleep in Rosemary's bed. I'm enjoying cleaning up the yard, but her muddle is everywhere inside. I try to sort out one box every night, but I'm usually too tired."

"I'd go right through that dreck." Stephanie wagged her finger at Jessamine. "I'm not sentimental."

Jessamine wasn't sure what to say.

"And here's a minimalist." Stephanie pointed at Marilyn passing by, waving her travel mug. "We'll both help you clear out in no time."

Marilyn sagged against the desk. "I don't feel capable of helping with anything right now. I just endured another meeting with Kathryn. I was ambushed by Joshua. Why was he there?"

"He thinks he should be the star of everything in this county." Stephanie rolled her eyes.

"I'm trying to get them to concentrate on budgets, and the building plan for the new library, but they keep nattering about the bear." Marilyn paused and broke into a grin. "I don't think Joshua knows about the naming and dressing of the bear. Everyone's too scared to tell him."

They all looked toward the bear, sprouting pink bunny ears, and laughed.

"Here's a change from meetings." Stephanie patted Marilyn's arm. "Jessamine needs help going through the hodgepodge in her house." She opened her arms to Jessamine. "We've got to get this woman off her couch and into a bed so she can work hard in our library."

"I should do it myself." Jessamine grimaced. "It's my property now."

"We'll all pitch in." Marilyn stood up straight and looked happier. "I'm great at sorting out clutter."

"Woo, hoo!" Stephanie clenched her hands over her head in a victory dance. "It's settled. Are you free this weekend? They're forecasting more rain."

Stephanie was right about the weather, and on Saturday morning, Jessamine ran through the mud to feed the chickens, then lit the fire. She used her chicken's fresh eggs to make a quiche and stirred up some Anzac biscuits, carried along by Stephanie's idea of a potluck lunch.

Hermes ran yapping to the door as Stephanie and Marilyn shook off their raincoats and umbrellas on the porch.

"Let our guests in, beastie." Jessamine took their dripping rainwear. "Sorry, with your coats on, he thinks you're aliens. Come and get warm."

Hermes recognized the women in ordinary clothes and melted into a waggy, happy, licky dog, bumping his nose on their legs for attention.

"He's a sweet boy." Marilyn ruffled his fur then scratched the cat's chin. "And look at this cat. You've done a wonderful job. She's glowing with health."

"Would you like a cup of tea?" Jessamine stepped toward the kitchen.

"I know you're always parched for a cuppa." Stephanie rubbed her hands together. "But let's get right to sorting. My husband is watching the kids, so I have a day off. We'll enjoy tea as a reward."

Jessamine led them to the back bedroom. "Rosemary's distant relatives don't want anything—I asked her lawyer."

The women moved aside the gramophone and faun, then carried boxes, drawers, and odd piles into the sitting room. Marilyn perched on the cross-stitch castle stool. "I can get you a chair, Marilyn." Jessamine hovered.

"I'm fine down here. I can reach everything and I'm close to your wonderful fire." Marilyn scratched Hermes behind his ears until he shut his eyes and sighed blissfully. "Most importantly, I can reach this sweetie of a hound."

Stephanie relaxed on the couch in a scatter of Post-it notes, electronic cords, torn t-shirts, and a glass paperweight containing a maple leaf. "I know everyone liked Rosemary, but I'm starting to think she was a hoarder."

"I've made it worse, dragging things out of cupboards and plonking them on the floor." Jessamine poked her toe on a box overflowing with fabric. "My family moved all the time. We couldn't walk across the floor for boxes."

"What was it like living all over the world? Your travels sound exotic to me. I still live in the same county where I was born." Stephanie tipped her head. "Weren't you married to a guy in the military?"

"Moving was hard. We had to get rid of stuff I wanted to keep so we'd stay under the weight limit. We needed a lot of beds and furniture with five kids, so we couldn't keep many extras. I guess that's why I find it so challenging to get rid of stuff now." Jessamine stared at Hermes. "It was really hard moving pets."

"What pets did you have?" Marilyn scratched Hermes' ear.

"We had dogs, cats, guinea pigs, fish and lizards. And turtles once. We had to find new homes for them when we moved to a different country. We were down to one dog, Laurel, and she died just after Christmas."

"That's a difficult time to lose your dog." Marilyn put her arm around Hermes.

A jagged lump formed in Jessamine's throat, and she couldn't talk for a moment. "It was a horrible Christmas. I don't think Laurel dying was the worst part."

"What?" Stephanie and Marilyn exchanged a look.

"I…" Jessamine swallowed. "I was thinking about when I decided to accept this job. It saved me."

"Saved you?" Marilyn and Stephanie exchanged frowns.

"My dog died, and it was my fault because I was angry that my husband bought a boat." Jessamine stopped and smoothed Hermes' ears. "That doesn't make sense."

"No sense at all." Stephanie leaned forward and rubbed her arm. "Tell us. If you can explain, it might help you."

"He bought a motorboat without discussing it." Jessamine felt ashamed of the boat, and she didn't know why. "We couldn't afford it." She shivered, suddenly cold in the cozy sitting room. "In Kansas, I couldn't get warm even though I'd lived on the wintry plains for years. I wrapped myself in layers of fuzzy clothes under my flowery embroidered jacket, but I felt frigid winds whistling across everything."

"Come closer to the fire." Marilyn shuffled over.

"I was glad to go back to work at the university library after Christmas. I polished my desk and filed months of paperwork. It was silly, but I felt better that I could clean up *something*. I trimmed and watered my cubicle plants until my boss said the office looked like an arboretum."

"We know you like plants." Stephanie smiled.

"The kids were moving in and out. It was hard to keep track. I made meals in the slow cooker with leftover Christmas food, so there would be something warm to come home to. No one ate them." Jessamine scratched Hermes' chin. "I picked pieces of meat out for our dog, Laurel, and she vomited all over the carpet. She was thirteen, so I felt guilty for upsetting her stomach. She threw up every day until she vomited blood. I took her to the vet in the morning before work. The vet diagnosed stomach cancer and said heroic surgery and drugs for a thirteen-year-old dog would prolong her suffering. He said it was best to put her down right then. I texted my children and husband. My husband texted, *I don't care. You deal with your stupid animal.*"

Stephanie and Marilyn gasped.

"I knew the dog was old and it was inevitable, but I could barely drive to work. The university library was quiet, and it was only me working in the reference office. I huddled at my desk in my flowery jacket. I stroked a leaf and wondered why my silly houseplant was alive when my dog was dead. I was starting to admit to myself that my marriage was also dead. The snow on the roads thawed slightly, then refroze, so it was hard to drive over the icy ridges of filthy slush. I pictured myself sliding off the roads into a ditch on the way home and bonking my head sideways on the window, so I never woke up. It happened to someone I knew..." Jessamine trailed off, lost in her darkness.

"Jessamine? Are you okay?" She heard voices as if from a great distance. Jessamine shook her head and came back to the present. She found herself crouched on the floor clinging to Hermes, who vigorously licked her ear. Stephanie and Marilyn frowned at her in worry.

She gave them a shaky smile. "I'm alright. Do you want to hear more?"

They both nodded, so Jessamine stroked Hermes' fur and went on. "I was telling you about when I went to work. I felt compelled to clean and organize everything in my office. I was tidying up my personal emails and came across the job offer from Bent River County Public Library that I hadn't answered. I sat there with my hand hovering over the reply button. It was hundreds of miles away. I couldn't leave my children in Kansas, and I didn't know anyone in Virginia. I desperately wanted to go home, put on my pajamas, then spend five minutes cooking an egg. I pictured myself eating it in bed with the plate propped up on my knees while I read a children's book."

"Sounds perfect." Marilyn smiled.

"But our fridge was empty except for a crusting of ancient spills and hot sauce. I hate hot sauce." Jessamine laughed dryly at the irrelevant detail. "I thought maybe a nice meal might thaw things between me and my husband."

"It sounds like you tried with your marriage." Stephanie tapped a finger on the maple leaf paperweight.

"I just wanted to rest. But I had to get gas, or I wouldn't make it home. I hated grocery shopping after years of buying for five teenagers when the carts were so overloaded that I couldn't push them. I remember all the details of that night vividly. I forced myself into the slushy, half-plowed parking lot of the supermarket and soaked my work shoes. I wrenched my shoulder stopping the wonky cart from crashing into displays."

Jessamine wrapped herself in a quilt and pulled Hermes onto her lap.

"I knew our bank account was nearly as empty and crusty as the fridge after he spent it all on the boat, so I grabbed the cheapest store-brand pasta and sauce. When I heaved a twenty-pound bag of rice into the cart, it pulled my thumbnail down to the quick and made it bleed." Jessamine examined her nail for the long-healed injury, then smiled. "I'm glad I impulsively grabbed a value pack of granola bars. I needed those on this journey. But the fancy triple chocolate ice cream turned into an embarrassment, even though I thought I deserved a small treat."

Marilyn handed Jessamine a cup of hot tea she'd quietly brewed, and Jessamine wrapped her hands around it.

"I was so tired by the checkout line that I was glad to have the cart handle to lean on. A young man with a beard argued for ages about a price. Then the checkout woman told me that my loaf of bread was moldy." Jessamine shook her head. "I wanted to throw that bread and stomp on it. Or slide down to the floor and not move. But she'd already checked it out, so she said to grab another one. When I got back, the people in line glared at me. I cared what they thought. I thought everyone hated me."

Hermes wiggled up and licked Jessamine's eyebrow. She laughed and pushed him off her lap. "I know you're trying to help, but that's slimy."

"Then what happened?" Stephanie leaned forward, passing the paperweight from hand to hand.

"My card was declined three times. I tried two more cards. I finally pulled out the cash I carried for emergencies, but it was ten dollars short. I picked out the ice cream to return to the freezer, but the people in line behind me tapped their feet, so the checkout woman said she'd handle it. She called for backup on checkout two through her microphone and she sounded grumpy."

"So you succeeded in getting the groceries?" Marilyn put more wood on the fire and stirred it to burn hotter.

"I still had to get the food home and inside. I'm too short for our garage door. I can't reach it properly. My husband laughed at me for being short."

"Like you can help being short?" Stephanie shook her head.

Jessamine stared at her. With her husband's teasing, she had always felt vaguely guilty for not being taller. Something so simple and logical never occurred to her.

"The garage door was stuck. I had to reach up and lean against it, so the melting ice was all down my front as well as in my shoes. I was shivering. Then I saw the boat. I'd forgotten I couldn't park in the garage because the boat took up all the space." Jessamine laughed when she heard how slapstick this sounded but finished on a half sob. "When I parked outside in that weather, I had to scrape thick ice and sleet every morning. I tried heating the car up ahead of time, but my husband complained about me wasting gas." Jessamine frowned. "I shouldn't have done it, but sometimes I would leave the ice and drive slowly, peering out the side window. But I was scared of hitting something."

"What? That wasn't safe." Stephanie frowned.

"We hadn't shoveled the steps, and they were treacherous, so I only took a few bags of groceries. I left the front door open behind me to bring more in. My husband slammed the door, then stalked into the kitchen.

"'That's right,' he said 'We're made of money. Leave the door open and warm the front yard and use all the electricity in the universe.'"

Jessamine tried to laugh at his childish exaggeration, but she couldn't.

"I told him I had more groceries to bring in. I tried to step around him, but he blocked my way. He put his hands on his hips and rolled his eyes at me. I said, 'Please, I've got to get the rest of the food out of the car.' I heard the begging in my voice and hated myself for it."

Stephanie took a deep breath as Jessamine went on.

"My husband shook his head sarcastically. 'What? There's more? We're living on the high hog now.' I told him I had to buy food."

Jessamine scooted closer to the fire until she almost touched it. Hermes whined and backed up. "I was glad that the ice cream hadn't made it home."

"You're allowed to eat a little bit of ice cream." Marilyn pleated a napkin and smoothed it out roughly on her knee.

"Then he picked up a gallon of milk and lifted it over his head." Jessamine shuddered at the memory.

Marilyn gasped.

Jessamine stared down. "He said, 'I'm glad some of us feel so rich that they can buy whatever they like, even though some of us get nag-nag-nagged about our simple outdoor hobbies. I can't buy a boat, but you can buy whatever crap you like.' I was frozen. I thought he was going to smash the milk down on my head. Then he turned and pounded it so hard on the edge of the counter that the plastic bottle burst, and milk splattered across the kitchen. I just stood there. He picked up the next bottle of milk and smashed that. When he raised a glass jar of pasta sauce, I ran."

Jessamine sobbed, and Stephanie put her arm around her. "Stop talking if you have to but go on if it helps."

"Tell us the whole story without stopping if you can." Marilyn patted Jessamine's other shoulder.

"I ran to the bathroom and locked the door." Jessamine took a quivering breath. "I should have been doing something, but I collapsed on the edge of the bath and sobbed. My phone buzzed in my pocket. My eyes were bleary, but I made out. *When are you coming?* I completely forgot I'd arranged to meet Victoria and some library people for a post-Christmas girls' night out. I saw my red, puffy face in the mirror. I couldn't go anywhere.

"'Clean up this disgusting kitchen,' my husband screamed between swear words. Then the front door slammed, and I heard the roar of his truck starting.

"I paced around my bedroom. I picked up my copy of *Anne of Green Gables* that my grandmother gave me when I was a child. I carried that book around the world. I knew I should do something, but I slid down between the bed and the wall and began to read. It reminded me of when I visited my grandmother and the spot between her bed and the wall caught the sun. I don't know how long it was, but I heard my husband returning.

"I felt naked. Why hadn't I left?

"I thought of calling the police, but he'd say he just dropped some milk. I thought of calling Victoria, but what could she do to help? I didn't want to involve her.

"None of my children were home, and my dog had died. Clutching *Anne of Green Gables,* something jelled inside me.

"It was time to find my train place.

"I snatched my wheeled carry-on bag out of my closet and threw in random underwear and t-shirts. I picked up the entire shelf of children's books from my grandmother, hesitated, then poked them all in the bag. They took up most of the space.

"My husband appeared in the doorway. 'Why are you going out? I'll be all alone.' He was often contrite and needy after his bursts of rage.

"I didn't look up. 'I thought I told you. Victoria from work has a medical procedure. I'll need to stay the night at her place so I can take her to the clinic early in the morning.'

"'You didn't tell me that she was sick.' He narrowed his eyes. 'She looked fine at the work Christmas party. She doesn't need surgery.'

"'It's not surgery. It's a scope thingy. They have to drug her up so she can't drive.'

"He didn't seem mollified. 'Give me your phone. I'll ask Victoria.'

"I waved the phone screen showing Victoria's *When are you coming?*

"'See. She's expecting me.'

"'Why do you need so many clothes for one night? And why so many books?'

"'I'll read in the waiting room. And I might have to stay longer…'

"'You can't! I didn't say you could stay longer!'

"'And I need extra clothes just in case. You know, for the time of the month.'

"His mouth curled in disgust. He always hated my womanly functions.

"I pulled out my tampons and slid them into the bag, feeling that the cash I'd been hiding in the box for months would be visible through my fingers.

"I didn't pause. I felt that if I hesitated, I'd be lost. I rushed to the front door, and he followed.

"'Give me Victoria's address.' He sounded less contrite.

"I pictured him turning up at Victoria's house. I couldn't do that to my friend and colleague. I remembered the address of a plant nursery I liked and scribbled it on the back of an old envelope.

"'I'll see you in a few days,' I said without meeting his eyes.

"I jumped into my car and left, while he frowned from the doorway. I drove toward Victoria's house, then did a U-turn at stop lights and headed toward the plant nursery. Within a block, I passed his truck going the way I'd been going. He was following me. I ducked down a side street and pulled into a strip mall behind a pile of snow and straggly bushes. I scooted down in my seat and watched the road behind me in the mirror. His truck went past twice. I took a deep breath and pictured how to get to the interstate from here. When his truck gunned past a third time, I slid the car in the opposite direction. When I reached the interstate, I took any road that said *East*.

"All night I followed the interstates east, the white lines unspooling under my tired eyes with adrenaline keeping me awake. My neck prickled with the feeling of him pursuing me. I was thankful my purse and some of the groceries were still in my car.

"I stopped to pee and buy gas in a brightly lit gas station, worried about being safe, alone in the middle of Missouri somewhere, but the people were friendly and the bathrooms cleaner than the ones I'd abandoned in my house. I nearly used my credit card for the gas but remembered in time that they were useless at the supermarket. And maybe somehow he'd be able to see where I used it. I cut up my cards with nail scissors and stuffed them into a trash can. I sent the email saying I'd take the job at Bent River County Library."

"I wondered why it arrived in the middle of the night." Marilyn smiled.

"I was glad you said to start straight away. But I underestimated how long it would take to drive to Virginia." Jessamine caught back a sob again. "I texted my children. And I begged them to come with me. They replied at different times. I remember things like, *I've got a test next week. I can't come. Where are you? Dad is on the rampage.* I got text after text from my husband asking where I was. I needed to lose the phone as well as the credit cards. At another gas station, I emailed myself the best photos of my children and dog, then bought a cheap phone. My hands shook, but I set the new one up under the light in my car, then dropped the old phone in the trash. Then you know the rest. I arrived here."

"No wonder you looked stressed that first day I met you." Stephanie put her hand on top of her head. "That's why I made the joke about us all being short." She stopped and a look of horror spread over her face. "My gracious. You said your husband teased you about being short. I didn't mean to hurt you."

Jessamine burst out laughing and couldn't stop. She finally hiccupped and patted Stephanie on the shoulder. "Your joke was exactly what I needed. You weren't vicious. It was a warm joke from a warm person. Thank you." Jessamine took a deep breath and blinked as if coming from darkness into light. "Let's have lunch and tackle this crazy tidying."

Chapter 18

Marilyn held up a tiny, hand-knitted pale-green sweater with a yellow stain around the collar. "I remember those days." She scratched at the stain with her nail. "Baby spit up never comes off. I wonder whose baby this was for?"

"That person's probably no baby anymore. He's probably a grandfather now, as old as Frank, who works for the county." Stephanie poked through more baby clothes. "Could be him. Rosemary and Frank's mother used to be friends."

"He seems nice." Jessamine laughed. "I don't think it'll fit Frank now."

"He likes you, Jessamine," Stephanie said. "He told me that you remind him of his daughter, who died of a drug overdose years ago. And then his wife died of grief. They said it was cancer, but everyone thought it was grief. He had a great job in the city. Something in construction, but he moved back here."

The three women stared at the fire for a moment.

Marilyn put the sweater aside. "Rosemary might have kept it for a reason. Put it in the thrift shop pile. Someone may be able to use it."

"I'll wash it first to get rid of that stain." Jessamine took the sweater. "You have one child, don't you Marilyn?"

"Yes, I've got one. He's grown and working for a computer company." Marilyn pulled out a pair of tiny blue leather shoes from the pile and stroked them absently with a finger. "We wanted more children, but we couldn't have them. How many children did you say you have, Jessamine? Lots?"

"I have five. They're grown. My youngest is nearly twenty. I didn't want to leave them. Not everyone finished university and a couple have gone back to living with their father…" Jessamine faltered to a stop.

There was a short silence, and the women looked at the flames flickering shadows across the room. Stephanie stood up. "We need trash bags, a box for the thrift shop, and another box for what you might keep." She paused. "Marilyn's son is a pleasant young man. He came to the library to give her flowers on her birthday."

Jessamine felt bad about her disloyalty. "My children are nice. In fact, they're wonderful. But it was difficult…"

Stephanie patted Jessamine's arm. "I wasn't saying your children weren't nice. I know things aren't always easy with kids, especially after all you've told us. For goodness' sakes, I've got three of my own. Sometimes you have to hug them, so you don't strangle them." She looked thoughtful for a moment. "Not that I'd strangle anyone."

All three women laughed. "Of course, you wouldn't." Marilyn smiled at Stephanie. The tension lifted and Jessamine went to fetch trash bags and to put the kettle on for another cup of hot tea.

Marilyn sat in front of a shoe box of pens, notebooks, rulers, and packets of staples. "Do you mind if we keep this for the library? We don't have much of a supply budget."

"Of course! I'll be glad if it gets used."

"You did a great job using recycled bits and pieces for the jar craft. We might find more craft supplies."

"Jessamine is crafty alright!" Stephanie laughed.

The box of useful things for the library overflowed. "I don't want more clutter, but we can always use scratch paper," Marilyn said. "Do you mind storing this here in the meantime, Jessamine?"

"I don't mind. The mess here can't be worse than it looks now."

Marilyn held up a small onesie. "Why did she keep all these baby clothes? I know newborns are small, but this is tinier."

Stephanie looked at it. "The baby was born early; it's preemie size."

"My twins were premature," Jessamine said. "They made it to seven months, which was a big deal, but they had to stay in an incubator. That was hard when we already had two toddlers, and my husband had to keep going away."

"They made him travel when you had newborn twins? Holy moley!" Stephanie frowned.

"His job always came first. It was part of the problem."

"Do you miss them? Your family?" Marilyn asked.

Jessamine bit her lip to stop the tears that pushed behind her eyes. "Yes."

"It's okay. People wash up here in Bent River County. We'll look after you. Who's for another cup of tea?" Stephanie patted Jessamine's arm.

"And Anzac biscuits… I'm ready for more of that great food we brought." Marilyn stood up off the tiny stool and stretched.

"Yes, I'm quite peckish," Jessamine said.

Stephanie looked at her. "You're what? Going to be pecking like a chicken?"

"Peckish—it means I'm hungry." Jessamine pursed her lips and laughed. "I suppose it does mean I want to peck like a chicken."

"You're from Australia, you said?" Marilyn asked Jessamine. "You keep it very quiet. I want to hear all about it."

"No, New Zealand." Jessamine smiled. "Lots of people make that mistake. They're quite separate countries. And it takes three hours to fly between them. There's a lot of empty ocean down there."

"I knew it was New Zealand," Stephanie said. "Because you told me. I was picturing that place off the coast of Scandinavia. You know, halfway to England. Because you said it had volcanoes."

The three women exchanged puzzled looks. Then Jessamine waved her cookie in the air. "Oh, you mean Iceland! No, New Zealand's not anywhere near Iceland. They both have volcanoes. New Zealand's in the South Pacific."

"The Pacific ocean?" Stephanie lifted her eyebrows. "Like Hawaii? Like Fiji?"

Jessamine laughed. "Same ocean but different climate. New Zealand's too far south to be tropical."

"Do you miss it?" Marilyn asked.

"No. Yes." Jessamine laughed. "It's complicated. I love the forest here."

Marilyn smiled. "Complicated might describe life, especially in Bent River County."

The rain continued pouring, so they stacked five trash bags of crumpled lists, cracked picture frames, and broken bowls on the porch for Jessamine to take to the dump next week and piled three bags of usable clothes for the thrift shop in the hallway next to the table with the antique phone. The sitting room remained knee deep in detritus.

"We better get this floor cleaned off so you can use your house, or we'll leave you worse off than when we started," Marilyn said.

"I can finish the closet in the back room later," Jessamine said. "And we didn't look at the books."

"We'll come back to help, Jessamine," Marilyn said. "There might be books we can add to the library collection. Hopefully this gets you over the hump."

Stephanie opened the last shoe box. "Hey, look. This is full of those decorative rubber stamps and tons of ink pads."

They looked over her shoulder. "They say *Happy Birthday* and *Thank You*. These aren't just children's stamps," Stephanie added.

Jessamine picked one up. "I like these sunflowers. We could use them for a craft. These will be great for all ages."

Marilyn laughed. "And the cat ones must be for me." She examined one more closely. "They're a bit dried out. My aunt makes cards, and she puts oil on the stamps. I'll find out what sort it is."

"These will work for that craft you wanted to do at first, Jessamine,"

Stephanie said. "They'd make great greeting cards and bookmarks."

"With these stamps, we could make adorable bookmarks for the kids to take home." Jessamine smiled. "Kids love getting a bookmark. And it stops them turning over the corners of the pages or breaking a book's spine by sitting it face down." Jessamine hesitated. "I asked Drusilla about buying bookmarks, but she dismissed it and said it was a waste, and the library could never afford them and to never ask her again."

"Oh, Drusilla." Marilyn rolled her eyes. "I can roll my eyes since I'm not at work. I need to get her working on the team. She needs to learn where her lane ends. I'm not sure about buying bookmarks right now with everything that the library needs, but you can make bookmarks when it's slow on the circulation desk."

Before they left, Marilyn and Stephanie insisted on helping Jessamine move a mattress from the back bedroom and make up the bed in the front bedroom with one of Rosemary's handmade patchwork quilts. "If we don't get the bed, and *you*, tucked in, you'll sleep on the couch," Marilyn told Jessamine in mock severity. "You deserve a proper bed."

They both hugged her tight.

"Yes. Just like you deserve triple chocolate ice cream if you want it."

Chapter 19

The next week, Jessamine and Stephanie found the ink pads completely dry. "I was looking forward to using our new decorative stamps." Stephanie frowned.

"Let's add water." Jessamine lined up the pads, dripped water on them, then stamped on colored paper. "Argh! It's making a sloppy mess. Maybe it's not water soluble." She stood back. "I've spilled ink on the desk."

"You've got a green nose!" Stephanie laughed at her. "You must have touched it."

Jessamine tried to rub the ink off her nose.

"Stop!" Stephanie put her hand over her mouth. "You've given yourself a purple forehead."

"I'd better wash my hands." Jessamine put the stamp pads into a plastic box and headed to the kitchen.

She returned with splotches of green, purple, and red on her face, hands, and arms. "It's definitely not water soluble!"

Stephanie snorted tea out of her nose. "Oh, no! Let's try hand sanitizer."

After she attempted, and failed, to remove the ink, Jessamine pulled her mouth sideways. "How will we use our new stamps without stamp pads?"

"I know. We have a ton of pads for stamping the library's address and dates and things like that." Stephanie hurried into Drusilla's dark office and returned with a stack of different colored ink pads.

They were soon immersed in their project.

"I found a stamp that says *READ*. Perfect for a library," Jessamine said.

"Why don't you stamp the teddy bear on this green paper?" Stephanie squinted. "Then back that with a rough shape out of an old book page? And stick the whole thing to a dark blue cardstock bookmark?"

"That's a splendid idea. You make it, Stephanie."

"I'm more of an artist than I realized." Stephanie put her head on her side, admiring her work.

"You sell yourself short." Jessamine studied the array of bookmarks. "I told you the whole point of these crafts is to be fun and accessible for everyone."

Walter, the guard, came in to check out his weekly three thrillers and gazed at the completed bookmarks spread out across nearby low bookshelves to dry. "You mean I can have a couple for free?" He picked up an owl bookmark. "My daughters will think they're pretty."

"Be careful!" Jessamine said. "We learned the hard way that the ink doesn't dry straight away."

Walter looked at Jessamine's forehead and nose. "I can see that smudging can be a problem." He put his hand over his mouth to hide a grin breaking through. "I'll come and choose bookmarks later."

Marilyn hurried into the library. "I need to refill my cup. What a meeting! I'm going to implode or explode or something, the way they keep going on about that bear. They don't understand a thing about library budgets or what the state requires for their reports. I told them over and over again how to do it correctly. The Library Committee and the county's ideas are from another planet." She peered at the bookmarks. "Are these from the stamps we found at the weekend? They look great! People appreciate this creative personal touch."

"We're having fun." Jessamine stood up straight and smiled. "We saved a cat one for you."

"Wonderful." Marilyn looked up. She paused. "Jessamine, what happened to your face?"

"The ink pads were dried up," Jessamine started.

Marilyn tilted her head. "Did using your forehead help?" She grinned. "I'll have to try using my forehead on those spreadsheets since I've got to get more ready for another meeting this afternoon."

Jessamine and Stephanie spread completed bookmarks across all flat surfaces until Jessamine finally said, "Even with the ones that people are picking up on the way out, I don't think we can do any more today."

"Yes, we can be proud of the job…"

With a bang, Drusilla hurried through the door, stopped, and looked around like an empress surveying her domain. "What on earth is all this?" She picked up several bookmarks. "I thought I told you not to leave trash all over, Jessamine?" She swung a fluorescent green and orange scarf around her neck. "And you're old enough to know better, Stephanie."

Jessamine and Stephanie exchanged a look. "We're making these for the library," Jessamine started.

"I don't care. It's a mess. You need to clean it up. And look at your face, Jessamine. Trust you." Drusilla swept into her office.

Jessamine and Stephanie had time to exchange another look before Drusilla exploded out of her office. "Who's been touching my things?" She puffed out her cheeks. "What do you mean by touching my possessions? Those stamps and ink pads are important, and I had them set just as I need them to be."

Jessamine held out her hands toward the furious woman. "We're making these for the library…"

"I don't care! No one said you could touch my personal effects."

"Marilyn said to…"

"I don't care what Marilyn said. You have no right to touch my possessions. I will talk to Marilyn!"

Marilyn came out of her office with her cup. "Do I hear my name being taken in vain? Who's going to talk to me?"

Jessamine saw with astonishment that Drusilla stamped her foot. "They have been in my office! Touching my things!"

"What do you mean?" Marilyn set down her cup.

Drusilla swirled her green and orange scarf. "They've taken my ink pads."

"I don't understand why you're upset. They're using them for the bookmarks."

"But they're wasting ink! And they are *my* ink pads!"

Marilyn laughed. "How can you waste ink? We have decades-worth in bottles we can add."

"We've hardly used any ink." Stephanie grinned. "You've used some on your face, Drusilla."

"What?" Drusilla wiped her face and purple spread across her cheek. "They went into my office…"

"I thought it's supposed to be an office you and Jessamine share? And the ink pads are library property for legitimate library business. Come into my office, Drusilla, and we'll talk about this."

Marilyn and Drusilla disappeared into Marilyn's office. Marilyn stepped back out and handed Jessamine a box of baking soda. "Here, this removes ink. I had it in my purse." She returned to her office and shut the door.

Jessamine and Stephanie had barely had time to exchange another look before Stephanie said, "I can hear loud voices. Wowee!" She shook her head. "I'd better get back to my shelving."

"Yes, the fun's kind of gone out of the bookmarks now." Jessamine sighed. "I've got to get ready for story time."

Drusilla emerged from Marilyn's office with her mouth turned down and her brows pulled together. The purple stain across her cheek had spread to her nose. She went straight to her office and shut the door. All afternoon, she didn't look Stephanie or Jessamine in the eye or speak to them. Later, when Jessamine was walking across the foyer, she saw Drusilla coming out of Kathryn's office. Drusilla was grinning. When she saw Jessamine looking at her, she smirked, then quickly returned her face to its usual neutral expression and kept walking.

Chapter 20

Despite being surrounded by a knot of eagerly talking people, the lieutenant governor's head was always visible in the crowded courtroom. Jessamine recognized his air of authority from her years as a military spouse. He was like a general; as soon as he walked into a room, everyone knew he was in charge. The lieutenant governor made it to the lectern. The crowd thickened, and he was lost behind an ocean of backs. Jessamine stood on tiptoe to see.

Stephanie put her hand on Jessamine's shoulder and tried to raise herself up. "Stand still so I can balance!"

Marilyn propped herself up on Jessamine's other shoulder. "No, I'm the tallest. I'm five-foot-two. Let me see."

Jessamine giggled. "You're cheating, Marilyn. You've wearing heels." She looked around. "Look, there's the bear."

"They must have moved it out of the library." Marilyn grinned at her two employees. "I didn't go near the board books this morning." She did a dance with her shoulders. "Wonderful!"

"What about Ursilla's clothes?" Jessamine giggled. "And our display?"

"She's not wearing anything." Stephanie shuffled over so she could squint around the crowd. "She's 'bear' naked!" She pulled a long, mock-laughing face at Jessamine.

"If we could have your attention." A voice came through squealing feedback. "Please take your seats."

Well-dressed people shuffled toward the front, edging into the courthouse's wooden benches as more people crowded in. This was the first time Jessamine had entered the Bent River County courtroom. The dark wooden paneling, gray swirly patterned carpet, and high-backed wooden benches reminded Jessamine strongly of a church.

"When did you know that the lieutenant governor was coming?" Jessamine whispered to Marilyn as the volume in the room dropped.

"Ten o'clock last night."

"Who organized it? I thought we had to be on that list so we were allowed to see the lieutenant governor?"

"We had to be checked. I guess that's why Kathryn told me about it so late. She was trying to make sure we didn't get on the list and couldn't come. She said she told me last night, 'out of courtesy.' Courtesy my foot."

"Courtesy? You're…" Jessamine shook her head. Marilyn called her two hours before the lieutenant governor's imminent arrival. She'd needed to change a vet appointment at the last minute.

Joshua stepped behind the lectern, dressed in his usual polo attire. Drusilla pushed in behind him.

Stephanie's mouth fell open. "What's Drusilla doing up there with the dignitaries?"

"You're the library director!" Jessamine's voice rose and people glared.

Marilyn shook her head. "I can't imagine why she thinks it's appropriate for her to be there."

"Of course *he's* up there. He thinks he owns the county. But Drusilla, bless her scarf-wearing heart. Words fail me." Stephanie rolled her eyes.

Joshua boomed into the microphone. "We are honored to have the lieutenant governor of our great state here today." He smiled at another tall man, also in polo attire, standing to the side. "He knows our county well. He's honored our Hunt Club on many occasions. It's not flattering to point out that it's due to his skill that we got rid of that rogue bear, since he took the kill shot." He gestured at the bear and scattered applause broke out. He cleared his throat and went on. "Our county is moving forward in great ways. We know that our citizens need better access to world-class sporting facilities to move forward into the twenty-first century."

Twenty-first century? thought Jessamine. *This century started decades ago!*

Drusilla stepped forward and whispered in his ear. He added, "And our citizens need a tip-top library, of course." The crowd tittered. Joshua ignored them and beamed at the lieutenant governor. "I will pass you over to Lieutenant Governor Gray," he said and stepped back.

Jessamine leaned toward Stephanie; Marilyn was on tiptoe staring ahead and didn't invite comments. "I didn't know that this many people lived in Bent River County," Jessamine whispered. "Who are they all? I don't see our library patrons."

"You wouldn't see our library patrons or people like us here. We're only the hoi polloi. We're not important people according to the pooh-bahs of Bent River County!"

Marilyn may have been regretting inviting her two employees because they were getting glares for their whispered comments. Marilyn lifted her finger to her lips in a well-honed shushing gesture that carried librarian conviction. Jessamine paused in professional admiration of Marilyn's shush. Marilyn was right—they needed to show a suitably dignified front for the library, but it was hard to take this ceremony seriously. Suppressing the urge to giggle, Jessamine tried to concentrate on the speech. As the lieutenant governor spoke, her impression of a high-ranking military officer stayed with Jessamine but also the impression of a politician with bland, stock phrases. "Moving forward in our great state… Funding to help those who can't help themselves…" Her mind drifted.

"Who set up the extra chairs? When did they have time?" Jessamine whispered to Marilyn.

"The county staff." Marilyn held her fingers to her lips again.

"And I know Bent River County is a great place for sports." The lieutenant governor was movie-star handsome, but his benign expression bordered on vacuous. "As you already know, I helped rid the county of this pesky bear with my old family friend Joshua Oxford." He gestured to the side. "And now if the county administration will come forward, we'll present the check."

One of the lieutenant governor's many hangers-on stepped forward with a three-foot-long cardboard check. Joshua and Kathryn rushed forward. They angled for the best place next to the lieutenant governor, trying to look like they weren't elbowing each other. Kathryn won the coveted spot.

The lieutenant governor smiled at the crowd and pretended he hadn't noticed people jockeying for position next to him. He held up the check. "For their new polo grounds and library, I am excited to present Bent River County with the Governor's Galvanizing Grant of two..." He paused and looked at the check. "Two point six million dollars!"

There was a moment of stunned silence, then applause and a ripple of conversation broke out. Jessamine applauded with Marilyn and Stephanie.

"I hope it gets to the people this time," Stephanie leaned close and whispered. "Look, Kathryn's not going to let go of that check."

Stephanie was right. Kathryn stood at the front, clutching the huge piece of cardboard. The lieutenant governor and his hangers-on conferred for a moment, then the lieutenant governor came to the lectern and adjusted the microphone. "Now we'll have a few words from County Controller, Kathryn Slattery."

"Bent River County is pleased to have been recognized for this award," Kathryn said into the microphone. "I grew up here. And it is my county. Our new community polo park and our new library are something that I've wanted. And I always get what I want." Jessamine heard people gasp. A stillness fell over the courthouse. Kathryn noticed that she'd had an effect and looked pleased.

Kathryn went on, "The moral of this county has been low." Jessamine exchanged a puzzled look with Stephanie. Was Kathryn accusing the county of having low morals? Before she could ask, Kathryn continued, "This money will allow us to improve salaries and we'll have a better moral." Her whole face lit up and she wiggled. The only word Jessamine could think of for the strange wiggle was *sashay*.

A buzz of conversation went around the room.

Jessamine whispered to Stephanie, "Why is she saying that the county has low morals?"

Stephanie looked puzzled. "I don't know. What a strange thing to say. Even for her."

"I think she means *morale*," said Marilyn. "She used the wrong word."

The three women exchanged looks and burst into giggles.

As the lieutenant governor made his way from the lectern toward the doors, he greeted people and shook their hands. Two or three men in dark suits followed him. When he got close to Marilyn, she stepped forward and held out her hand. "Hello, I'm Marilyn Webster, the library director."

"Pleased to meet you, Marilyn. I am a great supporter of public libraries."

"Please have a small token to remember us by." Marilyn gave him a handful of their homemade library-logo bookmarks.

"Thank you. They'll keep place in my important books every day." He handed the bookmarks to a man in a dark suit and smiled at the next person.

As people swirled around them, Marilyn looked at Jessamine and Stephanie. "We tried. I know he's interested in libraries, or said he was. He came last year and donated a couple of boxes of books."

Jessamine was always interested in new books. "Did you add them to the collection?"

"Drusilla is supposed to go through them and catalog them, but donations pile up. They're in those blue boxes behind the desk."

"I kept tripping over those boxes, so I looked in them." Jessamine snorted. "There were a bunch of textbooks and spiral bound academic workbooks. They weren't suitable for a public library."

"I know they weren't great." Marilyn sighed. "He got to pose for a photo for the local paper doing wonderful things for the poor people of Bent River

County. That's what counted for him."

"Surely the money from the lieutenant governor will help the new library a lot." Jessamine clasped her hands together.

"You heard him," Stephanie said. "It's for the polo grounds *and* the library. And you know which one is the priority of Joshua and Kathryn and the people who get to choose how it's spent."

"They can only do so much." Marilyn's face brightened. "We have the architect's plans for the new library. The construction company's been hired. That part's settled, so they're obliged to build it like that. But I don't know why it has to have thirty-six cameras. It makes no sense."

"Thirty-six cameras? What on earth for?" Jessamine pulled her eyebrows together.

"How is that a good use of limited funds?" Stephanie put her hands on her hips.

"Here's something even weirder." Marilyn leaned in closer. "When I went to that meeting last week with the architect and the construction company, Kathryn said we should install dozens of phone jacks so the meeting room would be useful for office space when the building wasn't used as a library anymore. I thought she'd made a mistake, you know misspoken, like she does, but I'm not so sure. We have all that money. Are they planning to not spend it on a library?"

Chapter 21

*A*fter the lieutenant governor left, Marilyn leaned on the circulation desk and said, "Phew, at least that's over. That money will be glorious for the new library." She rolled her shoulders and took a deep breath. "Oh, there's Ursilla's disguise."

Ursilla the Bear had worn a rotation of costumes since they'd first named her. The teen Englebert suggested they call the quirky assortment of clothing the bear's "clever disguises." The idea and name caught on, and Jessamine set out one of her jars for suggestions of new themes and costumes. She was planning a story time about dogs, so Ursilla the Bear had been wearing Jessamine's flowery jacket, cut to fit, and carrying dog leashes attached to toy dogs, with an assortment of bowls, and rubber bones and books about dogs.

The items were neatly stacked on the circulation desk with a note from Frank: *Sorry, had to take this off. Will help re-dress Ursilla later. Frank*

"At least the bear is gone." Marilyn shook her head. "We can be thankful for small mercies. Frank doesn't have to help with anything." She rolled her shoulders again. "I need a break. I'm going to take a mental health day on

Tuesday. I have tons of personal days saved up that I never use, and the Library Committee have okayed it. I've got to take the dog to the vet. Then I'll have a long, hot bubble bath."

"You need a break." Jessamine smiled at her. "There are three of us to keep the library open."

"Drusilla is off, but Stephanie will be here." Marilyn turned to Jessamine. "Will you two manage on your own for a few hours?"

"We'll be fine." Stephanie smiled.

Jessamine nodded.

On Tuesday when Jessamine arrived at the library, Frank was coming out the door. "Morning, Frank," Jessamine smiled. "You're early. Have you finished vacuuming already?"

"I wasn't vacuuming this morning, Ms. Jessamine. I had to move that bear before the courthouse opened."

"Move the bear? Not back into the library?" Jessamine wailed. "I thought it was gone!"

"I have my orders." Frank shrugged. He counted on his fingers. "That bear's been in the county foyer, it's been in the school, the fire station, the courtroom." He laughed. "It's even been in the control room for the sewage works!"

"Why the library?" Jessamine tried not to wail again, but didn't succeed.

"Kathryn told me to get it in here this morning. She said Joshua ordered it." He leaned forward. "I did try to put it nearer the back, not right next to the kiddies' books, but there isn't much room. I hope that helps. Do you want me to help dress it again?"

"Thanks, I suppose every bit helps with the location." Jessamine drooped. "I can dress Ursilla, unless you're dying to help?"

"I better get on with the cleaning if you're okay. You take care now, Ms. Jessamine."

Jessamine thought about how to dress and decorate Ursilla. They had several bags of costumes ready to go. Jessamine's favorite was a swimsuit, Hawaiian shirt, sunglasses, swim ring, and flowery sun hat for summer reading. Marilyn thought they should surround the bear's head with giant yellow petals to make her a sunflower, while Stephanie leaned toward super X-L pajamas she'd found with a night cap, teddy bear, and slippers. They had oodles of picture books about going to bed.

While Jessamine was poking through the costumes, Josey came in. She whispered in her son Larsen's ear, and he came up to Jessamine and silently held out two stuffed tractors.

"They're lovely, Larsen." Jessamine crouched down to eye level with the small boy. "Are these your tractors?"

"Tell Ms. Jessamine what you want to do with them, Larsen," his mother urged.

He leaned forward. "They're for the bear," he whispered.

"For the bear? That's very good of you, Larsen. Are they toys for Ursilla the Bear to play with?"

Larsen shook his head emphatically and looked at his mother.

"Tell Ms. Jessamine what they're for, Larsen," she encouraged.

He shook the tractors for emphasis. "They're for her feet. When she goes to bed."

"Oh, they're slippers." Jessamine looked up at Josey and again at Larsen. "This will work perfectly. I have pajamas for Ursilla. Do you want to help dress her, Larsen?"

Larsen's eyes opened wide for a moment and then he nodded firmly.

"We'll all help, if that's okay, Jessamine?" Josey asked, looking at the other children gathered.

"Of course." Jessamine and Stephanie dug out the nightwear, and they formed a loose circle around the bear. "You start, Larsen," Jessamine said. "Give Ursilla her slippers."

Larsen took a deep breath, marched over to the bear, and put the slippers in front of the bear's feet. He poked the furry leg hard with his finger, then raced to his mother and stood behind her legs. He looked around and stuck his tongue out at the bear.

Josey laughed. "Good job, Larsen." She ruffled his hair.

Soon Ursilla was ready for bed with pink fuzzy pajamas covered in ducklings floating on clouds, a long triangular nightcap with a pom-pom, her own teddy bear, and a cardboard cup of cocoa. Larsen edged closer and finally patted the bear's furry leg. The slippers were worn out, so Jessamine was able to cut them and tie them over the bear's claws. "That looks better."

"It does," said Josey. "Say thank you to Ms. Jessamine and Ms. Stephanie, kids. We'll get home so I can make lunch. Maybe we can come back later."

After lunch, when Jessamine was shelving in the fiction section, loud crashes and bangs echoed from the door. She thought that Josey's stroller must be completely wedged, so she abandoned her cart and hurried over. Four people in black jeans and t-shirts were crowding through the door with mysterious electronic equipment that trailed cables and electric cords.

"Hello," Jessamine said brightly as they trooped past her. "Can I help you?" she added to their backs.

Frank arrived next, carrying a black plastic box. He waggled his eyebrows and winked at her. Then Kathryn came trip-trapping into the library in her high-heeled boots. "I'm taking care of this, Jeb, ah… Jezabel." She pushed her long nails, each painted a different color, into her bright leather purse and pulled out a small mirror, a powder puff, and a comb and began tidying up her makeup and hair. "You don't need to stare. I'm getting ready for the camera crew."

Jessamine raised her eyebrows without thinking.

"They're from our local TV station." Kathryn gestured toward the people with the electronic equipment. "Go and help Frank move things. The important people for the filming will be here soon. The news segment will be about my new money from the lieutenant governor."

Jessamine made a conscious effort to control her expression. "Marilyn must have forgotten to tell us about the TV news coming." Past Kathryn's shoulder she saw the teenager Englebert pile a stack of books on the desk. "I've got to get to the circulation desk."

"Oh, Marilyn didn't need to know." Kathryn frowned. "And I told you to help Frank."

Jessamine gestured to Englebert and his pile of books. He gave a slight smile and a wave from beside his thigh. "I've got to help the customer who's waiting. Then I'll see if I can help." Jessamine ignored Kathryn's glare and walked to the desk.

"What's going on?" Englebert eyed the chaos surrounding the camera crew with interest.

"A film crew, apparently. From the local news."

Englebert's face lit up. "Can I watch?"

"I don't see why not." Jessamine smiled, glad to see him taking an interest. "We're in a public library, and we're open. Go right ahead."

Englebert abandoned his books on the counter and headed to where the camera crew were trying to set up lights and reflective screens, tripping over each other, banging into the bear, and knocking over the board books in the inadequate space.

Jessamine was about to follow Englebert, when she remembered Kathryn's odd comment that Marilyn didn't need to be here. She slipped her phone from her bag under the desk and texted Marilyn: *Camera crew here. Thought you'd like to know.*

The answer came immediately, *What camera crew??? I'm in a scented, fragrant bath. Relaxing!!*

Jessamine wrote back. *Kathryn is here with a camera crew from the local TV station.*

What???

Jessamine started to answer and looked up. *Joshua and Drusilla walked in.*

The text came fast. *Double what??? I'll be there!!!*

Drusilla was laughing up into Joshua's face. She was tall, but he was taller. Jessamine couldn't hear what they were saying, but Drusilla's voice was breathy and high.

"Don't you have work to do, Jessamine, instead of standing around texting?" Drusilla's voice wasn't high and breathy now.

Kathryn hurried over. "Yes, Jeb, ah… whatever. I told you to help Frank." She turned to Joshua. "I'm glad you're here, Joshy. We'll start now."

Jessamine felt out of her depth, but she had to try for her friend the library director who was being squeezed out. "What about Marilyn?"

"I told you, I don't…" Kathryn started.

"Englebert!" It came out nearly a roar. "What are you doing here?"

Everyone followed Joshua's gaze to Englebert, who was leaning over an unfathomable box with one of the camera crew pointing to a switch. He saw everyone looking at him and his face closed up. He blushed and lowered his chin to let his hair fall over his eyes. "Hi, Dad."

"Don't 'Hi, Dad' me! And look at me when I talk to you. I asked you why you're here in the middle of the day? What are we paying that overpriced fancy tutor for?"

Englebert sent one searing glance his father's way. "I'm doing research. And reading."

Jessamine helpfully waved one of Engelbert's books. Joshua noticed everyone was staring. "We'll talk about it at home. You've delayed enough. Go home *now*."

"Hiya, everyone!" A pretty, heavily made-up woman paraded through the door. "Are we ready to film? I've got to get moving. Other segments to film today." She tossed her head and smiled broadly at the group. "I'm Diana Rand. You probably recognize me from the news."

People crowded her. Englebert slid away between tall bookshelves.

"What happened to my bear?!" Joshua's deep voice rose above the chatter and chaos. Everyone fell silent and turned toward him. His jaw was tight and his face was deep red. Jessamine thought she could hear his teeth grinding together. His next words were at a normal volume, but they carried around the library. "Take that ridiculous nonsense off my bear. Then we'll keep my bear in the frame for the news. I'll stand next to it here when you film me."

The newscaster turned her glowing smile on Joshua. "Are you the librarian?" She put out her hand to shake. "We're here to do a segment about the library's funding windfall, so we'll need the library director."

Joshua took a step closer to the bear and ignored the hand. "I represent the library. I'm the chair of the Library Committee."

Diana Rand looked at her own hand, wiggled her fingers as if to shake off water drops and said, "I need a spokesperson for the library. A public library! In this sort of sweet human-interest story, we've got to keep it wholesome and positive."

"Yoo hoo!" Marilyn threw her purse at Stephanie and Jessamine without stopping and zoomed over to the crowd. She went straight up to Diana Rand and put out her hand to shake. "Hi, I'm Marilyn Webster, the library director. Thank you for coming!"

After catching the purse, Jessamine noticed that Marilyn's blouse wasn't ironed at the back, and she was wearing one blue shoe and one black shoe.

Diana Rand smiled. "Okay, it looks like everyone's here, so we can get filming. We'll start with a statement from the director. Stand over here by the bookshelves." The assembled crowd shuffled toward the shelves. Drusilla hung off Joshua's arm, but he shook her off. "Tall man, yes you. You can't be in this shot." Joshua looked thunderous.

From Jessamine's angle, she saw Englebert laughing from behind the books, the happiest she'd ever seen him.

The filming didn't take long and the camera crew left in the same bustle they'd arrived in: with trailing cords and inexplicable shouted instructions about filtering and sound bites.

After holding the door open for them to leave, Jessamine stood in the hallway outside the library doors and looked through the floor-to-ceiling windows at storm clouds building. She saw Joshua and Englebert walking across the parking lot. Joshua was making choppy gestures and Englebert's head was bowed. Englebert turned away and Joshua grabbed his arm, nearly pulling the teenager off his feet and making him stumble.

"What? He can't…" Jessamine stood up straight, not realizing she'd said anything out loud.

Stephanie came up behind her. "I feel sorry for that kid."

"Isn't that assault? Isn't there anything we can do? The poor kid didn't take his books. And we spent ages trying to find anything about volcanoes that wasn't decades old."

"I don't think there's anything we can do. He grabbed his arm. And we'd report it to Joshua's nephew, Wendell, the deputy. Or if not him, then likely Joshua's tenant. Or school friend. Or polo buddy."

"What about Englebert's mother? Is she around?"

Stephanie pursed her lips. "Everyone says his wife only married Joshua for his money and the Oxford name. They don't like each other much. If you see them together, it's like the other one doesn't exist." Stephanie shrugged her shoulders. "They say his wife had to produce heirs to carry on the family name. If you ask me, there isn't much family there. It's those kids I feel sorry for. At least they had boarding school for a while. Or they did until Englebert got chucked out. You need to do something really bad to get chucked out of that school! Rumor has it that he tried to burn down the principal's house. He said the principal liked small children too much in a bad way. They never proved anything."

"I have trouble believing that of Englebert." Jessamine frowned. "He's quiet and shy, but he's always polite and respectful to me."

"You never know what people will do if they're pushed too hard. It can't have been much fun for Englebert to come home to those parents, especially with his brother and sister grown and escaped." Stephanie put her hands on the window and sighed. "Let's get back to work."

The library felt quiet after the hubbub, and the four women looked at each other.

"I thought you had the day off, Marilyn." Drusilla was obviously dressed up, but no one had suggested that she would be on camera, and she had been publicly rejected by Joshua.

"I thought I did too." Marilyn sighed. "Since I'm here, I'd better go and wrestle with those untamable budgets." Marilyn headed into her office.

Drusilla watched her go. She scratched one pointy heel on the other ankle and wobbled. She narrowed her eyes. "You two boss's pets sure made sure she knew about the filming."

"Didn't you have the day off as well, Drusilla?" Jessamine squinted back.

Drusilla snorted. She waved her scarf with a broad gesture and her elbow caught Jessamine's "World's Greatest Plumber" coffee mug and knocked it to the floor. The three women looked at the six pieces stranded in a puddle of tea.

"Hey, that was Jessamine's favorite." Stephanie put her hands on her hips.

"Oops! I must have bumped it." Drusilla smirked. "Maybe you can salvage it, Jessamine, since you like rescuing junk."

"There was no need to break it." Jessamine felt hot.

"It was junk from the kitchen." Drusilla rolled her eyes. "It was library property, since Marilyn gets so excited about library property." Drusilla swept off to her own office, swaying on strappy, bright-red stilettoes.

"I know the mug was worth nothing." Jessamine turned to Stephanie. "But I liked my jokes about me fixing everyone's leaking taps or running toilets." She felt like an idiot, blinking back tears over a coffee mug, and added irrelevantly, "Since I'm not a plumber."

Stephanie pursed her lips at Drusilla's office door. "Drusilla's neutral po-face is slipping now." She narrowed her eyes. "Like she's slipping on those stupid shoes. She'll break an ankle one day."

Jessamine looked down at her own shoes: flat black Mary Janes that she lovingly polished, with no pretensions to being anything but solid, sensible, and comfortable.

"I suppose if that's what she wants to wear…" she started.

"She uses them as an excuse," Stephanie said. "She told me she can't work on the desk with us because her feet hurt. It's really because she thinks she's a better person than us."

"I don't get it." Jessamine shook her head. "Her basis for thinking she's a better person than us is…um…She doesn't work hard. She doesn't seem to know what she's doing, but she won't let anyone help."

"Exactly!" Stephanie exclaimed. "Her only basis is that she thinks she's superior to us."

"Her argument's a bit circular, isn't it?" Jessamine usually felt solid, sensible, and comfortable like her shoes, but today she felt pushed by Drusilla. "She's getting worse. I feel like I'm in middle school. She's hated me since I walked through the door."

"Don't worry. It's not you. She wants Marilyn's job and always has. I think she's intimidated by your background and experience and never wanted to hire you. But I'm glad she didn't get Marilyn's job." Stephanie picked up a book and checked it in with finality.

Chapter 22

Marilyn put her travel mug on the circulation desk. "They *finally* might be listening to me." She turned the mug and studied the kitten motif. "I've told them over and over again that the budget for this library and for the new building didn't make sense. And I told them they were buying way too much tile and paint. My husband did construction project management for years. He said it was ridiculous."

Jessamine looked up from the story time flier she was designing. "They said you were right?"

"Not exactly… not right. But they have stopped arguing with me about it." Marilyn rubbed her chin with her forefinger. "They changed the subject when I brought it up. They asked how we are organized for moving to the new library."

"When will we be moving?" Jessamine looked around at the overcrowded shelves. "We don't look ready. We'll *have* to weed the books."

Drusilla came in and headed straight for her office with a quick nod of acknowledgement. She had been withdrawn since the visit of the lieutenant governor and the TV news. Jessamine saw her coming out of Kathryn's office several times.

Marilyn waved her mug. "Oh, Drusilla, since you're here, we'll have that meeting about the weeding now. We've been talking about it forever."

"I'm busy. I can't." Drusilla didn't bother to stop.

Marilyn's jaw tightened. She walked over to Drusilla's office door. "Come out to the library tables now before we open, and we'll talk about the weeding."

Drusilla pinched her lips together, then pulled on her blank face and followed them to the tables, carrying a huge book.

When they sat down, Marilyn said, "We need to deal with the weeding, Drusilla. Jessamine, tell us about your good ideas."

"We need to replace tons of books." Jessamine gave a dry laugh. She didn't know how to say this without being insulting. "We need to throw out a bunch. There's a moldy, fifty-year-old dinosaur book."

Drusilla lifted her chin. "I can't get rid of books until the library can afford new ones."

Marilyn put her hands face up on the table. "We'll make a plan. We'll work at it incrementally with what we can afford. We need to balance the collection and..."

Drusilla sat up straight and made a sharp noise with her chair legs on the floor. Despite being seated, she towered over Jessamine and Marilyn. The intensity in her narrowed eyes made Jessamine feel pushed back. Drusilla barked out, "I will make any plans. It's my job!"

"But we're saturated with obsolete and damaged books." Jessamine could not imagine why they couldn't see that the state and age of the books were the most important things. "Why do you want to keep an ancient, moldy dinosaur book?"

Marilyn was the peacemaker. "We can work this out. When we get rid of it, we'll have nothing about dinosaurs, so we must get new ones, so Jessamine can—"

"It's *my* job to choose which books we buy!" Drusilla's voice rose. "Look at this. She wants to withdraw this." Drusilla tapped her long, bright purple fingernail on a heavy textbook about knee surgery. "It's a two-hundred-dollar book!"

"Yes, I want to withdraw it. It's out of date. I don't understand why a poor public library with no money for books bought a horrendously expensive medical textbook, anyway." Jessamine screwed up her face in puzzlement. "It's a book for doctors, not a consumer, everyday-person book. We can steer people toward reliable online medical resources. MedlinePlus is created by the National Library of Medicine."

Drusilla scraped her nail on the book, making Jessamine think of her chickens scratching in the dust. "What's MedlinePlus?" She waved her arm in dismissal. "That's not important. I can't withdraw this book. It was expensive, and it was requested."

"Medical books go out of date fast." Jessamine was baffled. "Research shows there are lots of reliable online resources that we should steer our patrons toward. I have lots of experience…"

"Put a note on it." Marilyn pointed to the surgery book. "Put it on my desk and I'll look at it later. I've got to get to another meeting with the Library Committee now. Jessamine, pull the books you think we should weed, and we'll talk about them again next week."

Jessamine pictured Marilyn's desk. She doubted anything emerged quickly from under the piles of invoices, memos, and catalogs.

Jessamine delighted in a wonderful week, pulling the worst of the worn-out books. "Goodbye, you poor sad old thing," she said aloud as she placed the moldy 1973 dinosaur book on her cart first. She couldn't pull as many as she wanted because the library only owned one cart to stack the books. When she asked Marilyn about the big surgery textbook a week later, Marilyn looked flustered as usual. "I *must* finish a special report for the Library Committee. The County Council wants to meet with us again. I haven't had a chance to look at it yet. Can't you and Drusilla work it out?"

Jessamine continued pulling books that were yellowed, had broken spines, and claimed that the USSR was a current political entity. Every astronomy book in the library proudly asserted the status of Pluto as a planet, having been published too early to know anything else. The antique and collectable price guides went out of date in the 1990s. The dictionary was from the 1960s, and the *Chase's Calendar of Events* gave sterling advice about how to celebrate the upcoming millennium.

Jessamine checked the books out on a library account, so Drusilla couldn't claim that they were missing, and since there was no cart, she tucked piles of them away under the circulation desk and hid them behind boxes in the kitchen.

The fiction and children's picture books didn't go so obviously out of date, but Jessamine pulled paperback romances with covers repaired by so much different colored tape that she couldn't read the title, and middle-grade books that showed children wearing bell-bottom jeans from the 1970s. She checked series books and discovered that although the catalog claimed they owned *Anne of Green Gables*, it hadn't been seen for fifteen years, and two of L.M. Montgomery's lesser-known titles later in the series languished forlornly on the shelf.

When Drusilla was in the library, she watched Jessamine's activity with a sarcastic twist to her mouth. Jessamine saw the surgery textbook back on the shelf and clenched her jaw, ignoring Drusilla's gleam of triumph. Not being able to do anything about the ugly, unwelcoming shelves caused an actual pain in Jessamine's chest, but she didn't know what she could do, short of stealing the library's books and taking them home and burning them. Over time, the other books reappeared on the shelves.

A few days later, Stephanie twirled a lock of hair around her finger. "I'm worried about Marilyn."

"Why?" Jessamine paused in rubbing an Agatha Christie book with a damp cloth; she continued to clean the book covers, working through the entire library collection. If they couldn't replace any of the books, at least she could make the grimy collection more appealing.

Stephanie stepped from foot to foot. "These meetings are getting crazy. She's always in with Kathryn and Joshua and that crowd." She pulled her lips from side to side. "I hear things since I know so many people in the county."

"I thought it was part of her job to go to meetings? One reason I don't want to be a library director."

"I know, but these meetings are beyond normal. It sounds paranoid, but I'm worried they're out to get her."

"Is there anything we can do?" Jessamine rubbed at a stubborn coffee cup ring on a picture book. "We're not allowed to go to the meetings, so we can't support her that way."

Stephanie held up a finger. "We *can* go to a meeting! The quarterly Library Committee meeting is coming up next month. It has to be open to the public for a public library. No one usually goes because it's so boring, but we could go to show support for Marilyn."

"Committees are the dullest things in the universe. I like *doing* things, not talking about doing them." Jessamine paused in her rubbing. "I'll go to support Marilyn."

"We could tell our regulars about the meeting." Stephanie looked more hopeful. "I know they like Marilyn."

"That's a good idea. The craft is coming up. And story time. I'll mention it to them. It's a public meeting, after all. They probably don't know about it, and it's our job to share information since we're a library. They might be interested."

Chapter 23

Marilyn came out to the desk, her face pale and her voice frantic. "My father had a stroke. They're not sure if he'll make it. I have to go to Texas. My special needs brother lives with him." She paused and swallowed. "Since our mother died years ago, my brother needs help. He won't understand, and I'll need to stay to get things settled." She paused again and took a deep breath. "The Library Committee meeting's next week. After their nasty emails to me about the staff, I must come back."

"I'm so sorry to hear about your father." Jessamine gave her a hug. "Don't worry about us. This is the time to think of your family."

Stephanie hugged her as well. "Yes. The Library Committee can go hang!"

"If it's so important that you're at their meeting, won't they postpone the meeting?" Jessamine asked. "You can't help the timing. It *is* a family emergency."

Marilyn swallowed and tried a weak smile. "Thanks. They've been reminding me over and over that you're 'at will' employees, so I've been worried. Kathryn was sympathetic. She told me about her brother and how hard it was for their family to look after him. I'll ask them if they'll postpone the meeting." She rubbed her eyes. "Can you two hold the fort? I'd better go home and get packed and get my flights booked. I don't know where Drusilla is."

"We'll be fine, won't we, Stephanie?" Jessamine said.

"Of course we will." Stephanie patted Marilyn's arm. "You do what you need to do. Do you want me to watch your place and feed the cats?"

Marilyn gave a humorless laugh. "I hope you're right that they'll delay the meeting. Casey Chilton trapped me behind the shelf of cozy mysteries and hissed at me that I should 'just quit!' And you… she said you should both quit. I said that you can't quit, you need the jobs. She said that you'd be more suited to work at Walmart."

The Library Committee wouldn't reschedule the meeting. Frank, Eunice, and Jonquil agreed to come. Many people in Bent River County didn't like to drive after dark on the narrow, dark roads, crowded with wandering deer.

As the meeting started, Jessamine, Stephanie, and the three patrons waited outside the library door, looking at the parking lot through the window. Marilyn approached as if the air around her was thicker than usual. Jessamine gave Marilyn a quick hug. "Are you okay?"

"I left Texas really early this morning." Marilyn put down her large leather purse and rolled her shoulders. "I'm stiff from flying and driving and rushing." Marilyn looked like she was going to say more, then jumped. "There's Drusilla!"

Stephanie's eyes narrowed. "I've never seen her in the library in the evening in the, what, *decade*, we worked together." Stephanie put her hands on her hips. "Why is she here? This doesn't look good."

Jessamine watched Drusilla climb from her red Cadillac SUV. The tall woman retied a neon-green scarf, then pulled out a hand mirror and checked her face and blonde hair.

Marilyn stepped from foot to foot and smoothed her skirt over her hips. "And that job title, Chief Liaison of Office and Organizational Management. She had it before I started. It doesn't mean anything. I need to change it." Jessamine had heard Marilyn talking about changing Drusilla's job title and responsibilities since she had arrived at the library. She thought Marilyn was kind and smart and a great librarian, but because of the constant pressure and bickering from the Library Committee, there were a lot of things she never quite got round to.

"I'd better get into that meeting." Marilyn rubbed her already smooth skirt. "Wish me luck!" She paused halfway through a step and laughed. "It's just a Library Committee meeting. I don't need luck. What are they going to do? Take away my birthday?"

The Library Committee gathered in a semi-circle at the tables. Jessamine recognized Casey Chilton, who Stephanie had given eggs to. As the library director, Marilyn sat at the main table to present her reports and plans to the Committee. The half-dozen members of the staff and public perched on mismatched chairs, peering at the Committee from among the overcrowded bookshelves. The public could see the Library Committee, but they didn't feel part of the meeting.

"I feel like I'm sitting in the kids' seats, facing the adults at the big people table," Jessamine whispered to Frank.

He pursed his lips. "It's on purpose. Look at Joshua in his polo gear. He likes everyone to know he plays polo. And he's telling us he's so busy he didn't have time to change. It's a wonder he didn't bring the stick-thingy, the mallet."

Joshua looked straight at Frank as if he heard, although Jessamine knew he couldn't have heard over the hum of conversation. Joshua reached under the table and pulled out a wooden pole almost as tall as Jessamine. He dangled it by a leather loop for a moment, then grabbed the wooden head and thumped it on the table. She didn't know anything about the sport, but it could only be a polo mallet.

Silence fell, and Jessamine felt her repressed snort of laughter hanging in the air in front of her in a ball.

Joshua glared at her, then clunked the side of a pile of papers on the table. "As those of us *on* the Committee know, I'm Joshua Oxford, the chair of the Library Committee." He looked down his nose at the library staff and patrons spread out among the books. "Since Marilyn has a…um…*her therapy circle* here, I suppose we'll get started." He cleared his throat and looked at the assembled committee. "I'm sure we've all read the emails. Because we're short of time today, I move that the agenda is amended to go immediately into closed session to discuss personnel issues."

Nobody spoke.

He looked pointedly around the seated Library Committee members. "Does anyone second the motion?"

Three people spoke at once. "I second…"

"Fine, fine, good, good." He spoke fast, his intense gaze on each committee member in turn. "All in favor say *aye*."

The chorus of *ayes* came quickly.

Joshua smiled for the first time. "So, the *therapy circle* should leave. This is private. Kathryn and Drusilla, could you please stay?" He made a shoo-ing motion with his hands at the seated people. "Go out in the hallway."

In the hallway, Stephanie snorted. "You can't run a meeting like that. There's an agenda. And *protocol*…"

"Apparently they think they can." Jessamine felt confused. "Can we barge back into the library if they're not following protocol? What can we do?"

Frank screwed up his face. "What did he call us? A therapy group? What does that mean?"

"Don't worry." Jessamine ground her teeth and grimaced. "He was being insulting."

"There's one thing." Stephanie looked hopeful. "They have term limits. Joshua will be off the Library Committee after this meeting."

Through the glass library doors, they could hear a blur of angry sound. One committee member gesticulated. It looked like she was shouting.

Another person half stood up and gesticulated back.

After what felt like hours, Drusilla returned, her face dancing.

"What's happening? What are they doing?" Stephanie asked quickly.

Drusilla's joy showed in her voice. "I've got no idea."

Stephanie looked startled. "But you…"

A committee member appeared and gestured for Drusilla to come. "They *need* me again. I'd better go." Drusilla hurried off as fast as her overtight skirt and four-inch heels would allow.

She's waddling, Jessamine thought, even while she was scolding herself for being unkind.

Time dragged for the waiting people. Stephanie left; she couldn't stay up late because she had to take her mother to the hospital early in the morning for long-planned surgery. Several others gave up, murmuring apologetically about having to get up early. The remaining people sagged on the couple of narrow benches and against the wall. Conversation between them petered out.

Marilyn appeared in the doorway, pale, eyes wide. Everyone straightened up. "They said I should quit. I can do something called 'quit with restraint,' or they're going to fire me."

There was a shocked silence. Frank muttered under his breath. Jessamine stepped over and gave Marilyn a quick hug. "Why?" she asked. "What possible reason could they have for firing you?"

"They said I wasn't being a team player about Bent River County wildlife and the bear. Then Joshua said that wasn't it. It makes no sense." Marilyn held up a crumpled piece of paper. "They gave me a letter. It says, *You have shown unwillingness to collaborate in the facilitation of county goals and objectives.*"

Frank lifted his eyebrows and shook his head slowly. "All I can say is bless their little country hearts." He reached a hand toward Marilyn. "What are you going to do?"

Marilyn stood with her arms hanging at her sides. Her voice was flat. "Drusilla's advice was that I should quit and then I'll get unemployment benefits."

"That doesn't sound right to me," said Eunice from the craft group. She frowned.

Jessamine had the immediate urge to do the librarian thing and look it up. "I know you go to the state labor department for unemployment. I've helped lots of people with it on the public computers. But I don't know the details of unemployment benefits."

Marilyn leaned against the wall. "I don't know what to do."

"Marilyn, come back in!" Joshua stood at his most imperious—all of his six-foot-four frame towering over Marilyn. "Oh, and the *circle* can come. We've got an announcement."

The few remaining people perched on scattered, abandoned chairs. Joshua was brisk. "It has been decided that Marilyn will step down. Drusilla is now the Acting Library Director. We'll move along with the meeting, since it's already late."

And whose fault is that! Jessamine thought, but she hardly had the energy to think anything angry. *Of course it's Drusilla. We could see that coming a mile off. At least this prat will be off the committee shortly.*

"The next order of business is to deal with a new Library Committee chair." Joshua paused and looked at the committee members over his glasses. He cleared his throat. The pause stretched out. He pointed his chin at one of the women Jessamine didn't know.

"Oh!" the committee member jumped. She mumbled through the words quickly. "I propose the motion that Joshua Oxford and Casey Chilton are elected co-chairs of the Library Committee."

"Co-chairs?" Jessamine gasped. "What?"

"Can they *do* that?" Frank muttered under his breath.

"Anyone second the motion?" Joshua looked intently at each Library Committee member in turn. Two committee members quickly seconded, and it passed.

Joshua looked at the assembled staff again. "We've run out of time, so we'll adjourn."

"What about citizen comments?" Frank sounded angry.

"Sorry, we don't have time…" a sadly smiling committee member started.

"If you must, you have *two* minutes. It's late," Joshua snapped.

"I prepared a statement." Frank stood up.

The new co-chair looked down at her papers. "Yes, we have that. We'll… um… take it into consideration."

"Since it's after nine o'clock. And we're all busy, educated professionals, and volunteers on our own time." Joshua paused and studied the assembled Library Committee. He smiled with his mouth around the group, but the hard-edged coldness in his eyes showed. Several of the Committee Members stopped gathering papers and tittered appreciatively. "We'll call this a good night's work!"

Jessamine glanced at the agenda in her hand. Marilyn labored over it for weeks. Frank obviously had the same thought because he jumped up. "What about the five-year plan? What about the budget? You're supposed to be talking about those!"

"We're all tired and want to go home. We'll talk about those later amongst the committee." Joshua raked his eyes over the committee and got immediate acquiescent nods.

Jessamine felt lifted to her feet by something outside herself. "You're meant to discuss the five-year plan publicly! This is a public organization!"

Joshua didn't pretend to smile this time. "It's too late tonight. As stated in section fourteen, subsection five of our bylaws, I have the right to limit public speaking. I call this meeting to wrap up at…" He stared at Casey.

"Um." She grabbed her phone. "Um. Nine forty-seven p.m."

"Meeting adjourned." Joshua gathered his papers with finality.

Chapter 24

That night, the scenes from the library played over and over in Jessamine's head. Was Marilyn fired? Or quit? The meeting appeared so pre-planned. So darned dodgy. Was it legal? What was she going to do about tomorrow's programs and her shift? Should she fix things for Drusilla? Or should she, for the first time in her life, call in sick?

Jessamine practiced breathing deeply. She visualized a soft breeze fluttering the uppermost leaves on her tall trees against the deep blue sky. Nothing helped. Her eyes ached with tiredness. Shutting them helped the ache, but then visions of the Library Committee meeting became bold and full color.

She got up and made a cup of chamomile tea. It was two o'clock in the morning, a time Jessamine rarely saw if she could help it. She stirred up the fire and watched the flickering flames while she sipped her cooling tea and nibbled an Anzac biscuit. Her thoughts whirled.

Hermes lifted his head, looked vaguely offended, and went back to sleep. The cat, Gabriella, looked at her with ears slightly askew, cat bedhead.

She wasn't used to seeing Jessamine up in the middle of the night, but she took advantage of the opportunity to jump on her lap and bat at her hand, demanding to be petted. Jessamine laughed and scratched the soft fur behind the cat's ears, feeling the rumbles of her purr. Taking a deep breath, Jessamine finally felt as if air was entering her lungs after hours of tension. She grabbed her copy of *Anne of Green Gables* that was sitting on the side table and studied the inscription in spiky, old-fashioned script. "To Jessamine. Happy 7th birthday. With love from Gran." She read a few chapters, feeling her shoulders relax and her mind stop spinning.

When she read the same sentence over and over, she evicted the indignant cat and went to bed. Curled under her blankets, the Library Committee tried to push their way into her thoughts. She lay still and drifted off.

Jessamine popped awake in the dark, her mind already spinning. She never set an alarm since she was an early riser, but it was five o'clock. She'd only had a few hours' sleep. She rolled over to try to sleep more; it wasn't going to work. She got up, greeted the animals, and put the kettle on for her morning cuppa. The sky was getting lighter over the trees to the east. She put on her sneakers and went with Hermes on the first of their daily rounds of her twenty-five acres. The rhythm of walking and the beauty of the morning gave her renewed faith in the world. "We can fight the Library Committee!" she said to Hermes. She watched the dog race down the pine-needle strewn path, reveling in his body's athleticism and his sheer joy in being alive.

In the house, Jessamine texted Drusilla: *I don't feel well and won't be able to make it today. Sorry about the short notice.* She didn't put any emojis or exclamation points. She paused before she sent it. Despite everything, she felt guilty. She had never taken a "mental health day" because she loved this job so much. With her lack of sleep, she could feel a migraine gathering pointed sticks behind her eyes, but for incipient migraines she usually took an over-the-counter headache combo, drank lots of caffeinated tea, and went to work. *Not today,* she said to herself firmly and sent the text.

All day, Jessamine felt dislocated, like she was recovering from an illness. She kept thinking, *If I was at work, I'd be preparing for the book group now* or

I'd be meeting with the science teacher from the school. Many days the library was open and operated without her. Perhaps it was because she had expected to be there. Or perhaps it was the import of the news and how the library filled her every thought. She buttered her toast for lunch and thought, *How can I be doing these mundane tasks after that meeting? After they fired Marilyn?*

She carried her phone around all day. Usually she forgot it in her bag and missed calls and texts. She texted Marilyn and learned that Marilyn was going into the library to pick up her possessions. Later that afternoon, Jessamine made herself another cup of chamomile tea, thinking that she might need fortifying, and called Marilyn. Her former boss picked up immediately.

"How are you, Marilyn?"

"I'm great! They sent Drusilla to sit with me in my office while I got my papers and personal effects out." Marilyn was talking high and fast. "To spy on me. I stayed and looked at the same pieces of paper for seven hours. Drusilla wouldn't leave the room. I suggested that she could go to the bathroom. I heard her stomach rumbling."

Jessamine laughed. She couldn't have gotten a word in, even if she'd wanted to.

Marilyn went on talking fast. "This is exactly what Drusilla has been angling for. To give her credit, she's got a lot of patience to wait this long to get what she wanted."

"She certainly did…"

"And they won't let me look at my emails at all."

"What?" Jessamine was startled.

"Yes. There were only two administrators for the email, Stephanie and me. They had to change the administrator passwords."

"Isn't Stephanie at the hospital with her mother?" Jessamine asked.

"Yes, she's at the hospital, but Drusilla called her and made her change all the passwords."

"*All* the passwords? At the *hospital?*" Jessamine wasn't keeping up. "What passwords?"

"There's all the other accounts. The website, the catalog, the teleconferencing, all of it. My name's on all of them… was on all of them." Marilyn's voice caught.

"Oh." Jessamine paused. "If Stephanie was at the hospital, how could she do it? Did they ask her to come back early?"

"No, they're getting her to do it remotely."

"From the hospital?"

"Yup. Nothing I can do about it now." Marilyn's voice came out stronger.

"She needs to spend time with her family!"

"Any decent person would know Stephanie needs to be with her family. But you know her, she won't complain."

Jessamine realized that she had stood up and was pacing around her tiny living room.

"Couldn't *we* complain? Aren't they breaking labor laws? Are they at least paying her? Who do we complain to, the Library Committee?"

Jessamine heard Marilyn's sigh come down the phone. "You know how it'll go if you try to talk to the Library Committee."

"Arrgh! Those people are so awful!" Jessamine stamped her foot.

After talking to Marilyn, Jessamine paced around her kitchen, muttering, "I can't believe it! How dare they?" Hermes followed her and lifted his paw as if to beg Jessamine to stop.

"Poor puppy," Jessamine rubbed his ears and laughed at herself. She opened the door for the dog to go out and stood looking thoughtfully out.

Out of necessity, she had cleared a path to the chicken coop, one vine at a time. The vines caught on her clothes every time she went from her car to her door, but she had always found more urgent tasks than clearing them. Stephanie had sold her a cheap refurbished lawnmower. "It's old, but it works. My husband likes to tinker with their engines, and we end up with so many of them. If you want it, it's yours for the cost of the parts!"

The vines didn't look as if they could be mowed down by an ordinary red gas-powered push mower, so it sat unused next to Jessamine's parking spot under the giant tree. Jessamine hadn't expected to be home today, and she was too restless to sit down. She would tackle the tangled vines.

She pulled on Rosemary's green, frog-decorated rain boots and scrambled into old gardening clothes she'd rescued from the library supply closet months ago. The small machine looked helpless against the profligate nature, but she'd try. She tore at the starter cord again and again until it chugged dispiritedly, then roared into an audible assault on the peaceful afternoon. She braced her legs and pushed hard. The mechanical monster ate the plants, leaving a path of stalks. "You're mostly air!" Jessamine crowed. "You're goners, you tormenting vines!"

The engine struggled, and the lawnmower stopped; vines tangled its wheels and stretched across its front. They sought Jessamine's unprotected hands. "We're not done yet." Jessamine pulled the lawnmower to a clear place and tilted it back, so the blades tackled the vines head on. The vines fell under the onslaught. Piece by piece, she cleared a car-width path from the giant tree toward her house.

She mowed around the back and toward several outbuildings half-hidden behind a tangle of bushes to a greenhouse she'd never entered. Letting the machine go quiet, she pushed the door with her shoulder until it scraped open across the dry dirt floor. Inside, the smell changed from the damp, deepness of growing plants and earth to a dry, dusty place stuck in time. The plants on the outside pushed against the glass, rude with life. The inside was a plant graveyard of gray sticks.

Jessamine eyed the shelves stacked with clay plant pots, wooden seed trays, trowels, and rakes. Old packets spilled dried out seeds on the floor. They were dead, but seeds meant hope. She could get more seeds, and she had the perfect place to plant and nurture them.

That night, Jessamine fell into bed early, her legs and shoulders stiff, her hands numbed by the vibrating handle, and sweat and green plant juice staining her clothes. Satisfied that she had cleared the vicious, clinging vines out of her way, she lay in bed and planned the life she would nurture in her greenhouse.

Chapter 25

The next day, Jessamine went back to work.

"I hope you feel better." Drusilla smirked.

Jessamine knew that Drusilla knew that she hadn't been sick.

"Thank you, I feel better." Jessamine felt like an awkward actor in a bad play. Overcoming the vines *had* made her feel better, but she didn't want to share that with Drusilla.

With Stephanie away looking after her mother, Jessamine spent her days working on the circulation desk. She needed to leave the desk to run the book group and story time, but Drusilla told Jessamine to hurry back. Josey reported that Drusilla had been rude and impatient with her and her children. "She made Larsen cry when she snapped at him for not choosing a bookmark fast enough. Who does that to a toddler?" Josey said.

Jessamine was glad to be busy. Marilyn's firing floated above her head like a zeppelin. Drusilla spent hours chatting with Kathryn, then retreated into her old office and emerged with full trash bags that she called Frank to pick up. Frank always paused at the desk to joke and ask Jessamine how she was doing.

All that week Jessamine poked her lunchbox under the desk and ate her lunch with furtive bites, not wanting to ask for a lunch break and disturb the ringing silences stretching out with Drusilla. She felt Drusilla's eyes on her back, and she longed for her house and fireplace.

Drusilla spent a long afternoon with Joshua and Kathryn measuring the open corner behind the circulation desk. Frank and a county work crew hauled away cracked tables and piles of broken bulletin boards. Jessamine eyed them, puzzled, but all she heard were snatches of conversation about non-load bearing walls and the cost of two-way glass.

Frank came by and leaned on the desk. "How are you doing, Ms. Jessamine?" He gestured at ladders and masking tape on the floor behind the desk. "What do you think of all this rigmarole?"

"What *is* this rigmarole?" Jessamine pulled her eyebrows together. "What are you doing?"

"You mean you don't know?" Frank laughed and shook his head.

"No, Drusilla barely talks to me."

"We're making a new office for Drusilla. It'll have a big internal window overlooking this desk."

"Why? Drusilla already has an office."

"I don't know why." Frank shrugged and laughed again. "I just do what I'm told."

"Who's paying for the construction? Did the county agree to this?"

"No, I heard it's coming out of the library budget."

"Why?" Jessamine shook her head. "I don't get it."

Frank shrugged and lifted his palms toward the ceiling before turning away. "You take care, now Ms. Jessamine."

The rickety walls went up remarkably fast. By the time Stephanie returned, Drusilla was installed in her new office.

"How is your mother?" Jessamine asked Stephanie.

"She's fine now. She needs to rest." Stephanie leaned her elbows on the desk and sighed. "It would help if my sister was willing to do anything for Mama." She looked over her shoulder at the huge internal window, now dominating the circulation desk. "I don't get it. Why install a giant window and then put blinds on it?"

"Frank said that Drusilla demanded two-way glass." Jessamine gave the window a sideways look. "But it was way too expensive, so she made him install venetian blinds. He put them on the outside, and Drusilla threw a hissy fit, and he had to put them on the inside so Drusilla could control them."

The blinds twitched and they saw fingers poking through the slats. "She wants to control them alright." Stephanie said. "It's her 'spying office.' Can she hear what we're saying?"

"No, don't worry. Frank and I tested it. You can hear a mumble, but you can't hear what people are saying. We must have looked stupid, one standing in the office and one standing by the desk talking to ourselves."

"I thought the library was poor." Stephanie screwed up her eyebrows.

Jessamine resisted the urge to make a rude gesture toward the blinds. "I cannot *believe* that the *very* first thing she did as acting director was to spend library money on that 'office.'"

Stephanie waved a ragged book. "I know. I was flabbergasted."

Jessamine paused with her pamphlets and waved a tattered picture book they were trying to cobble together with tape. "We need new books!"

Stephanie shook her head. "Yes, this is a library! What does she think it is, the FBI? The CIA?"

"No, she's the Stasi! For goodness' sakes. As you said, it's a public library. Who in the world does she think will be seeing what she's doing? She has top secret business in the card catalog?" The women were grinning at each other now.

Drusilla came out of her office. "I'm going to an important Library Committee meeting. You two need to stop gossiping and work."

"Yes, we're getting these books cleaned and repaired, since we can't afford to buy new ones," said Stephanie.

After Drusilla left, Stephanie giggled. "Or is the top-secret business with the little green men?" She sighed. "She's the acting director. She can build a new office if she wants."

"We're so desperately short of money."

"I've been through five directors since I've worked here, but I don't like this." Stephanie sighed again. "I guess we'll carry on since there aren't many jobs in Bent River County for ordinary people. Everyone says that."

"I know." Jessamine paused in folding her pamphlets. "I've been looking at other jobs. But it's unjust. I don't understand what Marilyn did to get fired. Isn't there anything we can do?"

"Unjust or not, those polo people along the river always get what they want. And this time Drusilla got what she wanted from them. She wanted to be director all along."

"She did? You mentioned that, but I didn't believe it."

"Yes, she thought they owed it to her. One of our old directors was Drusilla's great aunt and told her that being in charge of this library would be an easy job for her. She's been trying *so* hard to get in with the polo crowd ever since we were at school together." Stephanie paused. "When I look back as an adult, I can see that Drusilla was pretty miserable at school."

"Weren't we all? Do you mean extra miserable?"

Stephanie looked down at the desk and tapped her fingers. "I'd almost feel sorry for Drusilla if she wasn't such a… such a *cow*. If she wasn't ruining the library."

Jessamine opened her eyes wide. "Those are strong words from you, Stephanie!" She laughed. "What do you mean?"

"Her family have always been awful to her." Stephanie looked thoughtful. "Her mother died when she was young. There was some drama with the police, but I never learned what it was."

"I don't know whether to be smug or feel sorry for her." Jessamine grimaced. "I'll listen to my better angels and feel sorry for her without a mother. How did she cope?"

"At elementary school she was the stinky kid. She smelled of pee. I guess there was no one at home who'd wash her clothes or sheets if she wet the bed." Stephanie paused. "She was pretty old to be wetting the bed—seven or eight? Looking back as an adult, I wonder what else was going on at home."

"Yes, it sounds like she was neglected. Why did she stay in Bent River County? Don't young people go to the cities?"

"She did leave. She came back when it didn't work out." Stephanie twisted her mouth. "Now, I feel bad about school. She was always tall, like she is now, so that made her stand out. She developed early as well. Some of the girls were nasty to her when she got boobs in elementary school. I remember one girl, Natalie, was going around asking would you invite Drusilla or Evan to your birthday party? Evan was a weird kid too. He ended up at Harvard or one of those places then murdered his girlfriend and committed suicide. It was a big scandal. What you were meant to say at school was that you'd invite Evan over Drusilla. She was at the bottom of the heap. Children can be so cruel."

"Yes, they can be cruel." Jessamine sighed. "But so can adults. I saw bruises on Drusilla's arm after the STEM program. It looked like someone grabbed her really hard."

"I'm not surprised." Stephanie shook her head sadly. "She got involved in some dodgy things in the city. At first, she got a modeling contract." Stephanie laughed. "I was jealous when I was twenty because she was a model. I didn't think she was pretty! The modeling business got shut down. There were rumors about the governor being involved and that some of the models were getting paid for more than photographs."

"Wow." Jessamine opened her eyes wide. "That's a big story."

"And I don't know how she got that fancy car she drives, since she couldn't afford it on what she earns here." Stephanie shook her head. "I see that car and it makes it harder to be sympathetic toward her." Stephanie frowned. "Especially on cold mornings when I have to talk sweetly to my thirty-year-old heap of junk, so I won't be stuck on the side of the road, feeling desperate about being late for work or a doctor's appointment."

Frank waved and grinned as he went past the library windows with a mop and bucket. "Lots of people have hard lives," Jessamine said, "and it doesn't make them cruel."

"I'm scared she'll do anything to get in with the polo crowd." Stephanie looked sad.

Jessamine opened her mouth and shut it again. "This place is feeling more and more like a medieval village."

"You might be right." Stephanie gave a dry laugh. "Drusilla was *not* happy when the county hired Marilyn. But don't worry, the county employee who made *that* decision is gone!" Stephanie paused with the book she was checking in, hovering in midair. "Technically the Library Committee works for the County Council. When these old families and plantation owners are involved, it's all different. There are still plantations along the rivers in the South. As my grandmother used to say, all that cattywampus was meant to end over a hundred years ago." Stephanie gritted her teeth. "What century are we in?"

"I thought it was meant to end *eons* ago with the Sermon on the Mount, do unto others and love thy neighbor. Marilyn's firing is *wrong*. We must be able to fight back." Jessamine felt an idea forming. "You said that the County Council are in charge of the Library Committee?"

"As I said, technically the Library Committee members work for the County Council. But in reality…" Stephanie shrugged. "Be careful, Jessamine. Try not to care *too* much. You don't know what these people are like."

"What do you mean, I care too much? Do other people think what is happening is right?"

"No, not right. But we need to live in the real world. To get along. They're only books. It's only a library."

"Why do people work in a public library if they don't care about books? If they don't care about serving the public?" Jessamine patted Stephanie's arm. "Sorry. I know you care. And I know you need the job, but…"

"It's not that I don't care." Stephanie screwed up her face, reaching for the words. "It's just that we don't care as much as you do. Or in the same way you do."

"I don't get it." Jessamine gathered a section of her skirt in her hand and twisted it into a knot. "I know a public library isn't only about books. It's a place of meeting, a place of community. At its best, it's a place of sanctuary. But books are the foundation. Books matter!" She waved the tattered copy of *Where the Wild Things Are* that they'd been trying to repair. Jessamine could see that it was hopeless for this torn, scribbled on, and crumpled book with missing pages; it needed to go into the trash.

"Yes, we could—" Stephanie tried, but Jessamine was on a roll.

Jessamine stood up straight. "I've had dark and lonely places in my life where books were… were my only friends, only guides. I've been the pig with the wise spider for a friend. I've been the Jewish Dutch girl hiding in an attic in Amsterdam." Jessamine waved *Where the Wild Things Are* again. "I've been the little boy who had the wild rumpus, then his mother brings him his warm supper. And for goodness' sake, when I became a mother, I was the mother bringing the naughty child his food and love."

"I know Jessamine. We've all read *Charlotte's Web*, but how—"

Jessamine put her hands out and her voice rose. "For golly gosh sake, I've driven racecars, and I've lived through the plague and been a Roman Centurion. I've been to other planets and lived with dragons—impossible things!"

Stephanie laughed. "Jessamine, you're ranting! I don't think—"

"Yes, I'm ranting! Don't they realize that the point of a story is to be another person? To see the world through their eyes? Or to feel part of a bigger story that other people share?"

Stephanie raised her hands in surrender and laughed. "Or to be a talking spider."

"If it's a good story, even about a talking spider, you might learn about being a better human. We have a responsibility—no, a *covenant* to make these treasures available. And to research and curate them for the public to the best of our abilities." Jessamine looked around at the shelves crammed with decades-old books and shuddered. "I'm *horrified* if this is the best of their abilities!"

"I don't think the best of their abilities has anything to do with it." Stephanie shook her head. "You can't make other people be better humans.

Even if you can convince them that they need to be better. I know you care, and our library customers know you care, but…"

Jessamine breathed in deeply. "It's not in me not to care."

"You're tilting at windmills!"

"There's a literary reference." Jessamine laughed. "I only tilt at windmills if they're full of books."

Stephanie laughed, then sobered. "Care, since it's all you are capable of doing. But as I said, be careful. I'm afraid it's you who's going to suffer over this."

Drusilla clumped into the library on her heels. "You ladies can't spend all your time chattering! I thought you had a lot of work to do."

"We're discussing how to deal with the library's perennial financial problems," Stephanie said.

"Hi, Drusilla." Jessamine remembered Stephanie's story about Drusilla's background and smiled at her new boss. "I hope your meeting went well?"

Drusilla stopped and stared at Jessamine. She snapped, "None of your business." She narrowed her eyes. "You should be worrying about the jobs I've told you to do." She smirked. "Not problems above your level."

After Drusilla walked away, Jessamine narrowed her eyes and pursed her mouth. "I'm coming back to my idea. You said the Library Committee work for the County Council? I'm going to look it up." Jessamine put aside the ruined copy of *Where the Wild Things Are* and her half-made, job-searching pamphlets.

"Remember, she's watching us," Stephanie said. They glanced at the internal window. Drusilla's eye glared, then the blinds twitched closed.

Jessamine still used her own laptop for all library work and she suspected Drusilla didn't know how to check what happened on the library internet. She searched and read bylaws and meeting minutes. Jessamine had no doubt that Drusilla would try to catch her out doing something wrong, but she felt the bylaws and State Library Standards were library business. The boring, pompous words came alive as Jessamine understood that citizens were meant to have a say about what went on in their county. Jessamine plotted.

The following week, Jessamine had the feeling she was about to do an exam. *I wish this was over,* she thought. *I wish I'd never had this completely stupid idea. Why do I have such stupid ideas?*

As she walked down the hallway, past the courtrooms in the County Administration building, the only comfort Jessamine could come up with was that it would soon be over.

She watched what everyone else was doing and stopped at the receptionist's desk to sign in to give a three-minute public comment. In the column label 'Topic' she wrote 'Library,' under 'Who are you representing?' she wrote 'Myself. Citizen of Bent River County.'

After a quick trip to the restroom—Jessamine was a nervous pee-er—she followed the other people into the small amphitheater. A tall bench ran across the front of the room and the names of the county councilors appeared on metallic signs in front of microphones on bendy tubes. People filed in, shaking hands and greeting each other. They knew where to sit, either coming into the audience or going to the County Council spots. *They're making it crystal clear who's in charge,* Jessamine thought, eyeing the height between where the councilors sat and where other people sat.

"I call the meeting of the Bent River County Council to order. First on the agenda is Grace Murdock to update us on roadworks."

Jessamine listened in fascination as the woman in a business suit talked knowledgably about the windy country roads. "We have complaints about trucks from the quarry making noise and ruining the roads. They are heavy and cause damage to the roads that they're not designed for."

Jessamine had never considered the upkeep of the roads. They were just *there.*

"Now the state department of zoning will give a presentation." This new presenter didn't have the previous speaker's panache, and when he read his PowerPoint slides, Jessamine eyes glazed. *What am I doing here?* she wondered. *Is it going to change anything?*

"We'll now have citizen comments. Um…" He looked down at his sheet. "First is Jessamine Sibley."

Jessamine walked up to the podium. The bendy microphone was set too high for her, so she pulled it down as far as it could reach. The crowd tittered. She looked up at the bench, not sure if she could start.

"State your name and address. Go ahead." The councilor sounded impatient.

"I am Jessamine Sibley of 456 Pinetree Lane. I choose to work at Bent River County Public Library." She put her notes down on the podium so no one could see her hands shaking.

Jessamine felt her blood begin to flow and her voice came out stronger. "We have a remarkable library. Public libraries provide services that cannot be provided privately. All the library staff, except the library director, are part-time library assistants and we achieve more than many nearby, better funded libraries."

She stopped and took a deep breath. She looked up at the councilors. One was scrolling through his phone.

"As library employees, we have given our best to our county and our library. Our hard work shows every day in the improvements we have made to Bent River County Public Library. The great things we have accomplished, and our new ideas are dismissed with disdain. I feel a lack of respect for the library profession, and most particularly a lack of respect for the professional degree. I see a constant challenge and demeaning indifference, and outright hostility towards standards of librarianship. Last month our library director was fired or forced to resign, I'm not sure which!"

The councilor looked up from his phone and stared intently at Jessamine.

Jessamine plunged on. "I believe we have been treated like second-class citizens. Library employees are disregarded and attacked. I ask the County Councilors and the citizens of Bent River County to investigate."

The councilor gave her a puzzled look, as if trying to work out which species, and not a wholesome species, Jessamine might be an example of.

"Thank you for your t—" A buzzer sounded. Her time was up.

The councilor poked his phone with a finger, then looked up and peered at Jessamine over his glasses. The audience watched him. He cleared his throat and said in a gravelly smoker's voice, "Are you sure this is the hill you want to die on?"

The crowd tittered. Jessamine stared at him. "What? I…"

"Your time is up. You can leave."

Jessamine gathered up her script and walked up the aisle to the exit, her limbs not fitting right in her clothes and not reaching the floor in the way they normally did.

Chapter 26

W*hen Jessamine arrived at* work the next week, Stephanie was talking to a petite young woman bedaubed with bright makeup and wearing tight black trousers and a shiny black top. Stephanie greeted Jessamine with a cheerful smile. "This is Tiffany Bartlett. This is her first day."

"Good morning, Tiffany." Jessamine held out her hand. "Are you volunteering to shelve books?"

Tiffany gave Jessamine a slow look up and down and didn't answer.

"Ah, no!" Stephanie coughed. "Tiffany is working here. She's finishing a degree in public administration. She said that'll help her run a library and she'll be running the genealogy assistance program. She was telling me about her uncle being involved in the construction of the new library building. They're moving right along."

"I didn't know anyone new was starting. We need help with the genealogy assistance and circulation desk. Welcome to Bent River County Public Library."

Drusilla poked her head out of her office. "I see you've met Stephanie and

Jessamine, Tiffany. Come into my office and we'll get started."

After Tiffany left, Jessamine turned to Stephanie and said, "I thought they didn't have money to hire anyone new? When did this happen?"

"I met Tiffany ten minutes ago." Stephanie shrugged. "It was news to me."

"I know we told Drusilla that a new genealogy assistance person could pay for themselves. Not that she listens to anything I say." Jessamine sighed and wondered why she came in, but the craft ladies, book group people and story time kids kept her coming back.

"She doesn't listen to either of us. I told her the steps to do the genealogy assistance properly." Stephanie frowned. "We want to do it right."

"I didn't understand how a public library could charge to help people with their family research, most libraries do it for free. But it's working and making money for the library." Jessamine paused. "I know Drusilla keeps wanting us to do more genealogy assistance appointments." Jessamine paused again and considered if what she was about to say was mean. It was uncharitable, but it was also true. "It would have helped a whole huge bunch if she'd been willing to do the appointments as well."

"She *said* she was willing but she was too busy." Stephanie shrugged again. "She keeps pushing me to do more. Finally, I had to put my foot down and say I wasn't doing any more than a few appointments."

"Good on you." Jessamine put her hands on her hips. "I've seen you doing them on your own time. It is a big job you're not getting paid for. That's not right!"

"I told Drusilla I've been staying late to finish them." Stephanie twirled her hair around her finger.

"What did she say?"

"She said I should get them done faster. They can't afford to pay me overtime."

"That's illegal! You know that not paying you overtime is against the labor laws."

Stephanie shrugged. "It's going to be hard to do anything since we don't have *any* computers that work."

"None?" Jessamine's voice came out high and squeaky. "Not a single one works?"

"No, they're all down."

"For goodness' sake!" Jessamine lifted her hands toward the ceiling. "I don't think they know how Marilyn's constant work kept those old computers going."

"It's not that they don't *know*." Stephanie shrugged again. "It's that they don't *care*."

They shook their heads. "Whingeing about it isn't going to help." Jessamine puffed out her checks. "I suppose we'll baby those computers back to life."

"I love your word 'whingeing.'" Stephanie laughed. "It describes exactly what I want to do about this situation."

They restarted computers and pulled on cords and connections. When that didn't work, they patted the old machines and resorted to the odd satisfying kick. They had asked Drusilla to request county help, but she said that the county wouldn't send a technician without the library paying for their time out of the library budget, which Drusilla refused to do. "You do it. I thought you were so good at libraries. At library *functions*," Drusilla said with a sneer.

"I'll try looking it up since I have my own laptop here." Stephanie opened the battered machine and waited for it to boot up. "I have to take my laptop home every day. It's the only one we've got and the kids have homework, and I keep track of Mama's health records. It's all online these days."

Jessamine pulled books about computers off the shelves but threw them down in disgust when she saw that they had been published decades earlier and talked about floppy disks. "They're so old! Do you know what a floppy disk is?" she asked Stephanie.

"What?" Stephanie didn't look up. "I've found something." She pointed at the screen. "I think we have to install new drivers?"

"That sounds familiar," Jessamine said slowly and grimaced. "I remember I had to do it when I bought a new printer. But drivers for what?"

"Just a sec. I'm looking it up."

"For the programs the computers need to run properly?" Jessamine suggested tentatively. "I don't know that I can help much. My children always teased me about my EMP poltergeist."

Stephanie looked up. "Your what?"

"My poltergeist that sends out electro-magnetic waves when I'm near a machine, so it breaks." Jessamine looked thoughtful. "It's a completely silly joke, but it's true that I'm bad at getting machines going."

"You're going to be good at it today." Stephanie rubbed her hands together. "I'm going to learn how to do this. There are a lot of video tutorials. These old computers may be hopeless, but we'll keep them going another day."

The women went back to wiggling cords and restarting, and enough of the old machines struggled to life to open the library. "If you call it life," Jessamine said. "I know they're machines and not actually alive, but these ones are far more dead than most."

In the following days, Tiffany's schedule became as mysterious as Drusilla's. Jessamine assumed that the new woman needed to settle in before she took on circulation duties and genealogy assistance.

Eventually, Jessamine screwed up her courage and knocked on Drusilla's office door. Drusilla pulled it open and looked at Jessamine without speaking. Jessamine swallowed. "Um. I'd like to do more programs now that Tiffany's working here. We've been talking about starting up a knitting and crocheting group for ages."

Drusilla turned away and stamped a book. "You need to cover the circulation desk and the genealogy assistance schedule."

"I always do. But my job is to do programs. That's what I was hired for."

"The library needs you to do the desk and the genealogy assistance. The genealogy assistance payments are essential and valuable for the library. I would have thought you realized that?" Drusilla stood up heavily and reached into a box of books. Even in the bigger office she took up most of the room. "I suppose you can do a few of your pet programs, if you must. Only schedule them when Stephanie is available for the desk."

"What about Tiffany? Couldn't she cover the desk when I do programs?"

"Tiffany is helping me with the collection."

Jessamine felt a lift of her heart. "I can help with the collection! I know you're busy with the director's work. I have lots of experience and I love—"

"No, as I said, make sure the desk is covered." Drusilla turned away to her computer. Then she turned back. "Oh, and remember to clean out that other office. Tiffany is going to use it."

"Tiffany is going to use it? Why doesn't she clean it out? And what about the third office? Can I use it?"

"The third office is for storage. That should make you happy since you like keeping junk." Drusilla rolled her eyes. "It was actually a closet originally, but you wouldn't know that since you've only been here for five minutes. Don't put any of your trash in there. It's for me and Tiffany." Drusilla turned to her computer. "Tiffany doesn't have time to clean out the office. She's busy."

Jessamine knew she was being dismissed, but the whole situation was so stupid. "When is Tiffany going to help with the genealogy assistance?"

Drusilla's poker face slipped and she spoke sharply. "I told you, she's busy. She's helping me. If that's all, you can go."

Jessamine stood in the doorway of Drusilla's old office. It looked like Drusilla liked to keep junk as well; the floor, desks, and shelves were covered in a jumble of crumpled papers, ragged books, and old maps. Jessamine saw the pile of glass sign holders that she had used for labels for the shelves months ago. Drusilla took them down in one of their first conflicts. Jessamine snorted and kicked at them. They spilled across the floor, exposing papers dense with numbers. She bent to pick them up and the word 'tile' caught her eye. Marilyn said that there was something odd about the way they were ordering the tile for the new library. Jessamine studied the pages.

"What are you doing? I thought you were told you had to clean up?" Tiffany appeared behind Jessamine and grinned openly.

Jessamine jumped and pushed the papers into her cardigan pocket.

"Drusilla, *our boss*, said you need to get back to the desk. People are waiting. You should work faster, so you can get this cleaned up." Tiffany giggled.

Interacting with Tiffany and Drusilla transported Jessamine to the bad part of middle school; she didn't want to play their games, but since they had power over her, they sucked her in to whatever they wanted to play. Jessamine knew Tiffany and Drusilla were decades younger than her, but so was Stephanie. Jessamine considered Stephanie her friend; the decades between them didn't matter.

Over the next days, Jessamine resolutely ignored the messy office. If Drusilla wanted to store old junk on the floor in there, then she could. At home, Jessamine looked for nearby jobs; she hated to leave her library community, but she knew this couldn't go on.

There were no suitable jobs within a reasonable distance.

Tiffany never managed to help with the genealogy assistance, but she had plenty of time to sit in Drusilla's office and chat. Jessamine glimpsed her through the blinds, glacially picking up one book and putting one sticker on it. Then putting it down and turning to Drusilla and talking.

Stephanie, sorting a huge pile of picture books that had been returned after the story time, saw Jessamine watching and said sourly, "Yes, I've actually timed it. I have seen her take a full twenty minutes to put two stickers on a book." Stephanie lifted a pile of picture books onto a wheeled library cart. "No rest for the wicked. Can you watch the desk? I'd better shelve these, or we'll be snowed under. I've got to leave early today to take my mother to her follow-up hospital appointment. Did I tell you? I told Tiffany to tell Drusilla." She jerked her head toward Drusilla's office window, where both were bent over in laughter. "I don't know why her majesty, or either of her majesties, can't shelve a book occasionally, but they're too good for the likes of us. At least Tiffany will be able to back you up on the desk this afternoon." She sniffed and maneuvered the awkward, heavy cart toward the shelves. "Thanks, Jessamine. You're a lifesaver."

Chapter 27

Jessamine gazed at the bookshelves, lost in thought. She loved her new home and the people in her library, but was it worth it?

"Could I please borrow this book?" She jumped when she realized a man was standing in front of her. The man unfolded a crumpled piece of paper, tilting it away from Jessamine and shielding it with his hand. He carefully read out the title and author, "*How Anyone Can Find (and Claim) Lost Government Money!* by Brett Toby."

She searched in the library's mucked-up online catalog. "I can't find it here. Would you like me to show you where to look on the shelves?"

"No. Can you just grab it?" The man looked eager.

"I'll have a look." Jessamine walked over to the 300s and searched without much hope and returned. "We don't have that book. We have, *Getting the Most from Your Government…*"

"That's not it! Can I borrow this one from another library?"

"We don't do Interlibrary Loan, I'm sorry." Jessamine pulled a rueful face. "We can't afford it. But I can search for the book, to see which libraries own it."

Jessamine opened WorldCat, the database of books owned by libraries worldwide, which she used almost daily. "By Toby who?" Jessamine hadn't kept up with her typing. "Can I see the author and title?" Eyes on the screen, she put her hand out.

"No!" The man slipped the piece of paper into his shirt pocket and held his palm over his chest as if he expected Jessamine to reach into his pocket.

"Oh." Jessamine pulled back her hand. "How to claim government money? Is that it? I'm finding a few here in WorldCat. Do you want the newest one?"

"It *must* be *this* book." The man scratched his ear. "Look, I'll write it down. Do you have paper?"

Jessamine gave him a small square of paper and a pen. He went to a nearby table and looked at the other people in the public computer area, quietly occupied with their own business. He hunched over and covered his paper with his hand as he copied the words quickly and brought it to Jessamine.

"This book was published in 1981. And only one library in the world owns it. I can look for a book we have here in our library about finding government money?"

He lowered his eyes, pulled on his tie, and fiddled with a button on his ironed blue shirt. "Well…" He glanced around the busy public computer area of the library. He leaned forward. "I need that book," he whispered. "You see, they've put the answers I need in it."

Clean-shaven, with combed hair and a faint smell of cologne, Jessamine thought the man was remarkably unremarkable, but she was beginning to wonder if this wasn't an ordinary library transaction. She looked the man in the eyes. "Who's put the answers in that you need?"

The man looked down. Then he hunched his shoulders again and turned to look at the library door and into the bookshelves. He leaned forward and lowered his voice. "They did. *They* put the answers in. The government people. The ones who live in the lines on the interstates."

"Ah." Jessamine struggled to keep her face neutral. "In that particular book?"

"Yes, in that book. I took a risk telling you the name of the book. Even worse, writing it down. You have a trustworthy face." He smiled at Jessamine.

"Um. What answers are you after? I can help you search online."

"I can't tell you that! They've got agents everywhere! It's *government* money. And the internet is worse." He leaned forward again. "They live in the *lines* on the interstates. So, they're not big people. And there are lines in books."

Jessamine knew the best reference interview technique was to ask the customer clarifying questions. She didn't think it would clarify anything if she asked this well-dressed and ordinary-looking man if he truly believed that the government had put messages, aimed individually at him, inside an out-of-print book. He obviously did. The only thing she could think of was to please the customer. "I'll write down which library owns the book. I'm not sure if you'll be able to get it. Possibly this library lost it long ago and haven't updated their catalog."

The man clutched his hands together and his face lit up with joy. "Oh, thank you! I know they'll have it!"

Jessamine had another thought. "Do you want to see if you can buy it second hand? There are a lot of places online that sell old books."

"A library book would be better." He pulled the scrap of paper with the book's title out of his pocket and covered his mouth and whispered to it. He crumpled the paper in one hand and tapped his knuckles three times on the desk. He turned and stared intently at the library door, considering. "Libraries are the best, but I *could* look at buying it."

Jessamine helped him sign in to one of the struggling public computers and showed him how to search for the book. He was excited to learn that several online companies sold only books, mostly secondhand. "I'd rather not use those *big* online selling companies. You know all about them and what they do." He tapped the side of his nose at Jessamine.

"And several companies buy books that libraries get rid of. It's a great deal all round," Jessamine told him.

Jessamine could see a librarian was not the professional help this man needed. When she worked in a big city library, so many homeless people had spent whole days there that the library had security guards. Jessamine vividly recalled several times that a quiet, if scruffy, library patron would suddenly break out shouting or a person she greeted everyday had become increasingly belligerent until they physically attacked staff or another patron and needed to be banned from the library building. They hated to ban people who came in every day because the library was obviously a big part of their lives, but the library had a duty to safely serve the quiet customers as well.

The man-in-the-blue-shirt, as Jessamine began to think of him, stayed on the public computer all afternoon. Jessamine stood behind the desk and worked on the fliers for the coming months' book groups, crafts, and the summer reading program. He called her over a couple of times to show her the books he was finding and Jessamine said noncommittal approving things. Other patrons came and went; Jessamine chatted to them and checked out their books and watched as they sat at the computers to check their email or social media or apply for jobs. As the afternoon wore on, the man loosened his tie and finally took it off and slung it over the back of his chair.

When a family arrived for a scheduled genealogy assistance appointment, Jessamine stuck her head into Drusilla's office, where Drusilla and Tiffany were sitting and chatting with a table of books between them. "I have a genealogy assistance appointment. Someone will have to cover the desk."

Drusilla looked up slowly and gave a repressed sigh. "Get Stephanie to cover it. That's what she's here for."

"She's gone to her mother's doctor's appointment, remember?"

"Why did you let her do that?" Drusilla snapped.

"I didn't let her do anything." Jessamine frowned. "Aren't you the… Aren't you supposed…"

Drusilla interrupted. "Is she going to be back soon?"

Tiffany finished placing one sticker on the spine of a book. She rubbed it with a long, colored thumb nail and said, "Oh, Stephanie said her mother was sick. Something about the hospital. I told her it wasn't convenient, but she said it'd taken her months to get this appointment, and she couldn't change it. Didn't I tell you?"

"My genealogy assistance family is waiting." Jessamine turned and walked away, leaving Tiffany and Drusilla arguing about who would go out to the desk. The genealogy assistance appointment turned out to be long and complicated. An extended family had long-ago ancestors from the area of Bent River County, and they had been planning this trip for months and had driven in from several states. They had only a single appointment when they should have scheduled several, but since they had driven a long way and wouldn't be able to find another time to get the family together for weeks, Jessamine stayed to help them. It was more than an hour later she headed back to the desk, escorting the family to pay. She promised to look up more enticing historical leads and sat the paperwork on the desk. They cheerily wished her well and thanked her.

She drew a deep breath. She felt pleased about providing good customer service, but she was worn out. Tiffany was over by the computers, helping the man in the blue shirt. The light was out in Drusilla's office, which meant she must have gone home early again. Jessamine had heard her say that she did lots of work out of the library, so she could take flexible time. Jessamine knew that Drusilla had dumped a lot of Marilyn's administrative work onto Stephanie, so she couldn't picture what Drusilla actually did.

Jessamine helped a family check out a stack of picture books, then Tiffany came stalking over. It was the only word Jessamine could think of to describe Tiffany's furious waddle.

"I don't know why they let people like that in the library!" Tiffany sniffed.

"It is a public library. Everyone's allowed in. That's the whole point."

"Well, he shouldn't be here." Tiffany sniffed again and Jessamine wondered if Tiffany had sinus problems. "It's been awful with you gone so long."

Despite her irritation with Tiffany, Jessamine felt concerned. "What happened?"

"He's had me over there all the time you were gone. Help with this. Help with that. What took you so long anyway? How long does it take to do one stupid genealogy assistance appointment?"

Jessamine felt a pulse of exasperation. Tiffany had that effect on her a lot. "You'd know how long genealogy assistance appointments take if you finished the training and started doing them, like you were hired to."

"I'm too busy to do that." Tiffany tsked.

The man stared intently at the two women and waved his arm. "Excuse me, ladies!"

"You go and help him." Tiffany pursed her lips. "Now his credit card won't work." She paused and folded her arms. "I bet there's no money on it."

Jessamine needed to tidy up her genealogy assistance paperwork, but more urgently she needed to pee. She looked at Tiffany's pursed lips and folded arms and sighed. "I'll go and help him."

In the hours that he had been there, the man had grown more relaxed and more expansive. "Oh, thank you! You ladies are so helpful!"

"We're here to assist." Jessamine hoped it was a quick question so she could get to the bathroom.

The man pointed a bitten-short fingernail at the screen. "I put in my card number and it says, *Not Accepted*." He picked up a worn credit card and peered at the numbers as if his close attention would make them behave. His voice rose. "I don't know what to do!"

"Try typing the number in again. And..." Jessamine began.

"I already tried that! She told me to." He pointed to Tiffany at the desk. "She isn't nice!"

Jessamine looked over at the desk and saw Tiffany heading into the office.

The man thumped the keyboard. A large pop-up box appeared on the screen. "Now it's timed out!" *We're sorry, your transaction has expired. Please return to your cart to continue shopping.*

"Try clicking the grocery cart icon in the top right and put the payment in again," Jessamine suggested.

"I already did that! It won't work!" Sweat formed on the man's red forehead, and he rubbed his hands through his dark hair and made it stand on end.

She looked up from the computer and saw Tiffany wearing her coat, with her purse tucked under her arm. Jessamine felt a lurch in her chest and headed toward the desk. "What are you doing? You can't leave," she hissed.

The man looked between the faces of both women. His expression changed. His frown relaxed and he lowered his hands from the keyboard and laughed. "The line people, they send *me* the messages. I see that they haven't been sending *you* the right messages."

Tiffany walked toward the door.

Jessamine followed her a step. "Tiffany, I …um…" Jessamine looked toward the man, who gazed intently at them. He moved his head to follow their conversation and his slight smile kept breaking into a grin.

Jessamine gestured to Tiffany to move back to the office and lowered her voice. "Come here. We need to talk."

Tiffany pouted out her lips and tossed her head. Jessamine would have been amused at such a childish gesture at another time. Jessamine whispered, "Is Drusilla here? She's the director, she'll need to talk to the difficult…"

"No. She's already gone. And I'm going. You *know* I *must* get my girls to gymnastics. Constantina can't wait for…"

Jessamine's heart lurched again. "You can't leave…"

"Yoo hoo! I'm ready to check out!" Eunice from the craft and book groups waved cheerfully from the circulation desk. "Sorry if I'm too close to closing time. I lost track of time because I was lost in the books!" She laughed but stopped as she eyed their faces. She put the book on the counter. "Or I can check it out next time?"

"No, we're not closed yet." Jessamine looked toward the man. "We have things to finish."

The man waved, grinning openly now. Jessamine was sure he could read what was happening in the group of women and was enjoying their discomfort.

"I'm leaving." Tiffany sniffed. "I've got important things to do."

"But it's better if you stay." Jessamine eyed the man again, knowing he could hear everything she said. "Um, you're… ah…" While she was turned toward the man, she heard the door opening and in her peripheral vision she saw Tiffany's departing back.

Chapter 28

The lurch in Jessamine's chest turned into a lump; she wanted to kick something.

"Yoo-hoo!" the man called out, echoing Eunice. He pouted. "I need more help on this computer! I need librarian help!"

Jessamine hovered behind the desk, reluctant to walk back to the computers. "Check out my book, sweetie." Eunice winked. "Pass me a scrap of paper, sweetie. I need to write the author of a book before I forget." Eunice held out her hand, and Jessamine automatically handed her a scrap of paper and a pen. She wasn't sure what to do. The hair on her neck stood on end. Should she call the police if the man wouldn't leave? He hadn't done anything wrong yet, but she didn't want to be alone in the library with him.

Jessamine checked out Eunice's book and Eunice handed her a note. "Here, can you find this for me?"

In large block letters Eunice had written, *DON'T WORRY! I'M STAYING.*

"Oh!" Jessamine couldn't help a squeak of surprise. Eunice winked again. "I'll do some shelving for you." Eunice pointed behind Jessamine. "Let me have that full cart over there."

Eunice was two or three decades older than Jessamine and probably weighed half as much, so the older woman wouldn't be able to move the loaded cart. As a shelving volunteer, Eunice usually returned the books a few at a time, so she could chat with the staff. Jessamine thought it was fine if chatting was the reason Eunice volunteered—the library served its many customers in many ways. Jessamine leaned in to push the squeaking, wonky cart toward the computers.

"Sorry, we're closing soon." Jessamine spoke to the man from the other side of the cart. "You can come back tomorrow, and we can search again. We open at ten."

The man clutched the arms of his chair as if he was frightened that they were going to bodily remove him. He pulled his eyebrows down. "But they have my credit card number now!" His voice was rising again.

Eunice came closer, hugging a huge art book to her chest. "Well then! They can't do anything with your credit card."

"Why not?" He ran his hands through his hair again.

Eunice glanced at Jessamine. "Um, because the library's closing."

The line of computers all flashed a warning in a pop-up box: *The Library will close in ten minutes. The public computers will shut down in five minutes. Please save your work. All data entered is automatically cleared from the public computers every night.*

"See," said Jessamine. "It all disappears automatically."

"But what about the government?" The man looked confused again. "What about the messages?" He stared at the two women. "I can't leave if I don't have something to take with me." His voice rose. "I need the messages!"

"We're closing in a few minutes, so you can search again tomorrow." Jessamine wondered how long it would take her to get behind the circulation desk to call the police. The library had panic buttons under the desk, but nobody had known if they worked. Eventually Bobby, the Sheriff, had pushed them. They went nowhere.

Eunice stepped closer to the man and lowered the huge book. "This is a good book for you, sweetie." She placed the big art book on the desk. "It has black and white photos of statues all over Europe. They're just the sort of old-fashioned ones you'll need."

The man frowned and cocked his head as if he was listening to something in the distance. "You're not pulling my leg? This book will work?"

"Oh, yes. It has statues and churches. It's got gargoyles."

"Gargoyles?" The man looked interested and paged through the book.

Jessamine let out a long breath and felt her shoulders go down.

Eunice winked at her again and went on. "It's in the sale, sweetie, so you'll have to take it home. You can look at all the pictures there."

The man picked up the book and held it to his chest. It was a much-hugged book, Jessamine thought irrelevantly.

"And I can keep it?" The man looked at Eunice to ask. He eyed Jessamine sideways. "The library lady won't think I'm stealing it?"

"Oh, no," said Jessamine. "We have coupons for everyone to get a free book from the library book sale. They're for the summer reading program, but you can have one early. You can have one specially. A special coupon."

"A special coupon? Can I see?"

The women exchanged glances. "Of course you can, sweetie," Eunice said. "Pack up your papers and things, and we'll go up to the desk and get the coupon. The coupon's at the desk, isn't it Jessamine?"

"Yes, it's at the desk. I'll print a new one on yellow paper quickly for you."

The man frowned again. "I don't like yellow. I like blue paper better."

Jessamine let out her breath. "Blue paper. Of course!"

The two women went over to the desk and Jessamine quickly found the computer file of the coupon she had been working on and put blue paper in the printer.

The man placed his papers into neat piles. As he worked, he picked up papers and whispered to them. He gave Jessamine an unfriendly sideways glance when he caught her eye, so she quickly averted her gaze to the screens as she shut down the desk computers, locked away the cash box, and tidied away the day's detritus. After the papers were in piles to his satisfaction, the man pushed them into various worn envelopes and colored file folders. He stacked these up, then put them neatly into his backpack. He stowed his tie in his backpack and swung it onto his back. He came over to the desk, clutching the huge art book to his chest.

"Here you go." Jessamine handed him the half-page coupon on blue paper. He held a finger under every word with his lips moving as he sounded them out. "Entitles the Bearer to One Sale Book." The man got near the bottom and frowned again. "Hey! It says it's not valid until August. And it's only June. This won't work!"

Jessamine opened her mouth, but no thoughts came into her head.

"It's a special coupon, remember?" Eunice's voice was bright. "It's a special coupon for you!"

"Oh! Special for me?" The man's shoulders relaxed, and he looked at Eunice questioningly.

"Yes, sweetie. Just for you. But take it home."

"Yes. I'll take it home." The man folded the coupon over and over until it was a tiny blue square. He unbuttoned his shirt pocket, pushed the piece of paper in, and rebuttoned it. He eyed the women. "I'll need to keep that coupon safe."

"Yes, of course you do. You take it home." Eunice put out her hand in a patting gesture, without connecting with the man's arm.

The man headed toward the door. "I've got what I need now," he said, nodding his chin toward the art book clutched to his chest. He was disheveled compared with the dapper man who asked Jessamine for an interlibrary-loan hours earlier.

After he went out the door, Jessamine dashed over and turned the lock. She sagged against the frame and a flow of relief lightened her tight chest. Both women watched as the man walked across the parking lot with his mouth moving as he talked to himself. He drove away.

She turned to Eunice. "Thank you. Thank you. How did you do that? I was frightened."

Eunice's shoulders sagged.

"Are you alright? Can I get you a cup of tea?"

"I'll be okay after a short rest, sweetie." Eunice rolled her tiny shoulders. "I'll take you up on the offer of tea." Her eyes twinkled. "Since we're in your territory, we'll do the tea your way and have it hot."

Jessamine laughed. She could think of ordinary life again. "I better make sure the library's closed properly. I'll pay a quick visit. Then I'll make tea. That genealogy assistance paperwork will wait."

Jessamine rushed around the library, checking no one was still there. It was easy in this tiny library. She remembered in a big city library poking her nose into the bathrooms, and calling out, "The library's closed!" She would look under the toilet stall doors and push them open with a foot. She felt like she was in a bad movie, but once she found a runaway teen sitting hunched with her feet up on the toilet. Today she checked down the rows of silent bookshelves, the clicking of the heating system loud in the empty building.

Jessamine made sure all the computers and most of the lights were turned off. "You're technically not meant to be here when we're closed, but I won't tell if you don't."

Jessamine and Eunice sat away from the door, in a small ball of light, safe in the middle of the library contained in the large, dark county building, and sipped their hot tea. Eunice looked tiny perched on the edge of her chair.

"I worked in the state psychiatric hospital for years," Eunice told Jessamine. "Until I wasn't strong enough to do the hard physical work." Eunice looked down at her own legs barely reaching the floor from the office chair. "I was always little. Some of those big guys would force the patients. Or they would try to force the patients. Everyone knew who would win in a fight. I had to learn how to read them. I had to see what a patient was likely to do and lead him in the direction I wanted to go. I think that was kinder."

"Yes, you were kind." Jessamine felt teary after the stress of the afternoon. "I don't know what I would have done."

The man didn't return the next day. When Stephanie was shelving books, Drusilla emerged from her office and loomed over Jessamine. Jessamine sat nervously, hiding her hands under the folds of her full skirt. Her back felt stiff and her legs wanted to run, but Drusilla trapped her behind the desk.

"You need to do genealogy assistance appointments faster. Tiff… people are complaining that they take too long. I thought you understood that the money they bring in is important to the library. Our new building is finally going ahead after years. Can't you see the construction across the parking lot? I thought you could at least understand that?"

"What?" Sweat prickled in Jessamine's armpits. "Yes, that's exactly why everyone should do these appointments. To help the library."

"Everyone has their own duties that help the library. I'm the director, so I wouldn't expect you to understand…"

Jessamine had enough. "I thought that was what you hired Tiffany for!"

Drusilla gave Jessamine a slow look. As usual her face betrayed no emotions. "Tiffany is working with me. She's helping with the collection development."

Jessamine rolled her eyes. She hated being drawn into making the childish gesture like she was back in middle school. "We should all be doing collection development, the same as genealogy. In my experience—"

"We need someone younger and um… fresher to help with the collection."

Jessamine's resentment at being left with the difficult man in the blue shirt boiled over. "Tiffany left when we had a customer who wouldn't leave and was getting belligerent. We're not meant to be alone in the building. One of the book group ladies had to stay. And she's eighty if she's a day!"

"I told you to do that webinar about difficult customers. You should be able to deal with um… unusual people. I thought you'd at least know how to do that with all the experience you say you have? Tiffany is extremely busy with the collection development and helping me with special projects. Stephanie is supposed to help you."

Jessamine's chest and forehead tightened. "Stephanie took her mother to a doctor's appointment. Tiffany was meant to be here."

"Tiffany needed to leave. Her daughter had gymnastics. You should have timed it better to be kind and cover for your colleagues when they need help."

Jessamine narrowed her eyes. "You live close by, don't you? Shouldn't your cell phone number be behind the desk for emergencies? Next time we're short staffed, I'll call you to come and help." Jessamine relaxed her voice to voice to be purposely innocent. "Since you're the acting library director, isn't that the right thing to do?"

Drusilla's emotionless mask slipped. "No, you can't call me at home!"

"Why not? You called Stephanie at the hospital."

"I did not! You'd better get back to work, Jessamine."

Jessamine restrained herself from sighing again. "I am working." *Yes, Drusilla, this is what work looks like.* She almost said the last bit out loud.

Chapter 29

Jessamine stood at the library door and stretched. She gazed unseeingly at dark storm clouds piling up in the sky outside the hallway windows. She wasn't sure what to do. She told herself that she was passionate about her job. She yearned to create the welcoming place she could picture for her community of patrons. She delighted in sharing recommendations for books. She loved learning about people in the growing story time, crafts, and book group. And she was finishing her plans to start a knitting group and run a plant swap.

But she woke up every morning at three o'clock. In her dreams she traveled endlessly on winding roads that narrowed the farther she went. She couldn't find where she needed to be. She was a passenger in the back of a car, and the space shrank until her face was pressed against the upholstery, and she couldn't breathe. She told herself that these weren't nightmares. She told herself that she didn't have nightmares anymore. It was her psyche sorting things out.

No one was in the library or the county hallway, so she stretched her arms up and breathed deeply. *It's okay*, she told herself. *It'll all be okay.* She watched as a truck pulled into the parking lot and a hunched figure emerged. It wasn't until he came past the security guard that she recognized him. "Hi, Frank," she said and stood back from the library doors to let him past.

"Hey, Ms. Jessamine. How you doin'?" His eyes met Jessamine's briefly and slid away. He stood in front of her, arms hanging.

"I'm great," Jessamine replied. "Are you feeling okay?" His face looked gray. Every day he went briskly about his cleaning and fixing with a grin and a joke. Something was off. And Jessamine realized he'd come in the front door, not the employee entrance near his supplies like he usually did.

"Can I help you, Frank?"

He jumped, like she'd shouted. "Can I use one of them computers?"

"Of course, anyone can use a public computer."

"How do I get on it?"

"Do you have your library card?" Jessamine settled Frank on the computer. He obviously wasn't accustomed to using one. He looked at the mouse as he moved it and plucked the keys one by one as he typed. She left him to it and returned to the desk.

"Ms. Jessamine?" Jessamine looked up from the pamphlet she was making. "Sorry to disturb you." Frank looked miserable and she walked over to him.

"You're not disturbing me. You always help me. How can I assist you?"

"I need to find the job people."

"What job people?"

Frank squirmed and looked down. Jessamine could barely hear him. "You know, the unemployment people."

"You're applying for a new job?"

"Yes, but first I've got to apply for unemployment."

"Unemployment! Why?" Jessamine realized she wasn't being professional. "Yes, you go to the State Employment Commission."

Frank gazed at the computer screen, baffled.

"Would you like me to type it in for you?" Jessamine asked. Frank only nodded. He looked like he was going to cry. Jessamine didn't care if it was unprofessional, she *liked* Frank. "What happened? Why are you applying for unemployment?"

"They fired me." His voice cracked and he cleared his throat.

"Why?! What the…"

"They wanted me to keep moving that bear. And I dropped it."

"What do you mean?"

"It fell off the dolly." His voice rose. He cleared his throat. "Into a puddle. I laughed, but Joshua Oxford saw and he was furious."

"Why? It's a stuffed bear. Why would falling off the dolly hurt it?"

"The stitching came undone and papers flew everywhere."

"Papers? What do you mean?"

Frank clutched the arms of his chair. "All sorts of printed papers. And handwritten papers. I don't know why they were sticking papers in the bear. I've never seen Joshua so angry, and I've known him a long time. He yelled at me while I picked them up. I found papers behind a bush afterwards. I'm not giving them to him so he can yell at me again." Frank fumbled for a worn cardboard folder. "Here, I don't want to look at them. I know they're not good people. I'm not doing three hots and a cot for them!" He took a deep breath. "You take them, Ms. Jessamine. The papers say something about the library. You'll know what to do with them." The old man bowed his head.

Jessamine took the papers without looking at them. "Holy moley! And then what happened about your firing?"

"They said the bear would get moldy and they'd have to send it to the taxidermist for repairing and cleaning. And that I owed hundreds of dollars."

Jessamine's mouth opened. "Hundreds of dollars for that?"

"They said it was all about the bear," Frank scratched his head, "but I think it was about the papers. They said I 'hadn't lived up to professional expectations.' And I was 'insubordinate' about that stupid bear. I wouldn't pay their cleaning fee. They fired me. Can you help, Ms. Jessamine? I don't know how to do this." Frank gestured at the computer screen as if he expected the machine to fire him.

"Of course I can." Jessamine saw Josey and her usual four or five small children lining up to check out books. "Stephanie will be here later to cover the desk, and we'll help you with the job thing."

Jessamine helped Frank for over two hours. He didn't know how to fill out an online form or go between tabs. He typed slowly, but with perfect spelling. After he laboriously typed answers that didn't go anywhere, Jessamine reminded him to click in the box.

"I'm sorry Ms. Jessamine. I'm taking up all your time. I'll be okay."

"No, I'm here to help. This is what we do."

When Stephanie was free from the desk, she came over. "How ya doing, Frank?" she asked. "My grandmother was asking after your mother. Is she out of the hospital yet?"

Jessamine whispered to Stephanie what had happened to Frank.

Stephanie was indignant. "They can't do that!" She settled in a chair next to Frank. "We'll work this out. What should we start with? Have you got a lawyer?"

"What do I need a lawyer for?" Frank asked.

Stephanie exchanged a look with Jessamine. "Believe me, you need a lawyer. Look what they did to Marilyn."

"I'll text Marilyn and get the name of her lawyer." Jessamine grabbed her phone.

A sharp voice interrupted them. "What are you doing?" Tiffany stood behind them with her hands on her hips.

"We're helping Frank."

"You've got work to do."

"This is work. Helping patrons on the public computers is part of our job."

Tiffany tapped the pointy toe of her glittery shoe. "You can't spend so long helping one customer. You've got books to check in and shelve."

Jessamine narrowed her eyes. "Why don't you shelve the books, Tiffany?"

Tiffany sniffed, but after looking at all three of them down her nose, she trotted to the office.

"I don't want to get you ladies into trouble." Frank looked worried. "I can finish here."

"Don't worry, Frank. She's not our boss."

Stephanie put her own hands on her hips. "No. Miss Prissy is not our boss. She can always help check out books if she thinks it's so desperately busy."

"Anyway, Frank." Jessamine looked around. "I don't think Drusilla is here."

"Yes, she is." Stephanie snorted with laughter. "I saw her lurking in the back room and peering at us through the blinds again. She sent her lackey out to tell us off."

Jessamine tried to keep her eyes on Frank's screen and not peek toward the blinds twitching on the internal window, but she couldn't help it and turned. Frank also cast quick glances toward Drusilla's office. Fingers poked between the blind slats, then abruptly disappeared. The three of them caught each other's eyes and burst into giggles.

Frank clicked send and sat back, looking exhausted. "Thank you. I feel like I can move ahead now." He packed up. "I'll find the info I need and ask about references, and I'll be back to work on my resume."

As Jessamine worked at the desk that afternoon, she laughed when she thought about the fingers poking between the blinds. Having the internal window behind her gave her a vulnerable feeling; she didn't like being watched. Being able to laugh about it with Stephanie and Frank put it in perspective.

After a genealogy assistance appointment, Jessamine returned to the desk and saw Stephanie grinning and hopping from foot to foot. "We've gotten end of year spend-now-or-you-lose-it money from the state! Drusilla said I can choose items to order."

"That sounds promising." Jessamine grinned back. "How does it work?"

"They've got money left in the budget at the state level, so they're dividing it up between public libraries. The problem is, we have to spend it really quickly."

"We can spend it!" Jessamine's head whirled with visions of books to buy. "Think of the subjects we can replace. I can't believe that everything is donated or grant funded."

"We can replace the toddlers' puzzles." Stephanie jiggled on the spot.

"The ones with the chew marks and missing pieces."

"How much are we getting?" Jessamine laughed. "I've got dollar signs in my eyes like a cartoon character."

"I don't know exactly." Stephanie tapped a pen on the desk. "In the thousands."

"Wow! How do we order?"

"Drusilla's the only one with the authority to spend money. But we can find things the library needs." Stephanie patted the desktop computer with duct tape holding down a button. "We sure can do with new public computers."

"Let's search now." Before Jessamine could open the website of a book vendor, Tiffany appeared with a stapled pile of papers for each of them.

"Is it more things to buy?" Stephanie asked.

"No." Tiffany smirked. "You have to sign this to be *official* employees like I am."

The paperwork contained library employee policies for them to sign, full of obvious rules like not selling drugs at work. Jessamine read the boring words until her eyes glazed. They both signed quickly then returned to searching for new books and library materials. They exchanged comments: "I can't believe they're asking that much," and "I bet we can get a discount for a whole set."

They were still searching when Drusilla's fancy SUV backed out of the prime parking space in front of the library. The other staff were expected to park farther away, to save the best parking spots for the public, but Drusilla didn't follow her own rules. It made it easy to see when she went home. The atmosphere lightened every time she left.

"We need more books about art." Stephanie hopped from foot to foot. "And the DVDs desperately need updating. We haven't got a TV series that's less than twenty years old. So many people around here can't stream movies with our bad internet. They love the DVDs."

Jessamine and Stephanie worked on their lists of essential materials. They couldn't keep their excitement in and told their patrons about the windfall, so everyone gave lots of suggestions.

When Jessamine arrived at work the following day, Stephanie was banging on her keyboard. Before Jessamine said anything, Stephanie thumped the computer with her fist and exclaimed, "Crappy equipment in this crappy library in this crappy county!"

"What's wrong?" In the months they had worked together, Jessamine had seen Stephanie excited, but Stephanie had never raised her voice.

"This stupid keyboard doesn't work." Stephanie jabbed the keyboard rapidly with one finger. "I can't type *p*." She leaned over and pulled the electric plug out of the wall. "That's really bad for it, but I don't care! I guess I'll never be able to type *p* again."

"What's going on?"

"We have to put up with these crappy computers. Apparently forever. Did you hear what Drusilla did now?"

"What? I've never seen you look so angry! Would you like a cup of tea?"

"Wait on the tea. Let me tell you this." Stephanie took a deep breath. "She spent the state money on a desk."

"Huh?"

"You heard right. All the money for the new books and the new computers." Stephanie gritted her teeth. "On. A. Desk."

"How could a desk cost that much? We've got plenty of desks and tables, even if they're a bit battered."

Stephanie's face was red. "Oh, I'm too furious to talk!" She clenched her fists in front of her chest and shook them. "A fancy-schmancy shiny rosewood desk set with a bookcase and a credenza for her office! I'm spitting."

"I don't understand. Why did she think she needed a desk?"

"I don't know. Why did she think she should spend library money—taxpayer money—on building a new spying office? It looks ridiculous and it serves no purpose. But it was peanuts compared to this."

"She spent *all* the state money?" Jessamine frowned in confusion and growing anger. "How much is left for books and computers?"

"None! Even the Library Committee is annoyed about this, and I thought she could do no wrong in their eyes. But they're backing her up."

"Can't she send the desk back?"

"No. It's too late. The money had to be spent fast before the end of the fiscal year, so it's done. And she wants me to stay late to take the delivery."

"I hope you told her no?"

Stephanie grinned wickedly. "I did! I finally did! I told her I was scheduled until five and I'm a wage employee. I told her that they'd better pay me time and a half if she's making me work more than eight hours today. I said that since they keep telling us we're at-will employees, we're not *obliged* to work here either. I told her that I could make more money working in fast food and that they wouldn't make me do illegal overtime."

"You didn't!" Jessamine laughed. "What did she say?"

"She said 'um ar'. You know how she doesn't like to be held down to anything. And she hates to spend any library money on anything except her. I'm leaving at five o'clock on the dot!"

"Good on you! And she's the one who's salaried. If anyone should stay after hours, it's her. She got the director's job that she wanted. She should do *something* for it!"

Chapter 30

"*What's up with her?*" Surrounded by her gaggle of small children, Josey piled a stack of picture books on the circulation desk. "And I'll try these for me." She added half a dozen dystopian and apocalyptic teen books.

"How are you, Josey?" Jessamine smiled at the young woman then leaned toward the children. "Who wants a bookmark?" She handed the eldest child a decorated jar. The children spread the bookmarks across the low counter and gravely sorted through them. The eldest held up samples. "Do you want a cat or a tractor?"

Jessamine turned back to Josey. "What's up with who?"

"Drusilla. She walked by without answering when I said 'Hello.'"

"I think she…" Jessamine paused and considered what might be considered professional. "Things are challeng… um, different with Marilyn gone."

"Yeah, this place has had its ups and downs." Josey sighed. "I need our library visits. Now I'm reading Larsen those books about bears like you suggested, he's excited about going into the children's section." She patted the toddler's head. "He pokes his tongue at the bear, but we're making progress."

"We're always glad to see you and your little ones. We couldn't get the bear moved out. Marilyn tried and look where… And we've been told in no uncertain terms that we're not allowed to dress it anymore. But…" Jessamine paused again and decided she could reveal this to Josey. "Stephanie and I have ideas about how to get rid of it."

"I'll sure be glad if it gets moved." Josey shook her head slowly as if contemplating the mysteries of the world.

"This is a good series," Jessamine said as she checked out Mike Mullin's *Ashfall* series about survival after a super-volcanic eruption.

"I didn't think I had time to read for me, but it helps me sleep if I read before bed. It's my treat after all the kids are settled. I know it's silly." Josey laughed. "These disastrous, end-of-the-world books make me feel better. At least my life's not as bad as that!"

"I enjoy them, too." Jessamine smiled back. "Maybe that's why they're so popular. If we have the health and leisure to read it, then our lives aren't as bad as the characters' lives."

"Say 'thank you' for the bookmarks, kids." Josey picked up a complaining toddler. "You all take care now."

After Josey left, Drusilla emerged from her office. "You need to stop talking to customers."

"What?" Jessamine looked at her blankly. "I have to talk to people, or I can't serve them."

Drusilla rolled her eyes, her unreadable poker face gone. "You're spending too long prattling with them."

Jessamine drew in a breath. "Of course we chat. We talk about the books and the programs. This is a library."

"We're down a staff member because Marilyn quit. I'm too busy for you to gossip. I thought you'd realize that since you're so experienced?"

Jessamine opened her mouth to say sharply Marilyn didn't quit. And then ask how they were down a staff member since Drusilla had hired Tiffany. Was Drusilla admitting that Tiffany was useless? "Okay," Jessamine replied. She had no intention of changing the way she talked to library patrons, but she wasn't going to be sucked into Drusilla's game.

"And here." Drusilla handed Jessamine a sealed envelope. "This is from the Library Committee. Mr. Oxford asked me to give it to you."

"What is it?" Jessamine took the envelope.

"I don't know." Drusilla's face melted into a smirk. "I'm just the messenger. It's officially from the Library Committee." Drusilla headed back to her office.

Knowing that Drusilla had been watching her and Josey through the tightly shut blinds made Jessamine's back prickle, but she had no choice except to keep working at the desk. She opened the envelope.

"Up to and including termination." The words sprang off the page. Jessamine tossed the letter on the desk as if the paper had burnt her, her heart pounding. When she glanced toward the internal window, the blind twitched. Drusilla was watching her. Jessamine rammed the envelope in her pocket, then pushed a cart of books between the shelves. Surrounded by the 500s, science, on one side and the 700s, art, on the other, she looked around to see if she was alone and felt idiotic, then pulled out the envelope and finished reading the enclosed letter.

"You have failed to comply with the rules as set forth in the Staff Procedures Guide by speaking to the County Council. You have brought disrepute on the library and caused a hostile work environment by your thoughtless actions of not following the chain of command and… You are requested to come to a meeting with the Library Committee on Wednesday at 9 a.m. in county meeting room two."

Jessamine had never had words like this aimed at her. For the rest of the day, she forced herself to look Drusilla in the eye and speak to her as if nothing had happened. She shuffled through her daily library duties. She felt perched on the ceiling, looking down at her own meaningless movements.

Sheriff Bobby came in to check out his weekly books about gardens and small engine repair. Jessamine suggested mysteries or thrillers, and he replied, "I get enough of that in real life. I want my reading to be different."

Eunice, Kelly, and Jonquil, regulars at Jessamine's craft programs, came in to look at books about knitting. Their plans with Jessamine to start a knitting and crocheting group at the library were nearing fruition.

Jessamine didn't know what to do about the letter. Her first impulse was to talk to Marilyn and Stephanie. Marilyn hadn't found another job and was fighting the Library Committee to get the money she was owed. Jessamine invited her over for a cup of tea and Marilyn let it slip that she was worried about being able to pay her mortgage. Jessamine couldn't disturb her.

Jessamine opened her mouth several times to tell Stephanie. After all, Stephanie knew everyone in the county and could spin a positive light on almost anything. Jessamine told herself that she didn't want to upset the new uneasy equilibrium. Or she was distracted by Stephanie complaining loudly about her sister not helping with their mother. She typed texts and emails to her children about it, then deleted them without pushing send. It took a few days for Jessamine to realize that she was ashamed—ashamed of having done something so wrong that she had been summoned to the principal's office to be told off. So she stayed quiet.

Jessamine longed to nurture the struggling Bent River County Public Library, but she needed a job to support herself in her railway station. She continued to search for local jobs. She found great librarian job listings, but when she searched online maps, they were an hour and a half drive each way. She nervously counted down the days until the meeting.

Chapter 31

At the appointed time, Jessamine found the meeting room in the county complex. Joshua Oxford stood by the door and rubbed his hands together, causing a dry, slightly scaly scratching sound. He stepped closer, towering over her. "Ah, Jessamine. Sit there."

Jessamine sat at a battered conference table facing a row of bright windows and pleated her skirt. She put her hands on the table and told them to behave themselves.

Joshua turned his head quickly and craned down the hallway. Jessamine was reminded irresistibly of a heron about to stab its beak into an unsuspecting fish.

Kathryn and Drusilla came along the hallway, laughing together. They sat in front of the glaring windows, across from Jessamine.

Casey Chilton from the Library Committee hurried into the room. "I hope I'm not late? I had trouble getting away from work."

"We're all busy, educated, professionals, Casey. Thank you for taking the time to come. We'll get started." Joshua stopped rubbing his hands together and leaned forward to look over his glasses. Jessamine's feeling of a predator stalking its prey grew stronger.

"As the chair of the Library Committee, I have been asked to meet with you today to talk about a serious situation that has arisen as a result of you talking to the County Council."

He paused, so Jessamine said, "Okay." She understood why Drusilla was there; she was Jessamine's boss. But why was Kathryn there? Jessamine gave Kathryn a puzzled look.

Joshua caught her look and said cheerfully, "Kathryn has kindly agreed to be here. She was an HR professional at a shoe store for many years. And Casey was an assistant manager at that exceptionally prestigious men's clothing store… what's it called? With the branch in New York City. They're particularly experienced with this sort of thing and they'll get us going forward from the, um, difficulties that Jessamine has created." He beamed around the table. Now he looked like a happy predator. The hairs on the back of Jessamine's neck prickled.

Kathryn looked at the papers in her hand. "You made some statements." She paused.

"Yes?" Jessamine wasn't sure where this was going.

Casey spoke, and everyone turned toward her. "Yes, you know you went against the rules for staff. It's laid out in the *Staff Procedures Guide*."

"What's where?" Jessamine couldn't follow.

"In the *Staff Procedures Guide*." Joshua tapped his long finger on a pile of papers. "It says that staff are not allowed to speak directly to outside bodies on behalf of the library without permission of the library director."

Jessamine clenched her fists under the table to overcome her urge to run out of the room. "You mean the guide thingy we signed a few days ago?"

Joshua tapped the papers again and craned his long neck forward. "It's *all* in there."

"I signed it days ago and the County Council meeting was weeks ago," Jessamine struggled to explain.

"That's not important. Your statements have created a very uncomfortable environment." Kathryn pursed her lips.

"I don't know what you mean." Jessamine squinted at them.

"You should have come to the Library Committee." Casey stretched her lips across her teeth. Jessamine couldn't describe it as a smile.

Jessamine's nails dug into her palms. "I couldn't go to the Library Committee. The Library Committee just fired Marilyn."

"Marilyn's not relevant." Joshua pressed his fingertips together and looked at Jessamine over them. "I don't know how an old English woman in her sixties thinks she's *allowed* to say things about our county."

"What?" Jessamine put her head on the side. "I don't suppose anyone living in England could know much about Bent River County. It's not famous."

Kathryn pointed at Jessamine's chest. "So, *you* shouldn't say things!"

"Why not? I live here and I work here." Jessamine frowned, trying to follow. "You're calling me old? That I'm not young and fresh?"

"You must listen!" Joshua snapped. "I just said what I mean! No English woman gets to make comments about us. We've been doing fine for a long time."

Jessamine puffed out through her nose. "I don't get what this has to do with me."

"Since you're an English woman…"

Jessamine screwed up her nose. "No, I'm not."

Casey shook her head, as if at a slow child. "Yes, you are! You have that accent."

"Yes, I have an accent. But what's that got to do with anything? I'm not English."

"Yes, you are!" Joshua narrowed his eyes. "Everyone refers to you as that English woman with the short hair in the library."

"They do?" Jessamine shrugged. "How odd. I've been to England. In fact, I once had a work permit there in the 1990s. I loved the double-decker buses in London. I used to ride around on them. But I didn't work there long…"

"What are you talking about? What we're saying is an outsider like you from England can't—"

"I'm not from England! I don't get it. Are you trying to say there's something wrong with my national origin?" Jessamine narrowed her eyes. "It's actually illegal to…"

Casey leaned forward and spoke directly into Jessamine's face. "Here's the thing with human resources issues." Jessamine was so much shorter than Casey that she felt as if she were back at kindergarten. *My feet actually don't reach the floor on this chair,* she thought irrelevantly. Casey went on. "I'm sure that those of us who have worked in the human resources field know what we're talking about." Casey laughed to the other three people in front of the window, and they chortled back. "We who *know* human resources, know that decisions made regarding people's employment cannot be discussed."

Jessamine swallowed. She put her hands on her lap to hide their trembling. She was on quicksand, and she didn't know how she got here. She opened her mouth. She didn't know what would come out. "That makes no sense. I don't understand how…"

Casey continued as if Jessamine had not spoken. "*And* you not only told your *stories* to people inside the library, but made it public to County Council, who provides funds for the library. How would you feel about that? We're in this cultural situation now that there's tension on the team. Drusilla is upset."

Jessamine felt that the quicksand was soon to close over her head. "But none of it would have happened if the Library Committee hadn't…"

Casey spoke over Jessamine again. "We're not talking about any of that." She cleared her throat and picked up a pile of papers and tapped their edges. "Change is hard." She leaned forward and showed her teeth. "Because of your thoughtless actions, you ruined the library."

Jessamine considered herself a nonviolent person, so she was astonished at the restraint it took to dampen her urge to leap up and slap the Library Committee member. She said nothing.

"The Library Committee only meets once a quarter, four times a year," Kathryn said.

Jessamine frowned. Were they sitting in front of her, wielding their authority over her like a big stick and trying to claim that they didn't control the county because they only met a few times a year? "Yes," Jessamine tried, "but the Library Committee has a lot of power."

The Library Committee members exchanged looks. Casey leaned forward. "You know power is a very big word."

"A big word?" Jessamine didn't know if she'd followed Alice through the looking glass. "It has two syllables."

"Don't be stupid!"

"You know what she means!" The two exclamations whipped out so close on top of each other that Jessamine didn't know where they came from. Jessamine stared at the surface of the table. Suddenly the swirls in the pattern were the most important thing in the universe. She took a breath in. She remembered going to a counselor years ago. The sessions hadn't saved her marriage, but they had taught her many things that she continued to digest. One of the things was that she suddenly found trivial things, the pen or the curtains or the pattern on the table, compellingly interesting if the conversation or the situation became too intense or too frightening. It was why she was staring at the table. It was called dissociation. Jessamine hadn't wanted to believe that she dissociated—she still didn't. It sounded crazy. But if she stepped away from her own reactions and tried to view herself dispassionately (and who can do that?), she could see that she was doing it now. She wanted to run from the room, but it wouldn't be the action of a grown woman.

Joshua sat back. "So, rather than thinking about this as a power structure, you must think about it as a team. Drusilla now leads your team."

"We *were* a great team with Marilyn. We achieved so much."

"Success isn't everything." Kathryn shook her head. "We keep telling you Marilyn doesn't matter. What I'm saying is that in your day-to-day work, the staff is empowered to change the environment."

The women looked toward Joshua. "Yes, empowered," he said. He leaned forward and narrowed his eyes. "And if you want to be frank about it, the library staff doesn't have control over the Library Committee. Correct?"

Jessamine felt like she was spinning. Hadn't he said the direct opposite a moment ago? "Yes. No." Jessamine stuttered. "Like I said, the Library Committee has power over the staff." Jessamine took a deep breath. "Except through our elected representatives. Aren't you appointed? We can vote and talk to our elected representatives."

"You can vote however you like." Joshua smirked. "But," he narrowed his eyes again, "you must not talk to the elected representatives."

Casey gave him a startled look. She went on, "The one thing that I would recommend, like my colleagues, is that you are empowered to create the environment here that you want. You should look at it as a new day in the library."

Jessamine sighed.

Casey leaned forward again. "You know, what I'm hearing you say is that you have built up an awful lot of hurt and um…"

Jessamine snorted. Even in this situation, she could hear how manipulative it was for Casey to pretend to be concerned about her feelings.

Casey pursed her lips and drew her eyebrows together. "I don't know what you'd call it? I keep thinking of the person who walks around with a knapsack on their back and every time something happens that doesn't, you know, they find *incongruent*, they throw it in their knapsack. And they throw more in their knapsack and pretty soon their knapsack is full of all these wrongs."

Jessamine knew this wasn't fair, but with the cold stares of four people on her, couldn't articulate it. "Doesn't that also apply to Drusilla then?" she said tentatively. She paused. "Since she feels upset like you said?"

Casey clicked her tongue. "No, I'm talking about this conversation that we have had now for a half an hour. What I am hearing you say…"

Jessamine knew this wasn't right. "I work hard in the library. I built up the programs from nothing." Jessamine could feel her teeth grinding together. "The Library Committee unjustly fired one of the staff for no reason. And all the nonsense about the bear. I don't understand it."

Joshua tapped the side of his papers on the table. The four women immediately looked at him. "This has come up multiple times, as you know. How to move beyond this."

Jessamine frowned. It was like they had a convoluted plastic puzzle made out of sticks and rings that she could almost solve, then they turned it upside-down and the parts she thought she understood were gone. "What's come up multiple times? Why is 'upset' different from 'carrying a knapsack'?" She was genuinely puzzled by this question.

"Jessamine." Kathryn stretched her lips over her teeth again in a poor imitation of a smile. "At the end of the day, Jessamine, we need to move forward. I have good faith that our committee that is presiding over this organization would not take an action that wasn't warranted. I don't think you are fully considering the stakeholders in Bent River County. There are important people relying on our… I mean, we have modalities that we must synergize to move the organization forward."

"What?" Jessamine frowned. She knew Kathryn was speaking English, but the words conveyed no meaning. She looked around; she didn't know where they'd attack from next.

"Jessamine, what we're saying is that you have a problem with communication." Kathryn looked up at Joshua for confirmation.

He lowered his glasses with his hand. "Numerous people have said your communication leaves a lot to be desired."

Jessamine screwed up her eyebrows, trying to work out this new attack. "You mean my accent? That's what you said earlier."

Joshua picked up his polo mallet and leaned forward. "This meeting is off track. I have important things to do." His voice came out deeper and louder. "Jessamine Sibley. You will do better in the future. You will come to the Library Committee with your petty concerns. You will not go further up the chain of command if you feel slighted." He narrowed his eyes and tapped the head of the polo mallet on the table. "You will work diligently to further the aims of my… of Bent River County!"

The room sat silent for a heartbeat.

He stood up straight and his voice lashed out at Jessamine. "Do you agree?"

Jessamine jumped. "Yes," she stammered. Her breath was gone, and she could barely hear her own words.

"What?" Joshua's eyes narrowed, and his voice was spiky and forceful. "I can't hear you."

Jessamine opened her mouth and croaked. She swallowed and licked her lips. "Yes."

"Yes, what?"

"Yes, I heard you."

"Will you do better in the future?"

"Yes."

"Yes, what!" This time the words cracked like a whip. Jessamine flinched and hated herself for it.

"Yes, I'll do better in the future."

"Tell everyone what you'll do!"

Jessamine pulled her shoulders forward and drew her arms across her chest to protect herself. But it was too late, the words were inside her.

"I told you to tell everyone what you're going to do in the future!" Like a club, Joshua's words beat on Jessamine's psyche. She felt herself shrinking into a small, lifeless rock, tight and enclosed. "Look up and tell them!"

Jessamine looked up at the women silhouetted against the bright windows. She was glad she couldn't see their faces properly. "I'll do better." She felt deeply ashamed of existing.

"Since you said you'll do better, you can go back to work." Joshua's lip curled. He picked up his papers and tapped the ends of them on the table, as if to neaten them, then gathered up his polo mallet and left.

Jessamine looked up. The three women's faces were hard to see against the bright window, but for a moment Jessamine thought she saw shock on their faces "I'm not sure he can… I mean, is it perfectly legal to…" Drusilla started. She looked at Jessamine, then looked away and shrugged.

Jessamine slunk to the circulation desk and pulled the full library cart close behind her. She felt the ridiculousness of her actions, but she couldn't help it: it felt like a wall of books protecting her in the castle of the desk. She imagined a moat full of crocodiles appearing across the tattered library carpet. The crocodiles would eat Joshua or Drusilla if they came too close. Jessamine smiled at the childish fantasy, then was abruptly overcome by an urge to cry. She thought about going home. But that would be a victory for them. That was what they wanted. She sagged against the desk and became hollow. She contained no thoughts. She picked up a pen as if the stained and pitted plastic surface was inscribed with the answers to the questions she didn't know how to ask.

Jessamine sucked in a deep breath. She was dissociating again. She stood up straight and pushed her shoulders back.

"No," Jessamine said out loud. "No, I won't!" she added more forcefully. A library patron looked at her from the public computers. Jessamine smiled at the patron and kept saying *No!* in her head.

They had ambushed her with overwhelming numbers. They had attacked her from several angles at once. She hadn't known what the meeting would be about. She could fight back, and she *would* fight back. She took another deep breath. She remembered the county attorney from her first day. He stood up to Kathryn when they were moving the bear into the foyer. He suggested the name for the bear and came in regularly to check out books. She could talk to him. She looked up his official phone number, called, and left a message. She went through the rest of the day's tasks buoyed by the thought that she knew she had the facts on her side, and surely she had the law on her side.

Chapter 32

Lost and late, Jessamine needed to find the meeting. She scurried down corridors and tiptoed at scratched windows on the doors into classrooms. In the first two rooms, people turned featureless faces toward her. The next three rooms were empty except for hastily pushed back chairs, bags and jackets tossed in disarray. The feeling swelled. She was too late. She had to find it.

Elevator doors loomed in front of her and relief bubbled up. *I'll find it here*, she thought. The elevator doors slid open and as she stepped in, a tall figure in a long coat turned around. It was Drusilla. Already much taller than Jessamine, Drusilla came forward, expanding as she came. At the same time the elevator shrank. The figure approached and the tall woman's face became smooth with no features, then morphed into Joshua's face. The roof and corners of the elevator pressed on Jessamine's head. From all directions Joshua crammed her smaller. She was about to be crushed. Jessamine heard herself make a strangled squawk as she woke up.

The feeling of pressure remained on her body. She lay flat on her back in bed with pearly moonlight creeping around the edges of the curtains, but the dream reverberated round the room.

It had taken Jessamine a long time in her adulthood to recognize this feeling as fear. Her body felt tight and still, but no individual parts existed. She couldn't feel a separate toe or a single ear. She lay rigid in her bed. Lying motionless was the only safe thing to do. Gradually her breathing slowed and her heart rate settled. She could feel the blankets on her and became aware that she needed to pee. She pushed the blankets off and headed to the bathroom, patting the whining dog on the way. In the bathroom, the fear clung to her sticky like cobwebs and dug into her flesh like the vines. The dream was vivid and fresh; it felt more like the real world than the solid porcelain, water, and scratchy towel. She had come to love being alone in her house in the dark forest at night, and she hated this clogging fear and feeling of helplessness.

Jessamine began to shiver. Her collar was sweaty—no wonder she was getting cold. She scurried back to bed, while a mocking voice from somewhere outside her laughed and belittled her for running and being scared of Drusilla and Joshua. She turned over her pillow to get away from the damp patch on her neck and slipped under the blankets. She usually hated having her face covered, but she pulled the blankets over her head with shaking hands. Slowly her shivering subsided as the warmth returned to her body. The blankets felt like safety from danger, although her mocking thoughts knew the flimsy cloth offered no protection against anything truly dangerous.

She pulled the blankets down off her face to breathe the refreshing night air. As the fear ebbed out of her body, she felt her limbs come back to her. Her pajamas pinched her leg where they were rucked up from jumping so quickly into bed. The seam on one of her socks twisted underneath her foot. She checked the time on her phone, although it barely felt safe to let a part of her out from under the blankets. Three-thirty. Still the middle of the night. The voices from the meeting the previous afternoon played in her head: angry, loud, condescending, and dismissive. She rolled over but felt too exposed. She rolled back and saw another angry face behind her eyelids.

Jessamine couldn't bear it, so she thought of flowers. She imagined the pictures on the seed packets and in the gardening books she'd borrowed from the library. The bright natural colors filled her inner vision. She pictured the trays of dirt she'd prepared in the greenhouse and how the tiny sprouts were pushing through the soil. How a seed given the right conditions will undergo a miraculous transformation from an inert blob into a living plant. Jessamine drifted off to sleep.

She woke with her eyes and mouth feeling sticky and heavy. The dog was whining. Her thoughts moved sluggishly to consider that he probably needed to be let out. "Wait puppy," she said groggily. She pushed herself out of bed and led the prancing animal to the door. She stood there, taking in the green forest and sparkling blue sky. The sleep fog in her brain didn't let the world become quite in focus yet, but there was something odd about the sun. It wasn't in the right place. Jessamine yelped. "It's too high! What's the time? I'm late!"

She ran and grabbed her phone. It was after eight thirty. She might be able to make it to work by nine o'clock if she skipped breakfast and zipped through showering. But she had to look after the animals. She quickly put food down for the dog and cat and went to let the hens into their run.

Her yellow Buff Orpington hen, Buffy the Worm Slayer, was lying under the perch, strangely long, with her scaled yellow legs sticking straight out below her. Jessamine nudged the hen with her foot. The bird was stiff and quite dead. The other hens rushed out to their food in the run, completely unconcerned. Jessamine heard a strange sound come out of herself. She had as little control over it as she'd had last night during the nightmare. She turned from the hen and left the chicken coop. She began to sob. As she staggered to the house, the only thought she had was that she had to get to work.

She sobbed all through her quick pits-and-bits wash, and feeling half-blind, she grabbed the first clothes she came across in her closet. She was still sobbing as she turned on her car. "Ping, ping, ping," it announced imperially. The tiny gas pump icon blinked, *low gas*. She put her head down on the steering wheel. She knew it was only a small thing, and she had planned to fill it on the way home last night, but it felt like an overwhelming problem.

She scrubbed her eyes angrily so she could see, but the tears wouldn't stop. She had to get to work, but she'd look like an idiot. They were sure to notice her red eyes. Since it was the day after the up-until-termination meeting, she had to go to work to show herself and them she wasn't scared.

If she stopped to buy gas, she would be late. It couldn't be helped. She pulled into the gas station on the corner. Thankfully the teen assistant came out to fill her car. He wasn't usually chatty and was incurious about the goings-on of old people, so she could sneak away quickly. Most mornings she enjoyed her morning waves and smiles to the coffee-drinking men as she had learned their connections within Bent River County, but not this morning.

Jessamine was about to drive away when a knock on her passenger window made her jump and slam her foot on her brake. She rolled down her window, and Frank leaned in and held up a paper cup of steaming liquid.

"Come over here and sit with us for a spell," he said. "You look like you need a break."

"I can't! I've got to get to work!" To her horror, fresh tears poured down her face.

"They'll cope without you for a few hours. And you don't look like you're in any fit state for work today." Frank waved the cup enticingly.

Jessamine gripped the steering wheel and tried to think straight. What more could they do to her if she didn't show up at work? And Frank's invitation was warmly meant. She relaxed her shoulders. "Thank you. I'll stop for a drink."

"We made tea." Frank smiled. "Just for you."

She parked next to several dented pickup trucks at the edge of the broken concrete. She got out and hesitated under the gaze of the cup-clutching old men sitting on benches made of planks across concrete blocks. Frank patted the bench next to him and the men shuffled along. "Come and sit here."

As Jessamine sat, Frank handed her a paper cup. "See, it's hot tea. I knew you liked hot tea."

She held the textured paper cup with both hands and rubbed it with a fingertip. She had watched this scene from her car many times, but didn't know she could be part of it. She brought the tea up to her face and breathed in the steam. Her hands were shaking, nearly spilling the drink, but the warmth and dark, sharp smell comforted her.

"How are you doing, Ms. Jessamine?" Frank asked.

"I've been having nightmares," Jessamine blurted out. She laughed at herself and caught back a sob.

"You don't have to be ashamed of having nightmares." Frank looked straight at Jessamine. "It's just your body's way of saying something ain't right."

"I know things aren't right," Jessamine wailed, "but I don't know what to do about it!"

Frank paused. "Weeell," he said slowly. "I know what it's like to work for this county. What I like to say at a time like this is, 'Not my circus. Not my squirrels.'"

A smile formed on her face, despite herself. She sipped her tea. The tea bag was stale and it had steeped too long in a sagging paper cup, but it was a gift, and she felt the warmth of it going down as a benediction that spread throughout her body.

They both followed the flight of a hawk swooping past the tops of the pine trees. "Sometimes you've just got to turn your back on it," Frank said. "It's hard, but you've got to do what is best for you right now. Otherwise, you'd drive yourself crazy. It's their circus, but you don't have to be one of their squirrels."

"Circus is about right." Jessamine sat up straighter.

"Yep," said one of the old men. "I can picture *us* as the little squirrels in *their* circus. How the poohbahs want us to be!"

"You're right," said another of the men, looking up. "They want us dressed in tiny, embroidered satin vests with miniature tambourines. They want to us put on a show for Joshua Oxford."

Jessamine laughed. "Poohbahs! They want us to call them 'elites' but that's not the right word, because elite means you're good at something."

"That's for sure." Frank grinned over his worn travel coffee mug.

Jessamine returned his grin. "It's about time their little squirrels fight back." Jessamine made an exaggerated throwing gesture, spilling her tea. "We'll throw away our tambourines," she stomped her foot, "and step through their skins."

"Yes! We're not their squirrels!" said one of the other old men.

He put out his hand to shake. Jessamine took it and felt warmed by his firm grip. "I hope things go well for you," he said. "Things aren't easy in this county."

Another man stared into his cup. "My daddy always told me I should leave this county. That the Oxfords and their kind took everything and only left the poisoned bits for everyone else." He lifted his head and his face was serious, but crinkles showed around his dancing eyes. "But I started my family early, before I could leave, and here we are."

"We know you've brought your crafts and story times and good things to that library. My niece told me about the way it feels like a community now, a *family*. We hear things," another said.

Jessamine sat up straight, her feeling of panic returning. "I forgot to text them." She stood up and patted her pockets, feeling for her phone. "I'd better tell them I'll be late."

Frank patted her hand. "After you drink your tea, I think you should take yourself home and get warm and fed. If they're going to treat you bad at that library, they can do without you for a day when you're in this sort of state."

"You're right." Jessamine sat down. "I'll tell them I'm not coming in today."

"Yes, finish your tea since we made it."

Chapter 33

Jessamine went home and spent an edgy day scrubbing her bathroom, digging her garden, and attacking the vines with the lawnmower. She texted Marilyn and Stephanie about not being sure what to do and they texted reassurances and promises to meet for lunch soon.

In the early evening as Jessamine sat at her table with her egg for dinner, a new text from Drusilla popped up, *The Library Committee have decided that due to your reprehensible behavior, you are required, on your own expense, to undertake a course in appropriate communication. Your tenure at Bent River County Public Library is under review.*

Jessamine felt numb. Her only thought was that she couldn't believe that they would send such a thing by text. Then she thought over the last months of Drusilla's behavior, and she could believe it only too well.

Decades of experience told her not to quit a job before she had another one. How would she support herself in this out-of-the-way place without her library job? At the moment, she didn't care. At least she wouldn't pay for any "appropriate communication" classes. She gritted her teeth and texted: *I hereby give my two weeks' notice. I terminate my services at Bent River County Public Library.*

The text came back so fast that Jessamine thought that Drusilla had it planned. *Your services are no longer required. You need not return.*

In the next weeks, Jessamine's despair grew as she sat at her computer and searched for jobs. Despite leaps in technology in the cities, to get slow internet that stopped when it rained, she had to rely on an unreliable scheme involving her phone, a box she didn't understand, and an expensive app.

She found no jobs within an hour's drive that paid well enough to cover the gas, but she had to find work, so she applied anyway. From her years of helping public library patrons search for jobs, she felt confident about her searching ability and how to write a good, individualized cover letter and resume to maximize her chances. She applied for everything, but she knew that many HR departments moved at a glacial pace, or perhaps they advertised a position that they were planning to fill internally. She looked at her bank account, hoping she'd misread the numbers, and they were higher. With a place to stay, she could last a while, but in a few months, she would literally eat up her savings.

She gritted her teeth and vowed never to slink back to Kansas, so she needed to support herself. Her children told her about her husband's increased drinking. He bought a sports car, then it was repossessed for nonpayment. When she glanced at divorce laws, a strangled, panicked feeling compelled her to exhaust herself with hacking, digging, and planting.

Her garden responded by blooming beyond her wildest expectations. The spinach, tomatoes, green beans, and squash grew like weeds, then the weeds grew like an alien invasion. She labored in the garden from dawn to dusk. She subsisted mostly on her eggs and vegetables, but she needed tea and milk and flour, as well as the dried coconut and oats for her Anzac biscuits. One day, on her way back from buying the cheapest groceries she could find, she stopped at the gas station. She hoped the one and five-dollar bills she gathered from her purse and house would be enough to get her gas tank *almost* full. Frank came up to her window.

"Hi, Frank. How's your job hunt going?"

"Slowly, Ms. Jessamine, slowly." Frank shaded his eyes with his hand. "Ms. Jessamine, my mama would like to visit with you."

Jessamine leaned out the window. "I'd love to meet her. Do you want to come to my place? Or go out for lunch?"

"She can't get out much these days." Frank scratched his nose. "Would you be able to come to our place and see her? On Saturday afternoon?"

"Okay." Jessamine gestured to the trees. "You live behind the gas station?"

"Yes, that's us." He stepped back to avoid a car arriving for gas and waved. "See you around two, then?"

Jessamine returned his wave and drove off, looking forward to visiting. She loved the way locals used the word "visiting" to mean sitting and chatting and getting to know someone, not just the bald act of going to a place.

After lunch on Saturday, Jessamine picked a small bowl of the nicest tomatoes and grabbed handfuls of green beans. Her garden was producing in such abundance, she had plenty of vegetables, maybe too many. She loved to share them. The sunflowers nodded their cheerful yellow heads near the top of the fence, so she cut three. She went outside the fence and gathered wildflowers, laughing at their names; black-eyed Susans like miniature sunflowers, tiny, purple tinged, daisy-like flea bane, handsome purple stalks of spider wort.

Inside she checked the Anzac biscuits cooling on the rack and stacked them into a cookie tin decorated with a Scottish Castle that she had found among the treasures in Rosemary's laundry. She hoped that the sweet coconut and oat cookies, with a history stretching back to World War I and the battlefields of Turkey, would be unusual enough to spark conversation.

Once she put the vegetables into a basket and the flowers into a decorated jar, it looked like too much. She laughed at her own indecisiveness and drove the short distance to the gas station.

Jessamine knew Frank lived down one of the long driveways that wound into the forest behind the gas station, but when she examined the row of five black D-shaped mailboxes on metal poles, she realized she had been overconfident about knowing exactly where. She should have gotten directions. She looked round for the gas station regulars but saw only the teenage worker pumping gas for a shiny SUV with out-of-state plates.

Bent River County was thick with driveways disappearing enticingly into the forest. At the other end could be a settlement of broken-down trailers, or a shiny, white-fenced horse farm, like her neighbors through her forest. Or in Jessamine's case, an unexpected and unconnected railway station. People valued their privacy, and Jessamine was wary of simply driving down and seeing who lived there. Then she noticed the sixth mailbox, bird house shaped with a faded sunflower matching the painting on Jessamine's box. This must be Frank's.

Paths into the shadowy forest split off the shared driveway, labeled with names, numbers, and "No Trespassing" signs, but she couldn't see Frank's. The driveway narrowed until she couldn't go further when she spotted a vine-covered wooden sunflower with "Pearson" painted in the middle.

Jessamine bumped down another forest path and emerged into a riot of multicolored flowers. They burst from the ground, trailed over boxes, and waved from above, fighting and shouting in their exuberance to reach the sun. She wound down her windows and bathed in the crick of cicadas and a jumble of warm, sweet smells, like a candy jar. She struggled with the heat and humidity of her new home, but she loved the verdant growth it brought.

As she eased farther along the path, Frank waved from the porch of a small house covered in vines and bright-red, trumpet-shaped flowers. He leaned over a white-haired woman, tucked into a chair with a blanket over her lap despite the July heat. "Welcome, Jessamine," he called. Jessamine noticed that he had dropped the 'Ms.'

Frank walked over to her car. "Sunflowers!" Frank said, lifting them from Jessamine's arms.

"I feel silly bringing sunflowers to this garden."

"They're perfect. Mama loves sunflowers, and she didn't grow any this year."

"I'm glad she'll like them. And I brought Anzac biscuits." Jessamine patted the cookie tin.

"Wonderful! I told Mama about them. She'll appreciate cookies with a story. Mama doesn't get around too good now, but she loves to see people."

Jessamine followed Frank up a gravel path, bordered with delicate yellow cups, sturdy white daisies, showy red roses—far more flowers than Jessamine could absorb or name. Cucumbers, basil, and giant purple eggplants grew among the flowers. Bees, butterflies, and other insects flew, collected, and worked over the flowers, humming and buzzing.

"Mama, this is Jessamine, who I was telling you about. Jessamine, this is my mama."

Jessamine put the basket of vegetables on a cushioned porch chair and took up both hands of the wizened, white-haired woman who barely came up to the top of her chair. "Hello, I'm very pleased to meet you, Mrs. Pearson. Thank you for inviting me."

"We're pleased to have you, honey. Call me DaisyMae. My Frank has told me a lot about you," she said, her voice as sweet as her flowers. "These sure are pretty sunflowers, honey." DaisyMae stroked a petal. "They're such cheerful, in-your-face flowers. Nothin' shy about sunflowers."

"Oh!" exclaimed Jessamine, distracted. "There's a hummingbird."

"Stand still and watch them," DaisyMae said.

Jessamine focused and saw four or five finger-sized, glittery green birds flitting around the vine. One hovered outside a red flower, and its tiny needle beak disappeared inside as it drank. Two darted at each other until one turned and whizzed away so fast Jessamine could barely see it go.

"They're fighting!" exclaimed Jessamine.

DaisyMae laughed. "Yes, they're territorial little scraps."

"I… sorry…" Jessamine wanted to be polite and talk to DaisyMae, but the hummingbirds were entrancing. One hovered in its otherworldly way, barely an arm's length from her face, with an audible burr like a tiny motor. It turned its head, and Jessamine could swear that the tiny wild bird was looking at her.

DaisyMae laughed. "They're territorial about their people, too. These ones come here all the time, and they know me and Frank, but you're new. Sit down, honey." She gestured to covered porch chairs. "So they can have a good look at you and decide if they like you."

Jessamine sat on a cushioned porch swing. "How can you tell if they like me?"

"If they don't like you, they'll go away. They love my trumpet vine, but they're fickle if they don't like a visitor. But look at them! They like you, honey. You must be one of the good ones."

"Thank you," Jessamine said faintly, not sure what else she could say.

DaisyMae leaned over and took Jessamine's hand. "I knew that you were a good one when my Frank told me your name: Carolina Jessamine. We have flower names." She nodded and smiled. "Me and my sisters, we all had flower names: LilyMarie and PoppyJane and DahliaStar. Our names meant beauty and strength and connection." DaisyMae's hold on Jessamine's hand was tight. "We women named after flowers. They think we're delicate and decorative. But we're strong like plants. We put our roots down into the good earth, and we bring up the goodness. We turn our faces to the hot sun, and we drink the fine, clean rain. And we grow. We get strong. The world relies on plants. And the world relies on us."

Jessamine smiled at the old woman. This wasn't the small talk she had anticipated. "How did you know that my name is a flower name?" Jessamine asked. "Most people don't realize that."

"Your namesake grows everywhere around here, honey." She smiled at Jessamine. "My name is a strong plain flower. I am the daisy, and I ended up stronger than all my sisters. And you, honey, are the Carolina Jessamine. You're strong and you smell divine." She narrowed her eyes while she smiled. "You have a secret weapon. You look weak, and you grow up on other plants or on fences, but every part of your plant is poisonous. That makes you strong, honey. No one can fool with you. Woe to those who try."

Jessamine laughed.

DaisyMae sat up straight. "Where are my manners? We haven't given you any tea." She shook Jessamine's hand, as if for emphasis. "Frank, bring out the tea and we'll have Jessamine's heavenly cookies."

"Thank you. I'm appreciating cold tea more and more in this climate," Jessamine said.

When Frank left, DaisyMae leaned forward again. "Thank you for helping my boy, honey." She looked into the distance. "He's been lost. His daughter was such a beautiful girl." She swallowed. "But she got in with a bad group of kids. With their girl gone, he fell apart and his wife faded away. His son wouldn't talk to him. He was alone and low. So low. He told me that you remind him of his daughter. She loved animals and she always had her nose stuck in a book."

Frank arrived with a tray of icy, clinking tea glasses. They sipped and watched the hummingbirds for a few minutes, and then DaisyMae told Jessamine about the flowers and plants growing in such abandon in front of them.

As the hot afternoon faded into cooler dusk, DaisyMae directed Frank to get plants for Jessamine to take home; he clipped pieces off plants that would grow from cuttings and dug up other plants that were lost without their roots.

"People say this isn't the right time of year for transplanting, but my experience is that it depends on how much care you give the plants. And I'd offer you vegetables, honey, but it looks like you've got a lot." DaisyMae laughed.

"Yes, I feel silly bringing tomatoes now." Jessamine laughed too.

"We have been blessed with such an abundance. I know we should share." DaisyMae smiled.

"Yes, I love to share my plants. Like you do."

"We need a more organized way to share them. I hate to see them go to waste," DaisyMae said.

Jessamine sat up straight. "I saw a sign about a new farmer's market."

DaisyMae stared at her. "What did it say, honey? July is late in the season to think of starting at a farmer's market."

"I know it's late in the season, but it said they were looking for vendors."

"Who's running it?" Frank frowned. "I went to the county's market and it was no good."

"It's one of the new families who bought land to build a homestead. They've got a big field that opens onto the highway," Jessamine replied.

"I've seen that." Frank's face lit up. "We could do it! Mama, do you want to be in on it? You could sell your flowers."

DaisyMae shook her head. "Frank, honey, I know we call them my flowers, but we know who does all the planting and weeding and watering. I'd be honored if we can share our flowers and plants with other people and help you both while you're between jobs."

"And Jessamine can put them in her jars!" Frank stood up and paced in the small space of the porch.

"Yes, I could." Jessamine grinned.

DaisyMae grinned back. "We can see if we're allowed to sell things that we cook. I have the most divine recipe for pickles that we call Christie's Eight-Day pickles. Your Anzac biscuits will be a winner, Jessamine."

"And I've got a recipe from my grandmother," Jessamine said. "In my family we call them Great Granny Gwen's Mustard Pickles."

"Great name!" Frank laughed.

Darkness came down, and fireflies flickered. Less appealing invertebrates arrived, and Frank lit a citronella candle in an attempt to keep the mosquitoes and midges at bay. They talked about their plans for setting up a farmer's market stall; Frank had an old folding table, DaisyMae had embroidered tablecloths, and Jessamine's greenhouse meant that they could grow plants all year.

DaisyMae yawned and Jessamine realized that she had stayed a long time and the old woman was tired. "I better go," Jessamine said. "I'll come around soon, and we can talk about it more after we've had a chance to think."

"Yes, honey, we'll do that."

"Stephanie's bingo is coming up. She's been talking about it ever since we met. And she's been texting me about it. Do you want to come?"

When DaisyMae spoke up, her voice sounded stronger. "We should all go to Stephanie's bingo. It's our county, too, and we'll support Stephanie and Cyril! It's time I got out more."

Chapter 34

Every morning Jessamine woke up at dawn. She pulled on ragged shorts, grabbed a cup of tea, and headed outside to weed and plant and water and nurture. She crouched in the rows of swelling plants and watched the wild hawks swoop above the trees. The crows croaked their displeasure at the hawks, and when the pressure rose for reasons Jessamine could not see, the crows noisily mobbed the hawks and drove them away.

"There's drama in the avian world, as well," Jessamine told Hermes, who gazed at her with lifted ears and waved his plumy tail. With Jessamine at home nearly all the time, he had become less clingy.

Jessamine ate cherry tomatoes and green beans straight off the vines for her breakfast. She lost weight with her fresh diet. "You can't get any fresher than that," she told the plants. But she realized she could get slightly fresher and bent down and nibbled a bean still growing. She laughed at herself and tension eased from her shoulders and stomach and into the earth and away.

She worked outside until the sun climbed above the trees and caught her in its penetrating rays. Sweat soaked her old t-shirts and dripped off her nose. During the heat of the day, she retreated to the shade under the trees or inside. Jessamine's railway station didn't have air conditioning, and at first, she found it hard to sleep. But no air conditioning meant modest power bills—it was all she could afford. She set up an old picnic table under a tree outside her back door and sat there to make her covered jars and painted pots to sell with her flowers and plants at the market. In the late afternoons, once it cooled off a bit, she headed back into the garden and worked outside until it got dark. She fell straight into bed, exhausted from physical labor and the heat. She slept better and worried less about nightmares.

The farmer's market succeeded beyond Jessamine and Frank's dreams. Jessamine got used to winding into Frank and DaisyMae's bright oasis of flowers. She was so busy that it wasn't until a rainy afternoon, searching for a raincoat in the laundry room, that she came across the cloth carrier bag she had taken into the library every day. Her stomach lurched; she hadn't touched the bag since the day she quit. More than one counselor had told her she couldn't hide from her problems and that putting things off made them worse, but for the last month Jessamine pretended everything from the library, except her friends, didn't exist. Merriam, the county lawyer who had phoned Kathryn on Jessamine's first day when they'd all been stuck outside because of the delivery of the bear, sent a strange handwritten letter in reply to her long-ago phone call about legal help. *I can't do anything, Jessamine,* it said. *Be careful. Don't stir up anything you can't handle in this county.* The ominous words, echoing what Stephanie had said, made Jessamine uneasy.

In her laundry room, the work carrier bag was a miniscule whirling black hole that sucked in all light and hope. "This is ridiculous," she told herself out loud and grabbed the bag, pulling out her insulated lunchbox. It didn't smell good. She contemplated throwing it out, but her natural thriftiness and the fact that her middle son had given her the volcano-decorated lunchbox with money made from his first job inspired her to save it. She grimaced at two rotten apples, a rotten avocado, and a less-identifiable slimy thing that may once have been a sandwich. She took it outside and hosed out the lunchbox and left it to rinse in the rain.

Inside, Jessamine turned the cloth bag upside down, and papers and pens and paperclips fell out. She threw out supermarket receipts and old library fliers, then sat on the couch to scrutinize the rest. Old instructions from Marilyn about the intricacies of state funding for public libraries were crumpled around printouts of information for Bent River County Public Library grants she'd been researching before she left.

The folder Frank had rescued from the bear stared up at her. She'd glanced through it but none of it made sense. It looked like personnel records and included the names of people who worked for the county. The information connected to the names was unintelligible, so she'd dampened down her guilt about returning it. What were ordinary human resources records doing inside a stuffed bear? It was inexplicable. She should have done something with the papers, but the library remained such a toxic malignancy that she pushed it out of her head. Now on her couch, she held the folder and sighed. The market was doing so well that she was building up a small backup savings account. She thought she'd buy stamps and mail the folder anonymously to the county.

Jessamine's phone rang. She smiled when she saw it was Stephanie; her young friend always had a cheerful word.

"Hi Stephanie, how are…" Jessamine started.

"I can't believe they did it!" Stephanie was talking fast. "After all I've done for them! How are we going to pay the car loan? We had to replace the car. It was thirty years old and didn't work anymore."

"What's wrong?" Jessamine couldn't make head or tail of it. "Are you okay?" She grimaced at her stupid question; it was obvious Stephanie wasn't okay. "Tell me what's happened."

Stephanie sobbed. "They fired me!"

"What?"

"The Library Committee and Drusilla fired me for 'sabotaging library property' they said."

"What? Why?" Jessamine felt stupid repeating herself, but she was dumbfounded.

Stephanie was crying in earnest now, but Jessamine made out the words.

"They said that by dressing the bear, I'd sabotaged library property."

"What? I can't believe…" Jessamine felt the Library Committee and Drusilla again bringing her as close to swearing as she'd been in decades. "But we dressed the bear months ago… and we all dressed it! Me, Marilyn. The customers."

"I don't think that mattered. They said I didn't have permission to touch their stupid bear. I've worked there for over ten years!" Stephanie's voice rose to a wail. "I volunteered there when I was at school."

"You do so much for the community working there. Much more than Drusilla. I can't believe them!" Jessamine paused. "You'll get another job. You're a great worker. I'll be a reference for you."

"Thank you. That means a lot right now." Jessamine heard a smile creeping into Stephanie's voice through her tears. "Josey told me that she saw Drusilla and Tiffany screaming at each other in the hallway outside the library. Drusilla broke a heel on one of her stilettoes and threw it at the wall." Stephanie giggled. "Josey *and* Eunice say the library didn't open on time for several days. They're stopping *all* the programs. There's a rumor that the county is talking about getting the Department of Motor Vehicles staff to open it in their spare time. Like that'll work."

"What? That's absurd." Jessamine shook her head, even though she knew Stephanie couldn't see her. "The only reply to that is what we said when I was a kid, 'Yer what mate?'"

Stephanie laughed.

"I know." Jessamine perked up. "In the meantime you can join me and Frank at the market. You've got lots of eggs and feathers. I'll plant more seeds. Come over soon and we'll talk about setting up the stall."

"Sounds great, thank you." Stephanie paused. "There is good news. They wanted to stop all the programs, but so many customers asked about the bingo that when I went in to pick up my stuff, Drusilla rolled her eyes and said that if I must, I could run the bingo as a volunteer."

"As a volunteer? If you're lucky? As a favor to you?" Jessamine shook her head. "Drusilla raises condescension to an art form."

Stephanie laughed. "Yes, she does." Then she sighed. "But I said I'd do it since so many people were excited about it. I know we'll both miss our poor old library."

"Yes, we will," Jessamine said. "But we'll carry on."

Chapter 35

After they hung up, Jessamine realized she was clutching the folder from the bear. She thought of how upset Frank had been the day he was fired. She thought of them firing Stephanie after ten years for the farcical charge of "sabotage." She thought of them firing Marilyn for murky reasons. They didn't think they had to give any reasons to the yokels. She thought of her own exit—she had quit, so she hadn't technically been fired, but she knew her firing had only been days away.

She gritted her teeth. She would study the papers and find out why Joshua had his knickers in a twist about the papers and the stupid bear. Determined, she put on the kettle for a fresh cup of tea and got to work.

She remembered sticking other papers in her work cardigan pockets. She hadn't worn her cardigan since spring, and they were crumpled at the bottom of her closet. She pulled out the strange papers she had seen in Drusilla's old office and smoothed them out.

Jessamine sat on the couch and started reading. She compared numbers and her mouth fell open. None of it made sense. The rain cleared, but instead of heading out to her garden, she spread papers out across her sitting room floor. She found two copies of the same bill of lading for the same supplies and compared them line by line—except they weren't the same. The name of the contractor, date, and everything else was the same, but the amount and cost of the materials and labor were orders of magnitude different. Both copies had Kathryn's and Drusilla's signatures. Jessamine stared at them, wondering which one was right.

At her computer, Jessamine found the website of the state library and was daunted by the sheer volume of information. The state library accepted, disbursed, and spent public money, so the public had a right to know how it was done, but their website was bogged in details. Jessamine clicked on a one-hundred-and-sixty-page PDF of one of the state library's meeting minutes and stretched while her slow internet connection chugged along, trying to download it.

She doubted many members of the public could get this far; she was struggling, and she was an experienced and tenacious reference librarian who had worked helping students and faculty doing research in university libraries. She gave the bureaucrats the benefit of the doubt. It wasn't that they were hiding the information; it was so obscure, no one would find it. Gabriella the cat sat contentedly curled with her fluffy bottom protruding onto Jessamine's keyboard, the armistice-line location of the cat in their constant battle about the cat's right to sit directly in the middle of the keyboard. Gabriella stood and stretched. She put her front paws on the keyboard and the screen flashed across several websites that Jessamine had been searching. A loud ding announced a pop-up box asking Jessamine if she was *really* interested in Caret browsing. Jessamine had no idea what Caret browsing was, but the cat made the offer appear quite often. Maybe because the word sounded a bit like "cat"? Jessamine pushed Gabriella off the keyboard and onto the table. The cat turned her back on Jessamine and stuck her head in Jessamine's water glass with her fluffy tail slashing in front of the screen. Jessamine moved her head, trying to read the PDF that was now loaded. Then she laughed at herself, picked up the indignant cat and placed her on the floor. Gabriella hissed at Hermes, made a half-hearted swipe at the curled-up dog's nose, and stalked out of the room.

Jessamine sighed with relief and scrolled through the PDF. She sat up with a jolt. This made less and less sense. The state library had given Bent River County Public Library far more money than Jessamine knew that the library had spent. The library struggled desperately for money the entire time Jessamine worked there. She remembered when they got the end-of-year windfall that Stephanie said Drusilla was the only one with the authority to spend money. But the documents showed many other people connected to library money. It mentioned Merriam, the lawyer, which made sense, but also Frank, Stephanie, and Agnes, Kathryn's assistant, which defied logic.

And it kept talking about thousands of dollars for the "Library Annex." What was the Library Annex? Jessamine had never heard of it. It had to be something big because it received most of the library's funding.

Jessamine pulled up the computer's calculator and started adding. She grabbed an old envelope and repeated the calculations by hand. Then she dug in a drawer and found Rosemary's old solar-powered calculator. It didn't matter how she did it, the figures all said *millions* of dollars were missing.

Jessamine leaned back and tapped her fingers on her desk until Hermes and Gabriella poked their ears forward and stared intently as if they might pounce. After Jessamine won a big grant, Drusilla authorized Jessamine to select new books. It was glorious and she remembered her excitement when the boxes of new books arrived. Drusilla and Tiffany processed the books with stickers for the shelves excruciatingly slowly, while Jessamine waited with growing anticipation.

Drusilla finally gave Jessamine permission to weed. After Jessamine threw away books over thirty years old, the library had nothing about dinosaurs at all. When Jessamine showed the moldy dinosaur book to Drusilla, the tall woman said, "I don't want to touch it. That's disgusting. Why didn't you get rid of it already? I would have thought you would have known better, since you went to a fancy library school?"

Jessamine selected fifteen new dinosaur books, but only one emerged to be shelved. Drusilla said the rest were coming.

At home on her computer, Jessamine wondered if the books ever appeared. She checked the library's online catalog; only one dinosaur book. Jessamine checked for *Anne of Green Gables;* also, not there. The first in the timeless series had been missing from the shelf because the library didn't own it, not because it was checked out. Although they owned many later in the series, and people asked for it, Drusilla didn't want to buy it. It was one of the first books Jessamine had ordered with a suitable grant. If these books weren't in the library, then where was the money for them?

Jessamine compiled all her research and numbers into a hundred-page document. She got it ready to send to Marilyn and Stephanie and Frank. They needed to know this. She paused and added Bobby the Sheriff's name to the list. She sat at the computer until Hermes ran in circles yipping and Gabriella climbed onto the back of the couch and clawed. She let out a big breath and clicked the send button.

Chapter 36

The papers stayed a constant tug at the back of Jessamine's mind; they were so bizarre she thought she must have misinterpreted them. But she was too busy to dwell. Stephanie was so upset about her firing and so excited about the bingo in a week that Jessamine and Frank invited and cajoled everyone they knew.

"Bingo isn't really my thing," Marilyn said when Jessamine saw her at the market. "I'm more of a book group person."

"Come along to support Stephanie," Jessamine said.

"Yes, promote what the library used to stand for and what it achieved," Frank added.

Marilyn laughed. "Okay. Your proselytizing worked—I'm a bingo person now."

Late summer storm clouds piled up above the trees as Jessamine drove down Frank and DaisyMae's driveway on bingo day. She loved the drama of bright, sunlit leaves slashing against a lowering, gray sky. DaisyMae was finding it harder to drive, so she put off long-delayed repairs on her temperamental car. She found it much easier to climb into Jessamine's car than Frank's truck, so Jessamine was picking her up.

As they assisted DaisyMae down the porch steps with her walker, Frank looked up. "Are you sure you want to go, Mama? The weather might get rough."

"Oh, hush your mouth, son. A little rain hasn't melted me yet, and I'm going to stand behind Stephanie. I'm ready, and I'm going."

In the county building parking lot, blobs of summer rain stained the cracked concrete, and the sky grumbled. Figures jumped out of old cars and pickup trucks and hurried to the doors with their heads bowed against the wind.

Walking alongside DaisyMae, Jessamine glimpsed the half-built walls and roof of the new library building going up across the parking lot, but there was no time to stop and examine it. She felt her body's reluctance to enter the library that had meant so much to her for months, which she hadn't set foot in since the day of the up-to-and-including-termination meeting. *This is my library. I live in this community,* she lectured herself.

Jessamine added an armful of sunflowers to Stephanie's arrangement of prizes. Stephanie had worked magic to make the table of dusty vases, decorated popcorn tins, and ceramic ducks from Rosemary's cupboards look appealing.

"Look at all the people!" Stephanie's face was alight.

"They came to support you, Stephanie."

"They did?" Stephanie's eyes went wide and shiny. She blinked.

"What did you think of the papers I sent?" Jessamine stepped aside to let Cyril, Stephanie's cousin, go through with a huge box.

Stephanie grimaced. "I haven't had a chance to read them. Have you seen Kathryn? She was adamant…" She turned away to Eunice with a big cardboard box of prizes. "I'll take that. It's heavy."

Relieved of her box, Eunice raised her eyebrows and tilted her head at Stephanie's handsome cousin. "Hi there, Cyril. It's great to see you! I'll sit up the front near you."

The rain beat on the windows in the hallway but didn't dim the party atmosphere inside. Josey bounced up to Jessamine with a slightly older, slightly taller version of herself. "Hi Jessamine. This is my sister, Christa. We got a babysitter! We couldn't miss this for anything."

"Are you the caller, Jessamine?" asked Bobby the Sheriff. "I miss you at the library. That Tiffany isn't helpful."

"No, Cyril is calling today." Jessamine gestured to Stephanie's cousin, who was going over the bingo cards with Stephanie. "What did you think of the papers I sent?" Jessamine asked.

"That *really* long document? I'll um, get to it. Ah… soon. Have you seen Kathryn? I needed to talk to her," Bobby said before calling out, "Cyril! How are you?" He turned to Jessamine. "Cyril and I went to school together," and headed across the room.

A knot of the men from the gas station shook Jessamine's hand. "Good to see ya. How ya doin'?"

Jessamine greeted her old boss with a quick hug. "Hi, Marilyn! How's your new job?"

"Great! They appreciate me working out the budgets and the computer contracts."

"What did you make of the papers I sent you?" Jessamine asked.

"Yeah. The papers. They look interesting. I'll get to them as soon as I've finished fixing my new library's computers. It's overwhelming."

Josey shook her head. "Better than here. The computers hardly ever work now."

They looked at the line of handwritten *Out of Order* signs taped to the computers.

"I know they don't," Marilyn said. "Drusilla called me and said that I was allowed to come into the county if I agreed to fix the computers as a volunteer. She said if I cared about the library as I *said* I did, then I could give back to the community by doing this service for them."

"She was always good at that manipulative garbage." Jessamine sighed. "She's as lazy as a post herself."

Marilyn laughed. "I told her that my new library director job is going extremely well and I'm remarkably busy. And I said that if the computers need fixing, then as director, she should fix them herself."

"Good for you." Eunice stood with her hands on her hips. "I don't approve of what's been going on in this county. I'm glad someone's finally standing up to them." She tried to squint over the crowd. "I thought Kathryn would be here."

"If I can have your attention!" Cyril formed a megaphone around his mouth with his hands. The room hushed. "It's great to see everyone here today." He gestured to the rain pouring down the hallway windows. "We better get started before the flood arrives!"

The tables soon overflowed. Clipboards, which Jessamine and Stephanie had made from old book covers, were balanced on people's laps. Jessamine found a seat next to Frank and laid out her multi-colored plastic chips. "It feels weird to be here in the audience."

"I'm glad to see you here." Frank grinned. "Enjoy it!"

"What did you think of the papers I sent?" Jessamine whispered.

"I haven't been able to download the file. I'll need help. And with Mama needing to get to the doctor…" Frank broke off and pointed to Cyril starting to spin the cage for the bingo numbers.

The chattering died down; the people of Bent River County took their bingo seriously. But they knew it was for fun and to support Stephanie and the public library. Jessamine cheered with everyone else. She found herself relaxing into the rhythm of placing the plastic chips and soaking up the company of a room full of happy people. She anticipated what prize she could choose—everyone won a prize. She told herself it was silly since she had donated three boxes of knick-knacks, glad to get them out of her house. Who cares, she asked herself, why not enjoy it?

The crowd cheered the loudest when thirty-something Amelia with Down syndrome won, with help from her mother, as always sitting at her side, closely attending to her. Amelia looked surprised by the cheers but went happily up to the front to choose Jessamine's sunflowers as her prize.

Cyril gestured toward the tables at the front. "A big thank you to everyone who donated our prizes today." He turned to Stephanie. "And an even bigger thank you to my own cousin and our local gal Stephanie, who made a beautiful display of them." He paused for effect. "We have more." He looked toward the kitchen door. "After our break, Stephanie will bring them out."

The promised break came with homemade sweet tea and homemade cookies. Stephanie told Jessamine that customers had asked after her Anzac biscuits. Jessamine wasn't sure if it was true or if Stephanie was being kind, but she made a quadruple batch of the oaty, coconutty treats.

"And now," Cyril announced. "What you've all been waiting for…"

"Come on, Cyril!" a voice shouted. "Don't keep us in suspense."

Cyril smiled mysteriously and gestured dramatically to Stephanie hovering by the door to the kitchen. "Stephanie will reveal our premium prizes."

Stephanie disappeared into the kitchen and emerged, needing both arms to carry an enormous box of chocolates tied with a floppy red bow. She set it on the table and went back to the kitchen for a suitcase-sized car tool set in its plastic. The crowd buzzed. "Look at that! I'm going to win that!"

"And now for the pièce de résistance." Cyril held his arms out.

"Speak English, Cyril!" someone shouted. Everyone laughed while Stephanie once again disappeared into the kitchen. They all watched the door and waited. "Has she gotten lost?" another person asked, while a couple of people got up to help, when Stephanie emerged backwards pulling a garden cart with the taxidermied bear. Stephanie held her arms above her head in a victory gesture and the sky boomed and rumbled. The noisy crowd was shocked into a brief silence, then the room broke into catcalls.

"I'm going to win that bear! Just watch!"

"No, I'm having it. I won't be able to bear it, if it isn't mine!"

"Quiet. Quiet!" Cyril used his six-foot height and considerable presence to subdue the uproar. "Don't be un*bear*able!" He paused for laughter. "We'll play another round, and if you *bear* with me, maybe we won't lose all our stuffing."

As Cyril called the numbers Jessamine noticed Frank's hands were shaking. She thought it wasn't surprising, considering how much the long-dead creature had put him through. With a plunge in her chest, Jessamine spotted a two on her card, that would give her a bingo. Out of the corner of her eye, she saw that Frank was close too. She hesitated. Frank *deserved* the bear if he wanted it so much. She kept the plastic chip squeezed in her fist.

"Bingo!" yelled Frank. He jumped up and waved his arms as the room erupted into cheering again. Stephanie checked his card and nodded to Cyril.

"Ladies and gentlemen, we have a winner. Our great friend and loyal Bent River County hero has won!"

Frank whooped and raised his fist in triumph. His grin split his face wider than since his firing. Walter won the chocolate. Eunice clutched the tool set, a gleam in her eye as if she pictured bolts to be tightened and rivets to replace. The bingo wound down. The men from the gas station swarmed forward and together they pushed the bear like a Roman triumph to the parking lot and loaded it into the bed of Frank's truck.

"I've had to give up beer, but at least I've got a bear," Frank said cheerfully.

"Why did he give up beer?" Jessamine asked DaisyMae quietly.

"He's been struggling hard since he was fired, honey," she said. "He wouldn't admit it, but he couldn't afford beer." She patted Jessamine's hand. "But a mother tries to look on the bright side. At least he's lost weight."

The rain was clearing and a stab of sunshine highlighted Frank as he drove out of the parking lot with a toot and a wave out the window. The stiff, furry legs of the bear stuck up out of the bed of the truck, as if the vehicle was growing a jaunty tail.

Jessamine helped DaisyMae into her car and followed him. In the last few minutes of bingo, she had formulated a plan.

Chapter 37

Flames flickered above the trees and sparks spiraled into the midnight sky. Sirens and shouts disturbed the night. The pickup truck stopped on the bank above the river. Jessamine got out and turned toward the sullen orange horizon.

"Hurry up!" Frank called from the truck cab.

Jessamine directed the backing vehicle, then they both climbed into the bed of the truck. She coughed on the rancid smoke clogging the air. "The fire's getting bad. I don't think they'll be able to save the library."

"Don't worry about that! We've got to get rid of this!"

They maneuvered a bulky bundle out of the bed of the truck until it thumped on the ground. They each grabbed an end and stumbled, barely able to drag it, toward the crumbling riverbank. They tried to swing the bundle out, but it fell and lodged halfway down. Frank crouched down and pushed it with his foot.

He teetered and she grabbed his arm. "Careful, Frank!"

They stood on the top of the bank and watched as the bundle slid into the water with a slight splash. Caught by the current, the white shape floated a short way, and then disappeared into the dark, shiny water. They turned and Jessamine wiped her hands on her pants.

Search lights blazed. "Stop! Show your hands!"

Jessamine froze as Sheriff Bobby appeared through the glare.

"Jessamine Sibley, you're under arrest for the murder of Kathryn Slattery. Anything you say…"

"Oh, botherations!" Jessamine said and lifted her hands into the air.

Jessamine looked around. The search lights pinned them like bugs in a display. The river was on one side and several figures silhouetted against the glaring lights were on the other. Jessamine squinted at them. She had an urge to laugh. She couldn't believe it wasn't a movie as Sheriff Bobby continued reciting the Miranda rights. "You have the right to an attorney. If you…"

"Hey, Bobby. It's *us*! It's Jessamine and Frank!" The smoke caught at her throat and she coughed.

Bobby rubbed his eyes and coughed. "I know it's you and Frank. Are you going to come quietly?" Bobby sounded miserable. "We've got to get back to that fire. Did you set the library on fire, too?"

"I would never set the library on fire, Bobby! You know that!"

"Yeah, well. I kind of do, Jessamine. But the library's on fire, the same night you're throwing a body in the river in the middle of the night."

"I'm not throwing a body in the river."

"Jessamine! Remember them Miranda rights?"

"Okay, okay. I'll come quietly or whatever you want."

Jessamine regarded the handcuffs on her wrists with interest. She'd never been arrested before. She remembered her one speeding ticket in forty years of driving almost with fondness. The cuffs were heavy and cold against her wrists and then she forgot them as she climbed into the back of the sheriff's car awkwardly without using her confined hands. She saw Frank pushed into another car and they all drove off, leaving behind his pickup truck.

As they drove into the county complex, Jessamine saw that the flames no longer reached far above the roof of the partially constructed library. The building was surrounded by four or five fire engines, and dozens of figures in bulky fire suits blundered about with hoses and mysterious equipment. As she watched, a figure slammed the back doors of an ambulance, and it veered into the night, lights and sirens blaring.

"Was someone hurt? Who was hurt?" Jessamine leaned forward, but Bobby didn't hear her through the plastic barrier in the police car.

They parked around the back of the sheriff's department, out of view of the library. As Bobby opened the doors, Jessamine tried again. "Was someone hurt in the fire? Who was hurt?"

Bobby sighed. "Jessamine, remember your Miranda rights." He led her down a long, narrow hallway and through a door. "Sit here." He pulled a chair out from the table and Jessamine sat down. "I don't know how long we'll be. I have to go to the fire. We're waiting for the state police. I mean…" Bobby stopped abruptly. "Jessamine… why did you do it?" He suddenly looked sad and much older.

Jessamine tried to stand. "Bobby, I didn't…"

"I gotta go, Jessamine."

The door closed and Jessamine heard a key turn in the lock. She looked around. She was being held in a windowless storage closet. Chairs were stacked along one wall and old bulletin boards leaned against another wall. She squinted and turned her head sideways. They were old bulletin boards from the library. The light was bad, but she could make out a colorful border with cartoon books repeating the words, "Make Reading a Habit!" With more squinting she could see that the worn and broken chairs were also from the library. She sighed and put her head down on the table. It had been so hopeful when they thought they'd be moving from the cramped library into the new building.

Jessamine liked to go to bed by nine-thirty every night. It was far past her bedtime and resting her forehead on the table felt good. She shut her eyes and sighed again.

Jessamine was dreaming that she was in the library. She was decorating bulletin boards, but it didn't matter how many she did, more boards kept coming. They needed pictures, they needed fliers about programs, and Jessamine couldn't find any of them. And the worst part was that she needed to pee. The white, shiny toilet was right in the middle of the library floor. She wanted to use it, but she knew she couldn't pee until she had finished the boards. And how could she pee in front of all the people?

Jessamine heard herself give a last half snore and jerked her head on the table. She opened her eyes. Her neck was so stiff she could barely turn it, and her face and mouth felt puffy. *I'm parched for a cuppa.* The statement repeated in her head. She wiggled uncomfortably on her chair. Her need to pee was becoming so urgent that she could barely think of anything else. She craned round toward voices and movement in the distance on the other side of the door. "Hey, I'm still in here. I need to go!" Her voice came out cracked and quiet, so she tried again, "Hey, Bobby! Whoever. I need to go!"

Raised voices came closer along the hallway. She strained to hear, ready to call out again. *Thump!* Something heavy hit the door. Jessamine twitched in her chair and struggled to stand up, pushing up off the table with her hands handcuffed in front of her. Her wrists felt bruised and her thumbs nearly numb. She staggered over to the door. Sleeping properly in a bed meant she was stiff in the morning, but sleeping for a few hours propped up on a table meant her left hip and right knee were hardly able to bear her weight. She leaned on the door, preparing to bang on it and shout again.

Angry voices penetrated the door. "What are you doing? Don't hit me!" A female voice sounded near hysteria.

"I'm not hitting you! You've got to tell me what the hell is going on? Why are you here, Agnes?" The second voice was male, and lower. Jessamine put her ear right up to the door to make it out. The words were said slowly, but with such menace that Jessamine shivered. "*Where* is *my* money?"

"I don't have your money! Don't hit me!"

"I told you I'm not going to hit you! Calm down! I only hit the door, you idiot. If you don't have my money, where is it?"

"I don't know!"

"How can you not know? It would be good for you to know." Jessamine realized that the male voice was Joshua. This was worse than the up-to-and-including-termination meeting. She had never heard him sound like this. The quieter he spoke, the colder she felt, and the more the base of her stomach told her to get away. But she was on the other side of a locked door from him. She clutched the door handle with her handcuffed hands.

"I don't know where the money is!" The female voice was sobbing now. Jessamine realized it was Kathryn's assistant, Agnes.

Thump! The door jumped under Jessamine's leaning head and shoulder.

"Don't…" Agnes's voice was hard to make out.

"I didn't hit you." The male voice was contemptuous. "But that can change if you don't tell me what you know."

"I don't know anything!"

"You do know. Even if you don't have the money. And why would a pathetic mouse like you have my millions? But you know where it is. Who has it? Where is it? Who has it? Who? Where?" The voice was getting louder.

"I don't…"

Thump!

"Don't lie to me! You know where the money is!"

Thump!

"Kathryn has it! Kathryn has it! She made me promise not to tell!" Agnes sobbed.

"And where is Kathryn?" Joshua's voice was quiet again.

"She told me she was going to Hawaii. She went to that meeting for county controllers. She took all the money. I don't know when she'll be back."

"She won't be back, you moron…"

Jessamine heard another voice. "Uncle Josh, what's happening? What's wrong with that woman?"

Although she'd gotten to know Joshua more than she wanted, Jessamine could hardly believe the difference in his voice. "Well, hi there, Wendell. How are things? Poor Ms. Agnes here seems a touch upset about the fire and all. I was seeing how I could help her."

"Everyone's at the fire." Wendell sounded confused. "I'm the only deputy here. Maybe you should give her space, Uncle Josh?"

Jessamine couldn't stand it anymore. She banged on the door. "Hey, let me out. He was attacking her! I need to pee!" She rolled her eyes at herself for saying the last bit out loud, but despite everything, her need to pee was taking up ninety percent of her thoughts.

Wendell's voice came through again, "Move back, I've got the key."

The door opened. Jessamine looked out at three shocked faces. No one spoke.

Agnes was the first to break the silence. "What are you looking at, Jessamine! This is all your fault! You and that Marilyn, coming in from the outside."

"Our fault? My fault?" Jessamine felt herself grow taller. "Marilyn was fired! I was arrested! I spent the night in jail." She paused. "I need to pee since no one let me out."

Joshua was urbane and smooth again. "You were arrested for good reason. You ruined the library, Jessamine. You know you did."

"*I* ruined the library? What the… what the f… what the fluffy-doodle-heads do you mean?" Jessamine never said words like that. She felt vaguely surprised to hear the curse word nearly come out of her mouth. She knew she should stop talking, but she didn't seem to be able to. "Did you say that Kathryn Slattery ran off to Hawaii with millions of county funds?"

"That was a private conversation. That was private infor—"

"It is *not* private! That's the point. This is public money. This county is corrupt." Jessamine stomped her foot.

Joshua was slick again. "What would you know? You're not from around here."

"I'm not from round here, so I know how towns are meant to function. Kathryn said that she runs the county to Marilyn and all of us in front of the lieutenant governor. That's not right. Kathryn *works* for the county."

"I better be going." Joshua was all business. "It's been a hard night on all of us, and I must see about the insurance for the library that Jessamine burned down. That's why I'm out here in the middle of the night."

"I didn't burn down the library!"

"Uncle Josh, don't you know?" Wendell stepped forward. "Engelbert was in the library with a gas can and rags. It looks like he burned down the library."

In the harsh light of the hallway, Jessamine saw Joshua's color change. He swayed and put a hand out to the wall. "Engelbert did what? Wait, don't say more. I'll get our lawyer, Merriam."

"We've been trying to call you. Engelbert is in the hospital. He suffered burns and smoke inhalation."

"I've got to get the lawyer. I've got to…"

Wendell looked uncomfortable. "Cousin Englebert might be hurt bad. Aunt Elmira is out in the foyer. She's looking for you, so you can go to the hospital."

Joshua turned to walk away.

Jessamine blurted out, "What about him assaulting Agnes? And the county money? I know what happened to the money. He can't leave!"

Joshua gave her a narrow stare from his height. "I didn't assault anyone. I don't know anything about any county money. Jessamine, I'm tired of you. I own—"

Wendell interrupted, "Uncle, this is the sheriff's office. I'll deal with Jessamine. You better go."

Joshua left and Agnes hurried after him. Wendell stayed.

Jessamine jiggled from foot to foot. "Where's the bathroom?"

Wendell pushed her back into the room. "I wasn't told I could let you out."

Jessamine heard the key turn in the lock and his footsteps disappearing down the hallway.

She sat down and then stood up. She couldn't settle; her mind was a snarled mass of competing thoughts about the money, the corruption, the burned library, and needing to pee.

She sat at the table and nodded off when she heard another key in the lock.

Sheriff Bobby came in and took off Jessamine's handcuffs. "Sorry. You'd better get to the restroom." He pointed the way to the bathroom, and she rushed in. The sink water ran brown from her filthy hands, and her face in the mirror was baggy eyed with smears of mud. She smelled awful. *I'm parched for a cuppa.* The phrase kept popping into her head. She hadn't been escorted into the restroom; maybe she was free. She lifted her shoulders, breathed deeply, and walked slowly to the lobby.

Bobby waved her over to him from behind the reception desk.

"Am I under arrest?" she asked.

Bobby rubbed a hand over his eyes. "I don't know."

Jessamine hesitated, confused. "What?"

"We got an anonymous tip that you were going to throw a body in the river. I think I know who sent it, but when we drove up, it *did* look like you threw a body in the river." His hands and face were dirty. He looked like he could barely stay awake. "I know Kathryn's in Hawaii, or she had plane tickets to Hawaii for the county conference thing. So, who did you throw in the river? We haven't had a chance to get out the divers to search the river."

"I didn't throw anyone in the river."

"You and Frank threw someone in the river."

"Frank?" Jessamine was horrified to realize that she'd forgotten Frank. "What happened to Frank?"

Bobby looked down, then pinched his nose between his fingers. "He's... Don't you worry about Frank."

"Didn't he tell you what we threw in the river?"

"Right now, I need to hear what you have to say, Jessamine." Bobby rubbed his nose again.

"We..." Jessamine paused. It didn't matter now. "It was the bear."

"The bear?"

"We threw the bear in the river. The bear from the library. That Frank took all over the county. Joshua Oxford's bear."

Bobby began to laugh.

Jessamine giggled. "Frank won it at bingo and we decided it needed a burial at sea."

Bobby snorted. "A burial at sea?"

"All rivers go to the sea eventually. We thought nobody would see if we threw it in the river in the middle of the night. What's happened to Frank?"

"Frank called his cousin and he lawyered up. We had nothing to hold him, so we took him home."

"You took him… wait, why did you keep me all night?"

"Sorry about that. With all that was happening, we sort of forgot."

"You forgot!?"

Bobby looked away. "Jessamine, you look more suspicious doing something in the middle of the night than at any other time. Didn't you realize that?"

"No, I didn't realize that! I don't live a life of crime. Joshua's not going to be happy about his precious bear."

Bobby straightened. "Talking about a life of crime, Joshua's not going to be happy about a lot of things. I read your research. Thank you for working all that out, Jessamine." He hesitated. "Merriam the lawyer has been talking to us."

"What's going to happen to Joshua now?"

Bobby appeared to remember that he was the Sheriff. "I can't discuss an ongoing case. I'll take your witness statement, and then you'd better go home and get cleaned up."

"Why do I have to do a witness statement if I'm not under arrest?"

"We'll need to know formally what you did and what you saw and heard. We saw a bunch in the command room from the cameras in the hallway. Joshua punched the wall above Agnes's head. That was assault. And it's all on tape." Bobby gestured toward the hallway. Four or five cameras blinked their cold, red eyes. "It's going to be a big case against… It's going to be a new day in this county."

Jessamine stood up straight, wincing as her back and hip twinged. "It's about time something new happened in this county."

Chapter 38

After sleeping all day to recover from her out-of-character nocturnal adventures, Jessamine went to her greenhouse to plant seeds. She needed to fulfill her promise to Stephanie to grow more plants to sell in the market. She smoothed a tray of dirt, enjoying the rough feeling on her palm. She poked twenty-four holes in the dirt with an old pen; six along and four up, then dropped a small black basil seed in each hole. "Grow well and strong! Photosynthesize and prosper!" she sang as pushed soil over each seed with the tip of her finger. "You need to grow for me, Frank, *and* Stephanie now."

Jessamine and Frank sold plenty every week. With her greenhouse protecting them, Jessamine grew plants that other people couldn't. She set the hose attachment to the mist function and dampened the tray. "Here comes the spring rain. Slurp. Drink up!" Maybe she should stop talking to plants, but now she wasn't begging them for solace, she was enjoying their company. She felt lighter than she had for months. She was in constant contact with all her children now, and they were all talking about visiting her when they could arrange it. She had finally contacted a lawyer in the city about divorce and found she didn't have to pay anything up front. Soon she could put him completely behind her. It was almost dusk, and the birds were singing their last songs. Hermes poked at the edge of the forest, finding compelling squirrel-related smells. And her eggy supper waited inside for her after she finished today's planting.

As Jessamine smoothed the third tray, she stopped moving. The back of her neck suddenly felt vulnerable. Had she heard something? The birds were silent.

Hermes erupted into frantic yapping. Jessamine swung around. Joshua's height filled the greenhouse's small doorway.

"What…" Jessamine began.

Time moved slowly as Joshua turned to the darting, snapping dog. Each event fell into Jessamine's horrified eyes like the slow, inevitable dripping from a water wheel. He lifted his arm, revealing the polo mallet he'd been carrying alongside his leg.

"No!" Jessamine screamed, at the exact same moment that he braced his feet, lifted the mallet, and brought it down on the dog's head with an audible thump.

Hermes yelped once, almost a scream, and was instantly silent. It felt like years to Jessamine as Joshua turned to face her. Her mouth opened, but no sound came out. He raised the mallet again and Jessamine realized she was trapped in the small greenhouse.

She lifted her hands and stepped back, almost falling over the hose. The hose! She had a flash of spraying him in the face but pictured the fine mist she had been using on the seeds.

Then she thought of the hatchway that the hose came in through, and she dove under the wooden bench just as Joshua's mallet whistled down to give her a glancing blow on her shoulder, then bounced onto the side of her head. She saw flashing lights and heard a tray of seeds go flying with the patter of the dirt falling. It must have gone into Joshua's face because, at the same time that she pushed her hands and arms through the hole in the side of the greenhouse, the loop of the mallet fell next to her leg. Somewhere above herself, the same Jessamine who had been laughing at herself for singing to her plants knew that she would never fit through the small hole, but she had to try.

Joshua's hand grasped her bare ankle. She kicked up with her free foot, and he grunted as her heel connected with something soft, but her flip-flopped foot couldn't do much damage. Jessamine heard the swish of the mallet coming down in the same instant the back of her legs burst into flame. Jessamine had a moment's confused thought that Joshua was setting the greenhouse on fire to burn her up, as she heard the wet thwack of the mallet hitting her legs. Jessamine screamed and grabbed the wooden sides of the hole. The mallet came down on her back and head. She heard the thwacks but no pain registered.

Joshua swore. "There isn't any room to swing," he snarled.

He grabbed both her feet and pulled, and with a splintering of wood, the panels along the edges of the hatch came away in Jessamine's hands and she skidded backwards across the dirt floor. Her sudden movement toward him put Joshua off balance, and he fell with another grunt, letting go of her feet.

Jessamine lunged forward and scrambled through the enlarged hole, ignoring the poking splinters. She ran straight into the forest, expecting one of Joshua's large hands to grip her shoulder, or his mallet to swish down. As she entered the forest, glass crashed behind her, and Joshua gave out muffled curses.

It was almost dark and Jessamine ran blind. Her bare feet skidded on the wet leaves, and she slid into shallow water. She gasped and looked around; she knew exactly where she was. The heavy rain of the last few days had made the ephemeral stream flow, so she was in the gully near the old tree house. She could hide in the tree house. It was off the ground and invisible from below. She didn't have much time—Joshua hurtled over the dead leaves toward her.

Under the trees, the darkness was complete. She saw a tiny flicker of Joshua's cell phone light as he searched for her. Jessamine crept toward the fallen trunk that led to the sanctuary of the tree house, careful not to disturb the leaves and make a sound.

Joshua got closer. "Jessamine!" he called. "I won't hurt you. I just want to talk." She heard the soft swish and thwack of his mallet as he tapped it on the side of his leg.

"Jessamine," his voice was lower, trying to use its radio-star timbre and his charm to persuade her. "I know this forest. I played here as a child. It belonged to my family. It all belonged to my family."

Jessamine stopped crawling. He was so close; he might hear any movement.

"I bet I know where you are, Jessamine. You're up in my old tree house, over the stream. We built it, and we loved to play there as kids."

Jessamine held back a sob, weak with relief that she hadn't already gotten to the tree house, but with no idea of where to go.

"I'm here now," he said in his new persuasive voice. There was a pause and a grunt and Jessamine pictured him climbing. He went on conversationally. "You know I lost my virginity in this tree house. Rosemary said she didn't want to, but really, she did. Her family complained." He sounded aggrieved. "Can you believe it? You'd think trash like that would be pleased to be connected to Oxfords. We got rid of her then. We got rid of her whole family. They needed to move away."

Jessamine shivered in her wet clothes, frozen in place. She couldn't stay here. She would be found, and he was much bigger and stronger than her. With him up in the tree, now was the time for her to go. Her brain cleared enough for her to picture the Sheriff's office next to the burned library. Bobby would help her. The way was much shorter through the forest, so she could run there. She wouldn't be able to be quiet, but Joshua would be delayed by getting out of the tree.

"Jessamine, Jessamine," Joshua called between grunts. He was about to slide out of the tree. "You should have minded your own business. I know what you did. Wendell sent me all your figures and calculations and the fussy librarian research that you sent to Bobby. It pays to have family in the right place. I always manage that." He cackled. "The library budgets aren't your business. Bent River County isn't your business. The bear was mine. My insurance. All the names of the people I'd caught were in the bear. I have so much on them. They know that. That's why I had to keep moving the bear around to remind them what I had on them. It was my joke that the papers were *in* the bear!" He chuckled. "They'll pay now. I'm sad, Jessamine, but you must pay the price, too."

Jessamine leaped up and stumbled and pushed through the forest. Branches slapped her face. It was too dark to run. She was lost, but she hoped to find the road or Frank and DaisyMae's house and get help.

It was a short distance in the daylight, but in the dark, it felt like another nightmare of invisible vines and bushes, scratching her face and tripping her. She whimpered in relief when she saw house lights and heard voices. She had found her neighbor's horse farm. With a gulp, she headed toward the signs of civilization. She was about to cry out for help when she realized that one of the voices she heard was Joshua's.

"Yes," he was saying in his smooth, confident way, as if any reasonable listener had to agree with anything he declared. "Yes, it's that little English librarian. She's gone crazy. We had to let her go from the library. It wasn't dignified for the county. She drank, you know." He laughed and his voice became lower and more intimate. "She was chasing me with a shovel. Look what she did!" There was a pause while Jessamine imagined him displaying a scratch from clambering out of her greenhouse or chasing after her. Another laugh. "You know how women can get when you take away their hobbies and pet projects."

Jessamine had an urge to run out and shout that she hadn't been chasing him, he'd been chasing her. It wasn't fair that her neighbors would think that she drank and hit people with shovels. She pushed away childish thoughts like unfairness. She had to get away. She had thought the rumors that people who annoyed Joshua disappeared on boat trips had been exaggerated, but now she knew. She spared a moment to wish well on poor drowned Malcolm. With Joshua off her property, she longed to go home, but she couldn't risk it. It wasn't safe.

Her neighbor's house oriented her. She turned toward the road, shivering at the cold of the night through her wet clothes and the jab of fallen holly leaves.

The road wasn't far, and Jessamine climbed up beside the bridge, the gravel sharp under her tender feet. She heard the sound of a car. As its lights flickered closer through the forest, her first impulse was to slip into the trees and hide. But she was cold, wet, and without shoes in the middle of the night. Joshua's low murmurs were not far behind her. Surely someone could help her.

She stood at the entrance to the bridge and waved as the car lights came down the dip. The car didn't slow, so she stepped to the side. It would be easy to accidentally run someone over on the country road in the middle of the night. The SUV came to a stop beside Jessamine and the window rolled slowly down. Drusilla's long, white face looked out.

Jessamine took a step back.

"Oh, Jessamine. We've been looking for you. Are you alright? Joshua's gone crazy, and he said he's going to kill you." Drusilla's voice was sympathetic.

Jessamine stood poised, uncertain whether to run or believe Drusilla.

Another face appeared over Drusilla's shoulder, and with a start, Jessamine recognized Stephanie. "Jessamine! Come in out of the rain. You're all wet and muddy. We'll drive you to the police. We need to do something about Joshua."

Jessamine took another step back, touching the concrete barrier of the bridge. Stephanie came around the side of the Cadillac with a blanket. "Come here, Jessamine. We'll look after you."

Jessamine held the scratchy fabric against her skin, instantly grateful for the warmth. "But what about Drusilla? What's she doing here? I know she doesn't want to help me."

Jessamine let Stephanie put her arm around her and lead her to the SUV. Before Stephanie opened the door, she said, "Drusilla said she'd help. She said she knows what Joshua has done."

The effort of moving or standing became too much; Jessamine let Stephanie open the door and help her in. She sagged against the car seat.

Stephanie leaned across her and gently buckled her seatbelt.

The short, windy drive to the sheriff's office made Jessamine feel like a small child, strapped safely in the back of the car, with no control of where she was going. The competent adults would take care of it all.

As they went across the parking lot to the brightly lit building, Drusilla put her arm around Jessamine and helped steer her to the door. Jessamine wanted to shrug away from Drusilla's touch, but she supposed it was kindly meant, and she didn't have the energy to resist. Jessamine caught sight of her reflection in the glass door. She was wet, muddy, and scratched. Leaves poked from her hair and her clothes gaped holes. Her bare feet left a trail of blood spots from where they'd been cut on sticks and stones.

Wendell, Joshua's nephew, stood on the other side of the counter. His collar was sticking up and his shirt was buttoned wrong. He had the ruffled look of someone who had gotten out of bed and rushed into work. The young deputy looked Jessamine up and down. He spoke like a disapproving teacher. "Have you been drinking, Ms. Sibley?"

"I don't drink. I haven't for years." Jessamine felt unmoored. "My idea of a wild night is to skip flossing."

The young man pursed his lips and lifted his nose as if he smelled something bad. "I've heard all about you. You…"

"Who from?" Jessamine felt the world sway and sink. It was more than exhaustion.

The young man stood up straight. "You don't get to question me! You're staying here. I heard about your drunk spells. My uncle Josh said—"

"Shut up, you idiot!"

The sharp words were right in Jessamine's ear. She had forgotten that Drusilla was beside her. Jessamine tried to step back, and Drusilla's arm went tighter around her shoulders. Jessamine turned to get away. "No! I…" but Drusilla's other hand came up to her other shoulder.

Out of the corner of her eye Jessamine saw the young deputy trying to simultaneously draw his gun, pull out his radio, and open the folding counter to get to them.

Stephanie's indignant voice rose. "What are you doing? You told me that you were going to help her!"

A sharp shove from behind broke Drusilla's hold on her. "You're free Jessamine! Run!" Stephanie tore Drusilla's car keys out of the tall woman's hand and tossed them to Jessamine.

Jessamine caught the keys as she had a confused image of Drusilla falling into a chair, knocked off balance by another push from Stephanie. The young deputy was tangled in the counter with his radio cord.

Jessamine threw her weight against the glass door and stumbled into the night. Drusilla's red Cadillac's doors were open, so she jumped in. She must have squeezed the fob in the right place, because the vehicle started automatically. The seat was set far back for Drusilla's long legs, so Jessamine perched on the edge. She pushed the accelerator with her bare foot as she struggled to put it into gear with the unfamiliar controls. In her peripheral vision, she had a confused impression of people spilling out of the bright building behind her. Stephanie was trying to hold back Drusilla, but Drusilla was much taller and heavier. The deputy had his radio in one hand and his gun in the other. The sharp retort of a gunshot made her jump and yelp.

Jessamine got the car into gear and her foot on the accelerator. She pushed too hard and the wheels spun, spitting up gravel into the faces of the people wrestling in the parking lot. The car headed straight toward a light pole, but Jessamine wrenched the wheel round just in time and sped over the grass berm. The car sank and spun momentarily in the wet grass, but Jessamine remembered all her years in the snow on the plains and turned the wheel slightly until the tires found traction and sent her shooting forward onto the road.

Chapter 39

Perched on the edge of the seat, with no seatbelt, and bare feet cold on the pedals, Jessamine's wild careening didn't feel like her everyday staid driving.

She had no idea where she was, and tree trunks and mailboxes whizzed by, as if of their own volition. Finally, her heart slowed and she became aware of what she was doing. She slowed to a crawl. Her shivering intensified in her soaked clothing. She felt like her brain started to work again and she considered her options. She was in Drusilla's car. She supposed she had stolen it, but maybe it didn't matter since Drusilla might have kidnapped her. Jessamine's tired brain couldn't work out the convoluted legality of it. She didn't care.

With a lurch in her stomach, a picture of Hermes flashed into her mind, whacked on the head by Joshua's polo mallet. His scream replayed in her ears. The small, unwanted creature was probably dead, but she had to check on him. She had to give him a proper burial at least. Tears streamed down her face. She knew it was the middle of the night, and there were lots of urgent things that she should do, but burying Hermes became imperative.

The forest unspooled down an endless, featureless tunnel, then through her tears she saw the gas station. She thought of winding down Frank's long drive. DaisyMae was physically weak, but she'd know what to do. Jessamine hesitated, but the urge to take care of her dog was stronger. She drove home.

Her tears wouldn't stop. She left Drusilla's Cadillac in front of her railway station, vaguely thinking she should hide it, but not caring. The night was inky, so she went around to the back door to get a big flashlight out of the kitchen. Her house didn't welcome her as one of its own. She felt like a trespasser.

She slipped her gardening sneakers over her cut feet and went out to the greenhouse. The dog wasn't there. She threw up on the ground.

She flicked the light this way and that, thinking she was in the wrong place. Then, poised at the edge of her hearing, she heard a low whimper. She paused her own ragged breathing and focused on her ears, trying to locate the sound.

She heard it again. It was coming from the chicken coop. She darted over and shined her shaking light into the small wooden shed. Indignant chickens blinked in the light and squawked softly. Hermes crawled out from under the chickens' roost into Jessamine's lap.

She laid her head on his side and sobbed until he yelped. She felt him all over and found a huge lump on his head. He whimpered and pulled away when she touched it. "Poor puppy," she whispered. "Let's go inside."

Hermes followed her out of the chicken coop, his nose tight against her leg. Jessamine paused to latch the doors against predators and said, "Thank you, ladies," to the oblivious sleeping chickens. With Jessamine gone, the dog had crawled to the safety of the feathery members of his family.

In the dark house, she offered Hermes food, but he turned away from it. Jessamine threw up again, barely making it to the bathroom. The mirror above the sink showed her hair tangled full of sticks. Scratches marched in lines down her gray face. A huge bruise on her shoulder showed above her ripped shirt. Her head pounded.

She stood in the sitting room doorway, clutching the frame and swaying.

Hermes's left ear was drooping and blood was caked around his eye. "We need to go to the vet, pups," she said, her voice a strange croak to her own ears. She had memorized the directions to the emergency vet in the city from a magnet on her fridge. Her jumbled mind considered if she should go to the doctor.

She found her car keys. She thought she was missing something, but her head hurt too much to work out what else she needed.

Jessamine ignored Drusilla's Cadillac and lifted Hermes into her own car. She climbed stiffly into her driver's seat and pulled out of her driveway in the opposite direction that she usually went. In her rearview mirror, she saw a commotion of lights and official vehicles converge on her driveway. She heard faint sirens. She kept on driving.

Jessamine drove straight to the emergency vet in the city, keeping all thoughts out of her head. She felt nothing. Feeling anything would be too dangerous and might unleash all her fears and all her fury.

The vet office was dark. Jessamine squinted at her car's clock. It said 2:30. Jessamine wondered why they would be shut in the middle of the afternoon, when her befuddled brain circled and settled on the idea that it was the middle of the night.

She went up to the door to read the notices taped there, the print going in and out of focus in an odd way. The notice gave a number to call after hours. Jessamine went back to her car and searched for her phone. She couldn't find it. She didn't remember leaving the house with it.

Jessamine sat in her car and put her head on her steering wheel. She heard herself whimper. Hermes was sleeping on the back seat, his breath steady.

Bright lights shone into her car as another car pulled up next to her. She opened the door.

"Are you the vet?" a man asked without looking at her, before he climbed out of his car and reached in for a cat box.

"No," Jessamine said slowly. "I'm not the vet, but I'm looking for one."

Another car pulled in and a rumpled woman in a track suit climbed out. "Hello. I hear we've got a very sick cat. I'm the on-call vet. We'll go inside as soon as my assistant gets here." The man followed her.

"And a sick dog," Jessamine said from her car.

"Did you call?" the vet asked.

"No, I don't have my phone."

"I'll see Cally the cat first, since he called. Wait here and I'll see your dog afterwards." Jessamine waited in her car and watched as a young woman in scrubs arrived, and they all entered.

Jessamine had nearly nodded off but startled awake when the assistant knocked on her window. When Jessamine staggered into the lighted waiting room, the assistant's eyes widened.

"Are you okay?" she asked Jessamine. "You look terrible. Were you and your dog in a car accident?"

"Not a car accident. We… I…" Jessamine didn't know what to say.

"I'll get your dog's details, then we'll be ready for the vet."

As they were finishing the check in, the man emerged without the cat box.

"We'll keep her a few days, but we've caught it early and I think she'll be fine," the vet said.

The vet looked at Jessamine and winced. "Come back and we'll look at…" the vet glanced at the clipboard the assistant handed to her, "Hermes."

"Thank you." Jessamine stood up, and the sides of the world went dark. She felt herself toppling over and put a hand on the wall.

All three people rushed over and helped Jessamine sit back on the plastic waiting chair. "I'm a vet, not a doctor, but you need to see a doctor."

"No, no! I can't go. What about Hermes? I can't leave without him being looked after."

"I'll check Hermes," the vet said, leaning down. "What happened to him?"

"He hit him." Jessamine began to cry again.

"What did he hit him with?" the vet asked while her fingers gently probed over the whimpering dog, starting with his blood-encrusted face.

"A polo mallet. He always carries a polo mallet," Jessamine said.

"Did he hit you with the polo mallet too?"

"What?" Jessamine looked up. She tried to stand up. "That's not important. What about Hermes?"

"Hermes will be fine. It's you I'm worried about." She pulled out a small flashlight and peered into Hermes's eyes. "I don't think he's got a concussion." She looked up. "But I'm not sure about you. I can keep Hermes under observation, but you should talk to the police."

"I went to the police," Jessamine said, staring at her feet. Her voice was without emotion. She needed new shoelaces. She could see that the laces on the old gardening sneakers that she had thrown on to leave the house were nearly worn through. It suddenly felt urgent. She'd stop at Walmart on the way home and buy laces. Or had Rosemary left some in a drawer? Rosemary was sure to have stocked up on something as practical as shoelaces.

"Ms. Sibley? Jessamine?" The vet's calls brought her back to the present. "What happened to you? I'm a vet, so I'm a mandatory reporter for animal abuse. But I will tell the police if someone hurt you."

"I already talked to the police. They told me to go away." Jessamine continued to stare at her shoes.

"What?" The vet, her assistant, and the cat owner exchanged looks.

"In Bent River County. I went to the sheriff's office and he told me I was drunk and sent me away." The accusation of being drunk felt more unfair to Jessamine than anything else. Tears came more thickly down her face. "I don't drink. I haven't for years. For decades."

"Bent River County? We're not in Bent River County. We'll call the state police."

The vet assistant brought her a paper cup of sweet tea that she threw up. Soon a police officer arrived. People kept coming and going: the vet, the assistant, and a parade of unidentifiable faces. Jessamine could barely remember what she told them, but she did remember that the policewoman put a gentle hand on her shoulder and said, "It's okay, we'll take care of it. Is there someone to come to the hospital with you?"

Jessamine looked at her blankly. "I... I don't..."

"We'll sort that out later. Right now, an ambulance will take you to the hospital. The vet will keep Hermes here for observation and you can pick him up later."

"Okay." Jessamine wanted nothing except to sleep and she let herself be helped onto a stretcher and away. At the hospital, after too many hours of poking and prodding and photographs and bright lights, Jessamine was allowed to lie still on the hard, narrow hospital bed. They dimmed the lights for her headache, and she fell with relief into the encroaching darkness.

Jessamine climbed up through layers of sleep

"Jessamine, I can't believe it." Stephanie clutched Jessamine's hand and wept. "I thought Drusilla was going to help."

Marilyn came in behind her. "They said you have a concussion and rest is the most important thing."

"When they release you, we're taking you to my house to rest up for a few days." Stephanie squeezed Jessamine's hand. "I brought your clothes from home and a toothbrush. And I grabbed sunglasses. They said you shouldn't be alone."

Jessamine felt like a newly hatched chick on wobbly legs as the nurse helped her into a wheelchair and she left the hospital, tucked firmly under their wings.

Chapter 40

Lying in a single bed in Stephanie's darkened daughters' room, time flowed in a strange way for Jessamine. The shelves of stuffed toys, boxes of building blocks, and a frieze of cartoon zoo animals made Jessamine feel that she had gone back decades. She floated on a soft film of waking and sleeping. Somewhere at the back of her mind, she felt she should wonder what Joshua was doing, and all the other things that had been so important, but she didn't have the energy to care about them.

Her voice sounded croaky when she asked, "What about my animals? What about Hermes?"

"Frank and Marilyn are feeding the cat and the chickens. I've talked to the vet and Hermes is doing fine. Marilyn said she'd look after him. Or do you want him here?"

"It's a lot to ask, but could he stay here with me?" Jessamine felt tears sliding down her face again, but the tears were coming less often. "Thank you for taking me in like this. It's more than I could expect."

"I let Drusilla get you." Stephanie stepped closer and tears glinted in her eyes. "I feel so bad. I trusted her."

"It's not your fault." Jessamine put her hand out, her tears coming thicker. "Drusilla is so manipulative."

Stephanie fetched Hermes from the vet, and he lay curled up tightly under Jessamine's arm. Stephanie's two big retrievers wanted to play, but they were hushed away from the door. Stephanie's daughters were at their grandmother's so the house would be quiet.

As Jessamine's headache slowly faded, she realized that they were keeping things from her. Frank and Marilyn stopped talking in the hallway when she tottered out on her way to the bathroom. She didn't care.

One morning, Jessamine woke up and her headache was a whisper at the back of her skull. She had room in her head to wonder what had happened. Stephanie drove her to a checkup from her doctor, and she was given the all-clear to go home.

"Stay one more night," Stephanie said on the way back. "Since it's already afternoon, I'll invite Marilyn and Frank around and we'll talk. You lie down now and rest before they come."

Jessamine opened her mouth to insist that she help Stephanie prepare for visitors, but she was overcome by a need to sleep, so she didn't argue.

Feeling raw and weak, like a plant that's been out of the sun too long, Jessamine sat at Stephanie's kitchen table.

Marilyn said, "Everyone knew something was going on, but it's out in the open now."

"What do you mean?" Jessamine knew her mind was moving slowly, but she couldn't grasp this.

"They've unraveled the corruption," Marilyn said.

"*You* found all the proof, Jessamine." Stephanie piled their plates with spaghetti.

"You found out what they were doing and put it all together. The state police were after Joshua Oxford. They knew he was up to no good, but his network was hard to crack." Frank rubbed his forehead. "He had a lot of people in Bent River County under his thumb."

"They were embezzling money and laundering it through the fund for the new library. Particularly for the library annex that didn't exist. That's what you figured out. And that's what Englebert knew. Englebert found out that his father was going to use the new library building as a polo club house. And keep a few old books in a corner to get away with it. They didn't care anything about the books or running a library." Stephanie smiled in a sad way. "Englebert loves books. That's why he burned down the new library building."

"How is Englebert? Was he hurt?"

"He's fine. The fire didn't hurt him. He bounced straight back, but he'll probably be in trouble. It's not settled yet."

"Why didn't you tell me sooner?" Jessamine poked her fork into a piece of broccoli.

Marilyn shook her head. "You had to rest. The doctors were adamant."

"The police wanted to talk to you again, but the doctors wouldn't allow it." Frank said. "The police had enough to work with at the time, but you'll have to give another statement."

Jessamine paused to absorb all of this. "What will happen to Joshua and Drusilla and Kathryn? Will they go to jail?"

Jessamine's three friends exchanged looks.

"No, not jail." Frank hesitated.

"Joshua is dead," Marilyn said.

"Dead? What happened?" A spike of headache pushed behind Jessamine's eye.

"He drowned in the river. It's not officially out yet, but that's what we heard," Stephanie said.

"What was he doing in the river?" Jessamine felt that reality was slipping away again. "I didn't think anyone swam in it? Was he looking for the bear?"

"He wasn't swimming. He drove his car off the Windsor Bridge." Stephanie put her arm up over her mouth. "It's terrible when a human being has died. But they said that he was drunk." Stephanie giggled. "They said that Drusilla's monogrammed bra was tangled around the steering wheel, and that might have made him crash."

"What a horrible way to go. And it will probably get in the papers about the bra and the drunk driving and…" Jessamine couldn't believe that a giggle escaped her. She considered the information with her slow-working brain. "He liked to think he was so proper and dignified. He'd hate that."

"And more is coming out about poor Malcolm drowning." Stephanie offered sweet tea all around. "Everyone knew that Malcolm was a champion swimmer. No one believed he drowned."

"It looks like Joshua whacked him with his polo mallet and pushed him off his boat." Marilyn waved a forkful of spaghetti until sauce spotted the table.

"I thought he carried that stupid mallet everywhere because he was vain and wanted to show off that he played polo." Frank frowned darkly at a piece of carrot. "But it was a warning. Like the bear, he was telling everyone what he could do and laughing at them."

"Poor Malcolm." Stephanie sat down abruptly. "He was ahead of me at school, so I didn't know him well. He found out about some of Joshua's shenanigans and was whistleblowing." She shivered and looked at Jessamine. "Joshua planned for you to be next."

Stillness fell over the table.

"What about Drusilla? And Kathryn?" Jessamine broke the silence.

"They've disappeared." Frank rubbed his eyebrow.

"Drusilla sent a postcard from a place called Roto… something. Rotorua." Marilyn scratched her head.

"Rotorua? In New Zealand?" Jessamine blinked. "I've been there. New Zealand's not big. Surely, they can find her?"

"She's not in Rotorua anymore. It was a tease." Stephanie stood up to replenish the pitcher of tea. "They're not sure if Kathryn was with her or not. The bank accounts were emptied. There were shell companies and all sorts of rigmarole I don't understand. The money's hard to trace."

"They're going to be working on it for a while." Frank shook his head. "I hope the county gets its money… I mean *our* money back."

Chapter 41

The next day, Stephanie said, "Why don't you stay for lunch, Jessamine? Then I'll drive you home."

"You've done enough for me. I'll drive myself."

"You can't. Your car is at your place."

But after lunch Stephanie said, "You look tired. Why don't you take a nap?"

"Just a short nap. Be sure to wake me up so I can go home early in the afternoon." Jessamine screwed up her eyes at her friend.

When Jessamine woke up, it was getting dark. She went out to the kitchen where Stephanie was stirring a pot.

"Why didn't you wake me? Can you drive me back now?"

"I'm in the middle of cooking now." Stephanie didn't look at Jessamine.

"What about after you've cooked?"

"Weeell." Stephanie drew out the word.

Jessamine felt hurt and then realization dawned. "Stephanie! You're putting me off. There's something else you haven't told me."

A knock sounded at the door and Marilyn poked her head in.

"You planned this if you invited Marilyn around." Jessamine looked at her friends, and put her hands on her hips, not sure if she should be annoyed or grateful. "What is happening?"

Stephanie screwed up her face. "You can't live in your house."

"Yes, I can. I have to. It's my house." Jessamine paused as a horrific thought occurred to her. "Did it burn down, too?"

"No. It's fine." Stephanie put her hand on Jessamine's arm. "I'm not saying it's not your house. We're worried about you. If you'll be scared being there after… after everything that's happened."

"You can say it." Jessamine sat and squeezed her fingers together on her lap. "After I was assaulted and chased in my own forest." The tears that were close to the surface squeezed into Jessamine's eyes. "But that's the point. It's my forest. It's my refuge. It's where I want to be."

"See, you're upset. I'd be scared to live alone there now." Stephanie turned back to her chopping.

"I won't be alone. My kids are coming to visit soon."

"Shouldn't you wait?" Stephanie stirred the pan hard.

"No, I've got to plunge in and stay there straight away." Jessamine screwed up her mouth, trying to work out how to articulate her feeling of certainty. "I'd be dishonoring Rosemary if I ran away now. And Joshua would win. Even though he's dead, it would be a victory for him."

Marilyn gave Jessamine a searching look. "As long as you're sure."

"Remember that we're a phone call away. I live close," Stephanie said.

"You could stay with me," Marilyn said, "Or I could come and stay with you for a while."

"You don't need to. I need to look after myself." Jessamine smiled. "Besides which, who would look after your cats if you're not there?"

Marilyn laughed. "You've got a point about the cats. But make sure you contact us if you need us, like Stephanie said."

Despite her brave words, as darkness fell on her first night at home, claws of fear dug into Jessamine's intestines. Autumn was starting and she told herself the nights were cooling, so she lit the fire in the afternoon and made sure that there was plenty of wood stacked in the sagging basket in her sitting room. She cooked a big pot of minestrone soup in the slow cooker. The warm aroma of tomatoes and herbs filled the house, an olfactory protection against bad things in the night.

As darkness fell, Jessamine went to every window and door three times to check that they were locked. She knew after the second time that nothing could possibly be undone or loose, but she felt that Stephanie's and Marilyn's concern had given her permission to coddle her fears.

It was too quiet after the bustle of Stephanie's house, so she wound up Rosemary's antique gramophone and listened to the scratchy singing from over a hundred years ago. She thought of the singers, who must be long dead, sending a hopeful message to a future they couldn't imagine.

She almost fell asleep on the couch watching the fire, but she told herself sternly that her days of sleeping in the sitting room were over. Without looking at the blank faces of the windows, she forced herself to visit the bathroom and get into bed. She slept instantly and deeply and woke up to sunlight prodding around the edge of the curtains and Hermes whining to go out.

Jessamine let the dog out and went out to feed the chickens. She stood by their run and wrapped her arms around herself. "It's a good thing I have to look after you. I can't cower in the house," she said to them out loud. They scratched and pecked, completely unimpressed. Jessamine found their unconcern comforting.

She went into the greenhouse and picked up the seed trays that had spilled everywhere when Joshua attacked her. For a moment she couldn't breathe, but she saw that one of the seeds, lying in a pile of dirt next to the broken tray, had germinated.

"Life goes on," she said aloud and looked up. Joshua had smashed several panes of glass. The holes let in rain that provided the life-giving water for the seed to grow. She cradled the tiny plant and transferred it to another pot. She found several tiny seedlings and set them in pots to grow. "I guess my work wasn't for nothing, after all," she said to Hermes, who stood alert in the doorway, his eyes on her face.

The dog growled low in his throat and Jessamine's heart hammered. He yipped and streaked around the side of the house to the front. Jessamine heard a car coming up her driveway and followed him. It was unlikely that the ghost of Joshua Oxford would drive up in a car.

Frank was helping DaisyMae out of her old car, which Frank had fixed so the elderly woman didn't have to climb into Frank's tall truck.

"Come in," she greeted them. "I made a whole pot of winter soup."

They gathered in the sitting room round the fire and ate bowls of leftover soup with Jessamine's homemade bread studded with her own dried tomatoes. For dessert, they nibbled on Anzac biscuits. After lunch, Frank had to go to an afternoon shift at the library where he now worked. Jessamine played the gramophone for DaisyMae. "My grandmother had one of those," DaisyMae said, her face lighting up. "I never thought I'd hear one again."

The music reverberated in Jessamine's head, clearing space for her lurking fears to come to the top so she could articulate them. "I don't know if I want to go back to a library," she said and rubbed Hermes's ears. "It's too hard. I love libraries too much. I don't think I can make enough money to live on with just the farmer's market. And I feel guilty about Drusilla and Joshua. It's turned out so bad. Could I…"

"Hush child," DaisyMae said. "As my grandmother used to say, when you engage with she-dogs, you might stand up with fleas. And those Oxfords were prime she-dogs!"

Jessamine snorted.

DaisyMae put her hand out toward Jessamine. "But sweetie, you always have a choice about working at a library. You're the strong Carolina Jessamine vine with the beautiful yellow flowers. You use the support of others to reach up to the sun. But the bad ones, they can't eat you—you'll poison them. Remember that girl."

"I suppose Drusilla and Joshua did try to consume me. But all the options are difficult." Jessamine could hear the whine in her own voice. "What if I get it wrong? What if I make bad choices?"

"Sometimes you can see only bad choices. But you have choices." DaisyMae put her hand on Jessamine's arm. "Thinking you have no choice. That's the road to despair, Jessamine. Don't tell yourself you're a victim, or you *are* a victim. You win by standing up to them, no matter what they did to you."

"I suppose I can choose?" Jessamine wasn't whining now, but she sounded doubtful.

"Be definite about it, girl." DaisyMae waved her small, wrinkled fist at the ceiling. "You're stronger than that, I know you are! Say, 'I choose!'"

Jessamine smiled at the old woman and raised her own fist. "I choose."

DaisyMae was grinning now. "Make me believe that you believe it, Jessamine."

Jessamine laughed. She pumped her fist at the ceiling. "I'm not going to sit in that comfy victim chair. I choose. I choose! I choose!"

That night, after Frank picked up DaisyMae, Jessamine faced the dark blanks of the windows. She took a deep breath and opened the back door. The restless silhouettes of the trees heaved against the scudding clouds. Hermes cocked his head at her and then stared into the night. Jessamine laughed. "Okay, beastie. We'll go out." The dog pranced while she laced up her shoes.

She left without a flashlight. She knew the small cone of light would make the surrounding dark feel more impenetrable. She stepped outside the circle of electric light spilling from the kitchen and let her eyes adjust. The dog's progression was marked by the rustling of the leaves and the white tip of his tail waving. He wasn't worried about being in the forest. Jessamine sniffed deeply, wondering what the dog could smell. She walked farther until she could let go of all feeling and become a small part of the living forest.

When they reached the dip of the ephemeral stream, dark panic clutched at Jessamine. She stopped and breathed in the sweet, cold air the concavity held in its cupped hands, until the scent of leaves and soil and life slowed her banging heart.

The moon rose. In the cleared spaces, she and the dog cast sharp black moon shadows against the buttery light. She put her hand flat on the rough bark of an ancient tree. It felt like a friend. The whole rustling, alive night felt friendly. Jessamine didn't know if it was because Joshua Oxford was gone and could never chase her through her own forest again, or it was because she had struggled and overcome. She had stood up for herself so the dark places didn't hold so much terror. She knew she could fight again if need be.

Epilogue

Jessamine admired piles of colored paper, old book covers, ribbons, string, and an old food processor laid out on the library tables. "Frank, your homemade book is going to be Bent River County Public Library's best craft ever."

"I can't beat your crafts, Jessamine." Frank grinned at her. "Keep coming back, because this will take several sessions." Frank held up a pile of thick homemade pages joined with loopy stitches. "We'll enjoy your sweet tea and Anzac biscuits on the break."

"This is pretty." Eunice turned over the decorated book covers.

"We'll make paper, then we'll decorate covers, then we'll sew the whole thing together." Frank's eyes twinkled. "You'll be able to write your secrets in it, ladies."

His tiny mother, perched on a tall chair like a queen beaming at her beloved subjects, paused her smiling to frown at him but said nothing.

"I don't know that any of us have any secrets after everything that's happened," said Marilyn.

"It's not just ladies." Stephanie leaned across and peered at the door.

"Here's Walter, Bobby, and the guys from the gas station."

"Hey all. I hope y'all are keeping warm? It's been freezing right much lately, ain't it?" said Bobby.

"Yes, things are looking up all around," Stephanie said. "I'm enjoying being back."

Englebert squeezed into a seat, looking down after a quick nod and smile around the group. The tables grew crowded as Josey and Christa joined them. They left their toddlers playing with the toys across the room and kept an eye on their babies in strollers nearby.

Marilyn turned to Jessamine and Frank. "You two looked busy at the Christmas market."

"We *were* busy." Frank handed out piles of old colored fliers. "Those Christmas decorations Jessamine made out of recycled books sold like hotcakes. And we're working on more ideas." He gestured over the table.

"I'm glad it was the last farmer's market of the year." Jessamine puffed in mock exhaustion. "I need the break until spring."

"We have to get more seeds planted in Jessamine's greenhouse to get our early plants for sale in the spring." Frank sat up straight.

DaisyMae wagged her finger at her son. "Now, Frank, don't talk market shop at your library job."

"I'll talk about the other shop, then." Frank laughed. "My new job in the library is fantastic. Thank you for suggesting it, Jessamine."

"I knew you'd be perfect for it." Jessamine grinned. "You're in your element with all these people to talk to."

Frank grinned back. "I don't know about that, but it sure is easier on my back. It beats going up and down all those ladders."

"Even this library hasn't put in ladders." Stephanie shook her head. "Don't give them ideas."

"I'm learning how to use the computers." Frank gestured to the row of public computers. Only a few of them wore *Out of Order* signs. "Stephanie's helping there. I'm enjoying reading all the books and telling people about them."

"You're reading *all* the books?" Marilyn laughed.

"I'm getting to know my library. I'm starting at the beginning of fiction and nonfiction and I'm going to read one book off each shelf. I'm too busy at work to read, but I've got plenty of time at home."

"That's impressive." Jessamine beamed again, feeling her face falling into a new configuration.

"I'm talking up a storm about those books I read. The people who come in think it's great." Frank grinned at Stephanie. "I love working with Stephanie. I would have hated it if I'd had to work with Dru… Um." Frank paused. He held up a thick sheet of textured paper and went on quickly. "We rip up the old paper and transform it into this homemade paper."

"I know what you mean." Stephanie tore a sheet of blue paper down the middle then narrowed her eyes. "Tiffany didn't last long when she was forced to actually exert herself. It's working out a lot better without Drusilla being the shark in the tank."

"We *thought* Drusilla was the shark in the tank." Marilyn waved her travel mug. "It turns out that she was just one of those little sucky hanger-on fish. What are they called?"

Everyone paused, trying to remember the word.

"A remora?" said Englebert.

"Yes, that's the one, Englebert." Marilyn warmed to her theme and a drop of sweet tea fell on the table. "They hang out with the big scary fish and slurp up the trash."

"I'm Bert now," the teen added and blushed.

"Joshua was the big scary fish all along." Jessamine narrowed her eyes. "He had all that money behind him. And generations of people sucking up to his family."

"Ahem!"

Jessamine gave Marilyn a startled look and followed the direction of Marilyn's urgent nod. "Oh, Englebert, I mean Bert," said Jessamine. "Sorry. I don't mean you. You want to help the ordinary people in the county."

"I *do* want to help ordinary people," said Bert. He put his head down and muttered into his paper.

"What was that, sweetie?" DaisyMae said. "Speak up! I'm old and hard of hearing."

Bert looked up with tears in his eyes. "I'm doing community service for setting the library on fire. And I'm on probation. I know I deserve that." He swallowed. "I got Ms. Marilyn fired. I'm sorry."

The adults exchanged looks.

"You didn't get her fired…" Frank started.

"But I did!" Bert wailed. "I stuffed the ballot boxes when we were naming the bear, so the bear would be called the name that sounded like Drusilla, so it would be Ursilla the Bear. I made lots of extra ballots. It made my father so angry." He sniffed and wiped his nose with his sleeve. DaisyMae handed him a tissue. Bert blew his nose and went on. "I knew that they were having an affair, him and Drusilla. I wanted to punish them both."

There was a long pause.

Frank clapped Bert on the back. "Son, I'm proud of you." He guffawed.

Stephanie laughed until tears ran down her face. "We wondered about the name Ursilla winning, didn't we Jessamine?"

"We did." Jessamine tried to hold in her laughter and snorted.

Marilyn put down her cup and looked seriously at the quivering teenager. "Englebert. Bert. You shouldn't feel guilty. They fired me because I was close to understanding how they were laundering money through the library budgets."

Bert looked down again. "But Ms. Jessamine was right. The plantation owners have always banked on their… on our ancestors. An ordinary person would be ashamed of that background. They brought me up to do whatever I like in this county. That because of the land that we own, we were *chosen* to rule the little people." He paused and poked a finger in his wet paper pulp. "I don't think that's right."

"Good on you for going your own way," said Jessamine. "You can rise above being one of those sucky remoras."

Bert gave her a watery smile. "I will go my own way. No sucky fish for me!"

"Drusilla wasn't the only remora." Stephanie tore her paper with so much force that her elbow hit the table. "The other sucky fish were Kathryn, Casey, and oooh, I could name a few."

"Yes," said Frank. "They took over Bent River County and made it a big steaming, stinking heap of b—"

"Frank!" his mother exclaimed.

Frank laughed. "It was a big stinking pile of *bureaucracy*. What did you think I was going to say, Mama?"

The rest of them laughed. "A stinking pile of bureaucracy. That sums up a lot!" Jessamine held up her paper.

"They thought they'd have it all their own way when they got rid of me." Marilyn narrowed her eyes. "But they found out that's not how it functions. There are laws and the state and other people interested in the library."

"Cheers to us." Jessamine raised her plastic tumbler of sweet tea.

"Yes, cheers! They couldn't beat us into submission." Marilyn raised her travel mug.

Everyone else raised their plastic tumblers.

"No, you can't keep us down," agreed Frank.

They tapped their cups against their neighbor's and laughed.

"Are you thinking of coming back to the library, Jessamine?" Stephanie asked. "There's new management. It's like a breath of fresh air."

"Yes," said Eunice and Josey together. "We miss you."

"No. Not for now. I'm flat-out getting ready for my family coming in a few days for Christmas. My middle boy is talking about starting a master's degree here on the East coast, and three of the others are talking about moving here. They like our cities. We're going to be driving around a lot and exploring for the next month or so."

"It's winter again, so you've been living here for almost a year." Stephanie looked thoughtful.

"Yes, a whole year. What a change," Marilyn said.

"We'd better go home," said Josey. "It's getting dark early."

The library patrons left their home-made paper drying, ready to work on the next week, and filed out.

Jessamine stood entranced in the broken parking lot. "Look, snow!" Flakes appeared from the dark sky and tumbled end over end in the halo of a light. "I was sick of it out west, but it's lovely."

Marilyn shivered and wrapped her arms around herself. "Brrr. You can keep it. I've got to get Frank's mama home in this since Frank's working."

Jessamine laughed. "Bring your car up to the door, and we'll help her."

Everyone gathered around, and they almost carried the old woman out to Marilyn's car and bundled her in. With the heater blasting and Christmas carols playing on the radio, they drove off waving.

The people turned to their own cars, the biting wind making them reluctant to stay and chat.

"Say hello to your family from me, Jessamine," Stephanie called over her shoulder. "I can't wait to meet them. I'll tell them stories about you!"

Inside her car, Jessamine turned on her own heater and fiddled with the radio to find carols. She headed down the now-familiar winding, forested roads, her mind overflowing with joyful plans for baking, and making up beds, and stacking firewood to be ready for her family to arrive at her new home for the holidays.

Jessamine reveals that before the story started, she ran away from her home and family in Kansas. Have you wanted to run away from your current situation? Do you think this was the best thing for Jessamine to do?

Have you worked with someone like Drusilla? What would have happened if Jessamine had talked to Drusilla about their conflict? Do you think that Jessamine could have handled Drusilla's hostility better? Why or why not?

Do you know any military families or other families who have to move often? Do you think that the book represents the isolation that these families feel? Or is the isolation that Jessamine describes about her past not because of moving? What do you think caused her isolation?

Frontline library workers and other public-facing workers have to deal with customers who behave badly or bizarrely, perhaps because of mental illness. What do you think is the best way to handle this?

Jessamine loves nature and animals, and these are important to the story. Did you connect with this? How does nature or do animals enrich your life?

Throughout the story, Jessamine connects to books she remembers and loves. Are there books you remember from childhood that you return to for comfort or that have revealed important life lessons to you? What are these books and why do they resonate with you?

The public library setting is central to the book, and Bent River County Public Library could be seen more as a character than a backdrop. What do you think is the ideal relationship between a public library and its community? Has your library achieved this?

The book explores the situation of hereditary and unearned power. Do you think this still exists? If so, what can be done to improve this?

Throughout the book Jessamine rebels against other people's desires and achieves victory, such as the jar craft, dressing the bear, or quitting after the bullying meeting. Do you think Jessamine could have been more proactive and stronger? Do you think women are socialized to go along with other people's wishes, or is it Jessamine's individual nature to want to please other people? Have you gone along with something you weren't enthusiastic about to please someone else and then resented it? What victories have you achieved?

Through the library programs and connecting with each other through the difficult situations Jessamine makes close friends in her new home. These close friends can be called a 'found family.' Do you have people in your life who are found family? What did you go through together to become close?

Anzac Biscuits Recipe

Controversy surrounds the question of whether Anzac Biscuits were invented during World War I or soon afterward. They are strongly connected in the Antipodean mind to Anzac soldiers, Australian New Zealand Army Corps. Anzac Day is still commemorated on the 25th of April every year. Whatever their exact history, Anzac Biscuits are over a hundred years old, are tasty, and are filled with coconut and oaty goodness. Many recipes exist but this is the recipe Jessamine uses that she adapted from childhood recipes, with ingredients that are easy to find in her new home, and to her taste.

1 cup flour

¾ cup brown sugar

1 ½ cup oats

1 ½ cup shredded or flaked coconut

4 oz butter

3 Tbsp. maple syrup and/or honey (or traditional golden syrup if you can find it)

1 tsp baking soda

2 Tbsp. boiling water

Preheat oven to 350 [degrees] Fahrenheit.

Line a cookie sheet with parchment paper.

In a large pan on the stovetop melt the butter and syrup / honey together over a low heat. Remove from heat.

Dissolve the baking soda in the boiling water in a small bowl.

Mix the baking soda mixture into the melted butter and syrup. It may froth.

Stir in the sugar.

Stir in the oats and shredded or flaked coconut.

Lastly stir in the flour to make a sticky paste.

Form into tablespoon-sized balls and put on baking sheet.

Bake for 10 to 15 minutes until golden brown.

Enjoy with a cup of piping hot tea or a tall glass of sweet tea!

A librarian for more than two decades, Jan Marry ran hundreds of library programs and in 2021 she was named the Donna G. Cote Virginia Librarian of the Year.

She has a Master of Library Science from the University of Illinois and a Master of Arts in science writing from Johns Hopkins.

She has published in *Nature Futures*, *The Hopkins Review*, *Virginia Libraries*, and *Library Journal*.

Originally from New Zealand, she lived in six countries before settling on a small farm in Virginia. She has been making Anzac biscuits for over forty years and is ecumenical on the question of crispy versus chewy.

9 781961 548237